Though still caffeine-deprived, Grace's hunger had at least been satisfied. Now she could focus on the next item on her to-do list—finding a safe place to stash her life savings.

As the bell on the bakery door jingled behind her, she gave her money belt a reassuring pat. She'd made a habit for months of keeping important documents and cash safely nestled at her waist. The stack of bills currently crammed into the pouch represented nearly all she had in the world, and she cringed at the thought of anything happening to it. She wouldn't be able to relax until it was safely stowed away in a bank—under her assumed name, of course.

She started down Main Street, which was more far-reaching than she'd realized. The businesses spanned two full blocks, but she couldn't spot a bank in either direction.

A familiar sensation breezed through her like a whispered warning. Adrenaline flooded her system. She hated this feeling so much she had flown clear across the country in the hope of shedding it. Slowing her steps, her eyes darted from one side to the other. A few people milled about, but would anyone help her if she screamed?

Panic rose in her throat as it became obvious that someone was following her.

Madison Falls series
Christian Women's Fiction

Saving Grace
Book 1

Jill Came Tumbling After
Book 2

Lefty Lucy
Book 3

Other Books by Lesley Ann McDaniel

Montana Hearts series
(Heartsong Presents)

Lights, Cowboy, Action
Book 1

Big Sky Bachelor
Book 2

Rocky Mountain Romance
Book 3

Holiday Hearts series
Christian Romance

Christmas Bells are Ringing
Book 1

Heavenly Peace
Book 2

Home for the Holidays
Book 3

Comfort and Joy
Book 4

Crescent Cove series
Christian Romance

Testing the Waters
Book 1

Oceans Apart
Book 2

Sink or Swim
Book 3

Islands of Intrigue: San Juans series
Christian Romantic Suspense

The Unrelenting Tide by Lynnette Bonner
Book 1

Tide Will Tell by Lesley Ann McDaniel
Book 2

Find out more at www.lesleyannmcdaniel.com

DEDICATION

This book is dedicated to my mom, Virginia Even, who encouraged my love of reading, which led to my love of writing.

Saving Grace
Madison Falls, Book 1

ISBN: 979-8-9988488-5-8

Cover design by Lynnette Bonner of Indiecoverdesign.com
images ©
www.fotolia.com, File: #30097055_L
www.shutterstock.com, File: #shutterstock_537119
www.shutterstock.com, File: #shutterstock_98954030 Photoshop
Swirls by Obsidian Dawn, www.obsidiandawn.com

Printed in the U.S.A.

By Lesley Ann McDaniel

Chapter 1

Warm air prickled the back of Grace's neck. The porch creaked under her feet as she stole a glance over her shoulder at the dark street. *Nothing.*

"...excited to have you here ...."

The real estate agent's lilting voice hummed in Grace's ear. She turned, marveling not only at the whiteness of the agent's slacks, but at the boldness of that fashion choice for a woman whose figure resembled that of a snowman.

"...cab ride even longer than your flight."

Something pinged against the wooden planks. Grace jolted, dizzied by days of wakefulness. The agent dipped down gracefully as her plump fingers extended.

Just a dropped key.

"I know you'll fall in love with this adorable house. The pictures on our website don't do it justice."

Her chipper tone set Grace's tired nerves on edge. Why couldn't the woman move a little faster? Casting a wary eye down the shadowy street, Grace eased the strap of her computer bag off the tense spot on her shoulder. Her overworked adrenal glands pulsed as the agent—what was her name...Cookie? No. Spritz. Spritz Cole, that was it. As Spritz righted herself and lifted the rescued key toward the mahogany Craftsman door.

"Of course," Spritz lobbed her an encouraging smile. "Most people want to actually see a house first before signing the papers. You must be anxious to start out fresh."

"Yes." Grace coerced a steady tone. "This place just *felt* right."

An air of confidence spread over Spritz's carefully made-up face. "You won't be disappointed." She clicked the key, and the deadbolt gave an obliging swoosh. Pushing the door open, she took a theatrical step back. "Welcome home."

Grace's heart made a thump that could have come from the score to a Hitchcock movie. She peered in. Her lungs filled with paint-infused air as she took a careful step across the doorsill and into the foyer.

She blinked away welling emotion, plunking her suitcase down on the polished wood floor of the vacant bungalow. Her chest ached as she perused the living room, which looked bigger than her entire studio apartment back home. Its white walls stared at her like a vast canvas.

"Well?" Spritz's voice glistened with just enough gusto to instill consumer confidence without falling into phoniness.

Grace forced a step further into the house which now bore her name on the title—or rather her chosen name. She found it impossible to whip up much enthusiasm when all she really wanted was her life back. "It's...adorable. Just like you said."

The door *ka-thunked* shut, sending Grace's heart into her throat.

Spritz let out a pleased breath. "You were smart to snap it up. Houses like this don't come on the market very often. Why, folks in Madison Falls tend to stay put till they die."

Grace shot her a fretful glance. Was she being funny or merely factual?

Apparently oblivious to Grace's unease, Spritz breezed into the living room. "Let me just give you a quick tour."

Exhaustion jabbed at Grace like a maestro's baton. "No, you don't have to—"

"You've come all this way," Spritz cajoled. "I can't just abandon you at the door. I don't mind at all."

Too weary to argue, Grace ran a jittery hand through her hair. Startled once again by the shortness of her cut, she flinched. "All right then."

As Spritz took center stage with a clearing of her throat, Grace backed up just enough to secure the deadbolt. She forced attentiveness, though frankly her only architectural concern was the structure's ability to keep danger at bay.

Spritz stepped seamlessly into tour guide mode. "The key feature of this cozy room is of course the striking Craftsman brick fireplace." She recited the painstakingly penned text of her own website.

Feeling like a reluctant audience to a friend's baby-picture slideshow, Grace swallowed her protest and stepped into the living room.

"...loads of light from this generous picture window." Spritz pulled a cord, sending the front blinds clattering upward.

Grace shrank back, feeling the same vulnerability she did whenever someone burst into her dressing room unannounced. The darkness outside chilled her. Why hadn't she planned for a day-lit arrival?

"...cut glass...original to the house." Spritz dropped the cord. Her arm extended toward the smaller windows above the built-in bookcases which flanked the fireplace.

Keeping a polite focus on her guide, Grace slid toward the picture window. She felt for the cold metal of the latch, breathing easier at its firmness. She gave the cord to the blinds a quick yank then twisted the wand to smooth the slats.

"...nineteen twenties charm." Spritz clasped her hands in front of herself, clearly moved by her own narrative of the home's features. A well-rehearsed pause, then a twirl toward the dining room.

Forcing her tired eyes to stay focused, Grace pulled shut the blinds on the smaller windows. *Nineteen twenties charm, indeed.* Feigning cheerful interest, she crossed under the wide arch which separated this room from the next.

Spritz drew her arm with a flourish in the direction of a built-in china hutch. "This room is perfect for entertaining."

Grace huffed at the suggestion that she would actually invite people over. Spritz's eyes narrowed.

"I...I..." Grace stuttered, dismayed that fatigue had wiped out her ability to self-censor. "I just never had my own dining room before. I didn't know I needed one."

Spritz's face lit like a make-up mirror. "Our neighborhood progressive dinner is coming up. I'll be sure to add you to the circuit."

Grace shivered, giving in to a long blink. Just what she needed. An invitation to the biggest event of the Mayberry social season.

Spritz swung open a double-hinged door, taking a calculated step through it as she spoke. "I just love the charm of this vintage-style kitchen."

Grace cast a polite look through the doorway. *Vintage style?* Was that real estate lingo for badly-in-need-of-an-update?

"Cute." Too bad she couldn't cook. All those years of dorm food and take-out had made that skill superfluous. At least she knew how to make coffee.

Thoughts of a comforting beverage warmed her momentarily, then vanished as her inaugural step into the kitchen almost sent her plummeting.

Spritz let out a yelp, catching her by the elbow. "Sweetie! Are you okay?"

Her heart racing, Grace clutched Spritz's arm as her feet surfed for solid flooring. "I… I'm fine. Thanks." She let go, testing the tiles using the care of a person treading through a minefield. One tile near the door had a definite trampoline-like quality. Funny that hadn't made the website's list of fancy features.

Spritz gave the floor a healthy stomp with the heel of her Easy Spirit pump. "I really had no idea there was a problem here." She patted Grace's bicep. "Not to worry. We've got a wonderful handyman in town who'll fix it for a song."

Grace's stomach fluttered. The last thing she needed was some strange man in her house expecting her to sing. "I'm sure I can take care of it myself."

"Oh, a DIY girl, huh?" She looked impressed. "Why not let Sam handle this, and put your energy into the fun projects?"

With a decisive nod, Spritz stepped over the aberrant flooring to the rectangle of a hallway. Grace followed, anxious to finish the tour and get on with her plan. All she needed was to be left alone, to let down her guard at last, and fall into a deep sleep.

"Storage closet. Linen closet. Basement." Spritz flung open each door in turn. "The floor is original to the house, but it's been refinished. Let me show you the back bedroom." She disappeared, rattling off facts as if her audience still needed convincing.

Grace's body followed her eyes to the cracked-open bathroom door. A golden trail of light across the floor taunted her. Flashes of that last moment before her life had changed for good. She looked intently at the light—an eerie implication that someone else had recently been in the house. *Be strong.* What other choice did she have?

She reached out. A light touch to the crystal doorknob. *Good grief, it's only a bathroom.* Wouldn't be practical to avoid it indefinitely.

Shoving the heavy door with one hand while instinctively clenching the other, her own breath threatened to choke her.

The bathtub held a dead body.

No! Reflexively, her hands shielded her eyes. Then through parted fingers, she forced a second look. It was just a bathtub. Clean, white...and empty.

It had been more than two years now, but the image of the blood-splattered porcelain still haunted her.

"Don't you just love the claw-foot tub?"

Grace sucked in a sharp breath, jolted by the perky voice from behind. She shook off the memory. Why couldn't the place just have a shower, like her apartment?

"Let's take a look at the front bedroom," Spritz chirped with an air of unruffled confidence. She stepped into the room to her left, flicking a switch to illuminate it.

Grace followed, heavy with fatigue. She hovered in the doorway of the big white box that would be her bedroom, piqued by Spritz's unnecessary perkiness.

Spritz beamed with professional pride. "The bedrooms are the same square footage, so it really depends on which view you prefer."

Grace heaved an anxious sigh. She had already decided she'd sleep in this room. Best to keep track of the world out front—as if anything would happen in a town this size. Yawning, she lifted her wrist slightly, shocked at the hour—nearly eleven. One o'clock in the morning back home. Her eyelids felt like they had stage weights in them.

"Where's my head?" Spritz crossed toward her, hands outstretched. "You flew all the way from Seattle, then had that long cab ride from Missoula. You must be dead on your feet."

Grace's stomach pitched at the ill-chosen words, but she coerced a smile. Spritz had shown such kindness without even knowing how much Grace had needed it. She allowed the realtor to enclose both her hands in a solid, warm grasp.

"I'll see myself out." Spritz gave Grace's hands an extra squeeze. "You just call if you need anything." She turned for the door, speaking over her shoulder as she walked. "Or stop by my office. It's on Main, right across from the park. You can't miss it."

Grace chuckled to herself. As if finding anything in this town would require the use of MapQuest.

Grateful for her long-awaited solitude, she bolted the door after Spritz's exit and lowered the blinds over its small cut glass pane. Talk about impractical. Why would anyone want a window in their front door?

Looking around the quiet house, she surrendered to a welcome yawn. She hadn't been this tired in a very long time. All she needed was a refreshing night's sleep to plan her next step for surviving this ordeal.

She dragged her feet back to the bedroom and stopped. Looking down at the hard wood of the floor, she let out a throaty moan. Where had her head been? She had always prided herself on her ability to think things through down to the minutest detail. How could she have neglected to arrange for a bed?

She sat down with a thud and buried her face in her hands, not knowing if she would burst out in laughter or sobs.

"Good grief, Grace Addison." A quiet laugh escorted her words. "Or whatever your name is. Get your act together, would you?"

Chapter 2

Stepping onto her front porch and into the morning sun, Grace groaned. She rubbed her aching shoulder, making a silent promise not to spend another night on the floor. By comparison, her Murphy bed back home was a feathery cloud. She pulled the door shut and locked the deadbolt, vowing to add *get some kind of bed* to her to-do list.

As she turned to face the street, her stomach roared like the lion at the beginning of an MGM movie. Even though she felt like signing up for the hermit's union, survival forced her to plunge headlong into a limited exploration of the town.

Taking the initial tread down the steps that bridged her front porch and the rest of the world, she scanned the tree-lined street. Two women with strollers, and a couple of kids on stingrays. Just an ordinary summer day in Small Town, U.S.A.

As her foot left the bottom step, a movement caught the corner of her eye. Someone sprang up from the flower bed, as if they'd been lying in wait. Terror shot through her.

Her heart could have auditioned for a seat in the timpani section as her body propelled forward. The heel of her sandal hooked her pants hem, landing her face down on the pebbly pavement. Panicked, she pulled her legs under her and scrambled to her feet.

Stumbling ahead, she threw a glance over her shoulder, then lurched to a halt and reeled around. As she looked down into a pair of deep brown eyes, a wisp of relieved laughter escaped with the breath she'd held for the past several seconds. Scruffy fur, coffee-brown with clouds of cream, covered a scrawny knee-height frame. Her guest gave a tentative wag of his long ratty tail and Grace tittered. If the former homeowner had left this forlorn canine behind, that couldn't be her problem. She could barely take care of herself, much less a dog.

"You're a pretty boy, but I can't keep you." She gave her linen pants a quick swipe. "You wouldn't want in on my life anyway if you knew what a mess it is. Go on!"

He cocked his head with a questioning whimper.

"You heard me." She made a shooing gesture with her hand. "Go find someone who has their act together."

He gave one more high-pitched plea before lowering his nose and ambling down the walkway. When he was several houses away, Grace set off in the opposite direction, chuckling to herself. Clearly, she'd have to adjust to being out west where packs of wild dogs roamed the streets.

There had been a time when a walk, or better yet a run, on a clear early summer day like this would have soothed her soul. Now, as she strode under the arch of trees that enclosed the street, she wondered how hard reclusiveness would be, what with the internet and home delivery.

Taking care not to trip where a tree root had turned the sidewalk into a roller coaster track, she rallied her thoughts. Had it really only been three days since she had shut her eyes and circled her finger over a map of the United States? Madison Falls, Montana, had seemed like such a good idea at the time. Now the reality seemed strikingly unromantic.

Still, she had to go somewhere. Kirk had left her no choice.

A few minutes later, she looked up at the street sign on the corner of the undeniably charming main street. *Main Street.* At least something in this new world made sense.

Her nose caught a distinctive scent. Pleasant...oh yes very.

Instinctively, she turned to the left and inhaled her way past quaint little shops until the spicy sweet aroma enveloped her. As it became clear that the Madison Bakery was to be her first stop of the morning, she did a quick calculation. Twenty hours since that skimpy little sandwich at the airport. No wonder the fresh-baked smell lured her like a carnival barker.

The creak of the old wooden screen door announced her entrance, and the dozen or so people seated at café tables turned on cue to look at her. She stopped cold, overtaken by stage fright. It wasn't an audience she craved. Not anymore.

Forcing a feeble smile, she homed in on the pastry case just a few feet ahead. *Get a bagel and get out*. Her will to live instructed her to stay nourished and, besides, she smelled coffee.

"You from out of town?" The chipper young girl behind the counter greeted her.

Grace sputtered. Did she look out of place? Why weren't these people going back to their newspapers and small talk? It felt as if they were all waiting for her response.

"Yes. I mean, not anymore. I just moved here."

"No kidding. Oh, you must be the woman who bought the Miller place. I heard about you."

What had she heard? Grace's mind raced as she tried to recall every detail she'd given to Spritz. Most of it had been made up, but still. Her palms grew clammy and her appetite slipped into hiding.

"Coffee?" the girl chirped. "First cup's on the house."

Relief swept through Grace. Coffee would do the trick. "Sure. Coffee. And a bagel with lox please."

A delighted clucking erupted behind her and she turned to face her spectators. Laughter in the wrong place had always been a sign of an off performance.

"Where do you think you are, miss, New York City?" A jovial looking older man in grubby overalls seemed to take great joy in her awkwardness.

Warmth washed her cheeks as she looked at the counter girl again. "No bagels?"

The girl shook her head, as if she'd never been asked for such a thing and had no appropriate comeback prepared.

Grace glanced down at the case and pointed at nothing in particular. "One of those then."

"Oh, a bear claw." The girl brightened. "Those are fresh out of the oven." She beamed with some sort of yeast-induced pride as she brandished a pair of tongs.

Grace released a lungful of air. She had pleased a local and today that felt like hitting a high C.

"Here you go." The girl presented a chipped, pastry-adorned plate. "Have a seat and I'll bring your coffee out. I'm just brewing a fresh pot."

Heartened by the promise of nourishment, Grace accepted the plate and scanned the room. Her recent victory faded. All the tables were taken.

Clutching her claw, she made eye contact with a woman who also dined solo but had evidently arrived early enough to commandeer a table. The empty chair across from her opened its arms wide and Grace nodded toward it with her best non-threatening expression. The woman smiled, and Grace took a step toward her, stumbling over an uneven floorboard. Gasps erupted from the audience as she fumbled with her free hand to prevent her bear claw from attacking an innocent bystander.

Just as gravity threatened to get the better of her, someone gripped her upper arms from behind. Her heart slammed against her ribs. She let out a relieved breath, realizing that she'd been saved from toppling headlong into the half-devoured cinnamon roll of the man in the grubby overalls.

She pulled her arms free, whirled around and looked up into a pair of eyes the color of a dark chocolate mocha.

"Excuse me, ma'am." The possessor of the eyes took a step back. "I just hate to see a lady in distress."

She clasped her plate with both hands and surreptitiously assessed her rescuer. He was about her age—twenty-five or so—clad in what was probably typical local garb, faded Levi's and a light-blue work shirt. A faint hint of stubble shadowed his strong-jawed face, and his dark hair needed a cut. He reminded her of the stagehands back home. The ones who looked for any opportunity to slip a hand around her waist or stand a little too close in the wings. *Distress?* Just who did this guy think he was?

"You could sit here, if you'd like." He gestured toward his table.

He expected her to sit with him? A diffident sound escaped her throat as her eyes darted around. "I... I really..."

"What I meant was," his voice sounded smooth, like a cappuccino. "I was just leaving and you look like you need a table." He picked up a mug and a crumb-covered plate, then set them on the counter behind him.

In spite of her desire to appear aloof, her eyes locked onto his. Dark chocolate had always been her weakness.

"Thank you."

She set her plate down and took a seat as the stagehand wannabe nodded toward the counter girl and hurried out of the bakery.

Feeling like a reluctant Lois Lane, Grace let her eyes linger on the screen door after it had banged shut. A murmur rumbled through the room. What was with these people? Didn't they have cable?

Remembering her empty stomach, she glanced down at her plate. Mouth watering, she lifted the sticky concoction to her lips and took an eager bite. Her eyes closed as her head tipped back slightly. It tasted like heaven with extra icing.

"Good, isn't it?" The young girl arrived with a large mug of welcome brew.

Grace smiled and took the handle. She hadn't had a decent cup of coffee in days, what with the throng of details she'd had to attend to. Now, as she inhaled the wonderful rich smell and put the cup to her lips, she felt for the first time in months that life would be good again. She drew the liquid into her mouth and wanted to cry.

That was the worst coffee she'd ever tasted.

Chapter 3

Though still caffeine-deprived, Grace's hunger had at least been satisfied. Now she could focus on the next item on her to-do list—finding a safe place to stash her life savings.

As the bell on the bakery door jingled behind her, she gave her money belt a reassuring pat. She'd made a habit for months of keeping important documents and cash safely nestled at her waist. The stack of bills currently crammed into the pouch represented nearly all she had in the world, and she cringed at the thought of anything happening to it. She wouldn't be able to relax until it was safely stowed away in a bank—under her assumed name, of course.

She started down Main Street, which was more far-reaching than she'd realized. The businesses spanned two full blocks, but she couldn't spot a bank in either direction.

A familiar sensation breezed through her like a whispered warning. Adrenaline flooded her system. She hated this feeling so much she had flown clear across the country in the hope of shedding it. Slowing her steps, her eyes darted from one side to the other. A few people milled about, but would anyone help her if she screamed?

Panic rose in her throat as it became obvious that someone was following her.

She had to act quickly, and with nowhere to run she decided to take a chance. She whirled around with a rush of anger-fueled bravado, ready to unleash the wrath that had been brewing in her for the past two years.

She froze. There, just a few yards in front of her, stood her tracker, looking up at her with deep brown eyes. His long scraggly tail wagged tentatively.

Grace laughed as relief cleansed her veins. "You again?" She put her hands on her hips, not wanting to encourage him. "That's twice now you've nearly scared me to death."

The dog sat and held up a paw, by way of gentlemanly introduction.

"Small-town hospitality, huh?" She folded her arms and smiled in spite of her unsteadiness. "Well, do yourself a favor and shoo." She took a step away, then looked back. "Oh, but before you go, can you point me in the direction of a bank?"

He cocked his head, then looked across the street and barked.

She followed his gaze. "You're kidding me."

There up the street stood a beautiful old brick structure with a sign over the massive doors that read "Banque."

As she looked back at her obedient guide, he offered a cheerful wag. She waved him off and darted across the street.

She climbed the hefty stairs to the imposing double doors. How old was this place, anyway? It looked like something out of an old Gary Cooper western. Her heart jumped to her throat as she heaved one of the doors open. Showtime.

A rush of cool air ricocheted off the gray marble floor as she stepped inside and scanned the room. It looked bigger than it had from the outside. A soothing sigh slipped from her throat as she noted that not one customer or clerk seemed to notice her. Feeling safer now, she moved toward a desk marked *New Accounts.* The man plunking at a computer keyboard didn't even look up.

"Excuse me." She spoke *sotto voce*, so as not to attract unnecessary attention.

"Yes?" His eyes grew wide under his round spectacles, as if he wasn't used to interruptions. "May I help you?"

"I hope so." She took a seat opposite the desk. "I'd like to open a checking account."

"You would? Oh, well then..." He dug through some papers on his desk, finally pulling one from the stack. "You must be new here. Name?"

She floundered. "Grace. Grace Addison."

"Middle name?"

"Oh...no middle name."

He shot her an inquisitive glance. Why hadn't she thought of a middle name? Didn't everyone have one? Now she had raised a red flag with a banker, and that wasn't good.

"Middle name, none." He scribbled on the paper. "Address?"

"Eighteen twenty-seven Pine Vista Avenue."

His head snapped up again. "Oh, of course. The Miller place." His face relaxed into a smile as he extended his hand across the desk. "Welcome to Madison Falls."

"Thank you." She accepted his welcome and nodded at the paper. "Is there much more?"

"Let's see..." He scanned the document. "Not much. It's been so long since I've done a new account. We don't get a lot of people moving into the area."

"It's a small town." As if he wasn't aware of that.

"Yes, and we like it that way." He looked beyond her, his brow lifting. "Joanne, come meet the gal who bought the Miller place."

Suddenly surrounded by outstretched hands, it felt like her dressing room on opening night. Several customers lingered on the outskirts looking at her the way fans sometimes did when they were too timid to ask for an autograph. She drew in an impatient breath. If she had wanted to stay center stage, she'd still be in New York.

"Where did you move from, honey?" The woman named Joanne seemed genuinely friendly.

"Um...Seattle." Her throat clenched at the sound of the lie.

"Beautiful city." Another woman—Tina, according to her name tag—nodded. "I went there once for high school choir. Why would you leave such a great place?"

Grace had chosen Seattle as her fictitious hometown because she'd spent enough time working there to be able to fake a familiarity. She forced her fists to unclench. She was an actress, after all. It wasn't lying so much as role-playing.

"I needed a slower pace, I guess." She hoped she sounded earnest.

Heads bobbed on all sides of her.

"That's what you'll find here," Joanne said. "Our pace is so slow you could take a nap for a year and pretty much not miss a beat."

Grace coerced a smile. *Sounds exciting.*

"You know," Joanne's intent look had become disconcerting. "You remind me of someone."

Grace's heart galloped but she forced her expression to remain dispassionate. "Oh really?"

Joanne snapped her fingers. "I know. Anne Hathaway. In that movie *Rachel Getting Married*, where she had the short cut."

Grace let out a tiny titter and touched her hair. Warm Cinnamon from a box would not have been her first choice. She shifted in her seat, anxious to pick up the pace on that paperwork. A couple strolled past on their way to the door, stealing a quick look at her.

Joanne leaned in. "Don't mind us, Miss Addison," she said with a hint of candor. "We're just not used to seeing such fancy attire around here."

Grace glanced down at her favorite spring-green linen pants and matching silk short-sleeve sweater. The heels of her white sandals were only two inches high. Flat-out casual.

She quickly assessed the costume-plot of the scene in which she seemed to be starring. The customers all wore shorts or jeans, and the bank employees looked as if they'd extended casual Friday to include Monday through Thursday. The men weren't even wearing ties.

Great. If she had any hope of blending in, she'd have to learn to dress the part.

Chapter 4

An hour later, Grace wrote her first check from her new account made out to *Sylvia's Closet.*

She exited the store, laden down with several bags full of jeans, T-shirts, socks, and sneakers. She drew in a satisfied breath. Small-town life at least weighed in on the plus side of the comfort scale.

Her heart lightened as she toted her new wardrobe down the street. She'd only been able to bring one suitcase. She needed new clothes anyway, so that justified the expense.

Casting a look at the vibrant blue overhead, a spark of homesickness jolted through her. She pinched back a tear. If she was home right now, she'd more than likely be on her way to her voice lesson, glancing up at the same sky, albeit a narrower strip of it.

She looked around, noticing for the first time that nobody seemed to be in much of a hurry. She slowed her pace, mimicking that of the dozen or so people who meandered along Main Street. Of course they weren't in a hurry. Where did they have to go? She smiled lightly. Walking at her usual rate, she'd have run out of sidewalk and stumbled into that park up ahead as if she were running a race. That was no way to blend in.

The eclectic display in an upcoming store window brought to

mind another item on her list. She tipped her head back to read the sign over the door. *Roberts and Son Hardware.* Surely someone here could instruct her. Struggling, she got hold of the door handle in spite of her bulky bags.

The place looked surprisingly tidy, considering the crammed-full shelves lining its aisles. Having no idea where to even begin looking, she started on one end, taking care not to knock anything over with her shopping bags.

Suddenly, her breath caught in her throat. Blinking back threatening tears, she set down her bags, freeing her hands to pick up a water globe from its place on a top shelf. Its smooth coolness mesmerized her as she rolled it over in her hands. It felt heavy, not like some cheap souvenir. Its base was real wood, and the simple treble clef inside looked like brass. She held it close to her face, as if she might melt into its magical world.

Her fingers found the key protruding from the back of the base. She hesitated only a moment before turning it. Eyes closed, she released the key.

At once the music swept her away, washing her with vivid memory. The tinny tune played a full symphony to her heart.

"Sounds like opera."

A voice jarred her back to reality, and her eyes snapped open.

The warbled features of a man's face projected through the glass globe in front of her. She lowered the orb as her stomach jumped to her throat. It was *him*—the stagehand wannabe.

"Nice." He nodded at the globe, flashing a dimpled smile. "If you like that sort of thing."

"That 'sort of thing' is called music." Her words dripped icicles.

"Yeah, so I've heard." He ran a hand across his dark, tousled hair. "Can I help you find anything, or are you just here for the concert?"

So, the guy worked here. Irritation boiling in her veins, she put the globe back on the shelf. Was that any way to talk to a customer?

"Yes," she said, folding her hands in front of her. "I seem to have a small problem."

"Most people do. That's what keeps us in business." He winked, his roguish brown eyes drilling into her. "What can I do to help you?"

She wavered. Her rush of emotion had thrown her off-balance, and now this man had muddied her thinking. Resolving not to play along with his familiar bantering, she firmed her mouth. "It's my kitchen floor."

He nodded, placing one hand on his hip and the other on a shelf edge. "I'm going to need a little more detail."

Her annoyance brewed. "It's squishy." She felt ridiculous, like one of those women who didn't know a wrench from a pair of pliers.

"I see—"

"Just in one spot. Under a tile. *Two* tiles. Anyway, I need something to pull them up with so I can put in some kind of support." She smiled, satisfied that she'd sounded like a knowledgeable homeowner.

"Okay." His head bobbed agreeably. "Or you could actually fix it."

Her jaw tightened. Once again, this guy had brought to mind those stagehands who always tried to impress the *little ladies* with their knowledge of construction. Their technique might be more effective if they'd bother with a close shave and clean shirt.

"Fine." She dipped down, reaching for her bags. "If you don't think you can help me, I'll—"

"No...sorry." He held both palms up in surrender. "Spritz called me a little while ago." His face softened as he offered his hand. "I'm Sam."

Teeth clenched, she allowed his hand to hover for a moment before lowering her bags and accepting his handshake. "Grace Addison."

"Grace..." His eyes latched onto hers a little too intensely. "Miss Addison." He let go of her hand. "About your floor—"

"I can fix it myself," she said. "I just need a crowbar."

He looked like he wanted to either argue or laugh, then held up a just-a-second finger. "I'll meet you at the counter."

She moved to the front of the store, still stewing, and waited while an older man helped a customer at the till.

"Did Sam take care of you, miss?"

She looked up to see that the older man had finished his transaction.

"Yes, I..." Her voice seized up with unexpected emotion. It was like looking at a *ghost*. She forced a steady tone. "He's getting me a crowbar." She looked away, unable to meet his gaze.

"Oh, well you're out of luck then." His soft voice revealed a caring spirit. "I sold the last one this morning, and I'm not sure when our shipment's coming in. You might want to borrow one from a neighbor."

Tears stung her eyes, and her throat threatened to close. "I see. Well, thank you." She hurried out the door, anxious to get away before her emotions overtook her again.

When she was well out of view of the store, she set down her bags and brought her hands to her face. This would have to happen to her now, on top of everything else.

What was it about the older man that had jarred her memory and jolted her heart? A quality in his voice, or the gentleness in his eyes? Whatever it was, it had caught her completely off guard. She hadn't expected to be reminded of her father.

"Excuse me...miss?"

A deep male voice brought her sharply around, alarmed by its propinquity. Only when she saw Sam standing in front of the hardware store holding up the water globe did it register that she'd heard the bell over the door signal his exit.

Her face flushed. Giving her eyes a casual dab with the back of her hand, she forced the emotion from her voice. "Yes?"

"Did you want this?" He spoke haltingly. "I forgot to mention it's on clearance."

Debating, she inched closer. She did want it, even if it meant prolonging their conversation. "How much?"

"Six bucks." He closed the gap between them. "But you can pay when you get your crowbar. Sorry we were out."

"It's okay." She took the globe, kneeling to place it snugly among her clothing purchases.

"I'm not sure when we'll get our shipment." He wavered. "You're in the old Miller place, right?"

Her head dipped tentatively as she stood.

"I drive down your street on my way home. I could bring it by when it comes in."

She pulled back her shoulders, not knowing how to respond. It chilled her to think she'd only just arrived in this town and already she had no anonymity. Complete strangers seemed to know more about Grace Addison than even she did.

She shot him an admonishing look. Why would he just assume he could come to her house after she'd refused his help? A protest formed in her throat, but when her mouth opened to release it, she swallowed hard. The last thing she needed was to develop a reputation as the town diva.

"That won't be necessary, thank you." She grabbed her bags and spun around, hoping this creep got the point. Who did he think he was, anyway?

As she marched back up Main Street, she vowed to avoid the hardware store. From now on she'd keep to herself as much as possible.

She'd never fit in here, that had become painfully clear.

Chapter 5

Glitter rained down around the treble clef as tears dripped from Grace's cheeks.

Barely making it home in time to keep her emotional outburst private, she had fished the water globe out of the shopping bag, knowing its tune would help pull every bit of sorrow from the corners of her soul. She'd slumped against the living room wall where she remained now, at least an hour later. What else did she have to do besides wallow in grief?

As if her life hadn't been bad enough—with the murder, then the ordeal with Kirk—it had only gotten worse with her dad's diagnosis. She'd been so wrapped up in protecting herself that she hadn't realized till it was too late how sick he was. Her mom had tried to tell her, but Grace had been too absorbed in her own problems. Besides, she hadn't wanted to endanger her parents. If Kirk knew where they lived.... A tremor shot down her back. Her intentions had been good, but would she ever stop blaming herself for not being there when her dad died?

She rubbed her eyes as the question ran through her mind for the millionth time.

Exhausted from the flood of feelings that had been building for months, she wiped her eyes with her fingertips and scolded herself. *Would it really hurt you to buy a box of Kleenex?*

Looking around, she realized this was the most time she'd spent in this stark colorless room, which actually had some cute features. It certainly deserved more attention than she'd given it. She pulled herself to her feet and placed the water globe ceremonially in the center of the mantel. Taking a step back to admire it, she had to admit that this tiny bit of home decor had been a good idea. It lifted her spirits just looking at it.

She let out a sigh. What a wasted day. Bad enough that she'd plummeted into unexpected emotional despair at the reminder of her father, but she'd neglected the most important item on her to-do list. *Find gainful employment.* She rubbed her temples. True, her savings were now safely tucked away, but they wouldn't last long, especially now that she had a house payment.

The *ping pong* of the doorbell nearly propelled her out of her skin. She stared at the door. What was she going to do, run? She didn't have an escape plan. This *was* her escape plan. How could a person flee any further than the middle of nowhere?

"Yoo hoo!" A female voice sounded from the front porch.

Grace took a careful step toward the door. Any person who would utter the phrase *yoo hoo* couldn't be much of a threat.

Biting her lower lip, she twisted the lock and pulled the door open a few cautious inches. There stood a pleasant-looking, thirty-something woman with honey-blonde hair pulled up into a ponytail and a plate of large brownies in her hands.

"Hi!" she chirped. "I'm Lucy Branigan. I live right across the street. Welcome to the neighborhood."

Grace willed the adrenaline in her system to return to its holding tank. "Uh...thanks. I'm Grace."

What now? Should she invite her in? She would never do such a thing back home, but then people there didn't generally appear at a stranger's door wielding baked goods. This was a different world.

She took a step back. "Would you like to come in?"

Lucy and her sunny disposition stepped inside and looked around. "Sure looks different. I guess the real estate agency thinks no one has an imagination. White, white, white. Reminds me of the hospital."

"Yes." Grace forced a casualness she wanted to believe. "It's very healing."

Lucy chuckled with a friendly, Kate Hudson kind of lilt. "Oh, these are for you." She handed over the plate as if she were presenting an award.

Grace inhaled the chocolaty aroma, remembering that she hadn't eaten in a while. The tension in her shoulders eased. It might be nice to have a woman to talk to. "Why don't you stay and have one? I could make some coffee."

Lucy smiled. "Anything to keep me away from my pile of laundry. The glamorous life of the American housewife."

They moved to the kitchen. Grace's nerves pinched at her sparse furnishings. "I'd offer you a chair, but..."

"It's okay." Lucy waved a dismissive hand and leaned against the wall where a table would go if there was one. "When does your stuff arrive?"

"Actually," Grace went to the sink and filled her camping saucepan with what she hoped would make two cups of Nescafé. "My 'stuff' arrived when I did. I didn't bring much."

"Oh." Lucy's tone dropped, then lifted. "Well, lucky you. You get to buy everything new."

"Uh-huh." Grace's hands started to sweat as she put the pan on the burner. How could she lie to this nice woman? She had no interest in filling this house with a lot of stuff. As far as she was concerned, it was just a place to stay while her life sorted itself out. "I can't do too much though." Did she sound casual enough?

"I hear you. Everything costs." Lucy's face brightened like a follow spot. "Our church is having a huge rummage sale this Saturday. I'll bet you could find everything you need there."

A rummage sale? Was she kidding? Grace swallowed a laugh. "That sounds like fun."

Lucy beamed as she stepped over to the counter and removed the saran wrap from the brownies. "So, have you decided on a color scheme?"

"A what?" Grace picked up her Nescafé jar. "Sorry I don't

have any real coffee."

"No problem. You're not leaving it white, are you?"

Grace set the small cup from the camping kit next to the Montana mug the bank had given her for opening her account. "No, I...I mean I haven't really thought about it." She plopped a spoonful of brown crystals into each vessel. "I'm not much of a decorator." She bit her lower lip. She was actually much better at decorating than she was at lying. She'd have to get better at rearranging the truth if she expected this to work.

"Really?" Lucy turned, her ponytail snapping like a flag. "I'm kind of a Martha Stewart wannabe, if you'd like any help."

"Great." Just what she needed, Montana's answer to Adrienne Neff.

"It would be a good way for us to get better acquainted." Lucy looked around, grabbing a couple of paper towels off a roll that sat on the counter. "Besides, now that my kids are getting older, I have time. And who couldn't use a creative outlet?"

Grace's stomach twisted. The idea that decorating a house in a middle-of-nowhere town where she had no desire to live could even come close to qualifying as a creative outlet made her eyes sting. Forcing a weak smile, she poured the bubbling water into the cups. "Coffee's ready. Such as it is."

Lucy traded a brownie on a towel for the mug. "Smells delicious. My husband prefers instant so that's all I ever buy. I guess we have something in common."

Grace smiled tightly, then took a sip of the bitter brew. Lucy seemed nice, but it was improbable that the two of them shared very much in common.

"Oh, I'd better warn you." Lucy took a drink, making a pleased face. "The young single guys in town are going to be clamoring to meet you."

"Great." Grace cringed involuntarily. Just what she needed—a bunch of cowhands with bouquets of wilted daisies stepping over each other to ask her to the town dance.

"Don't worry." Lucy must have picked up on her sarcastic tone. "My baby brother is ten years younger than me—probably about your age. He's been friends with all these guys since we were kids. I'll let you know which ones are worth the bother."

Grace offered up a feeble smile. *Bother* would be an understatement. What she didn't need was a romance to muddy up her life right now. That was absolutely, without question, the last thing on her mind.

Chapter 6

Eager to get this day off to a better start than the one previous, Grace settled into a booth at the Country Kitchen, Main Street's equivalent of the Carnegie Deli. She'd given herself an attitude check before setting out that morning. All she needed was to find a sense of purpose here while she waited it out. She'd be just fine.

With a heartening inhalation, she flipped open her copy of the local paper. She puckered her brow. Were they kidding? The *Madison Falls Gazette* was so puny, the ads from the *New York Times* would have laughed at it.

She flipped through it, easily locating a scrawny column of want ads.

"Coffee, honey?" A waitress straight out of *Alice* approached her table.

"Thanks." Grace smiled as the liquid promise of a better day flowed into her cup.

"You must be the new girl in town." The waitress nodded toward the paper. "Looking for work?"

"I think so." Grace smiled wanly.

"You're in luck if you'd like to waitress. We could use some help."

Grace gulped, hoping for some better options. "Oh, I would never do *that*."

"Oh?" The woman put a hand on her hip and looked down her nose.

Warmth flooded Grace's cheeks. Her tone must have betrayed her repulsion at the woman's suggestion. "I mean, it seems so hard. I just don't think I could do it." She gave her menu a quick go-over. "I'll have a spinach and cheese omelet and country potatoes, please."

The waitress firmed her jaw as she grabbed the menu and walked away.

Great way to start the day.

Grace really hadn't meant to offend the woman, but she had always considered that type of job to be subservient. She was used to being doted over. Now she felt terrible. And a little afraid to eat that omelet.

She looked at the mug in front of her with renewed hope. Could her quest for a decent cup of coffee culminate here at the Country Kitchen? She lifted the cup and inhaled, prolonging the anticipation, then let some of the liquid slip between her lips.

Her mouth pursed. Had she been in an appropriate social setting, she would have spit it out. How was it possible that this could be even worse than the coffee at the bakery? And how could all the other diners consume it without gagging? Didn't these people know mud when they tasted it?

She plunked the cup back down, letting out a loud breath. Her disappointment as bitter as the coffee, she turned her attention back to the want ads.

Gas station attendant. Not in her wildest dreams. *Dental hygienist.* Not likely. *Floral designer.* Now that seemed promising. *Must have three years floral experience.* She'd received five or six years' worth of opening-night bouquets. Would that count?

Heaving an uneasy sigh, she set down the ads. She'd better find something, and not just to keep her mind occupied. Who knew how long she'd be stuck here?

Too bad she didn't have unlimited funds, like Kirk, so she wouldn't have to work. Of course if that were the case, she would have just hired someone to protect her.

She huffed out a sigh, wanting nothing more than to forget about him. Why did he still permeate her thoughts? Would the day ever come when she could just live her life free of him?

As the bell over the door jingled, her gaze lifted and her heart all but stopped. In strutted a man in tight-fitting Levi's and a muscle T-shirt. He paused just inside the door to peruse the place as if making sure his entrance had been noticed. He looked right at Grace and for a split second, in spite of the casual attire, she could have sworn it was Kirk.

She gaped, too stunned to look away. It wasn't Kirk, she saw that now, but he had the same James Dean swagger and carefully coiffed sandy blond hair. The same air of self-importance.

He swaggered in, straddled a stool at the counter, and whistled to the waitress as if she were a cocker spaniel.

Grace breathed deeply, telling herself she was safe. It was just a weird coincidence coupled with her heightened awareness of her own personal danger zone.

The bell jingled again and she held her breath. *Oh no.* Was she doomed to run into Sam everywhere she went? What were the odds that they'd both choose the same place for breakfast two mornings in a row? She grabbed the paper, pulling it up close to her face and praying he wouldn't try to sit with her. Could she pretend to be waiting for someone? Could she be any more pathetic?

She glanced up again and their eyes met. *Terrific.*

He flashed a reticent smile before stepping toward the counter. He stopped, his eyes fixed on the James Dean/Kirk look-alike. The man flicked him a cocky sneer, and Grace thought for a second she might witness her first ever diner brawl. Sam lingered a moment before slipping into a seat near the window.

Her shoulders fell. Her emotions had been so manipulated during the past two years that her sensors must need a tuning. Why should she feel disappointed that he hadn't tried to sit with her?

"Here you go, honey." The waitress returned with an omelet the size of Central Park. "See," she winked. "That wasn't so hard. Need a warm-up?"

Grace glanced at her still-full cup. "No. Look, I really didn't mean—"

"Not to worry." The woman shifted her weight onto one foot, clasping the rim of the coffee pot. "Waitressing isn't for everybody. It takes a special sort of skill. You kind of reminded me of that. It's funny how God sends us messengers just when we need them. I was having a real bad morning and you helped me remember my calling."

"Your calling?" Grace said, unconvinced that God would actually use *her* as a messenger.

"Sure." The waitress's face looked brighter than it had just minutes before, when she'd seemed to want to stomp on Grace's toes. "It might not seem very noble, but a good meal served with a smile is a gift I can give people every day. I'm where I'm supposed to be." She grinned and crossed to the window. "Morning, Sam."

Grace's thoughts staggered. It hadn't ever occurred to her that someone could find that kind of meaning in a service job. She had always thought you were either called to do something lofty and significant or you settled for earning a living.

Mechanically, she lifted her cup with both hands, taking a sip she barely tasted, as the waitress and Hardware Boy exchanged a laugh. She drew in a deep breath to keep from choking up.

She looked again at the man who wasn't Kirk and remembered how it felt to be where she was supposed to be. Would she ever get to feel that way again?

Chapter 7

Sated from the best breakfast she'd eaten in a very long time, Grace commenced with the Plan B she had developed while forcing down her second cup of morning mud. Forget about the skimpy want ads. She'd walk around town to scout for Help Wanted signs. It was either that, or take a quick correspondence course in dental hygiene.

Stepping out onto Main Street, she surveyed her prospects. With so many little businesses in town, there had to be something interesting she could do.

She walked slowly, peering into the shop next to the café. She was in luck already. A bright orange sign announced that they were *Now Hiring*. Optimism surged until her eye caught an image in the lower corner of the front window. She balked at the yellow outline of a man running in winged helmet and heels, with one arm strewn behind him and a bouquet of roses clutched in his outstretched hand. Her shoulders drooped. Too bad she hadn't pursued floral arranging in her spare time.

She gave herself a mental pep talk. If she wanted something badly enough, she just had to focus. That had always worked for her in the past—why should this be any different?

Standing on the curb and looking across Mountainview Avenue, her curiosity was piqued by the building on the other side.

From this angle, it looked like a long, narrow garage, but the square facade in the front gave it the look of a set from a John Ford western.

Intrigued, she crossed the street.

The front of the building was prettier than she'd thought from a distance. The upper portion consisted of horizontal wood planks with a window squared in the center. The bottom half was made up of soaring display windows which angled into the central narrow double doors. It looked a little weather-worn—nothing a coat of paint and an extended squeegee couldn't remedy. A sign in the lower corner of one of the large panes stirred her hope until she got close enough to read it. *For Lease*. Her hope faded.

Still, the building captured her interest. She cupped her hands and peered through the hazy glass.

A long counter extended the length of a large room, and she scooted closer to get a better look at the ornate antique cash register that sat on the end near the window. She breathed out awe. That thing must be worth a mint.

Charming fishbowl light fixtures hung at regular intervals from long rods, adding emphasis to what the New York real estate market would refer to as a cathedral ceiling and charge a king's ransom for.

Squinting to get a better look into the darkened back corners, she could see a half dozen or so steps leading up to a landing and an old door that looked like it had been designed for Miss Kitty's grand entrance. *Striking architecture*.

Remembering her mission, she sighed and stepped back onto the sidewalk. *There's nothing for me in this abandoned old shop, that's for sure.*

She turned her head. What was that next door? The hand-lettered sign in the window of the aged brick building did appear to be a plea to the unemployed. She squared her shoulders and took a few steps, anxious to see what kind of business it could be.

Visions of herself as manager of a day spa or saleswoman of chic housewares rolled through her head. Sure she lacked work experience in these areas, but her actual skills were of no use to anyone here. Besides, she was a new person now, with new abilities. She just needed to find out what they were.

Drawing closer, she read the neatly written notice. *Help Wanted—Desperate.*

Desperate, huh? She slowed her gait. *That makes two of us.*

The lovely brass-plated sign over the double doors announced the name of her potential future employer. The Madison Playhouse. Grace fought the urge to cry, letting out a weak little chortle instead. *The Madison Playhouse?* Her last remaining hope was a *theatre?*

Flinging back her head, she strained to hear God laughing. This had to be some sort of cosmic joke. How could she fall off the radar working in a theatre? That would be the first place anybody would think to look for her.

She shifted her weight. The *first* place, yes. But wouldn't Madison Falls be the *last* place? So even if someone were to look in the first place of the last place, that still left her pretty well hidden.

Examining the carefully lettered sign, she climbed the front steps. After all, they *were* desperate. With a strengthening inhalation, she pulled on one of the rustic iron door handles.

Stepping from the sun-drenched porch into the theatre was like traveling back in time a good hundred and twenty years. As the door swooshed shut behind her, she looked around a slightly frayed but otherwise perfectly preserved Old West theatre lobby. It was tiny, like a child's play theatre, but lushly decorated in warm shades of red and brown. The well-used velvet settees beckoned her to curl up and hide from the world, but that wasn't on her to-do list.

Her eyes moved languidly around the room for some indication of how she should proceed.

Something on the wall to her left caught her eye and she stepped over to get a better look. A painting about the size of a magazine hung between two tall velvet-draped windows. Just inches from the canvas, she faced it full-on.

She studied the image of a woman with upswept hair and a

rich burgundy gown, with a jeweled opera glass in her hand, leaned forward over a railing. It was striking, and oddly familiar—the brushstrokes, the colors, the theme. For a lovely moment, Grace was cast into its luxurious world.

"Oh, man!"

A female voice joggled Grace back into her own century. She jerked around, facing a window marked *Box Office*.

"Ow!"

Her nerves on edge, Grace stepped toward the door next to the box office. Its top half stood open to create a second window, over which hung a sign that read *Concessions*. There was a loud *crash*, and Grace tilted her upper body to get a look inside.

A petite woman hopped around a space the size of Grace's closet, trying to dodge a cascade of runaway soda cans.

"Excuse me." Grace hesitated. "I'm here about the job. Should I come back?"

The woman looked up, pushing a stray strawberry-blonde hair out of her widening eyes. "Are you serious? You're really here about the job?"

Hearing the incredulity in the woman's voice, Grace considered beating a hasty retreat. "Uh...h...." she stammered. "What exactly *is* the job?"

Through a series of staccato movements, the tiny woman worked her way to the window. "My concessions manager eloped and her husband won't let her work. As of yesterday she's living in wedded bliss in a trailer on a pig farm."

"Sounds romantic."

"Terribly. You'd think she could at least have waited until *Wait Until Dark* closed, but no." She scrunched her young face and rolled her eyes upward.

Grace let out an anxious breath, relieved that the woman was apparently too frantic to ask for references. She'd been prepared to say that everyone she'd ever known or worked for was now dead, but that seemed far-fetched.

"In the five years I've worked here"—the woman waved a can for emphasis—"we've never once not opened the concession stand. So here I am trying to juggle a thousand things and get the snack bar ready for the hungry masses." She looked at the can as if realizing she'd shaken it to within an inch of its fizzy life. "It doesn't pay a lot, and it's really only three nights a week, but like the sign says, I'm desperate."

Grace bit her lower lip and considered her options. Taking a theatre job didn't seem wise, but maybe it would work in her favor. It wasn't as if she'd be onstage. How hard could it be to stand behind a counter?

Her chest heaved with uncertainty. This job was subservient, but the waitress's prophetic words stuck in her mind. Could it be that God had used the waitress to deliver a message to *her?* She hadn't ever thought of God as being that proactive in her life, but hey, *maybe*.

She lifted her chin. "I'll do it."

"Yes!"

Grace had never seen relief and gratitude wash so completely over a person, as the tiny woman did a high-strung victory dance. What was Grace getting herself into?

"Can you come back tonight? That way you'll be all trained for tomorrow night's show."

Grace nodded. At least now she'd have a little something to supplement her savings, and to keep her busy while she waited for things back home to change.

Promising to return, she shrugged off thoughts of home. Something would change, she had to have faith. She just needed to distance herself from the problem, and it would work itself out. She had to believe that.

Lost in her thoughts, Grace pushed at the solid front door and stepped back out into the mid-morning glare. She paused on the broad front porch to let her eyes readjust. She'd always loved that about the inside of a theatre—it was its own world. Safe and separated.

The gentle rumble of a car engine jostled her and she squinted in an attempt to see where it was coming from. She had just enough automotive expertise to judge from its timbre that this was no beat-up wreck on its last leg before meeting its destiny at the salvage yard. This was the sound of a motor that had cost its owner a fine chunk of change. As if in salute, she raised her hand to her forehead to block out the sun. Her eyes at least doubled in size.

Glistening in the sunlight, a sleek silver-blue Lexus coupe rounded the corner like a diva making her entrance. A tingle shot through Grace as the car picked up speed. Not enough to create a hazard, but just sufficient to declare its right to do so. It traveled a half-block and curved its way into a parking space right in front of the theatre—*rock star parking*, as they called it back home.

Grace wanted to believe she was above staring, but found it impossible to pull her eyes from the car as the driver's door swung open. She held her breath. Out stepped a strikingly handsome man in a well-tailored, pale gray linen suit—the first evidence Grace had witnessed of actual fashion sense in this town. He wore his shirt open with no tie, and his light brown hair gelled back just a touch. He was probably pushing thirty, but Grace had always admired older men.

He gave the car door a gentle nudge then adjusted his silver shades with one hand while holding a sleek—probably Prada—briefcase in the other. He then stepped onto the sidewalk and toward the theatre—toward her!

Stepping backward for no apparent reason, Grace nearly lost her balance. Blood rushed to her face as she realized she'd held her hand visor-like to her face all this time. So much for discretion.

He bounded up the porch steps with an energetic air of clear purpose. He hovered at the top step, as if noticing Grace for the first time. In one fluid moment, he removed his silver Armani shades, flashed a chiseled smile, and spoke.

"Good morning."

Grace grappled for air. A small, unidentifiable sound escaped her voice box as he breezed past, drew open the heavy front door with ease, and disappeared inside.

Placing a hand on her hip, Grace expelled a breath. Who was he? Some rich donor, probably. Her head snapped toward the Lexus. Obviously not *from* here. Legs wobbling, she moved slowly down the steps.

Wavering, she made a thin attempt to pull her eyes from the car. Why did she find it so difficult to walk away? Maybe because this car reminded her of home. While she was far from wealthy herself, her job catered to those who were. She had grown used to the finer things.

Caving to curiosity, she eased her way toward the coupe. She wove her fingers together to keep from touching the sleek exterior that could well have been custom-tinted to match the eyes of its handsome owner. Casually, she craned her neck to get a peek inside.

Ecru leather gleamed, smooth and spotless. What she wouldn't give to feel its luxurious softness against her skin. She leaned in a little further. A large manila envelope sat on the front passenger seat under a thick stack of letters. *He must have his mail forwarded here.*

She took a quick look around. No one paid her any attention. Twisting her neck, she read the name on the top of the stack. *Devon Sinclair.* Her gaze lifted. What a distinguished name, mysterious even.

Her stomach fluttered. Was she really spying on this man to find out where he was from? She took a deep breath, as if about to dive underwater, then bent down slightly. She straightened with a gasp. New York, New York. She could have guessed. Another quick look. Park Avenue—in an exclusive neighborhood. *Wow.*

Reluctantly, she stepped back onto the curb and started toward home. It raised her spirits to see someone in Madison Falls she could relate to, even if only in passing.

Funny, she should have been startled by the similarities between this man and Kirk. The good taste and affluence. The charm and appeal. But there was no mistaking the missing element—Kirk's self-conscious desperation.

Clearly, Devon Sinclair was everything Kirk aspired to be but wasn't.

She smiled. Adjusting to her stay here suddenly seemed a whole lot easier.

Chapter 8

"I know it's a lot to learn all at once, but you'll get the hang of it."

Grace had figured out fast that Nancy, the high-strung house manager who had hired her, moved at a mile a minute whether propelled by desperation or not. She was in charge of all front-of-house activity, which probably explained her frenzied pace.

"We have two kinds of canned soda, and whatever cookies are on sale down at the Peach Basket Market." Nancy pattered like a sped-up voice on a Chipmunks record. "That's pretty much it. That and gum."

"Got it." Grace looked around the small stand. "No coffee?"

Nancy stopped moving and wrinkled her brow. "Nobody's ever asked for it. Why would anyone want to drink coffee at night?"

Hadn't she ever heard of decaf?

Nancy flicked a look at her watch. "Any more questions?"

Anxious to avoid any surprises, Grace pointed to a narrow wooden door at the back of the stand. "What's in there?"

Nancy squinted, as if seeing it for the first time. "I just about forgot about that." She took a step toward it, rubbing her fingers across its splintery surface. "It just leads to the place next door. It's been empty for years now, but it used to be the general store until they built the Peach Basket. Mr. R. owns both buildings so he lets us rehearse over there. Don't worry though." She rattled the knob. "It's locked."

Grace nodded at the reassurance, then creased her brow. "Mr. R.? What does the 'R' stan—"

"Oh, gotta run." Nancy glanced at her watch again. "I have to approve the costume designs for the next show."

"Costume designs?" Grace took a step back to accommodate Nancy's exit. "Aren't you the house manager?"

"Yep." Nancy scuttled into the lobby and turned to Grace with a fight-or-flight stance.

Grace spoke quickly. "Don't you have an artistic director?"

"What's that?" Nancy shifted her weight from foot to foot.

Grace spoke haltingly. "The person who makes the artistic decisions." What kind of amateur operation had she gotten herself involved in? "Who chooses your season?"

Nancy's face went blank.

Grace tried again. "Who picks out your plays?"

The light returned behind Nancy's hazel eyes. "A bunch of us get together."

"Oh. Well, who hires the directors?"

"I do."

"Who determines the budget?"

"I do, but just because I'm good at math." Nancy bobbed up and down on her toes as if revving her engine for a race. "So anyway, the lobby opens tomorrow at seven. We're in performance in the theatre Thursday through Saturday, and our new show rehearses next door Monday through Saturday. They're having auditions right now in the auditorium if you'd like to stick your head in the door. It's a really good play."

Grace heaved a resigned sigh. "I think I'll do that. What's the play?"

Nancy smiled. "It's really funny. It's called *The Pirates of Penzance*."

Grace's chest tightened. Was this just a cruel coincidence, or did God have it in for her? How could she possibly stand in a closet selling cookies while one of her favorite plays was being performed, however badly, in the next room? This might just be the straw that would put her on the next plane back home in spite of what awaited her there.

"I'll be in my office." Nancy skipped off, leaving Grace with the impression that her training was now complete. From the sound of it, the job would be a piece of cake.

Cringing at the reverberation of overacting that wafted out to the lobby, Grace traversed the room with care. Would this be too painful? She opened a weighty door and slipped through, thankful for the darkness for concealing the reflexive roll her eyes did at the sight of the amateurish living room set on the tiny stage.

Taking a careful look at an auditorium no bigger than the women's chorus dressing room back home, Grace flipped down one of the padded wood seats and admired the intricate ornamentation of its iron armrests. The threadbare cushion failed to inspire much confidence, but she sat anyway. Its base eased down slightly as she sat, as if deciding whether it would support her weight. How long had these seats been here—since the patrons silenced their six-shooters instead of their cell phones?

A row of women of various ages stood on a stage so small it would have been more at home in a children's playhouse. A hawk-faced young woman with a sumptuous brunette mane moved to center stage and flashed a self-assured smile straight out of a toothpaste ad. Grace pulled herself up in her seat, anxious to hear what was about to transpire.

The woman nodded toward an upright Baldwin piano which stood where an orchestra pit would be, had there been room. The instrument appeared to be about the same vintage as the gray-haired woman who began happily plunking at its keys. Grace cringed. Had it occurred to anybody that the ability to read music might be a necessary requirement for an accompanist?

The brunette gazed out over Grace's head, clearly oblivious to her presence, and filled her chest with a supportive breath. Grace held hers for a moment, in pained anticipation.

"*Poor wand'ring one...*"

Grace clamped her eyes shut as a discordant note reverberated off the room's aged wooden beams. This was just too painful to endure. Why on earth had Nancy put a musical in their season with no apparent musical talent to pull it off?

"Fine, Sophia." A man rose from the director's table at the center of the audience.

Grace perked up. It was Mr. Lexus himself. What was his name...Devon?

He made his way out of the row of seats and down the aisle. "I'd like you to take it again." He stood at the foot of the stage, looking directly up at the brunette. "Remember, nice and bright, just like we worked on."

Grace grimaced. He had coached this girl before the audition? Weren't the other candidates irked by that?

Actress Sophia flashed him a Scarlet O'Hara smile and sang again, just as before but a little louder. Grace resisted a scream. Gilbert and Sullivan would no doubt have denied any rumor of their participation in this.

Devon paced the short distance at the foot of the stage, his ear craned toward Sophia till she hit the final note. "Much better." He stopped, waving an approving arm.

Grace shook her head. Was he tone deaf?

He turned to retake his seat. Halfway up the aisle he stopped, his steel-blue eyes locking onto hers. She shrank back, her stomach suddenly aflutter. A smile played on his lips causing a dimple to materialize on his square chin. Grace smiled slightly. If Devon had been a movie star in the 1940s, Cary Grant would have been nervous.

"Oh, *Devon*."

The willowy actress called out from the stage, with a hand on her hip and a glint in her eye.

Lithely, Devon turned first his head, then his body. "Yes?"

Grace kept her eye on him, entranced by his indisputable manly magnetism.

Sophia gave him a look that dripped syrup. "Did my phrasing play, or should I go back to my original interpretation?"

He flicked a hand toward her. "I liked the old way, Sophia. Your instinct is brilliant."

She radiated her pleasure at that verdict as she glanced at the row of ladies behind her.

Grace clucked her tongue. *Yes Sophia, they all heard him.*

Devon returned to his seat, calling out over his shoulder as he did so. "Ruby. You're up next."

Sophia frowned slightly, taking a step back to allow a stout young woman in a John Deere cap to take center stage. Visibly shaking, Ruby clasped her hands at the level of the bib pocket of her well-worn overalls. Grace fought the impulse to raise her hands to her ears.

"Go ahead, Myra." Taking his seat, Devon looked at the accompanist, who gave him a grandmotherly nod of consent and began playing.

Ruby looked uncertain and jumped in a beat ahead of Myra, who made no effort to catch up. Grace sat forward, leaning on the seat in front of her. This girl was actually pretty good. She did her best to stay on pitch, and was mostly successful, no thanks to poor Myra, whose playing only fell further from the mark as the piece progressed. The dear woman didn't seem to realize it, judging from the smile which was a constant companion to her sour notes.

Ruby reached the end of the song, albeit a half-step shy of Mr. Sullivan's intended destination. Sophia emitted an audible jeer and Ruby's pleased expression melted like wax. Grace wanted to hiss. *The little diva.*

With a jolt, Grace glanced at her watch. Casting one last look at the back of Devon's handsome head, she stood and eased out of the theatre.

Anxious to return to her bland white sanctuary before dark, she stepped out into the early evening, taking a careful look up and down the street.

She'd seen enough to gauge the artistic level in this town, but all wasn't lost. At least it was a job. A job where she could hopefully blend in and avoid being asked any personal questions.

Chapter 9

Grace took a peek out the kitchen window at the vibrant blue backdrop. No wonder they called this place *Big Sky Country*. She lifted her mug of Nescafé, breathing in the promise of a new day as she enjoyed her morning swig of instant caffeinated bliss.

This had been her first morning since coming here that she hadn't been roused by a nightmare. Instead, she'd awoken with a pleasing sense of purpose, and a Gilbert and Sullivan tune in her head.

Now, leaning on the counter, she peered through the pane. She hadn't even bothered to look at her backyard until now. Talk about never stopping to smell the roses. Speaking of which, was that a rosebush by the fence? It was beautiful. Too bad she knew less about gardening than she did about cooking.

She caught herself in a sigh as she looked past her back fence and the neighbor's yard beyond. The mountains here were nothing short of majestic. The website had mentioned a view, but that had been of no consequence to her at the time. Now she drank it in.

Her spirits lifted at the thought of going to work later that evening. It was just a silly little community theatre play, but Nancy was counting on her to do her part to make it run smoothly. That felt good.

Sipping her coffee, she walked from the kitchen to the sun

porch. She stopped. Why hadn't she realized that this was an actual room? She had assumed it was just a back porch and was delighted to see an area almost the size of her bedroom. Windows comprised the upper half of three of its walls, and it even had a skylight, obviously a recent update. She went back into the kitchen, grabbed the camp chair she'd picked up the day before at the surplus store, and set it next to the glass.

As she lifted her mug to her lips, a knock at the front door shattered her serenity. She froze, listening in vain for Lucy's "yoo hoo." Suddenly her translucent surroundings magnified her vulnerability. If someone rounded the corner from the side of the house, they would see her, and—

A second knock came, even louder than the first. Shaking, she looked down at her watch. Nine a.m. Early, but not by small-town standards. Who could it be?

She crept back into the kitchen, setting her mug on the counter. Treading softly through the dining room, she lamented her door's lack of a peephole. Didn't people in this town believe in monitoring their visitors?

She tiptoed into the living room and snuck a quick peak from between the front blinds. She balked. What was *he* doing here?

Her pulse commenced running a marathon. He was no doubt harmless, but she didn't want to encourage him. Sort of like that stray dog.

"Who is it?" She tried not to sound too welcoming.

"It's Sam, from the hardware store."

She could either play twenty questions or just open the door, so she chose the less time consuming.

Even as the door inched open, she spoke. "Yes?"

He wore a half-smile and the same Levi's as the two days previous. Today's work shirt was green, so that, at least, had changed. "I'm sorry to bother you, but I wanted to get to you before your problem got any worse."

Her throat tightened. What did he know about her problem? "I...I don't..."

Slowly, he pulled a crowbar from behind his back and raised it to shoulder level.

Fear seized her. Her gut told her to slam the door but her arms felt paralyzed.

A grin tugged at his lips. "I could pull up those tiles for you, if you'd like."

She let out a long breath and put her hand to the hollow of her throat. "That won't be necessary. I'll just get my wallet. How much?" She stepped inside, trying to tame her quaking limbs as she reached for her purse.

"The bar's ten." He paused. "Love what you've done with the place."

She turned to see him looking around her unadorned abode with a slight smirk on his undeniably handsome face. "Uh...thanks."

"That adds a nice touch." He nodded toward the water globe still doing its solo show on the mantel.

"Yes well, I'm a minimalist." She flicked a ten toward him.

He took it, handing her the crowbar. "Apparently."

Flushed with an awkward irritation, she dug through the change in her wallet. "And the tax?"

"No sales tax." His face lifted in a disarming grin. "You're in Montana, ma'am."

She grimaced, returning her attention to her purse. "Plus the six for the globe."

"Consider that a housewarming gift. Doesn't look like you've gotten too many."

Jerk. "I don't exactly have a lot of friends in the area."

"Too bad. That'll change." His mouth curved up slightly as he slipped the ten into his shirt pocket.

She frowned. Why would he assume she'd want to get to know anybody around here? Even the highly cultured, educated people who populated her world failed to capture her extended interest. What made him think that this town could produce anyone worthy of the effort?

Angling a glimpse over her shoulder, he raised a brow. "Sure you don't want me to have a look?"

She reeled in her focus. “A look?”

He lifted a hand in the direction of the kitchen. “At your floor. You know, since I’m here.”

She shook her head quickly. “No. It doesn’t really matter. I won’t be staying that long anyway.”

He slanted her an inquisitive look.

Why had she said that? His presence on her porch was off-putting, and she felt a sudden need for him to leave.

Tipping his head back, he made a smacking noise with his lower lip and upper teeth. “Not too taken with our little town, huh?” His eyes lowered onto her face. They seemed an even darker grade of chocolate than the other day. “Maybe that’ll change too.”

He turned, leaving her to stare at his departing back. She leaned against the doorjamb as he got into a dinged-up, dirty blue pickup truck that sat in front of her house.

She bristled. *Maybe that’ll change*. What was *that* supposed to mean?

Chapter 10

"Don't you have any Fig Newtons?"

The determined expression on the ruddy face of the man in front of her made Grace highly value the counter space between them.

"No, I—"

"What about ice?"

Flustered, Grace shook her head. Why were people shouting at her like she was deaf? A sea of bobbing heads and fists waving cash crashed against her little window. How could this miniature theatre hold so many people, and why were they all so ravenous?

"I'm sorry, I'm out of ones." Grace pushed a stray hair from her eyes and plopped a fistful of quarters into an outstretched hand. She silently thanked whoever had voted down a state sales tax. If she had to make change for fifty people in fifteen minutes, at least it was with round numbers.

"I wanted chocolate cream, not chocolate chip."

A dour woman slid the offending cookie back toward Grace, who suppressed a shriek of frustration.

"I'm sorry ma'am, I—"

The end-of-intermission chime felt like a life preserver. The disgruntled cookie woman turned away with a sneer and the flow of patrons at last ebbed. Grace leaned her elbows on the counter, covering her face with her hands. She'd survived, but she couldn't possibly subject herself to this again.

"How did it go?"

Grace jumped at the sound of Nancy's pert voice. The woman had appeared at the concession window like a bird flitting to a tree branch.

"How do people do this?" Grace took a step back, looking around at the carnage she'd created in her quest to locate the last diet soda.

"You'll get used to it. It's a mad house at intermission and then you stock up for tomorrow."

"Tomorrow." Agitation flooded Grace's throat. "I really don't think I—"

Nancy put up her index finger and touched the other hand to her headset. She pressed the button that was clipped to her belt and spoke to whoever was on the other end.

Grace let out a slow, even breath. Why had she taken this job? She was accustomed to being the one served. How could she accept such a severe demotion?

Gathering her thoughts, she scanned the room. Her eye landed on the painting between the windows. It had calmed her that first day. Maybe it would help now. She focused on it with a meditative breath.

Desperation rose in her chest and she took it as a sign. She was meant to be the one viewed from a distance through an opera glass, not the girl in the lobby counting out change. She had to tell Nancy this job was not for her.

Nancy flipped the voice tube of her headset to her forehead, shifting her attention back to Grace.

Grace reined in her courage. "Nancy, I really can't—"

"I can't thank you enough for being such a life saver. Everybody would have been so disappointed if we hadn't been able to open the stand."

"Oh. Well, I—"

"We can't afford to disappoint a single audience member. Especially not now."

Grace corked her intended resignation with a strained smile. Nancy grinned, then charged off to her next important duty.

A lump the size of her fist sat in Grace's throat as she scanned the crumb-and-coin strewn counter. This was terrible.

Grabbing a damp bar towel, she recounted the events of the past fifteen minutes. It had been chaos. Surely there was someone in this town who could do a better job than she had. It was only fair that she free it up for them.

A few minutes later, Grace had the stand shipshape. With renewed determination, she strode resolutely toward Nancy's office.

"Nancy, I..." She stopped in the doorway of the surprisingly tiny space.

Nancy stood behind a desk so large it appeared that the room must have been built around it. Her face was as white as the paper she clutched in both hands.

"I'm sorry." Grace reversed her forward momentum, alarmed by the woman's stricken look. "I can come back."

"It's unbelievable. That's what it is," Nancy snapped, waving the sheet of paper like she was swatting at an insect.

Grace hesitated. Nancy clearly expected her to provide a sounding board. "Is something wrong?"

Nancy's cheeks turned fiery as she flicked the paper with her fingers. "I thought this was a joke, but now this guy has his lawyer in on it."

Grace took a slight step backward, not wanting to get involved. She had enough problems of her own.

Nancy thrust the paper in Grace's direction, apparently assuming she'd be anxious to read it for herself. Grace held a beat before giving in to common courtesy and stepping fully into the room to take the offending letter. She scanned it as Nancy continued.

"This guy Langley thinks he's going to buy this building and the one next door, *and* our parking lot. He's just about got the owner talked into it. I can't believe it. What is Mr. R. thinking?"

Grace examined the legalese. "So he wants to sell. Is that

really so bad?"

Nancy's face grew fierce. "It's bad if he sells to Langley. That creep wants to tear down the theatre so he can build a big ugly casino. Can you believe it? He says he wants to turn Madison Falls into the Las Vegas of the North."

"Oh." This *was* terrible. If Madison Falls became a trendy tourist destination, it wouldn't be much of a hiding place. "You mean the theatre might not be here much longer?"

Nancy's eyes welled and her voice caught as she spoke. "I know it doesn't bring in the crowds like it used to, but it's such a part of this town. How could anyone tear it down?"

Grace wanted to ask if they'd considered doing better shows. She chose her words carefully. "So, if *Pirates* is profitable, Mr. R. might reconsider?"

Nancy rolled her eyes in an arch as if considering the notion. "That would be a start, I guess. He knows no one would want that casino. Besides, it's got to make him sad to think about losing this building. It's been in his family for generations."

Grace weighed her words. "You could resuscitate the place, but it needs a facelift. It's pretty old—"

"Built in 1882. Same year the railroad came through." Nancy's face fell in defeat. "We can't afford to do anything to it. We're running with no profit margin as it is."

Grace's mind started to click. "Well, maybe he could find another buyer. Someone who wants to keep it going as a theatre."

Nancy shook her head. "That's no good. He's already had other offers. Trouble is, the highest was only two hundred thousand."

Grace cringed. That *was* low. About the cost of a storage unit back home. "And Langley?"

"He offered a *million*, give or take."

"A million?"

"Yeah. Give or take."

"Wow," Grace said. "That's quite a difference."

"I'll say. Nobody else is going to offer that much for these poor old buildings. I mean, look around. Nothing's up to code. The plumbing, the wiring. We're just lucky we haven't had a fire in all these years. Mr. R. can't afford to fix it." Nancy folded into her chair, burying her face in both hands.

Grace's heart fluttered in sympathetic vibration to Nancy's grief. "Isn't there some sort of historical designation—"

"We've tried that route." Nancy straightened, her arms flourishing in front of her like a novice maestro. "Apparently Montana has an overabundance of history. If the price is right, people will sell their souls."

A tremor shot across Grace's back. It was true. She'd learned that from Kirk.

Nancy covered her face again and Grace tried to think of something she could say to offer hope. "I'm...um...sure it will work out for the best."

Nancy looked up, her eyes rimmed with red, and her face drawn with pain. She held a beat before speaking, her voice now barely above a whisper. "I just don't know what I'm going to do."

Grace's chest tightened at the realization that this building meant more to Nancy than just a job.

Aggrieved silence hung in the air between them. *Poor Nancy.* Grace knew how it felt to have the one thing that meant the most to you ripped from your grasp. If only she could fix this for her. Take away that awful ache that had been her own constant companion for too long. Her eyes pooled with despair. She wanted to help, but the best she could do was to hold off on giving Nancy another dose of bad news. The resignation could wait.

"Look, I'm sure this will work itself out." Grace took a step back, her familiar anguish threatening to take center stage. She needed to get away before Nancy questioned it.

Nancy smiled sadly. "Thanks again for saving the day."

Offering a feeble smile, Grace turned to go.

"Oh, and Grace?"

She turned again.

Nancy looked drained. "Nobody really knows about this yet. I'd appreciate it if you kept it under your hat."

Choking back her looming emotional detonation, Grace

nodded agreement.

She took the few steps down the hallway to where it opened to the lobby. The muffled bellowing of the performance in the next room assured her of momentary privacy. Pausing to collect her emotions before continuing on outside, she lowered her face into her hands.

"Don't tell me they've reduced you to tears on your first night."

Grace snapped to attention at the velvety smooth male voice. The blood drained from her face as she looked into the silver-blue eyes of Devon Sinclair.

He stood just a few feet from her, leaning back slightly and peering around the corner by the box office. A genial smile spread over his face. "I didn't mean to alarm you." He took a step toward her, hand outstretched. "I'm Devon."

"Grace." She accepted his firm grasp, embarrassed that her emotions were so transparent. "I was just.... It was my first night manning the concession stand, and—"

He raised his palm. "I completely understand. I once did a stint at Streebecks Coffee."

She spurted out a laugh, her despair instantly defused. "You get it then." Suddenly in no hurry to leave, she folded her hands behind her. "So, how's the casting coming along?"

"Actually," he took a step back and pointed around the corner. "I just dropped in to post this."

She moved beside him and looked at the bulletin board next to the box office window. "Ah, the cast list."

His face shone with the satisfaction that comes with the completion of an important task. "Yes, thank goodness. This one was a challenge."

"Uh-huh." She studied the page. "I can see why."

"You should be flattered to be the first to see it." His tone was teasing.

She harrumphed. "You're casting Sophia as Mabel? Why?" She hadn't intended to sound so harsh, but if they wanted a successful show, it had to start with a capable cast.

His voice flickered confusion. “Why not?”

She lifted a shoulder as her mouth formed her well-considered argument. “It’s just that...”

He folded his arms good-humoredly. “Go on. Who would *you* cast as Mabel?”

She hesitated.

He leaned in. “Come on Grace. You can be honest with me.”

She breathed out in surrender. “Okay. Ruby has a lot of talent. It’s raw, but with a little work and a good corset, I think she could carry the show.”

Devon raised his brow, clearly considering her words. “To be honest, I hadn’t even thought of her. I think I was guilty of a little pre-casting, truth be told.”

She made a sarcastic show of raising her eyebrows as she turned her head away.

He chuckled as if to let her know her gesture hadn’t gone unnoticed. “I’m not exactly sure why, but I have a feeling you know what you’re talking about.” He popped the pushpin that held the paper out of the board. “I think I’ll take a little more time with this.”

“You won’t be sorry.” She smiled, then jolted, suddenly remembering her Cinderella-like need to get home before dark. She started for the door. “I’d better get going.”

Falling into step with her, he carefully slid the cast list into his black leather briefcase.

“If it’s any consolation—” He pushed the front door open and stood to one side while she walked through. “—the last concession girl cried on her first night too.”

“Terrific.” Suddenly self-conscious of her small-town-casual attire, she balled up her hands in the pockets of her new *I Love Montana* sweat jacket. Anxious, she looked out at the sky that was already a dark blue on the horizon.

“Seriously,” Devon said, “it’s a great little town. The people here are very friendly once they’ve been fed.”

She sniggered softly, then recalled her curiosity about him. As they glided down the steps, she pondered the perfect probe. “So you live here then?"

"Only temporarily. I'm staying with a friend."

Her head bobbed like a metronome. Somehow, he didn't seem like the staying-with-a-friend type.

"Actually," he continued, "I'm pretty anxious to head back home...when the time is right."

Grace nodded again. *You and me both.*

Devon held a hand out toward the Lexus, which gleamed even in this pale light. "I'd be no gentleman if I didn't offer you a lift."

Her stomach flipped. As tempting as it was to slip into that buttery-soft passenger seat, she couldn't possibly let down her guard. It wouldn't be prudent to get into a car alone with a stranger, however trustworthy he might seem. Best to play it safe. "No thanks. I don't have far to go."

He nodded in concurrence as he clicked the remote on his key ring. The Lexus flashed its headlights and bleeped a greeting. He opened the door and tossed his briefcase in.

She paused, reluctant to walk away from the sweet life on wheels. "Oh, by the way," she said. "How did it work out for you at Streebecks?"

Leaning on the top of the door, he smiled. "I always find a means"—his eyes locked onto hers—"of making things go my way."

Glinting her a wink, he slipped into the car, shut the door, and revved the engine to life.

Chapter 11

Renewed from what had felt like a taste of home, Grace started slowly up the sidewalk, measuring her thoughts. She considered the old brick building as she passed, and what a handsome piece of old architecture it was. Built in 1882, wasn't that what Nancy had said?

She pulled her hand from her pocket and let it glide across the rough brick as she walked. It felt dusty and rugged, like the face of a cowboy after a day on the range.

Looking back, she tried to picture the neon flash of a casino replacing the hammered copper electric lanterns that flanked the front porch. What history had it witnessed, this building? It would be sad to see it go.

Such a shame that this Mr. R, whoever he was, didn't seem to care what a loss it would be to the town. She looked ahead, noticing how the old-fashioned streetlamps created soft titian pools of light that spilled from the sidewalk into the street. Not that it really mattered to her, but a casino would change everything. It would ruin whatever it was that made this place special.

Special. The thought surprised her. She'd only been here for three days, and hadn't put much thought into the aesthetics of the place. She'd traveled to major cities all over the world. Why would Madison Falls strike her as particularly extraordinary?

Must be just a side effect of her emotional state. She shoved her hand back into her pocket, pressing against the knot that had formed in her stomach. This Mr. R. was no doubt one of those hard-nosed businessmen who cared more about his own assets than he did about people. She'd witnessed more than enough of that in her career.

Swallowing hard, she tried to quash the fire in her throat. She'd seen Kirk use his money—old family money that he hadn't even earned himself—to get whatever he wanted. That was how he felt accepted, *loved* even. By how much money he could get people to take. Of course, it came at a terrible price for the recipients. They became his puppets—eternally obligated to do whatever he wanted.

As she stepped across Mountainview Avenue, Grace wondered for the thousandth time if her life would be more bearable if she'd just taken Kirk's money and gifts. At least then she wouldn't be paying the price for what he saw as a rejection of him. That was a choice for which she had nearly paid with her life.

A movement on the other side of the street jarred her from her deep contemplation. A woman had dashed out onto the sidewalk, her fists balled up in front of her. Grace slowed to a near stop as a man followed.

The pair was silhouetted by a neon *Coors* sign that blinked in rhythm with the twangy country music which spilled out into the otherwise tranquil evening. Grace hadn't even noticed that there was a bar two doors down from the hardware store, but then that wasn't the kind of thing that normally drew her eye. She was more the cocktail lounge type.

Shouting incoherently, the man grabbed the woman's arm and whirled her around to face him. Grace froze. The tone of his voice conveyed out-of-control anger. She strained to hear, not knowing if she should help the woman or flee for her own safety.

The man released the woman's arms, thrashing his own about in obvious rage. She tried to get away but he grabbed her again, this time shaking her until she started sobbing. He lowered his tone, pulling her into a hug.

Grace nearly choked in disgust. It was *him*. So that Sam fellow had a girlfriend.

It was so transparent. She'd observed enough drunken abusive rages to recognize the pattern. How could that poor woman stay with a man like that? Didn't she know how dangerous it could be?

Keeping a protective eye on her in case she needed help, Grace shrunk back into the shadows. Flashes of Kirk's rage shot through her like arrows. Shouldn't she have recognized that same quality the second she saw Sam? He'd seemed so docile. Then again, so had Kirk until she'd unintentionally lit his fuse.

Calmer now, the couple continued to talk.

The shadows were lengthening, and anxiety pricked at Grace's skin. She needed to get home. She started walking again, slowly but with purpose.

Close to the corner of Pine Vista, it dawned on her that she hadn't done her customary safety check. How could she have forgotten? Scanning her surroundings had been habitual for so long now, like brushing her teeth. It was foolish to let down her guard.

She kept moving as she examined the setting. A couple of people went about their business in front of shops. A Toyota drove by. Nothing unusual.

Sam opened the door to the blue pickup truck and the woman climbed in. He crossed to the driver's side. He was going to drive in his condition?

Just before stepping into the cab, he glanced across the street, and his eyes met Grace's. She looked away. Now he knew she'd been watching him. What would he think?

Forget it. Who cares? That was the last thing she needed to worry about. Making a left-face, she crossed Main, as the truck roared to life behind her and pulled away.

The drone of the engine still echoed in the twilit evening as she took the final leg of her journey at a gallop. She fumbled for her keys in her purse as she bounded up the front steps.

Shoving the door open, she paused. At least that part of her safety ritual hadn't been lost. Thankful that she'd turned on all the lights before leaving that afternoon, she scanned the part of the house she could see. That was one thing she missed about her studio—keeping track of the entire space with one sweep of her eyes.

The distant sound of kids at play and a car driving by were music to her straining ears. Her house was a tomb. She shut, locked, then leaned on the door—her shield against the world.

What was she going to do?

Taking a cautious step, she peered around the corner till she had a clear view of the dining room. An awful memory fought for her attention. It had been a little over two weeks since that horrible night when she'd returned from her gig in South Carolina, where she'd had six blessed weeks of no unwanted surprises. She had dared to hope that her life had returned to normal, that Kirk had finally given up on his senseless pursuit of her. How could she have been so foolish? She should have known he had a plan for her.

A chill crawled up her spine now as she remembered opening the door to her apartment, prepared to enter the tiny space that was her home. Instead she'd stopped cold at the terrifying sight in front of her, her blood freezing her veins.

Panic had surged, instantly de-icing her immobility. Without thinking, she'd turned and fled, not daring to look back.

The shock of her decision to abandon everything that mattered for the sake of her own survival rose up in her again. Now was no time to second guess that decision. If she had stayed, there was no telling what would have happened, and no one could have helped her.

She shuffled into the kitchen, grateful that she had done a little grocery shopping earlier in the day and that Pinot Blanc had been on prominent display. She grabbed the bottle out of the otherwise bare fridge and thanked the makers of her camp knife for understanding that even an outdoorsman sometimes needs a corkscrew.

Pitiable as it seemed to drink wine out of a mug, she poured to the brim and slunk out to the sun porch. She dropped into the camp chair, disappointment racing through her weary body. Hadn't the chair been cozier that morning? She slumped down, taking a welcome sip of the heady liquid. Her lips tingled, and her muscles relaxed a little.

Leaning back as much as the seat would comfortably allow, she looked out at the crisp black sky jeweled with stars, and let the emotion she'd been holding in bubble to the surface. Her eyes stung with unwanted sentiment. It was time she faced up to the hardest part of this whole situation—she missed her life.

She made a mental list of who might report her missing. Her manager, maybe? Surely Lana, her vocal coach, would find it odd when she failed to show up for her lesson. Anybody else? Maybe a neighbor in her building, but that seemed unlikely. She was gone so much as it was that no one would take notice.

Her agent would at least notice if she didn't return his calls, but she wasn't one of his star clients. She was still just a baby principal in his book, and his efforts on her behalf had done little to change that.

She pinched back tears, but the pain in her chest grew fiercer. What was wrong with her life that she hadn't bothered to make any real friends? Obviously, if she didn't care about anybody in a meaningful way, that meant nobody cared about her.

There was her mother, of course. A tear trickled down Grace's cheek as she remembered how difficult it had been to tell her she was fleeing. Her mother was still so caught up in mourning that it had been hard to tell if she'd understood. Regret and worry strummed at Grace's heart. If only she could be with her mother without endangering her too.

Emotion caught in her belly. The only other person who would wonder where she had gone was the one person she didn't want to find her. Ever.

A gulp of wine warmed her throat but chilled her heart. Her mom would disapprove of her drinking alone, but what other choice did she have? She *was* alone. Without plan or purpose. Tipping back her head, she gazed at the crystal stars above and wanted to shout at God for abandoning her. If He was up there somewhere, why would He create the stratosphere and then leave her down here on her own?

She let out a helpless wail, like an animal caught in a trap. All she wanted was to go home, but she couldn't. Nothing had changed. Rocking gently forward, she shut her eyes. She was waiting for home to be safe again, but with no idea what would make it so.

Pulling her knees up to her chest, she allowed the tears to flow like Niagara. What was she doing in a nothing town with a job that she was incapable of executing? It was so unfair that Kirk had unlimited funds and infinite time and she had to sell Oreos to keep herself afloat while hiding from him. Where was the justice in that?

Blowing despondency out between her clenched teeth, she thought about the theatre. There was no way she could quit, not now. It would be downright mean to do that to Nancy. Besides, she needed the income.

She took a consoling swig. Her life had been going so well. How could it possibly have come to this...and what was she going to do to change it?

Chapter 12

"This is the best play I've seen in years."

Grace peered up at the gray-bearded patron as she knelt, digging around the fridge for a diet cola. The sport coat he wore over a plaid work shirt must have looked stylish in about 1973. This was apparently the local dress code for an evening at the theatre.

"They always do such a good job here," the woman next to him raved. "Any one of these people could make it in New York if they wanted to."

"Broadway quality." The man's head bobbed. "I've always said it."

Grace rolled her lips between her teeth to suppress a laugh as she stood and handed him the can. Clearly these people had never actually been to New York.

"Have you ever auditioned here?" The woman directed her serious query at Grace as she handed over her carefully counted change and picked up a cookie with a white cocktail napkin. "You look like you'd make a good little actress."

"No." Grace turned her focus to the next customer in line in hopes of discouraging dialogue. "Acting is quite a skill."

The couple nodded in the apparent belief that they were engaged in a serious discussion of the arts.

"Well, everyone here acts a good part." The woman took a delicate bite of her cookie. "We're lucky to have so much talent right here in Madison Falls."

Grace breathed a little easier as she served a root beer to the last patron in line. With the pressure off, she felt slightly more forthcoming with the chatty couple. "What about all the people behind the scenes?" Her question was met with blank stares.

"What do you mean?" The sport-jacketed man took a swig of his cola and looked at Grace as though she was about to let him in on some sort of theatrical secret.

"Well, you know..." She flicked her bangs from her eyes. Her interest in teaching an impromptu stagecraft class was practically zero. "The stage crew, the stage managers. Front of house staff. All the designers and light and sound board operators. Not to mention the director and producers. It takes a lot of people to put together a production, even a small one."

The woman eyed her intently, swallowing her last bite of cookie. "All these actors are so good."

Grace let out a sigh as the end-of-intermission chime sounded and the couple exchanged a look of lottery-winner merriment. She shook her head and watched them go, before turning to examine the mess she'd created. Her head ached, but at least tonight she hadn't run out of change and no one had shouted at her.

"You have a nice way with people."

She jerked around at the sound of Devon's voice. She hadn't even noticed him standing in the lobby.

"I'm sorry." He approached, his hands raised in contrition. "I'll have to start announcing myself."

She eased into a relaxed chuckle. "I guess I'm just jumpy by nature. Can I get you anything?"

"Actually, I'm hoping that you can rescue me from that torture to end all tortures called 'stagehand coffee.'"

"*Oh horrible. Catastrophe appalling*." She put her hand to her throat in mock dismay as she lilted one of her favorite lines.

He arched an eyebrow. "So you're familiar with *Pirates*. Why didn't you audition? I could use another daughter who actually looks younger than the Major General."

Warmth crept up her neck. "I...couldn't. I just..."

Devon tipped a knowing gaze. "Now, don't lie to me. You're a singer. I could tell the first time we met."

Her heart slammed against her ribs, threatening to break right through. "Me? I..."

He held up a hand. "No use denying it. I've directed opera." He leaned in, assuming a confidential tone. "A well-trained voice can't be easily disguised."

She sunk into her shoulders, her manner modest. "Oh."

A kind smile caressed his lips. "Don't worry." He winked. "I won't pressure you till I'm desperate for a decent soprano. Right now all I ask is for a decent cappuccino."

She drew in a breath, relieved at the change of subject but oddly comforted by his keen perception. "I'm so sorry." She cuffed the counter with her palm. "I *told* Nancy this stand needs coffee."

"And you're right." He mimicked her gesture. "I'm taking it up with the management." As he moved his hand away, it brushed against her arm.

Her knees buckled. This man was even more handsome than she'd remembered, with penetrating blue eyes, and perfect features could have been carved from granite. He exuded something that Grace had always thought of as *presence*.

His gaze grew distant. "That's one of the things I miss the most about New York."

Her face warmed. "What's that?"

"Decent coffee. I'm sorry, but the good people of Madison Falls don't know a Breve from a Macchiato."

She let out a laugh. "I'd have to agree." A momentary panic seized her. Her guard had slipped like a clumsy soprano on a raked stage. "About Madison Falls, I mean. I've never been to New York."

He folded his arms across the counter, clearly in no hurry to seek a satisfying beverage elsewhere. "And where are *you* from?"

Her heart jumped. "What?"

"Well, you're new here, and obviously no stranger to the

theatre business. I'm guessing Chicago."

The flush crept further up her cheeks. Was he onto her?

"Se...attle." The word crawled from her lips like the lie it was.

"Seattle." He arched an eyebrow. "Really?"

She nodded. It wasn't entirely untrue. She'd worked there several times and had lived in apartments. It had been home for those few weeks.

"Nice place." His tone was lighthearted. "I hear *they* have decent coffee."

She nodded, swallowing her trepidation.

He studied her. "So, you're an actress then?"

Was she? She hadn't really invented a résumé for her new identity, and her close proximity to Devon didn't lend itself to clear career planning. "No. Just a patron." Her words tumbled out too quickly. "I worked in a...in a pet store." Where in the world had that come from?

"Oh? Funny, I wouldn't have pegged you for the feather-and-fur type. You seem so..."

His eyes drifted up as if the right word might be etched in the ceiling.

Grace edged in, anxious to learn how her act was reading.

"So classy." His eyes lowered to meet hers, seemingly satisfied with his assessment.

"Thanks." She let go of the tension in her shoulders. "It was an *exotic* pet store."

Raising his eyebrows, he nodded interest.

Suddenly flustered, she grabbed for a bar towel. Overcome by a desire to overshare, she bit her lip. He seemed so insightful. If she said too much, he might see right through her. She'd have to keep the focus on him. "So you're *from* New York?"

"Lived there my whole life. With the exception of my years at Yale."

"Oh?"

"And my directing forays out of town, of course."

"Of course." It was her turn to study him. His presence here seemed as much a mystery as hers. What was he doing directing inconsequential plays in this practically nonexistent town? Clearly there was more to Devon Sinclair than met the eye.

She absentmindedly wiped the counter. "So, what brings you here?"

A sly smile played around the edges of his lips. "I felt the call of the wild."

She quirked an eyebrow.

"Seriously, I needed a break from the pressure. I just felt like I was missing something in New York. I mean, the money is great there, but I started to miss that grassroots artistry you get in a smaller community."

She allowed a long look at his face. Having heard people talk that way many times, she'd never actually met anyone who had walked away from a lucrative career in search of true art. Her gaze narrowed. "You wanted artistry so you came *here?*"

His chuckle was almost lyrical. "I know it sounds strange, but this place has renewed my spirit. This is my third show here, and it's changed my life. I'm very grateful I found Madison Falls, for reasons I would find *difficult* to explain."

Grace twisted the towel. That sounded benevolent and all, but had he really said goodbye to the high life in favor of the simple life? "But you said you were anxious to return home."

"What can I say?" He smiled. "True art doesn't support many luxury vacations."

She lobbed back his smile. "So what are you doing here tonight, Mr. Sinclair? Besides prowling for coffee, I mean."

He lifted a hold-on finger before disappearing for a moment behind the bottom half of the door. When he stood, he placed the black Prada briefcase on the counter and clicked it open. "I'm here for the express purpose of posting this." He handed a crisp sheet of white paper across the counter.

She wiped her hands on her jeans before taking the paper. "Ah, the cast list."

"Excuse me...*revised* cast list." His eyes teased.

She glanced at the sheet, mollified by what she saw. "A wise choice. Ruby's going to be just great."

“I have every confidence.” He flashed a playful smile. “By the way...”

She looked into his silvery-blue eyes. “Yes?”

“I’m waiting to hear about a directing gig with the New York Grand Opera. If I get it, I’ll be auditioning singers. Would you be interested?”

She sucked in her breath. “Me? I—”

“I wondered where you went.” A harsh female voice sliced into her answer.

Grace’s head snapped toward the hallway as Sophia marched toward them, eyes ablaze. Couldn’t the woman see she was interrupting?

Devon reached out for Sophia, as if she was a boat needing to be guided into port. “Ah, yes. I was waiting for you.” His eyes returned to Grace. “I assume you’ve met Sophia?”

“Not really.” Grace lifted her hand.

Sophia flashed a smug look, ignoring Grace’s offer to shake. “You must be the new concessions girl.” She looked up at Devon, her expression shifting. “Shall we?”

“We shall.” He took Grace’s hand, which Sophia had left untouched, and brushed his lips across the back of it.

A tingle danced up her arm.

Sophia’s eye’s bore into her but Grace didn’t care. Devon winked, then looked at Sophia and opened his palm toward the door. Sophia arched her overly shaped eyebrows and turned to go. Devon followed.

Grace rolled her tired eyes. A smile moved across her face, then quickly leveled to a scowl.

Devon had left the theatre with Sophia. Was that what he’d meant by “staying with a friend”?

Chapter 13

"You lied to me."

"What?" Grace's heart bumped against her chest cavity with what seemed like an audible *thump*. She pretended to focus her attention on the table of rummage sale goods in front of her.

"You heard me." Lucy folded her arms, scanning the load of furniture in the back of her husband Bob's pickup. "You said you weren't much of a decorator. Look at how all these pieces are going to work together. You have a good eye. You really ought to give yourself more credit."

"Oh." Grace took in a breath of relief. She *had* lied, but about more than just her knack for matching upholstery patterns.

"The least we can do—and by 'we' I mean Bob—is to set up the dinette set." Lucy blew Bob a kiss as he climbed into the cab of the truck. "I can't believe you weren't even going to put a table in there."

Grace tipped a shrug.

"Or that you don't have a bed." Lucy said. "For goodness sakes, no one over the age of twelve should be expected to spend more than one night on a cot. Bob will have our extra frame all set up by the time you get home."

A current of guilt flowed through Grace. Lucy had been so kind to her, with no apparent expectation of anything in return. "I appreciate all your help, Lucy."

"It's my pleasure. You know—" Lucy sifted through a bin of used handbags. "—now that you have all that chic furniture, you have to do something about those antiseptic walls."

Grace raised a shoulder. She was content with the neutrality of the house and saw no reason to change it.

Lucy continued, her tone tentative. "So, I've been thinking.... Please don't feel like you have to say yes."

Grace clenched her jaw. There was nothing like that phrase to make a person feel obligated.

"I've been praying for you, and the Lord told me I should offer to host a paint party."

Grace wavered at both the offer and its presentation. Lucy had seemed normal when they'd met a few days before, but this was kind of peculiar. What did she mean the Lord told her? Who did she think she was, Moses?

"It's perfect." Lucy seemed to take her silence as a sign of assent. "You could settle in and get acquainted with people at the same time."

"Oh...n...no. Really, I'm fine." Grace stumbled over her words, wanting desperately to squelch Lucy's enthusiasm. If there was one thing she wanted less than to settle in, it was to get cozy with the townsfolk.

Lucy gave her a reassuring smile. "It's not like we're implying that you're a charity case, but I know it costs a lot to paint a whole house. Everybody can pitch in and it'll be our way of saying 'welcome.'"

Grace let out the breath that should have voiced a *fortissimo* refusal, but Lucy was so sincere, she had to give in. "That sounds nice. Thank you."

"Great then, it's settled." With a satisfied look on her face, Lucy pulled a beaded evening bag from the bottom of the bin. "Bingo!"

Grace looked around, surprised at the quality of the merchandise here. What she'd expected to be a junk sale had turned out to be more like a vintage treasure hunt.

She looked at the park-like setting of the Life in Christ Church and allowed her mind to drift back. Not long ago she would have observed a sun-drenched Saturday morning like this with a run through Central Park. Her heart warmed with the memory. It had been one of her favorite activities before it had become unsafe for her to go alone. In the later days, before she'd given it up altogether, it had comforted her to believe she was in training for a quick getaway.

She squinted up at the leaves rustling overhead and the sky beyond. Her eye caught the towering blue church steeple which glistened as the sun attempted to hide behind it. Then her gaze fell on the church itself, a picturesque white concoction that brought to mind images of a wedding cake. Not only did the building itself resemble fluffily frosted pastry, but the covered porch conjured up an image of romance. She could picture an old-fashioned bride and groom emerging from the carved doors and being showered with rice as they descended the extensive stairs. She'd never been much for church herself, but this one seemed inviting.

"Pretty, isn't it?" Lucy must have read her thoughts.

"Beautiful. I feel like Anne of Green Gables."

"That's just about the right era. The main part was built in 1888, but we're especially proud of the addition."

Grace tilted her head in an attempt to see around the building. "There's an addition?"

"You can't tell, can you? The board wanted to replace the building about seven years ago because the church had outgrown it. Bob went to them with a plan to add on instead. It looks like it was made this way to begin with."

"You mean, Bob *did* this?"

"He's a contractor. His specialty is making new construction match old-fashioned style. If you ever want to add on to your house, build up a story or anything, he's your guy."

The thought implied a commitment to her house that Grace knew she'd never have, but it intrigued her nonetheless. "That sounds tough. Do people really do that?"

"We did. Our house used to be a little bungalow like yours.

Remember, if you ever need anything fixed, I'll send Bob right over." Lucy looked like a proud mother, regarding the church.

Suddenly, her smile evaporated, and she let out a breath so loud Grace's head jerked to follow her gaze.

"Oh, great." Lucy's tone grew ominous. "Remember I promised to tell you which guys to avoid?"

Grace wouldn't have needed the warning. The dead ringer for Kirk seemed to repel the crowd like a leper as he strutted through it. "Who is he?"

Lucy tsked. "Well, it depends on who you want to believe."

Grace instinctively wrapped her arms around her middle. "I'm not much for gossip."

"Me either." Lucy said. "But it's hard to stand by and say nothing in the face of pure evil."

"Evil?" Grace shuddered. "That sounds daunting."

Lucy blew out a restrained sigh. "Too bad guys like that are sneaky enough not to get caught."

"Caught?" Grace's stomach tightened. "Doing what?"

Lucy's voice grew low and dark, like a brewing storm. "I wouldn't say this if I didn't know it to be true."

Grace took a slight step closer, intent on catching every word.

"His name is Carson. We know about him because he's luring in a friend of ours. Someone who's always been a really good guy. A family man."

Grace felt a shiver in spite of the heat of the day. "Luring him in? That sounds scary."

"I'll say." Lucy tipped her head toward Grace, her tone confidential. "See, this friend has been really worried about money. You know how when people get desperate, they can be extra vulnerable?"

"Especially where money's concerned." Grace flinched at the reminder of how easily people were influenced by Kirk when he wielded his wallet. "So, what do you think is going on?"

"That's where this guy Carson comes in. I hate to believe it, but this friend of ours hasn't been himself lately. One minute he's normal, the next he'll flip out, like Jekyll and Hyde. We're so afraid—"

"You think your friend is dealing drugs?" The words tumbled out of Grace's mouth practically before she knew she'd made the connection. Money…uncharacteristic behavior…she'd seen the pattern before.

Lucy's eyes teared. "He won't talk about it, but we're pretty certain. It's bad, Grace. We all care about him, but he's heading down a destructive road. His wife is beside herself."

Lucy's words pricked at Grace's heart. "That's so sad."

Lucy nodded. "I'm worried about their kids. Nice Christian family."

"Oh?" That seemed like an odd contradiction. Then again, she'd known lots of so-called Christians who hid an abundance of unseemly behavior behind a cloak of piousness.

"It doesn't seem right, does it?" Lucy shook her head. "The Holy Spirit guides us, but we still have free will. It's easy for people to follow their own desires especially when they're tempted by money."

Disgust swelled in Grace's stomach. Money and greed did terrible things to people all on their own. She hated to think what could happen when drugs got added to the mix. "Is there anything you can do for your friend?"

"What can you do when someone can't be reasoned with? We pray for him every day."

Grace sighed. That was nice, but it didn't seem very helpful.

Silence held for a moment before Lucy drew back her shoulders. "It's almost my turn to man our table, but I think you should look around some more. You never know what buried treasure you might dig up."

Grace smiled a goodbye to Lucy and looked around. What else did she have to do while she waited to go to work? Besides, this was the kind of shopping she could afford.

Wandering through the crowd, she cast a glance at the line-up of folding tables piled high with wares.

"Grace!"

The unexpected sound of her assumed name drew her around.

There sat Spritz in a tangerine top as cheerful as her wave. Grace let out a pleased breath, darting across oncoming foot traffic to get to her.

"Are you settling in?" Spritz leaned forward in her folding chair. "I've been so worried about that floor. Has Sam taken care of it for you?"

"Sam?" She fended off a shiver of annoyance. "Oh, he, uh...stopped by."

"Good. He's the best."

Grace struggled to keep her expression neutral. She looked down at a display of vibrant baby sweaters on the table next to Spritz. "These are gorgeous."

"Thanks." Spritz looked humble. "It's a good way to keep my hands busy when I'm on the phone at work."

"They're hand knit?" Grace ran her fingers over the soft garments, flicking over a tiny white tag. She gasped. "Did you mean to price them so low? You could get ten times this."

Spritz's face flushed as rosy as the half-done sweater she held in her lap.

"Seriously, Spritz." Grace lifted one of the tiny garments for a closer examination. "I saw some just like this for forty-nine bucks in a shop on Madison Avenue." Her cheeks heated as she caught herself. Was the Madison in Seattle an avenue or a street?

Spritz tittered, apparently oblivious to Grace's gaffe. "There's a world of difference between Madison Falls and Madison Avenue."

Grace gulped. She had to be more careful.

"Oh my goodness." Her eyes lit on a gleaming ray of silver hope. A shining cube the size of a microwave glinted in the morning sun, taunting her with a promised end to her regimen of mud and Nescafé. "Is that for sale?"

"I'll say. I can't wait to get rid of that thing." Spritz stood, crossing to the commercial espresso machine which sat atop a TV tray a few feet away. "It's been taking up space in our office for months."

Grace ran her hand across the smooth metal surface. "How

much?"

"Ten dollars and it's yours."

Grace was inclined to think Spritz was joking, but that wasn't in accord with what she'd seen of her sense of humor. "Ten dollars? Do you know how much this is worth?"

Spritz jutted out her lower lip, blowing a wisp of bangs off her forehead. "Hundreds, I'm sure. Our broker is always throwing around money, trying out new things. He got it in his head that our clients would enjoy a lovely cup of espresso when they came into the office."

"Good thinking." Grace bit her lower lip, debating whether to clue her in to the machine's real value.

"It might have been if any of us had learned to use it."

"Why didn't you?" Why would the people of the town slurp down caffeinated poison while a perfectly good espresso machine went unused?

"Whenever we'd offer the espresso, people would laugh and ask if the Mr. Coffee was broken. It turned into a joke after a while."

Grace reached into her purse, her mind trekking back to a conversation she'd once had with the owner of her neighborhood deli. He boasted of the deal he'd just gotten on a new machine that looked very much like this one. "*Two Grand*," he'd proclaimed repeatedly. "*Worth at least three!*"

"I'll take it." She grinned. "But I'm giving you a twenty."

"Okay." Spritz's look of surprise appeared unrehearsed. "There's no instruction book, but I guess being from Seattle qualifies you to run it by intuition."

Grace felt almost giddy as she handed over the cash. "I'm naming him Salvatore."

"Well," Spritz tucked the bill into her pocket. "I hope you and Salvatore will be very happy together. He's heavy. Why don't we find a man to carry him for you?"

"I can get him." Grace hoisted him into her arms, her knees folding slightly under his unexpectedly ample weight. "I'm fine."

Struggling to see over her new acquisition, Grace took one

careful step at a time. Her arms shook and a bead of sweat dripped into her eye, but she focused on the edge of the parking lot. All she had to do was make it to Lucy's table and ask her for a ride home.

Just then, a whirlwind of child-chasing-child crossed the sidewalk directly in front of her. She put on her brakes, halting her feet but not the rest of her body. Salvatore's forward momentum continued, and for one awful second Grace felt him slipping from her grasp. There was no way to stop it. She was going down like a bowling pin and Salvatore was leading the way.

Chapter 14

Grace braced herself for the awful crack she knew Salvatore's metal casing would make when it hit the pavement. Without warning, someone grabbed the machine while simultaneously barricading her descent. She gasped, astonished that she had just avoided two skinned knees and a mangled mocha maker.

She looked up, prepared to thank her rescuer.

"You okay?" Sam's eyes were wide with concern.

"I'm just fine, thank you." She spit out the words as she attempted to pull free of his grasp.

His firm grip held on the machine. "Why don't you let me get this for you?"

Her mouth froze around her intended retort as her biceps begged for mercy. Reluctantly, she acquiesced.

He bowed back subtly at the transfer of weight, then set the machine down on a nearby table. "Looks like she's still in one piece. I hope we can say the same for you."

"She's a 'he,'" she snapped. "And I'm just fine, thank you."

He nodded. "Good. And you're welcome."

She sneered. She had no desire to have anything even remotely resembling a conversation with this guy. The last thing she needed was to invite the attention of an abusive drinker. She flicked him a glance, noticing something odd about his appearance. The area under his left eye resembled a plum, both in color and shape.

"Get into a fight?"

He nodded in seeming embarrassment. "My reward for trying to help a friend."

"Oh. Well. You are very *helpful.*" She shook out her quivering arms, then reached for Salvatore. "I'll just be—"

Sam put his hand on the top of the machine. "Let me get that...uh...*him* for you."

She firmed her hold. "No, really I..." She stopped, her voice catching in her throat. There on the ground on the other side of the table, propped up against an old wooden barrel, was the painting from the theatre lobby. She sputtered, letting go her hold on the machine. "W...what's that?"

"What," Sam's voice pitched. "That old painting?"

The ornate gold frame rested unceremoniously on the balmy blacktop. The opera lover in oil paint seemed to cry out for rescue. Grace knelt down and reached out, but her hand froze a scant inch from the canvas.

The floodgate broke and a torrent of memories inundated her mind.

Chappaquiddick. That weekend at Kirk's cottage.

"Nice, huh?" Sam stooped beside her.

Jarred momentarily by his voice, she honed back in on her thoughts. She could be wrong, but all at once it seemed so clear.

Sam flicked a hand toward the image. "It's really old. I don't know anything about art, but the frame is real nice. It would look good above your mantel." His tone taunted. "With this opera lady and the water globe, you'd have a whole musical thing going on."

Her mind flashed back. Two summers ago, shortly after she'd met Kirk. She'd so needed that weekend in the country to take her mind off everything. She could still picture the pair of paintings prominently displayed on his gallery wall, and the blank space all ready for his next acquisition.

The same style. The same brushstrokes. The same colors. *The same artist.*

Sam brushed a coating of dust off the frame's rim. "I don't

know who it's by, but lots of people come here to paint so it was probably a local artist."

Her mind raced. *A contemporary of Van Gogh. Limited body of work.* This was almost too much for her to fathom. She leaned in, double checking the signature. Her heart leapt. "Horace Blackthorn."

As if her word wasn't good enough, he bent closer to verify. "Oh, yeah. You're right. Ever hear of him?"

She straightened. "Um...no. Not really." Her throat pinched. This lying thing wasn't getting any easier.

If he sensed her duplicity, he didn't let on. "I'll give you a good deal."

Her excitement mounting, Grace struggled to recall Kirk's commentary. Most of the artist's works sold to private collectors, causing their value to skyrocket. His subjects were always opera-related, so it made perfect sense that Kirk would own two of them. He was obsessive.

Placing an elbow on his knee, Sam took in a breath and rested his chin on his hand. "If you want it, you can have it for five."

Her pulse thumped audibly. This guy was actually going to let go of a million dollar work of art for a measly five hundred bucks? She smiled.

He leaned back on his haunches. "Oh, but I forgot." His tone dripped of sarcasm. "You're not staying around long. You wouldn't have any need for—"

"I'll take it."

"Oh." His voice lilted with surprised satisfaction as he stood. "Great."

She pushed herself to her feet, stunned. He actually thought he'd made a deal.

He lifted the painting and set it on an already-jam-packed table. She took a fleeting look at the surrounding items while he searched, presumably for wrapping material.

"Hey..." She puzzled. "Where did you get all this?"

He tossed his head to one side with a look of lament. "I'm just helping my dad clear out some old stuff."

She frowned, running her eyes across stacks of old playbills and sepia photos. "But where did you get this theatre stuff?"

"Well, I doubt the guy who's buying the theatre will be interested in salvaging piles of old junk—"

"You mean before he tears it down to build his casino?" Her antagonism charged ahead of her mouth. "He might as well tear down the whole town."

Sam blinked. "How did you—"

"So you're helping this 'Mr. R.' sell out the town. Great."

Sam's shoulders visibly tensed. "Look, my dad is just doing what he thinks is best—"

"Your dad?" Her chest heaved. "You're Mr. R.'s *son?*"

He lifted his hands. "Just like it says on the sign."

"What sign?"

"The one that—"

"Sam!"

His answer was cut short by Sophia's unmistakable trill. Grace turned to see her approach at a rapid clip with Devon close behind.

"I have to have this." Sophia aimed her sinuous arms toward Sam's table.

Grace reached down at the very second that Sophia's hands touched the painting. She lifted the frame, realizing with irritation that Sophia had a grip on the other end. Their surprised eyes locked on each other.

"It's mine!" Sophia said through gritted teeth. "I saw it first."

"Hardly." Grace scoffed. "Did you see me standing here?"

"So you were standing here. What difference does *that* make?" Sophia yanked the painting toward herself, but Grace held fast.

"All the difference." Grace gave a tug to no avail. That girl was stronger than she looked. "Let go!"

Sophia's face tightened. "I'm not letting go. You let go!"

"Now hold on, Sophia." Sam stepped in like a referee. "Grace and I already made a deal. I'm letting her have it for five."

"Five!" Sophia's face glazed like a child about to throw a tantrum. "I can give you seven-fifty! Devon, grab my wallet."

Devon, clearly amused, threw his hands up with a staying-out-of-this look.

Sam's tone remained calm. "Sorry, Soph, but we made a deal."

"Did you shake on it?" Sophia pleaded.

"No—"

"Then it isn't a deal. Sam, you know how much the theatre means to me. I deserve to have this." She shot Grace an icy glare. "*She* just got here."

Grace wrinkled her nose and tightened her grip.

Sam looked apologetic. "I'm sorry, Soph."

"Sam, you're being unfair. Devon, *tell* him!"

Devon stepped forward and all eyes turned to him. As he looked from Sophia to Grace, his expression shifted almost imperceptibly.

His eyes met Grace's, causing her unguarded heart to pound out a staccato passage. Why would she react this way to his piercing gaze?

She held her breath and awaited the verdict. Her nerves pinched with the understanding that as important as the painting was, something else was also at stake. Sophia had asked him to choose, and Devon was evaluating the candidates.

Winner take all.

"I'm sorry too." Devon's eyes lingered on Grace before grudgingly shifting to Sophia. "The court rules in favor of the new girl."

Sophia sputtered like a motor boat. The anger in her eyes dissolved into hurt and she released her grip on the frame. Lip aquiver, she took a few dramatic steps backward.

Grace's insides reeled with twofold victory. Surprised by the flutter in her stomach that had nothing to do with the painting, she tossed Devon a glance. A smile played at the corners of his lips. Then his eyes lifted, and his look grew shadowy.

Grace's gaze flitted toward Sam, who was pinning Devon with a stare that could melt iron. A palpable tension hung in the air between the two men.

"Devon!" Sophia huffed.

Devon's eyes remained steady. He reached into his back

pocket, removing a thick, Dior-embossed leather wallet. "The least I can do..." He held out a crisp bill and steadied his gaze on Sam.

Sam's mouth tightened. "I'm not taking your money."

"Take it." One corner of Devon's mouth pulled upward. "On behalf of the lady."

Grace withered in puzzlement as Sam worked his jaw. After a moment, he reached out and took the money. Grace caught a flash of the bill as he wadded it in his fist.

Devon slanted Sam a look as he stepped away. "You can keep the change." He tossed Grace a wink and met up with the retreating Sophia.

Sam turned away, darkness overshadowing his demeanor.

Looking at Sam's hunched shoulders, Grace measured her words. "Uh...Sam?"

He kept his back to her, barely turning his head as he spoke. "You really don't have to take the painting, you know. I wouldn't want you to feel like you're contributing to the selling out of the town."

She bristled, mystified and disturbed by his dark mood swing. "No, I still want it." She reached for the frame slowly, as if he might snap it away. "So, can you take a check?"

He lifted his head slightly. "Why? Did you want to grab some more stuff?"

Grace furrowed her brow, wondering if he had even bothered to look at the money. "No, but he gave you a *ten*."

His shoulders lifted in a sardonic chuckle. "You're right." He turned to face her. "You know what, I'll give you a deal." He bent down and picked up an empty box. "You can fill this up with whatever you want and we'll call it even."

She tried to shake off her mental whiplash. "Sam, I don't get it..."

He let out a sigh, pressing his fingers onto the bridge of his nose. "I can't explain. That guy just..." He waved a hand over his head. "You don't need to know." His face lifted and he turned back to the table. "There's some great old theatre stuff here. I don't know what you'd do with it, but hey, for five bucks—"

"Five bucks?"

He quirked a confused look. "Ten minus five. Such a deal."

Realization spread through Grace like a cool breeze. He'd given her the painting for five. Such a deal, indeed.

Chapter 15

"One for dinner?"

Grace inhaled the intoxicating bouquet of roasted garlic as she followed a young man with a large menu. He led her to a table by one of the elongated windows at the end of a surprisingly elegant dining room. She had a lot to celebrate, and it was time she treated herself to a nice dinner.

As she opened the menu, a warm rush of emotion pervaded her being. *The Fountain Restaurant.* She couldn't believe this little jewel had been hiding all along just a block past Main Street. After five days in Madison Falls, she had yet to find any real take-out and had been mainly relying on cold sandwiches from the display case that passed for a deli at the Peach Basket Market. Now, her mouth watering, she hoped the gastronomic options lived up to her expectations. If their Sauce Mornay turned out to be Velveeta, she might just lose it.

Scanning the bill of fare, she mentally reviewed her new to-do list as she took a sip of icy water to quell her fluttery stomach. Reality was setting in. Soon she'd be going home.

Her head still reeled from her amazing purchase that morning, but now there was much to be done. First she'd need to take the painting to an appraiser. According to the online yellow pages, there were two in Missoula—both of whom specialized in real estate appraisal, but that would have to do. She'd spent the afternoon researching auctions. Online was out. She needed to go to a reputable auction house with something of this caliber. EBay—no way!

Shipping it to the auction house would be easy enough. All she needed were the right wrapping materials and a wooden crate. Surely someone in town would be qualified to build one for her.

As for getting to Missoula...should she ask Lucy for a ride? No, too complicated. It would be tricky to explain her need for an appraiser without revealing the painting's value. Her niggling guilt about letting Sam sell it to her for the price of a latte was bad enough. She didn't need anybody's judgment.

How could anyone else understand? For two years, her battle against Kirk had been like jousting using a toothpick. Now, at last, she could face her opponent properly armed. The money would allow her to build a fortress around her life in New York, surrounding herself with guard dogs and bodyguards. So what if she had to live like a reclusive rock star? At least she'd have her life back.

A quiver of fear shot through her. Was this really going to work? It was all she could do. Her only other choice was to stay hidden, and that was out of the question.

"Are you waiting for someone?"

Her heart skipped. Slowly, she lowered the menu and lifted her gaze. Devon stood next to her table in a tasteful cerulean blue suit that set off the hue of his eyes. He looked like he'd just stepped out of a French film. Museums had been built to commemorate lesser works of art than his striking form.

"Oh, hello, Devon." She flashed a coy smile.

He cocked his head with a teasing gleam. "I have to admit I'm confused."

Her stomach bobbed slightly as she set down her menu. "And now that makes two of us."

"I know *I* stopped by on a whim." He gestured toward the empty chair opposite her. "I can't think why a beautiful woman like you would be dining alone."

She drew her mouth to one side. “And how do you know I’m not waiting for someone?”

Raising an eyebrow, he looked at her sideways. “Optimism.”

A demure smile escaped her lips as she nodded toward the chair. “No sense in both of us dining alone.” She was grateful for the dim lighting. At least he wouldn’t see the color rush to her cheeks.

She admired the way he guided the chair back and sat, as if every fluid movement was designed to reveal a deeper subtext.

“Your first time here?” His gaze pricked her nerve endings.

She nodded, not wanting to explain her lack of a dining companion.

“In that case, may I recommend the Tartiflette?” His finger expertly found the item on her menu.

Her mouth tingled in anticipation. “Sounds delicious.”

“Or the Pieds Paquets.”

“Ooo, no thanks. I try to stay away from lamb’s feet.”

His smile illuminated the scene like a well-focused Fresnel. He raised a hand. “May I?”

She nodded as the waiter appeared like a genie out of a bottle.

Devon cleared his throat with an ease that made even that act seem appealing. “We’ll start with the Coquilles Saint-Jacques. The lady will have the Tartiflette, and I’ll enjoy the Pansette de Gerzat. Then two Salades Nicoise. Also, a bottle of Shiraz, and for dessert…” His vibrant eyes met hers. “Mousse au Chocolat?”

She smiled assent. Was she really still in Montana?

The waiter took her menu and made his exit.

Devon settled back in his seat, his eyes resting easily on her. “It’s been a red-letter day for you. Congratulations on winning the war of the watercolor.”

“Thank you.” She beamed. “But it’s not a watercolor, it’s an oil.”

“I know.” He smiled. “I just couldn’t resist the alliteration.”

She twisted her hands in her lap. “Is Sophia very upset?”

He tipped back his head with a faint smirk. “Who knows with Sophia? She’s always got a burr under her saddle over something.

She'll get over it."

Resting her elbow on the arm of her chair, Grace casually touched her fingers to her chin. "Are we still talking about the painting?" Her hoped-for patina of flirtation was just glossy enough for him to take a shine to if he so chose.

He took a sip of water, pausing just long enough to achieve the proper effect. "That, and more."

Her heart took off at a sprint. It was all she could do to keep her smile from overtaking her entire face. Sure, the last thing she needed was a romance, but the promise of a mutual attraction made her spirit sing.

"You know…" He laced his fingers together under his chin. "You have the advantage. I've told you about me, but all I know about you is that you have an ear for casting, an eye for art, and a heart for animals."

Her lilting spirit hit a sour note. She lifted her water glass and took a shaky sip. "There's not much else to tell."

"Oh, I don't believe that." He lowered his hands and leaned in. "Everybody has a story."

She breathed in deeply, pretending not to notice her turn to pick up her cue. As a silence began to settle, she blurted out the first thing that came to mind. "So, what's up between you and Sam?"

"That guy." Devon chuckled with a roll of his sparkling eyes. "He's the one who's got a problem with me."

Figures. "The problem being?"

He lifted a shoulder with an indifferent tip of his head. "Jealousy, maybe. Some guys just can't handle it when things don't go their way."

"Oh really?" She rested her chin on her palm. "What things?"

The waiter returned with the wine. He uncorked it and poured a bit into a glass, which Devon swirled and swilled like a pro.

"Perfect." He nodded.

The waiter filled both glasses before stepping away. Grace fingered the stem of hers.

"Let's make a deal." Devon lifted his goblet. "Let's agree to leave the past in its place."

That sounded good to her, but surely he had nothing to hide. She lifted her glass to mirror his.

He tapped it and flashed a debonair smile. "To the present."

"To the here and now." She smiled back and took a sip. It was refreshing, both the wine and the company.

He swallowed with a look of contentment. "Mmmm. Perfecto. I feel like I'm sitting in a café in Palermo."

Her spirit lifted. "Oh, I love that city."

He raised his eyebrows and lowered his glass. "A fellow world traveler. I had a feeling. My favorite thing about Palermo is the Palazzo dei Normanni."

She leaned her forearms on the table. "Yes. Yes, it's beautiful there."

"I'm a bit of an architecture buff and the Norman-Byzantine style is a favorite."

"No wonder you love Italy then." Her heart felt light, like a balloon about to float right out of her chest. She'd been transported out of Madison Falls and was home, in a fashionable bistro, talking with a colleague about things that mattered. "The architecture, the arts."

"Ah, the arts." His voice lilted. "Surely you went to the theatre there? I saw an amazing production at the Teatro Luigi Orione. Oh, but my definitive experience was at the Teatro Mass—"

"—Massimo?" A fluttering in her chest propelled her forward.

"Yes. So, you're a fan of opera?"

She pushed the curve of her back against her chair. How much did she dare disclose? "I haven't been entirely forthcoming."

His eyebrow cocked. "No?"

She shook her head.

With a knowing smile, he lifted his glass and studied the swirling liquid, as if the truth might be revealed therein. "I suspected as much. Let me guess...does it have something to do with music?"

She cautioned a nod.

His amused gaze flicked to her. "Aha I was right. You are a

singer."

A confessional nod. How could she refute what his expert ear had so skillfully discerned?

"Opera?"

Relief and beguilement overcame her reticence. "Yes."

"Professional aspirations?"

She let her smile answer for her.

"I thought so. The pet store was just a day job."

Again she nodded. Might as well cling to as much of her ruse as she could.

"I'd offer to take you to the opera some time," he said as he whirled his goblet. "But that would involve a trip to Seattle."

Her stomach squeezed. She gave up a feeble smile. "Home sweet home." She swirled the liquid in her glass.

"Ah, yes. You're from there." Confusion creased his brow. "Now I'm really mystified."

Carefulness colored her words. "Why is that?"

"Seattle has a reputable music scene. What brings you here?"

Her pulse quickened. "The power of garlic."

He chuckled. "I didn't mean *here*, and you know it. What brings you to Madison Falls, and do not say a Greyhound."

She lowered her chin in careful contemplation of her response. She wanted to open up to him. How much did she dare say? "Something happened to me, and I had to get away."

He nodded slowly. "Care to elaborate?"

She studied the wall behind him, words sitting idle on her tongue.

Rotating his wine, he smiled playfully. "I mean, did you break your umbrella, or get a bad latte—"

"I found a dead body."

His glass froze in midair. Silence fell across the table like an act curtain.

She felt compelled to continue. "Her name was Julie. I didn't know her. I just happened to show up at her place at the wrong time."

He set down his glass and reached for her hand. "Oh, Grace."

She enjoyed the warmth of his touch, the softness of his manicured fingers. Her voice calmed. "It was pretty awful. I was a suspect, since I'd found her. They grilled me for so long I don't even know what I said after a while. I was in shock, and they wore me down."

"They arrested you?"

"No, they let me go."

"So..." He gave her hand a squeeze before pulling his away.

"So they never found the killer." She toyed with a silver salt cellar, pleased with the rightness of her disclosure. "It's just bizarre to know that whoever did it is still out there."

He blew out a breath. "Wow."

Trembling with an unanticipated sense of relief, she forced a derisive smile. "So, top that, Director Man."

A small trench formed in his brow. "What do you mean?"

"Well..." Anxious to take the attention off herself, she playfully drew her finger along the rim of her wine glass. "Last night you told me you came here to get a break from the pressure. Care to elaborate?"

He paused. "Do you believe in fate?" He looked at her and arched an eyebrow.

"Fate? I don't know." Was fate the driving force that had forced her from the life she'd worked so hard for? Maybe there was something to that.

He continued. "I'm convinced that fate is what brought me here. I'm in town on a business deal that's about to come to fruition."

"Business, eh?" She cupped her elbows on the table's edge. "So you're not just here to lend your artistic talents."

"No, the directing projects just happened to fall into my lap. It was something much bigger that brought me out west."

"I'm intrigued."

With stylish stealth, the waiter placed a platter of cheesy scallops in shells at the center of their table. Inhaling their rich scent, Grace reeled her hands back in.

Devon spooned some of the appetizer onto her plate. "I don't want to say too much yet." His tone was tinged with anticipation. "But the best part is I'll be able to go back to New York with no worries. I'll be free to do whatever I want."

She swathed her lap with crisp linen. "Sounds like a great deal."

"'Great' doesn't begin to describe it." He served himself. "I don't mean to say that money is everything, but it's certainly a good percentage of the haul."

She took a satisfying bite of the delicious dish, savoring the complex flavors of the rich cream sauce for a long moment before swallowing. "So when does this deal close?"

Bemused aggravation danced across his face. "Soon, I hope. Small-town people really move at their own pace. In New York, we could have sealed the deal weeks ago, but out here it's different. I have to respect that. In the meantime, I'm taking advantage of some opportunities."

She arched an innocent eyebrow. "At the theatre?"

He lifted his wine glass and smiled slyly. "Some of them."

She returned his smile, pleased that he knew an opportunity when he saw one. She liked that in a man.

She brought another bite of satiny scallop to her mouth. It looked like coming to Madison Falls had been a tasty plan after all.

Chapter 16

"I'm so glad we're doing this."

Grace angled a sideways glance at Lucy. By *this*, did she mean walking downtown to get paint samples, or decorating Grace's house against her will?

No matter. Grace had resigned herself to this little project because fighting it wasn't worth the risk. She couldn't afford to raise any red flags. Besides, now that she wasn't so worried about money, she could justify giving the bungalow a makeover. It would be so much easier to rent out furnished.

"Oh, before I forget," Lucy interrupted Grace's meditative thoughts. "Our church is having a concert in the park in a couple of weeks. I'd love it if you could come. It's a potluck, so there'll be plenty of food."

"A concert?" Suddenly Grace's mood faltered. The thought of sitting in the audience while a bunch of amateurs played their idea of music was more than she could stand. Besides, who knew where she'd be in a couple of weeks.

"It's just our little quartet." Lucy lowered her eyes. "We need an excuse to perform apart from the full band at service. It's silly, I know, but we have fun and the people seem to enjoy it. Of course, they're always giddy from too many cupcakes by the time we play, but that's the result of a little calculated planning on our part."

"You're in a quartet?" Grace perked up, excited by the opportunity to discuss her favorite subject, but fearful of saying more than she should. "What instrument?"

"Piano." Lucy's voice warmed. "I've played it forever. It's my little escape."

Escape. Funny that the word could carry such a different meaning for different people.

"This will be fun." Lucy gestured toward the shopping bag that Grace swung by her side as they walked. "I'm so glad you brought along that throw pillow."

"I can't believe someone was selling it." Grace dipped into the sack that had held her new wardrobe just a few days before and now contained one of her rummage sale finds. "It has all the colors of the living room in it. I think I'd like to tie the rooms together with a unifying color."

"Listen to you, Miss I'm-not-really-a-decorator." Lucy backhanded Grace's arm with a playful tap. "This is going to be easier than I thought."

Grace gave a small smile of ascent. Things were looking up.

"Oh, I put out some feelers yesterday." Lucy's tone was as cheerful as her coral T-shirt that nicely set off her ponytailed tresses. "I'm sure we'll have a healthy turn-out for the paint party on Saturday." She pulled open a shop door, stepping aside as if she expected Grace to walk through it.

Grace's face dropped. "Why are we going in here?"

"Well, where else would we go to look at paint?"

Grace tipped her head back as if the sign reading *Roberts and Son* might have changed to something more inviting. No such luck. Swallowing a feeble protest, she took a few careful steps into the hardware store, her eyes darting around like a secret agent on a mission.

"Is something wrong?" Lucy's eyes narrowed with concern.

"No. It's just that—"

"Well, hello ladies." Mr. Roberts' warm voice was like cocoa on a cold day.

Grace turned to him as he stepped from behind the front

counter. A lump instantly materialized in her throat.

"I hope you didn't mind waiting for that crowbar the other day, Miss Addison."

"No." She rasped out a weak response. "It was fine, thank you."

"Hello Mr. Roberts." Lucy beamed. "Will we be seeing you at the town council meeting on Thursday?"

"Haven't missed a one in thirty-five years." He spoke with an air of humble satisfaction, then clasped his hands together as if to signal his shift to business mode. "What can I help you ladies with today?"

"My friend Grace here is painting her house." Lucy spoke with a soft enthusiasm. "You know, the old Miller place?"

Grace winced. When she went back home, would the house then be referred to as "the old Addison place"?

Mr. Roberts nodded sagely. "You're in luck. Sam just got back from his delivery." He leaned toward Grace in an aside. "He's my paint specialist. I'll go get him."

"No..." Grace reached out to stop him, but he didn't seem to notice.

"It's okay, Grace." Lucy patted her arm. "Sam really knows paint. In fact, he already said he'd be happy to come on Saturday."

She did a slow burn. "You asked *him?*" Did everybody really know everybody else around here? What was the population of this town, seven?

With an offhand shrug, Lucy turned her attention to a display of vintage doorknobs. "Well, word got 'round church."

Church? Grace frowned. She was supposed to buy that this flirtatious beer swigging louse with obvious anger management issues was a churchgoer? She believed it of Lucy—she just seemed the type—but Sam?

"Lucy, I really don't think that—"

"Morning, ladies."

Grace whirled around, finding herself face-to-face with the paint specialist. The "plum" under his eye had ripened slightly, its effect somewhat less alarming. His hair was tousled but at least this morning he had bothered to shave. He put his hands on his hips, throwing emphasis on his broad shoulders.

He tossed his head in the direction of Mr. Roberts, as the older man returned to the counter. "My dad tells me you decided to paint. Great idea."

His dad? But his dad was Mr...

A light went on in Grace's head that could have illuminated Manhattan. *Mr. R and Son, just like it says on the sign.* She wanted to kick herself. That sweet Mr. Roberts was the heartless businessman whom she had charged with selling out the town.

Pulling in her breath, she grasped the bag handles with both hands.

"She has a color scheme." Lucy sounded so chipper, as if she were auditioning for one of those decorating shows. The next Paige Davis. "Show him the pillow, Grace."

Grace held a beat before pulling the pillow from its nest. Sam took it, examining the embroidery. He chuckled.

She lifted a hand to reclaim the pillow. "I don't see what's so funny."

He shifted slightly, oblivious to her grasp. "I could swear I've clobbered Jill with this a hundred times. Her mom's redecorating?"

Lucy clucked. "She finally let Jill talk her into it. It'll do her good. She took such great care of her things that they're practically like new, in spite of Jill's hooligan friends." Lucy took the pillow and gave him a playful swat. "Grace made out like a bandit at the sale."

He looked at Grace with a disquieting ease. "A bandit, I know. I was an accessory to the crime."

A burn settled in Grace's throat. She felt like such a fool. Why had he let her prattle on like that the other day about his dad?

"She took all that old stuff from the theatre off my hands." Sam spoke to Lucy, but remained focused on Grace.

Lucy's eyebrows lifted. "No kidding." She snapped toward Grace. "You could use it for decorating accents. Maybe frame some of the programs. It could be a motif."

Just what she needed—a *motif.* "Maybe..."

"It would be great. Shabby Chic is definitely in."

Grace shrugged, looking at Sam with a mixture of resentment and regret. "I just couldn't stand to see all that rich history of the theatre get split up. Once I started shopping..."

"Don't think I don't appreciate it." Sam's eyes softened. Why did they seem to get more appetizing with each passing day? He looked at his dad, then lowered his head toward Lucy. "You know how much I need the cash right now. Every little bit helps."

Fear flecked Lucy's eyes as she lightly touched Sam's arm, then visibly calculated a change in tone. "So...paint."

"Right." He held his hand out in an after-you gesture, and Lucy strode down one of the overcrowded aisles toward the back of the store. As Grace moved to follow, Sam leaned forward and spoke in a confidential tone. "Decided to stick around after all, huh?"

She seethed, firing him a fierce look. She'd have to be careful not to let herself be manipulated by him.

She knew his type.

Chapter 17

"Careful, gentlemen, that's a valuable piece of equipment." Grace held her breath as two farmhand/ushers hoisted Salvatore onto the concession stand counter like a bale of hay.

"You want us to bring in those other boxes too, Miss Addison?" The one named Hank removed his trucker's cap and swiped a hand across his brow.

"If you wouldn't mind." Grace admired her acquisition. "I'll give you two the first samples for your efforts."

Hank exchanged a perplexed look with his buddy Carl before the pair headed back outside.

Buffing the fingerprints off the sides of the machine, she heaved a satisfied sigh. "Salvatore, you look right at home."

"Who are you talking to?" Nancy peeked into the concession stand, trepidation lining her sprightly face.

"You're just in time." Grace arched her arm à la Carol Merrill. "Meet Salvatore."

The diminutive woman eased into the tiny room "Okay.... What is it?"

Grace puffed mock impatience. "*He's* our ticket to concession-stand success. When people around here find out what coffee's supposed to taste like, they'll be lining up around the block."

"Around the block?" Nancy perked up. "Can we charge fifteen

bucks a cup and let them drink it in an audience seat?"

Grace laughed. "I don't think we'll have to be that sneaky. Once we lure them in with our new coffee house ambiance, we'll promote the show like crazy. We can even advertise some sort of deal...like a free 'tall' with each ticket."

Nancy's eyes glazed. "A tall *what?*"

"Latte." Grace held up a paper cup. "I'll have to teach you the lingo."

Nancy's expression crossed from confused to dubious. "Well, I hope you can return it if it doesn't work out."

"He'll work out." Grace smiled. "Trust me."

From the look on Nancy's face, that was close to the last thing she felt like doing.

"Where would you like this set, Miss Addison?" Hank and Carl stood at the door to the stand, laden with treasures from the hidden tomb of King Costco.

Nancy cast a wary eye on their load. "What's all this?"

Grace shot her an offhand glance as she calculated how to stage everything. "Supplies."

"You bought supplies?"

"Yeah. You know, coffee beans, grinders, cups. I got two kinds of syrup, and I even bought some biscotti. Look." She leaned over, digging around in the lidless box as Carl struggled to maintain his grip. She produced a wastebasket-sized container and held it up like a trophy.

"Biscuits?" Nancy seemed befuddled. "They look like cookies. You got all this at the Peach Basket?"

Grace twisted her mouth. *If only*. "No, I drove all the way to Missoula to shop at Costco."

"Costco!" Nancy's face blanched. "Wait a minute. You *bought* supplies?"

"Sure." Grace shrugged. "Right after I bought a car."

"You bought a car?"

"It made sense. Joanie from the bakery was selling her Beetle, so—"

"Oh," Nancy's face brightened—back to familiar territory.

"You bought Joanie's Beetle? Cute car."

"Yes. It's a little old, but it runs." Grace didn't really see herself as the Beetle type, but it would come in handy. She'd acquired a few things that would look adorable in her apartment in New York, and besides, she'd never driven across the country. It might be more relaxing than flying.

A bead of sweat formed on Nancy's upper lip as she perused the contents of the boxes. "So, how much did all this cost?"

"It wasn't so bad." Grace flapped a dismissive hand in the air. "Considering what I spent on the machine, I could splurge on the beans."

"But the theatre can't afford—"

"Don't worry." Grace raised her palm. "It will be my donation. I know the theatre needs money and every little bit counts." She paused, casting a quick glance at the clean rectangle of wall paper between the windows where her painting had once hung. "Which reminds me..." She vacillated. Did she really want to bring this up? "Sam was selling off some theatre things at the rummage sale, and—"

"Oh, don't get me started." Nancy rolled her eyes. Hurt and anger practically announced themselves in writing on her forehead. "It makes me sick to think of all those things that we've preserved for years just getting sold like junk." She waved the subject away as she turned her back and started out the door. "I'll be in my office."

"But..." Grace moved to follow, but stopped herself. She wanted to tell Nancy that all the theatre's precious memories were boxed up in her basement. That she was about to become a wealthy woman and that someday soon she'd make a sizable donation to the Madison Playhouse. If it still existed, of course.

No matter how badly she wanted to, she couldn't quite bring herself to tell Nancy the truth.

"Uh...Miss Addison?" Carl readjusted his grip on the box he held.

"Oh, right. Sorry." Grace scanned her minuscule space, then gestured toward the floor. "Why don't you just set those down over there. I'll have to make room."

"Good luck with that," Hank said, obliging. He looked around the booth. "You know you've got no power in here. You'll have to plug 'er in out in the lobby." He gestured toward the wall next to the stand. The men tipped their hats and returned to their regular duties.

Great. Grace scooted the machine clear to the end of the counter just inside the stand and draped the power cord down to the floor and around the corner. To her relief, it was just long enough to reach the brass-plated relic of a power outlet. She plugged it in, hoping the outlet still had some juice.

"Oh!" Yanking her hand back, she shook off the afterburn of a tiny shock. She pulled herself to her feet, then reached around and flicked the On switch. A red light came to life, and she let out a relieved breath. *We've got power.*

She folded her arms and surveyed her purchases. Now that she saw the bulk of supplies sitting in the tiny space, she realized how daunting the task of storing it would be. She looked around. At least the stand had a little storage space.

She yanked open a drawer so old she half expected to find a yellowed pamphlet from the Suffragette Movement or a "Vote for Grover Cleveland" button in it. To her disappointment, all it contained was a coupon for a free shave from Hector's Barber Shop, and an ancient ring of keys. She pondered. Could be a good place to keep the twist spoons.

She sat down on the rough wood floor and began removing items from the boxes. Soon, encircled by barista paraphernalia, she leaned back and thought about how the day had gone.

Buying a car had been surprisingly simple. She'd been nervous about using her fake ID for such a major purchase, but since she had the funds in her checking account no one had questioned it. She knew it was impractical to own a car in the city, but her mom had more than enough space at her house. A definite plus to living in the Jersey suburbs.

Shopping had been fun, but the appraisal experience had been questionable. She'd been scared off by the taxidermy display in the waiting area of the first place.

"The owner's hobby," the beaming receptionist had said.

The second place looked promising until the guy showed up in stained overalls and waders. Did she really want to trust the estimate of someone who spent their days measuring crawl spaces?

She entertained a tiny smile. She still wanted the opinion of someone whose specialty actually *was* art, but at least now she had something to go on. She reached for her purse, pulling out the neatly folded paper and opening it slowly. One point two million would buy her a lot of freedom.

She should be thrilled, so why was she letting that tiny twinge of guilt color her personal celebration? She deserved this. There was no reason why Sam or anybody else in this town ever had to know she had suspected the value of the painting when she bought it. They never had to find out anything, ever. So why did she still feel guilty?

Her nerves jumped as she remembered that the lobby would open soon. Giving her watch a quick check, she tucked the paper back into her purse and bounced to her feet. There wasn't much time if she wanted to be ready for the pre-show crowd.

She crossed to the edge of the stand, reaching out to shut the lower half of the door. Just as she grabbed for it, she lurched back.

Sophia had moved into the doorway, and stood there with arms folded and shoulders rearing up like a cobra ready to strike. "Thanks a lot," she hissed.

"For what?" Grace frowned. Like she needed *this*.

Sophia slanted an eyebrow in an apparent attempt to appear threatening. Her words stabbed. "For talking Devon out of giving me Mabel."

"I didn't—"

"Yes, you did. He told me." She balled up her fists like a child about to launch into a tantrum.

Grace huffed out an impatient sigh. "Sophia, he's the director. He cast the play, not me. I just made a few suggestions for the good of the show."

"Yeah, well thanks for suggesting me right out of the best role of the season." She edged further into the doorway, spreading her feet wide as if to make her petite frame appear larger. "I'm the one who told Nancy about *Pirates*. I've waited my whole life to play that role, and just in case you didn't know, I always get the lead."

"Apparently not *always*." Grace indulged in a touch of sarcasm. "Nobody always gets the lead. You're in a very small pond—"

"Maybe..." Sophia charged forward, quickly closing the three-foot gap that had separated them. "But it's my pond. And Devon is my..." She stopped herself, her eyes suddenly pooling with angst.

"Your what?" Grace folded her arms and jutted out a hip. Devon certainly hadn't been acting like he was committed to Sophia. If she believed otherwise, she deserved to be set straight. "What exactly *is* he to you?"

Sophia's eyes darted around the room. "He's been staying at my house."

"So that makes him what, your tenant?"

Her eyes zeroed in on Grace like lasers. "You have no right to horn in."

"Horn in? Aren't you being a little juvenile?"

"*Juvenile?* Is it juvenile to be angry at someone who breezes into town and starts taking away everything that should be mine?"

Grace rejected the little minx's attempt at intimidation. "You're exaggerating."

"Am I? Would you like a list?"

"Is this about that painting? Because—"

"The painting, the leading role. Now you're trying to take away my—"

"Your *what?*" Grace pinned her with her best diva glower. She hadn't set out to find romance, but if one unfolded, she had every right to know where she stood.

Sophia pursed her lips and spoke in a voice so hot it could have creased a pair of trousers. "You know darn well what you're doing, but it's not going to work." She took a step even closer, her words sharpening. "I saw him first."

"You *saw* him first? What is he, a parking space?"

Sophia breathed out a snarl. She shot Grace a glare that would have simultaneously scorched and flash-frozen a lesser competitor in the field of infatuation. Grace smiled to herself. Actress Sophia had no idea what she was up against.

Sophia shifted back. She held up a pointy-tipped finger and aimed it at Grace. "You're going to be sorry you ever came here." Her steely stare lingered dramatically for just a moment before she reeled around and stormed off.

Oh brother.

After all Grace had suffered in the last couple of years, Sophia's sophomoric ranting didn't seem like much of a threat.

Grace stooped to pick up her coffee goods. There was something troubling about her conversation with Sophia other than, of course, that Sophia had been in it. *You're going to be sorry you ever came here.* Was she just a pesky little gnat buzzing in Grace's ear, or was there actual meat to her menace?

It was probably nothing, but she did have to hand it to the little scenery-chewer. She had given quite a performance. Behind the infantile behavior lurked the spirit of a true diva.

Chapter 18

"Who wants a corn dog?"

Catching a drip of paint on her brush, Grace looked up to see Lucy setting lunch out on the new dining table. A flock of kids clamored around her like seagulls.

Grace sat back on her haunches. She had gotten so absorbed in painting the windowsill that she hadn't noticed her living room had been transformed from cold and stark to warm and homey. No wonder everyone had been so enthusiastic about her adding color to this room.

She hadn't expected so many volunteers to arrive at her door that morning. Didn't these people have other things to do on a sunny Saturday? They'd been hard at work for several hours now and they all seemed to be enjoying themselves. Much to her surprise, so was she.

She lowered herself to the floor, pulling her knees up to her chest. It felt good to take a little break, although she appreciated that the painting had given her time to lose herself in her thoughts. Everything seemed to be falling nicely into place.

"Oh Grace, I meant to warn you." Joanie called down from atop a ladder where she spread cherry-blossom pink on the wall over the front door. "My car...oops! I mean *your* car has a quirk."

Grace picked up her brush. "Don't we all?"

"That's the truth." Joanie crinkled her nose in a giggle. She looked like a person who would drive a Beetle. "Anyway, the passenger side door tends to stick, and the window crank is long gone. No big deal."

Grace shrugged. "It'll only be a big deal if my purse wants to bail out. So far that's been my only passenger."

"I meant to get it fixed before I sold it, but it slipped my mind. I never really had passengers eith—" Joanie launched backward as the front door opened beneath her. She gripped the top rung of the ladder just in time.

Sam looked up as he walked through the door. "Whoa. Sorry about that."

Joanie smiled and resumed painting. "No problem, Sam. Where've you been all morning?"

"Mostly out in the garage mixing paint."

Grace rolled her eyes. She wasn't exactly thrilled about having him in her house, but he *did* know paint. He'd appointed himself head of the work crew and everyone seemed to be fine with that. Either they didn't know what a jerk he was, or they'd reached a collective agreement to ignore it.

He looked around, saw her, and opened his mouth to speak. Without meaning to, she gave him the look that a critic had once described as a "searing glare," and he stepped back. He looked around again.

"Hey Luce," he said, shifting into the dining room and holding up a paint card. "This 'lilac' is for the front bedroom, right?"

Lucy nodded as she carefully took aim with a ketchup dispenser at a paper plate held by a bobbing tot.

"So," he continued. "Which wall gets the 'thistle'?"

"I don't know, Sam. You'll have to ask the lady of the house."

Grace cringed. Why couldn't Lucy just act as a go-between?

She went back to dabbing at the corners of her windowsill, sensing Sam's pending approach. Let him think she didn't know he was there.

"Gra...Miss Addison?"

Faking an intense focus, she kept her eyes on her detail work.

"Yes?"

"Sorry to bother you when you're in the middle of that, but would you mind coming with me for just a sec?"

She let the air exit loudly through her nose to convey her irritation. Why couldn't he just ask her here?

She made a little show of extracting the last bit of paint from her brush and dabbing it with a cloth before setting it on the edge of her paint can. She stood, wiped her hands on the ratty jeans that Lucy had insisted she borrow, and made a lead-the-way motion.

She could have sworn he smirked as he turned toward the hallway. She'd had stagehands put on probation for lesser offenses. Who did he think he was?

Keeping a comfortable distance between them, she followed him to the front bedroom, which seemed to be the only room in the house that wasn't overflowing with paintbrush-wielding good Samaritans. Sam walked to the middle of the room, then stopped next to the mountain of drop cloth that looked more like the Matterhorn than her Lucy-gifted brass bed. She remained in the doorway, determined not to make herself vulnerable.

"So I'm wondering..." He turned, looked amused by her choice of a stopping point, and motioned toward the open cans of paint which stood in a tidy row near the side window. "Do you want the lighter tone to be on your south-facing or east-facing wall?"

A harrumphing noise escaped her throat. Which was which?

"Uh...that one." She pointed toward the front of the house.

"Great instinct." He smiled. "That's what I was thinking too."

Was he making fun of her?

He stepped toward the window and looked out, as if he had all the time in the world. Didn't he have a room to paint?

"You're lucky to have this window. The sun rising over those mountains is the greatest sight to wake up to."

How was she supposed to react to that? It was none of his business what view she opened her eyes to and besides, she hadn't actually noticed that the sun rose on this side of her house.

"Was that all?" She folded her arms.

He turned, his eyes dropping to the plastic-sheeted floor.

"Yeah. Yeah, that was it."

She gave up a tight-lipped smile and turned on her heel. A thought flipped into her head and she stopped, spinning again to face him. "Do you think you could build me a crate?"

His eyebrows shot up. He opened his mouth but the answer took its time coming out. "I guess so. Why?"

She instantly regretted having asked. Why did people have to question everything? "It's just...something I need."

"Of course." His smarmy smile returned. "Ridiculous of me to think otherwise." He crossed to the paint cans and bent to pick one up. "How big?"

"Huh? Oh." Pleased that she'd actually measured, she spoke with authority. "Fifteen by eighteen inches. Six inches deep."

He nodded, his mouth pulling up at the corners.

She hesitated, feeling the need to add more but not knowing what. "Don't worry about a second coat in here. One should be plenty." She winced. Who did she think she was, Bob Villa? Sam was the paint expert, not her.

He tossed her a bemused look as he carried the can to the front corner. "Why don't we see how it looks before we make that call?"

"I just...don't want you to waste paint." That was stupid. Why couldn't she just leave?

"I don't want to waste either, but I want you to be happy with the result." He knelt down to open the can.

She pulled in a deep breath. "It doesn't really matter to me."

"Oh." He gave a perplexed nod. "Maybe we should just send everybody home now then. Tell them it doesn't really matter if they finish."

She creased her brow. "What's that supposed to mean?"

He tipped the can, pouring the rich liquid into a paint tray. "Nothing. It's just that the painting doesn't seem to have much value to you."

Anger gripped her. So, that was what this was about—the painting. Had he realized his mistake and now he wanted to have it out with her? She stepped forward, opened her mouth, then turned and stomped back to shut the door. The whole town didn't need to hear this. "What business is it of yours?"

"None." He seemed pretty nonchalant for a guy who'd just been pinned by her ire. "Except that I'm one of the people *doing* this meaningless painting."

Oh. Grace's argument caught in her throat. Of course. *That* painting. She slowly deflated like a tire with a tack in it. "I guess I have other priorities."

He nodded in understanding as he twisted a long handle onto a roller. "Anything I can help you with? Besides the much-needed crate?"

She mentally ran down her list of concerns. "Yes. You can. Answer something for me."

Anchoring the roller on the floor, he leaned on the handle. "Okay."

She mapped out her words with care. "Your dad seems like a really sweet man. He runs a business that's important to the community. He's on the town council, for goodness' sake."

His look confirmed her comments.

"So why is he selling the theatre?"

The sideways bob of his head held the answer to be obvious. "Simple. He needs money."

Money. *Of course*. Did he think she was dense? "I meant if he cares about the town, why is he selling to Langley?"

He huffed out a quick breath. "Nancy told you."

"Don't blame Nancy." She held up a hand. "She's really upset. And she feels powerless. She had to tell somebody."

He raised a warning finger.

She held up her hands. "Don't worry. I haven't said a word."

Relief eased his expression. "Good. If people find out about the casino—"

"It's a *casino*. Don't you think they'll notice when their town starts to be visible from outer space?"

He gave her an *of course* look then turned, dipping his roller in the paint. He reached upward and a beautiful shade of lavender began to transform her wall. "We just want to keep our business private till the contract is signed."

She perked up. "So, the deal's not set? There's still time for your dad to change his mind?"

"He's not going to change his mind."

"But—"

Sam snapped around so abruptly that a spray of paint arched across the room. "You don't know what we've been through to get to this point. Nobody else could possibly come near Langley's offer. Don't you think we've looked at all the options?"

She drew back at his unexpected outburst. "But less money for your dad would mean the town could maintain its integrity. Don't you think you're both being selfish?"

The tightness around his eyes and mouth intensified. "You have no idea what you're talking about."

Indignation lit a fire deep inside her. "Just because I'm new here? I still recognize greed when I see it."

Fury flickered across his face so intensely that she braced herself for a slap. She recoiled, remembering the kind of person she was dealing with. How had she been so careless?

As quickly as the anger came, it passed. He dropped his head back and appeared to be scripting his response. When he spoke, his voice was low and measured. "It's not what we expected, but at this point I'm not second guessing how God answers my prayers."

"Your prayers?" She frowned. "You were praying for a million bucks to fall out of the sky? How original."

"I have my reasons." His voice was so low she could practically hear the paint drying. He turned back to the wall, but didn't resume his work. "Look, let's just drop it, all right?"

"But—"

"Besides, what's it to you?" He dipped the roller and lifted it to the corner. "You're not staying long anyway."

Silence settled. Why had she thought she could make a difference in the way he chose to see this?

"Oh, look at him. Sam!" Lucy's muffled voice called out from the other room.

"Yeah, be right there!" He practically dropped the roller and headed for the door. He flung it open and charged out.

Befuddled, Grace followed.

Lucy waved a mustard-coated knife in the air as she huffed at the front window. "He's lifting that thing all by himself. Doesn't he know the meaning of 'take it easy'?"

"You kidding?" Sam wiped his hands on a rag. "Don't worry, Luce. I'll take care of this." With that, he rushed out the front door.

"What's going on?" Grace frowned as she joined Lucy at the window. Mr. Roberts was in the front yard, lifting a door onto two sawhorses. Sam hurried down the steps and grabbed one end of it.

Lucy sounded melancholy. "Mr. Roberts has such a kind heart. He'd do anything for anybody."

A question formed on Grace's lips, but before she could put voice to it, Lucy had returned to her lunch duty. Grace turned her focus back to the yard, where Mr. Roberts had started to sand the door, preparing it for paint. Sam stood over him, talking in what seemed to be a calm manner.

Mr. Roberts stooped slightly, blowing away the sawdust from the area he'd sanded, and Grace saw something else for just a flash. A brief memory of a night long ago. It had been a week or so before her seventh birthday and she'd snuck downstairs for a drink of water. She heard something, a grinding noise, coming from the basement. She tiptoed down, taking care not to make a sound. Peering around a dark corner into the space her father used as a wood shop, she saw it—an outline of a small house. The grinding stopped and her father bent over to blow away the sawdust and inspect his work.

Grace smiled at the memory. She had loved that dollhouse.

Looking out the window again, she felt her throat constrict around a lump she'd never learn to swallow. The guilt that had smoldered in her gut for a solid week flared like a campfire. There was no way to quench it.

For some reason that she might never understand, Mr. Roberts—that sweet man—was in serious need of money. What was she supposed to do about that?

Chapter 19

"You're in for a real treat." Devon's sly smile put her at ease as he skillfully maneuvered his Lexus down the curved country road.

"It's a treat just to get out of town for the afternoon." Grace subtly caressed the buttery-soft seat, inhaling the rich scent of the leather. The beautifully clear summer weather had her in a lighthearted mood.

"It's an idyllic part of the country, isn't it?" He propped an elbow on the window's edge, resting one hand across the top of the wheel. His suave manner made every move seem effortless.

"Yes, I never knew." She watched the forested hillside glide past her window. She'd seen so much of the world, and had generally considered countryside to be just the necessary space between cities. She had never really taken the time to appreciate the beauty of farmland and fields.

Her head rested on the padding behind her and she reveled in the moment. This felt right. "How are rehearsals going?"

He cast a quick glance from behind the taupe lenses of his Burberry sunglasses. "The good news is, you were right about Ruby."

"I knew she could do it."

"Yes, and the bad news, I'm afraid, is the rest of the cast. I'm pinning all my hopes on Mabel to carry the day. I hope that's not too much to ask of a woman who's up at four to milk the cows."

An easy chuckle lilted from her throat. She rolled her head to the left, stealing an eyeful of Devon as he spoke. Her gaze lolled back to catch the view out the driver's side. A rushing river paralleled the road, as if racing them to their destination. From the look of things, it was winning.

"And Myra." He continued his good-humored account. "From what I hear she used to actually know how to play the piano. I don't have the heart to tell her the notes should be played in the order in which they appear on the page."

Grace drew her hand to her mouth in combined amusement and exasperation. She wanted so much to see this show succeed, but sometimes she felt like she was the only one who did.

She looked out her window, unwilling to dwell on thoughts of the theatre. She wanted to relax and enjoy the drive, like a normal girl living a normal life.

Lush farmland gave way to rolling hills that abutted the roadway. She had never given much credence to the restorative powers of nature, but this drive was opening her eyes. She raised her head and leaned toward the windshield, intent on drinking in this scenery. Nature had carved the perfect path between river and hill, and they were exploring it.

Just up ahead, the road curved and something at the foot of the hill caught her attention. "Look at that."

"What?" Devon perked up. "And don't say 'that tree over there.'"

"No, that old cabin straight ahead." Her mind swirled with the romantic notion that a home built by a hearty frontier family could still sit on the spot where they'd chosen to live. "I'll bet it's been there since the original settlers won the west."

"Maybe." Devon jutted out his strong jaw. "Think that old pickup has been there that long too?"

As they grew closer, Grace got an eyeful of the clearly not-so-romantic ramshackle redneck hovel that looked more Viet Nam era than classic Old West. She turned away in disgust, then did a double take.

She leaned in as they drove past, not wanting to see but staring anyway. She wanted to be sure. Two men stood in front of the shack talking. One was unmistakably Carson, in the same muscle T she'd seen him in that first day. The other man she'd recognize anywhere. It was Sam.

Her eyes stayed glued to the scene even after they'd passed. If there had been any doubt in her mind, which there wasn't, there was no mistaking that old blue pickup truck.

"Something wrong?" Devon's voice was tinted with concern.

She sat back in her seat, wondering what to make of it. "No, nothing. Just curious how anyone could live like that."

Devon shrugged. "Takes all kinds."

He continued talking, but Grace had difficulty pulling her thoughts away from the scene she'd just witnessed.

"I was so pleased when you said you were available today." Devon eventually drew her back with his velvet voice. "Thank you for trusting me with the details and the destination."

"Why wouldn't I?" She shook off her disturbing thoughts from a few moments before. "So, can I ask where we're going?"

His look turned playful. "You can ask, but in a minute you'll see for yourself."

He made a sharp left into a dusty clearing and brought the car to a standstill. Holding up a wait-here hand, he opened his door and stepped out. Grace enjoyed his passage around the front of the car, appreciating his sleek GQ style. His peach polo showed his muscular form to great advantage, and casual gray linen pants fit like they'd been tailored for him.

Pleased that she'd made an effort beyond what had become her daily uniform of jeans and a T-shirt, she smoothed her gray Anatomie capris and tossed her short-sleeve retro hoodie on over her floral print sleeveless blouse. He opened her door, offering a gentlemanly hand as she stepped out into the crisp morning.

"Don't worry." He walked behind the car and clicked open the trunk. "It's just a short hike."

"Sounds like fun." She stood on her toes in a catlike stretch.

After grabbing a basket, he pushed down the trunk lid and

reached out to her. She took his hand, enjoying the smoothness of his skin. She delighted in the reminder that the tools of *his* trade were his mind and artistic taste, not the greasy kind that promoted calloused palms.

He led her gingerly down a well-worn trail edged by giant pines. A whooshing sound lulled her as she took in a cleansing breath of pure air.

Devon turned his head slightly as he continued to guide them down a rocky grade. "It's just round this bend."

The whoosh graduated to a roar, and as they came around a cluster of mammoth pines she saw the reason why.

"Oh, Devon. It's magnificent."

"Now you can say you've really been to Madison Falls."

They had come out right at the point where the rushing river plunged dramatically into a pool of cloudlike vapor. She held out her hands to feel the chill of the mist that hung in the air like stage smoke.

Devon carefully navigated the huge stone ledge at the peak of the clearing. He turned, reaching a hand to her. "Come on, I want you to see this."

Her heart hit her ribs as if warning her of an unseen danger. She dismissed the thought, stretching her hand toward his. *Be Calm.* She refused to believe that Kirk had ruined her ability to enjoy the company of men by hacking into her instincts, recalibrating them to a constant state of high alert. At some point she would have to learn to trust again, and this seemed like a rewarding opportunity. His assured grasp boosted her faith in her ability to get her footing on the slippery rock. He easily hoisted her up, and she witnessed the full expanse of nature's artwork.

"Impressed?" He shouted to be heard above the roar.

She smiled, shouting back. "Very."

He eased closer to the brink, his hold on her still solid. She resisted for a beat, then gave in to his lead, inching up as far as she could safely go. Looking straight down, she had the dizzying sensation that the rocks below were really only inches from the tips of her shoes. She felt herself sway, ever so slightly. Forward.

Suddenly Devon's hand touched her shoulder and she rebounded back, catching her balance on wobbly legs.

"Grace, you're not afraid of heights?" Devon put a comforting hand on her arm. "You should have told me. Let's go back over there."

She nodded, glancing down one more time. She huffed out a calming breath and tried not to dwell on what a terrifying place this would be under different circumstances.

Scolding herself for her momentary lapse, she stepped back from the edge and onto more level ground, where they still had an ample view of the upper part of the falls. The cold spray gracefully touched her skin, sloughing away her temporary doubts. She could trust Devon. She'd succumbed to a fleeting afterburn of fear, but who wouldn't after the torture she'd been subjected to?

"I hope you enjoy nature." He set the basket on the level top of a small boulder.

"Does Central Park count?" The intoxicating effect of the setting had begun its work on her mood.

"Aha, so you *did* lie to me."

Her stomach buckled. What had she just said? "What do you mean?"

Opening the basket, he took out a blanket and spread it on the ground. "You said you'd never been to New York."

Her chest heaved. "Oh..."

He glinted a handsome smile as he moved the basket to the blanket and sat on his haunches. "I suspected you weren't being entirely truthful. You've got the whole 'woman of mystery' thing down. I have to pay attention or I might miss something."

Her palms moistened. She sat on the blanket, desperate for a subject change. "So, I'm sure the play will come around. You've got a few weeks yet."

He tossed her a snide grin as he lifted several containers from their wicker carrying case. "It doesn't much matter."

"Doesn't matter?"

He shrugged. "It's not like we'll be plying any critics from New York on opening night."

"No, I don't suppose so." She brushed off her feeling of unease. "The lunch looks delicious. Don't tell me you made this yourself."

He shook his head, amusement creasing his brow. "I wouldn't know a fillet knife from a frying pan. The fine people at the Peach Basket deli actually stopped frying chicken long enough to pull this out of their hats." He lifted a bottle of champagne and two flutes out of the bin.

Her stomach fluttered at the romantic implications of his choice of beverage. "So, you don't cook. That makes two of us." She folded her legs under her, taking a proffered glass. "I must say, you do know how to show a girl a good time."

He lifted his glass. "I credit the company."

She smiled, taking a sip. The champagne warmed her, easing her into a sense of calm. He opened the containers and displayed each one proudly.

She raised her brow. "You're kidding me. The deli has smoked duck?"

"I wouldn't have believed it if I hadn't seen it. Not only that, but they iced the shrimp, and this puff pastry with balsamic onions and cheese is their own recipe."

"My goodness." This was like a dream. "We could be dining on the banks of the Seine."

His eyes washed over her as his mouth lifted in an impious smile. "And for dessert..." He took a vibrant fruit tart from its nest.

She was suddenly ravenous. "I'm so impressed. I really thought their creativity extended only as far as their chicken salad."

"Yes, well just as I was about to change my opinion of their level of sophistication, they tried to throw in a bag of barbeque chips, so you see what we're up against."

A lighthearted laugh that Grace hadn't heard in a while emerged from her throat. She felt so proud of herself for seeing past the obvious similarities Devon bore to Kirk. She must be stronger than she'd realized.

"Any word yet from the New York Grand?" A coyness had

settled in her manner that didn't altogether displease her.

The corners of his mouth lifted. "I'm impressed you remembered. They've been in touch, and I'm very encouraged."

"What's the opera?"

"It's *Carmen*. I've always dreamed of directing it."

Normal breathing ceased. She'd always dreamed of *singing* it.

Her face must have registered her reaction, as his smile broadened. "One of your favorites too?"

She managed a nod, shoving a cracker into her mouth to avoid saying something she shouldn't about lifelong career goals.

"You know, the Grand is famous for discovering new singers at the launch of their careers. You wouldn't happen to sing mezzo, would you?"

A long stare held on her face before she managed another dip of her head.

He tipped a knowing nod. "You'd make the perfect Carmen. If you can sing the role, I'd love to work with you."

Her heart fairly scrambled out of her chest. If she could sing it? Just ask her neighbors back home. They'd been the beneficiaries of her free recitals for years. "I...I'd love that too."

His eyes shone. "Good. We could meet before rehearsal one night, if you'd like. Without Myra's accompaniment, of course."

Grace let out a titter of anticipation. She'd sung minor roles at the Met and lots of other houses, but she'd dreamed of breaking out to the next level as a singer. Of being taken seriously as a major force in the world of opera. Mezzo-soprano leads were few in number and the competition was fierce. If she played Carmen for such a highly respected company, that could change everything for her.

Her eyes locked with Devon's. She was certainly due for some change.

Propelled by a sudden need to know if his interest in her extended beyond the professional, she spread some tomato Brie on a cracker and gauged her words carefully. "So, how did you come to be Sophia's roommate?" She shoved the cracker into her mouth, chewing but not tasting.

His face remained noncommittal. "It just worked out well for both of us. We...merged."

She tried not to cough as she swallowed. Suddenly her mind spun with unanswered questions. She had to know where she stood. There was no time to play games.

"So you two are serious then?" She feigned a focus on the food.

"Serious?" Innocence rode across his handsome face.

Be direct. "Seriously involved?"

He nearly choked on a shrimp. "Involved...as in *romantically?*"

"Well, yes." What other way *might* there be?

He chuckled, evidently finding the idea funny. "Sophia is very important to me. She's the only person in Madison Falls I've gotten close to."

She arched an eyebrow with the diplomacy of a person reliant on a ride back to town.

He snickered softly, his hand lightly glancing over hers. Leaning toward her in a motion that seemed both calculated and spontaneous, he brought her hand to his lips and kissed it.

"Until you, of course." He smiled. "I'm surprised I have to say it."

A tingle of excitement tangoed down her spine. Sophia was apparently a victim of unrequited infatuation. That was unfortunate, but Devon had a right to his feelings.

Looking into his striking eyes, she firmed her resolve. Her tide had finally turned, and Devon Sinclair was riding it with her.

Chapter 20

"Lucy! SOS!"

Backing up into the dining room with her cell phone to her ear, Grace set her dripping feet down gingerly on the hardwood floor. What in the world had she done to deserve this?

"What's going on over there?" Lucy's voice retained its usual perkiness even through its current edge of concern.

"Remember you said to call if I needed anything fixed?"

"Yes..."

"Well, let me just put it this way." She sat on a dining room chair and pulled her knees to her chin. "I never thought I'd own a house with an indoor swimming pool."

"Oh no."

"Yes, my trampoline turned into a pool overnight and I'm afraid of what it might evolve into next."

Lucy clicked her tongue. "I knew something terrible would happen if you didn't get that taken care of. Don't worry, honey. Help is on its way."

"Thanks Lucy. I owe you big time." She clicked off, then sprang to her feet. If Bob was coming over, she'd prefer not to be caught in her PJ's.

A few minutes later, the doorbell rang and she emerged from the bathroom in her hastily thrown-on clothes. She grabbed for the door, swinging it open with neighborly gratitude.

"Bob, you have no idea..."

She froze. There on her front porch, with an impressive metal box in one hand and a hefty tool belt around his waist, stood Sam.

"Sorry to disappoint you," he said, "but Bob's at work at the moment."

She eased the door back to a barely open position as she weighed her options.

"I hate to point this out," Sam stated calmly. "But you can either turn your kitchen into a water park or you can ask me in."

Grace let a long breath out through her nose before stepping aside to allow him to enter.

He slid past her, scanning the room with a pleased expression. "Place turned out nice."

"Excuse me?"

"The paint. You are happy with it, aren't you?"

"Oh. Sure. Of course." She tried to avoid looking at his eyes, but they drew her like two chocolate-brown magnets. "The kitchen's that way."

He nodded at her outstretched hand. "I know. I've been here before."

Wearing a smug grin, he crossed toward what might soon be the new community pool if he didn't hurry. She followed, not entirely trusting him with such a critical repair job.

"So why are you here?" Her voice crackled with early morning murkiness.

"I thought we'd covered that." His brow dented with sarcastic confusion.

"I mean, doesn't this town have a plumber?" She pushed a stray hair behind her ear.

"No, actually. There's a guy in Victor who'll come out if you need him, but he'll charge you for his travel time. I'm not licensed, but I am a bargain."

He pulled the kitchen door open, let out a grunt, and blocked it with his toolbox. "I saw this coming, you know. It's too bad Mrs. Miller didn't want to put any money into the place toward the end."

Grace stood awkwardly in the dining room, keeping a wary eye on him. "No?"

He squatted down and surveyed the floor. "We did what we could for her. You got that crowbar handy?"

"Oh, yes. It's in there, actually." She flicked her hand toward the kitchen.

Sam grinned. "What, you mean on the other side of the levee?"

She smiled, caught herself, then looked away. He rose to his feet and took a step toward her. She felt her stomach lurch.

He eased past, seeming to sense her discomfort. "I'll have to go around to the back door. That is, unless you've got a canoe."

She crinkled her forehead. "Oh right. Had I been thinking ahead...."

She walked behind him toward the front door, then grabbed her keys off the hook on the wall. They stepped out onto the porch and she pointed toward the side of the house. "The backyard's that way...or have you been there before too?"

He flashed a dimpled grin. "Only about a million times. Mrs. Miller was a real nice lady. I knew her my whole life."

As they walked down the front steps and around the side of the house, it occurred to Grace that as often as she'd heard the name mentioned, she hadn't put a moment's thought into who this woman was.

"Was she married?"

Sam hooked his fingers in the front pockets of his Levi's and slowed his pace. "Yeah. Mr. Miller passed away when I was about five. Funny, I couldn't tell you a thing about him, but I remember when he died like it was yesterday. That was the first funeral I ever went to."

They rounded the corner and Grace smiled lightly. Sam would think she was crazy if she admitted that this was her first time setting foot in her own backyard. She thought better of telling him.

"Did they have kids?"

"You bought the house from their son. He lives in Spokane, so I guess you didn't meet him."

Grace surveyed the place with fresh eyes. Mrs. Miller was more than just a name that the locals tossed around to keep each other clear on real estate exchanges. She was a woman who had lived a life in this town, and raised a family in this house. She had been widowed and had gone on solo for at least a good twenty years. There was something humbling in taking over as the next inhabitant of her home.

"When we were kids, the guys and I would stop by here and ask for a drink from the hose." Sam reached out his hand. "We knew we'd always walk away with a homemade cookie."

The image forced her to smile as she handed him the keys. "Sorry, I'm fresh out of cookies."

"That's okay." He smiled back. "Got any dog biscuits?"

Her face crinkled, and Sam nodded toward the side of the house. Perplexed, she turned around. There stood that same brown dog, wagging his shaggy tail and looking at them expectantly.

"Agh. I can't believe it." She raised her hands in frustration. "He keeps showing up. I think he's a stray. He wasn't Mrs. Miller's, by any chance?"

Sam knelt down. "No, she didn't have a dog. I've never seen this fella." The dog approached, sniffed Sam's outstretched hand, and offered his head to be petted. "Good boy." Sam ruffled his fur with both hands, and the tail doubled its tempo.

"He likes you." Grace folded her arms and observed the friendly exchange. "Maybe you should take him."

Sam smiled and shook his head. "I would, but my dad says no more pets. Our yard's too small."

Grace's forehead puckered involuntarily. This guy still lived with his dad? He had to be at least twenty-five. What was up with him?

"Why don't you keep him?" Sam stood and moved up the two steps to the back door. "He seems to like it here."

Grace let out a little sputter. That was completely out of the question. "Oh, no, I'm just...not a dog person."

Fido sidled up next to her and maneuvered her hand until it rested on top of his head. Grace caught a hint of Sam's cocky smile as he turned the key and pushed open the door to the sun porch.

He looked directly at her. "Maybe you oughta let him know that."

As he disappeared into the house, Grace gave the scruffy head a friendly pat. The dog beamed up at her.

"Sorry fella, but you're going to have to find another target. It's not nice to keep showing up where you aren't wanted. Believe me, I know."

"Ah, excuse me." Sam's stature seemed surprisingly heightened as he reappeared in the doorway. "Where did you say that crowbar was? I need to jimmy up some of the tiles so I can figure out the source of your leak."

"Right." Giving the dog's head another ruffle, she moved toward the house. She hesitated at the bottom step. Sam looked at her, seemingly oblivious to the fact that he was blocking the doorway.

She cleared her throat. Head down, she advanced up the steps. He took an awkward step back and, just as she was about to edge past him, a tinny tune gave them both a start. With a look of apology, he pulled a cell phone out of his shirt pocket and glanced at it.

"Sorry." His expression suddenly urgent, he moved around her and down the steps.

She lingered in the doorway, watching his back as he lifted the phone to his ear.

"Hey..." He stepped to the edge of the patio. "I was waiting for you to call."

A confusing sensation splashed in her belly. Disappointment? That didn't make any sense. She let out a breath and stepped inside. Where had she left that crowbar? She glanced around the sun porch.

"Yeah, I know, I know, but you can't just take off like that. What do you expect me to do?" His tone was hushed, but gruffness betrayed his anger.

Must be his poor girlfriend. Grace really didn't want to hear this guy yelling at her, but if she shut the door now, he'd probably realize she'd heard him. She didn't want him to think she cared.

"No. You're wrong about that. I've had enough of your lame excuses."

His obvious attempt to keep his voice low was trumped by his hot temper. What had that girl done to make him so angry? She was probably mad about his drinking, and who could blame her?

"Look, I don't want to hear it. You need to get your act together."

Her act? Mr. Pot, meet Mrs. Kettle.

Taking a step into the room, she tried to ignore the yelling. *Where in the world...oh, that's right.* She'd placed the crowbar on top of that old cabinet in the corner. She stretched up, taking a quick glance out the window. Sam had moved to the far corner of the patio, clearly wanting privacy for his tirade. His back to her, he waved an arm wildly. Lucky for his girlfriend she was out of arm's reach. He didn't seem like the violent type, but you really never knew.

"That's got to be the stupidest..." He seemed to catch himself. "I've got something to do, but I'll be done in a little while. You'd better be there when I get back."

He clicked the phone shut and Grace looked away, feeling for the wayward tool. Her jittery fingers enclosed it just as Sam reentered the house.

"Sorry about that." He walked in just as she whirled around. "Great, you found it."

He reached out and took a step toward her, but she clasped the bar with both hands. What was she thinking, allowing herself to be vulnerable to a man with such a volcanic temper? Hadn't she learned her lesson?

"Ah, you know..." Her voice wavered. "I really think I can take it from here. How hard can it be to pull up a few tiles, right?"

His forehead creased in confusion. "Right. Well, you're going to have to get something to suck up that water. Then once you find the leak you'll have to either repair it or replace the pipes. Do you have much experience with replumbing kitchens?"

She shifted her weight from one foot to the other. Was he

enjoying this?

"Plus, I hate to tell you this..."

A dull throb thumped at Grace's temple. Nobody liked to hear that phrase.

Sam's eyes wrinkled as he continued. "You have a nice little moat forming near the outside corner of your house."

"Oh no." She cringed. "A *second* leak?"

He smiled. "No. I'm sure it's part of the same problem. It might even be a clue to the source. Listen..." His eyes softened. "At least let me run to the truck and get my shop vac. That ought to help alleviate the flood damage in the kitchen, and I can tell Bob to check in on you when he gets off work."

Her chest felt tight. This definitely extended beyond her home repair know-how. "Fine. I mean..." She held out the crowbar and took a step backward. "Since you're here, you might as well get it started."

"If you're sure." He took the tool, a teasing glimmer in his eye. "Look, if it's the money you're worried about, let me check the damage and then we can talk cost."

"The money." Her mind raced as she forced back that annoying guilt. The floor would only get worse if she didn't deal with it, and the sooner the better if she wanted to rent out the house. Besides, at the rate she was going, she might wake up to find piranhas swimming around the periphery of the house. "Okay."

His smile was sympathetic. "I might even throw in a free look at that bathtub. Is the pipe still leaking in there?"

A jolt shot down her back. "It's fine." She hadn't meant to sound so abrupt.

He looked as though he'd just dodged an arrow. "Okay then. One room at a time." He turned and proceeded into the flood zone.

Grace perched on her camp chair and locked her fingers over her knees. A small scratch at the door forced her to shift her attention to her other unwanted guest, who stood in the doorway looking hopeful. She sighed. All that stood between her and her old life was a few phone calls.

Why was she letting herself get so distracted?

Chapter 21

"Unusual place to install a hot tub." Devon barely restrained a laugh as he stood in the doorway of Grace's still-soppy kitchen.

"You think?" She chuckled, stepping carefully around the stripped-naked area of the floor and maneuvering toward the stove. "Remember I told you the house was undergoing surgery? Well, welcome to the O.R."

"Nice." He moved around the damaged area with such poise, it almost looked choreographed. Once safely over the swamp, he held up his hands like a camera frame. "I see a beautiful fountain going in right about there. Maybe a replica of the Trevi."

Grace gave a pot of boiling fusilli a quick stir. "Nice, but don't you think that's a little showy?"

He considered. "Not if you put the Piazza del Popolo in the living room."

"Hmm. A theme. I like it." She picked up the pot and emptied it into a strainer she'd set over the large plastic tub that was acting as understudy for her sink till the pipes got fixed. Carefully, she set the pot down and reached for a bowl of sauce on the counter. Studying it, she gave its contents a stir, hoping she looked more culinarily confident than she felt.

Devon leaned in. "So, what's on the menu?"

Grace proudly held up the bowl. "I'm making honey chicken,

and pasta salad."

Devon dipped a finger into the sauce. "Wait a minute. You said you couldn't cook." He slid his finger between his lips.

She beamed, setting down the sauce. "That's what I said."

He made a sour face. "Apparently, you were right."

She playfully walloped him with an oven mitt.

"You know I'm kidding," he said. "Actually, I'm very impressed."

She poured the pasta into the bowl and swirled it with a spoon. "Would you mind grabbing this?" She took a step to the fridge and removed a dish of chicken, which had been marinating in salad dressing all afternoon.

"Of course." He angled his forehead toward the floor. "You know, you are a little handicapped by your work space."

"It's challenging not being able to use the sink." She headed to the sun porch, indicating that he should follow. "Which is why we're going to cook in the great outdoors." They moved through the porch, and she pulled open the back door.

Devon reached out to hold it open for her, then gazed out at the patio. "You bought a barbeque?"

"No." She set the chicken down on the edge of a grill the size of a golf cart.

Confusion colored his handsome face.

She grinned. "I *borrowed* a barbeque." She held her hand over the grill, pleased that she had succeeded in getting it to heat.

"Ah." He stepped out to join her. "So nice to have helpful neighbors."

"True." She thought about Bob pulling this monstrosity across the street three minutes after she'd hung up with Lucy. "They said I could use it till the floor's done."

"Generous." He drew a leisurely gaze across the yard. "What's that over there?"

She followed his line of sight to the corner of the house, where Sam had dug a trench to expose her problematic pipes. "Oh, that's my outdoor pool." She poured a tall glass of lemonade from a Tupperware pitcher she'd borrowed with the grill.

Devon took the glass. "I had no idea you were so aquatic."

She poured a second glass. "Seriously, it started out as part of the kitchen problem, but it turns out a big root is about to break through the pipe." Raising the glass to her lips, she took a pleasing taste of the tart liquid. "We made an appointment for the Roto Rooter guy to come from Missoula, but apparently you have to book him almost as far in advance as Placido Domingo. Why, Sam says—"

"Sam?" Devon's neck snapped like a cadet doing drills.

Her stomach lurched. She knew how he felt about Sam. Why had she mentioned his name? "Yes. He's fixing my floor."

"Why?" His eyes flared.

Hoping to soften his reaction, she smiled coyly. "Because the fountain really isn't practical."

Agitation tinted his skin a rosy pink. "Grace, I just don't think it's very smart."

She kept her tone steady. "I know you've got a problem with Sam, and believe me, he's not my favorite person in the world either, but—"

"He's trouble." His voice was stern with warning. "You have no idea."

"Oh, I have some idea." Her stomach listed. Finally, someone else who had judged Sam's true character. "What do you think I should do?"

"Just..." He waved a hand in the air as if discarding the dilemma. "Find somebody else to finish the job."

A twinge curled her insides. "Well, there really *is* nobody else. I mean, have you seen the Madison Falls Yellow Pages? It's not exactly Angie's List. "

"What about Hank? Or Carl?" Devon's eyes held a soft concern.

"Hank or Carl? Devon, they're farmers, not handymen." She quelled an all-too-familiar sense of dread. "I could call them if I needed my barn door fixed."

"Lucy's husband." He snapped his fingers repeatedly like he'd suddenly turned into Frank Sinatra. "What's his name?"

"Bob. He's working sixty hours a week right now on some ranch remodel. Besides, they've done so much for me. I couldn't possibly—"

"You've got to do something." His brow was sweating, which seemed totally out of character.

"Okay. I will." With an awkward twist of her wrist, she picked up a piece of chicken and plopped it onto the grill. "What's Sam's problem, anyway?"

"I just don't want you around him." His eyes sharpened on her face. "Have you...*talked* to him much?"

"No..." She shifted the chicken, recoiling when a drip of dressing ignited a sizzle underneath it. "He seems nice enough when he's here to work."

"Meaning?" His eyes suddenly turned as icy as the drink he held.

"Meaning...I don't know." Had she said something wrong? The conversation had taken an uncomfortable turn and her thoughts addled.

Devon searched her face with his eyes. "Meaning, you've seen him *otherwise?*"

She drew back at the intensity of his tone, nearly dropping the second piece of chicken onto the patio. "No, of course not. I bought paint from him. Lucy knows him, that's why he came over to do the floor. It's not like I'd socialize with someone like him."

Guarded relief replaced the urgency that had cloaked his features. "Good. Keep it that way." He took a sip of lemonade. "Actually, I'd prefer you didn't even talk to him."

Discomfort at his implied control over her personal interactions gnawed at her. No doubt another overreaction to her experience with Kirk. She shook it off. "Fine by me."

"Good." His eyes sparked. "Let me tell him, n'est pas?"

"Okay...?"

"I just don't want you to deal with him at all. Ever. Got it?"

She swallowed hard. "This seems really important to you."

"It is, believe me." His piercing gaze intensified.

"Okay, whatever you say." She subtly relaxed her stance. "I

trust your judgment."

"I'm glad. Trust is critical." At last his face softened. "So, let's not waste any more time on that topic. Let's talk about books, or movies, or—"

"Shoo!"

"Or *shoes*." He turned, following her gaze around.

The stray dog had just rounded the corner of the house and stood there watching them intently.

"Friend of yours?" His voice wavered with uncertainty.

"He seems to think so." She placed her hands on her hips. "Why do you keep showing up?"

"You're talking to the dog, I hope." A jittery chuckle didn't quite mask his unease. "Whose is he?"

"Nobody's. I mean, look at him." She lifted a hand. His scruffy coat had only gotten rattier since their initial encounter a couple of weeks before.

Devon tentatively approached the animal, who sniffed his hand and emitted a low rumble.

"Whoa." Devon retreated back a few steps.

Grace rushed forward and knelt down. The brown tail swished from side to side as the dog offered his head for a pat. She spoke in a low voice. "What are you trying to do, ruin this for me?"

His rough tongue lapped her cheek.

Devon held his distance. "It looks like you learned a trick or two working at that pet store."

She startled at the reminder of her little web of deceit. "Yes, I'm a real pro." She tipped her head close to the alert ear of her uninvited guest. "Whatever you do, don't blow my cover."

She stood, allowing the dog to follow her back to the grill to check on the progress of dinner. She smiled demurely at Devon and blew a stray hair off her forehead.

He smiled and she recalled his words. *Trust is critical.* Now was definitely not the time to let him know that Grace Addison was really a fictional character.

Chapter 22

"She's great, isn't she?" Bob inclined his head toward Grace.

She clutched the folds of her gabardine skirt and angled her head to get a better view of Lucy, seated at the piano onstage. Grace smiled her concurrence at Bob, who beamed from his place next to her on the pew.

"She's *very* talented." Much to Grace's surprise, the simple hymn Lucy played revealed genuine skill.

Fiddling with her church bulletin, Grace felt like a lighthouse, unable to keep her head still. The number of familiar faces around her was no surprise—she'd been in Madison Falls for three weeks, after all. There was Spritz, leaning on the shoulder of a dashing red-haired gentleman. Joanie nattered with the waitress from the Country Kitchen—probably an exchange of work stories. Hank, Carl, and Ruby were there too, with not a bib overall in sight. She even spotted the man who had helped her open her checking account.

Warmth bathed her senses. She'd never really been a churchgoer, and had hesitated to accept Lucy's invitation. Now that she was there, she felt surprisingly at ease.

A thought flitted across her mind. She craned her neck to see the front rows, immediately identifying Nancy by her bobbing strawberry-blonde plait. She casually scanned the room again, then faced forward with a frown. Of all the people she'd met in town, she would have pegged Mr. Roberts as a dedicated churchgoer. He was so much like her father, who had, according to her mother, picked up the habit of prayer in his final months. She sighed. It would have been nice to have seen Mr. Roberts there.

The song ended to a rousing round of applause, and Grace inclined her head toward Bob. "Before I forget, who do you know who can fix my kitchen floor?"

The corners of his mouth lifted. "Is this a riddle?"

"No, I'm serious. Sam started it, but I need someone else to finish."

Bob rotated toward her in his seat. "It's not like Sam to leave a job half-done—"

"Oh no, it's not that. He could do it, it's just that..."

Bob's brow creased. "You're unhappy with his work?"

"No, not at all. As far as I can tell he's done fine."

"Then why—"

"Well..." Confusion pressed at her temples. How could she make her reasons sound reasonable?

He seemed to sense her discomfort. "Let me put it this way. All my guys are pulling overtime right now. Sam's the best man for the job anyway."

There had to be an alternative. "Well, I hear there's a plumber in Victor."

"There is, but he's not cheap. Sam can handle the whole job for less than what you'd pay that guy just for the plumbing. I'd stick with him." Seemingly satisfied, he returned his attention to his bulletin.

"But—"

The opening notes of the high voltage, well-amped band startled her. Everyone around her stood and she halfheartedly followed suit. What was she supposed to do now?

The music pulled her mind from her concerns. She started to tap her foot, but shirked a little when a twenty-something man took a step toward the microphone. The band was good, but they really shouldn't press their luck by adding vocals. She looked down, embarrassed for the poor guy as he took a breath and let out his first phrase.

Her head snapped back up. He wasn't wretched. In fact, he had talent. He wasn't Pavarotti, but then again neither was Pavarotti toward the end. This man sang with such joy that the audience energy instantly escalated.

People sang along, buoyed by the supra-titles on the screen behind the band. Grace hummed in sympathetic vibration. She put her hand on her throat, trying to force the lump of emotion back down. This was not going to be easy.

Shifting to see around the man in the row ahead of her, she frowned. The guitar player onstage looked just like Sam. She squinted. It *was* Sam. He hadn't mentioned that he played an instrument, but then, why would he?

She clucked in disgust. It was funny that church people could be such hypocrites—act however you want all week as long as you pray for forgiveness on Sunday.

Failing to pull her eyes off him, she couldn't help but admire his form. Clearly, he was skilled at playing and he seemed to enjoy it. Why did that surprise her so much?

The song ended to wild applause. As it waned, the singer started to speak. "Lord, we praise You for this glorious summer morning!"

More applause. Boy, were these people cheerful.

"Father, we gather here to worship You, to honor You, and to thank You for all the blessings You provide."

Everyone seemed to have their eyes closed, so Grace did the same.

"We praise You, God, and thank You for dying on the cross for our sins."

Grace opened one eye, checking to make sure he wasn't joking. *Dying on the cross for our sins?* That was such a cliché. What did it mean, anyway?

"We know that we're all faced with our trials, Lord, but we take comfort in knowing that no matter what, You are always with us, and that You know exactly what path we should take. All we have to do is ask, Lord, and You'll lead us."

She frowned. If only it were that simple. *Ask and You'll lead us?* If the Lord was looking down on her right now, He was probably just shaking His head.

She opened her eyes a bit, stealing a peek at Sam. He had one hand on the neck of his guitar and held the other above his head. There was an intensity about him which implied that he took this praying thing very seriously. Was God somehow leading him to be a greedy hot-tempered louse? What kind of god would encourage that?

"Amen!" Everyone around her spoke the word in unison and she felt like a complete outsider for not knowing her cue.

The band resumed playing, a slower song this time. Grace perked up. She knew this one. She'd learned it in choir years ago. As the room filled with singing she joined in, unable to stop herself. "*Amazing Grace, how sweet the sound...*" She closed her eyes and set her voice free.

The music carried her out of her concerns, out of her prison of fear.

In her mind she was lifted up, as if she'd never walked into that apartment two years ago. Never let down her guard or been nice to the wrong person. Music had always swept her up into its magic, allowing her to soar. That was the most precious of all that had been stolen from her, and for this moment she found it again.

The final chord resolved and she opened her eyes. Instantly her heart took off at a full-on sprint. Why was everyone looking at her? Even the performers onstage stared. Her eyes met Sam's and he flashed an admiring grin. Just what she needed. She sank into her seat as applause again erupted around her. How could she have let herself get so carried away?

"You have a real gift." Bob spoke softly, leaning toward her as he took his seat.

Her stomach churned. What good is a gift if you can't ever take it out and enjoy it?

She had really blown it. It was only a matter of time before people started to question why she wasn't using this *gift*. She slunk down lower in her seat. What story could she make up to explain her way around *this?*

Chapter 23

Balancing a tray of mochas with one arm, Grace pulled open the front door of the rehearsal space. She shuddered. Inside, the pirates reached for each elusive note of the song they were attempting to learn as Myra plunked out her own version of the tune. True, they lacked proper instrumentation, but what passed for singing with them made Grace worry that her ears might bleed.

Scanning the room for a place to set her tray, she glanced up at the landing in the back corner and pursed her lips. Why was she going all the way outside and around when that door led directly into her stand? Too bad Nancy didn't have a key.

She crossed surreptitiously to the director's table, which sat squarely in the center of the room, and set down the tray. Devon turned his head and gave her a more-than-cordial smile that lingered even after his attention turned back to the taped-off stage area.

Feeling the heat of Sophia's malevolent stare, Grace looked up. She tossed the little prima donna wannabe a look that she hoped read as victorious-but-not-too-haughty. No point in encouraging enmity.

"Fine everyone." Devon's tone was commanding and upbeat. "Let's take fifteen." He stood and grabbed a cup from the tray, his face just inches from Grace's ear. "I'll be out front."

Her heart did a *ka-thump* that would have been audible if the room hadn't been abuzz with excited chatter. She longed to tag after him, but thought better of being too obvious. It seemed best to keep her private life private even when she wasn't playing witness protection program.

"Miss Addison." Hank tipped his cap as he approached the table and reached for a cup.

"Evening, Hank." She smiled. "Love your eye patch."

A hint of confusion crossed his face as he touched his cheek. "Oh, I almost forgot I had this thing on. Thought I should get used to it."

"A wise choice."

A hopeful glint pervaded the eye she could see. "Have you had much of a chance to hear us sing?"

With some difficulty, she kept her expression pleasant. She *had* heard. Every sour note. "You've all been working very hard," she encouraged.

"Aw, thank you, Miss Addison." He looked satisfied with the answer as he took a healthy swig. "Mmmm. Great cuppa joe."

"Thanks. Tell your friends." She puckered her brow, marveling at Carl's attempt to pick up a mocha with the hook he held in his hand. "Nice to see you guys are really getting into character."

"It's not every day we get a chance to express ourselves artistically." Carl gave up the piratical prop in favor of his field-roughened hand.

"For the life of me, Miss Addison," Hank flipped up his patch, "I can't understand why you didn't audition. After that beautiful singing you did on Sunday—"

"Oh, that." Her knees buckled. "I just really love that song."

"I'd belt it out too if it was called 'Amazing Carl.'" Carl chuckled in apparent delight at his own wit.

Grace let out a nervous titter as Ruby wedged between the two men. "Step aside and let someone else get some coffee, guys." She elbowed them playfully. "Grace, you really *were* amazing the other day, but I'm grateful you didn't audition. I wouldn't have had a chance at Mabel."

"Oh, Ruby." Grace waved off her comment. "You're doing a great job."

"Thanks," Ruby lowered her eyes. "But I'm not trained like you obviously are."

"You're kidding." Grace handed out a few more cups to enthusiastic actors. "You've never had voice lessons?"

"Nope." Her expression humble, Ruby lifted her gaze. "Besides church, the only singing I've done has been to the cows when no one else is around. When I saw the audition notice, I started to think..."

Grace smiled. "That you should be singing to people, not just livestock?"

A pleased sparkle glinted in Ruby's eyes. "Exactly. But I have a long way to go to be as good as you. Your voice reminds me of a singer I heard once." She looked at the boys. "Guys, remember a couple of years back when my mom and I went to Frisco and we got to see *Madame Butterfly*?"

A sudden jolt of nausea surged through Grace's stomach.

"I just love opera." Ruby looked dreamily back at Grace. "Do you know that one?"

Grace bit her lower lip to keep it from shaking.

"The woman who sang Kate Pinkerton was astonishing. Her voice was pure and clear just like yours and she was beautiful." Her eyes steadied on Grace. "In fact, you look a lot like her. What was her name...? Tracy something." She looked away, her brow creasing, then snapped her fingers. "I know. Tracy Fontaine."

The trio continued talking but for Grace, their banter blurred. Her throat closed and breathing became difficult. She needed to get outside. Gulping in a lungful of air, she reeled abruptly toward the door just as Sophia stepped into her path, her arms folded like a sentry.

"You look a little green." She sneered. "I think you've had too much of that awful coffee of yours."

Grace reined in her thoughts and forced a controlled smile. "Thanks for your concern, but I'm just fine." She turned back to the table, picked up the one remaining cup, and offered it to Myra as she passed by.

"Why, thank you, my dear." Myra's coarsely lined eyes widened slightly as she grabbed the cup and eyed it as if she'd never seen coffee before. She lifted it to her carefully painted lips and took a wary nip. Her eyes softened and she made a pleased sound as she swallowed. "My dear, that's the most remarkable coffee I've ever tasted." She patted Grace's hand. "This ought to perk me up to play all those fast notes."

Grace smiled weakly at Myra's departing back. If only that could be true.

A derisive snicker escaped from Sophia. "Some people have no taste." She rounded the table and looked at Grace head-on. "Take Ruby. So what if she thinks you look like some singer nobody's ever heard of?" She scoffed. "People always tell *me* I look like Jessica Alba."

"Hmm..." Suddenly lucid, Grace studied Sophia's harsh features. "I really don't see it. Jessica's so *pretty*."

A fire lit behind Sophia's eyes and she turned on her heel.

Grace twisted her mouth. *Nobody's ever heard of,* my eye. She'd honestly intended to steer clear of any low blows, but Sophia made it too easy.

Her tray now empty, she picked it up and headed for the door. In the commotion of the last few minutes, she'd forgotten all about Devon.

Her pulse played a staccato melody as she stepped out into the warm evening and saw him push off the brick wall he'd been leaning on.

He eyed her suggestively. "I was starting to feel stood up."

Assuming a demure attitude, she moved toward him, clasping the tray under her arm. "I never promised I'd come out."

"You can't blame a guy for hoping."

She sidled up next to him. "So, will I see you at the potluck tomorrow?"

His eyes bugged out in amusement. "Potluck's aren't exactly my style."

"Mine either. But Lucy's quartet is playing and I promised her

I'd go. I know it's not the Met, but..."

He chuckled lightly. "Or the New York Grand? If your audition for me the other day is any indication, you could be on the inside track at both."

She flashed a grin. He'd seemed impressed by her a cappella rendition of Carmen's Act I aria, but she hadn't wanted to push a decision. "So, have you heard any more?"

"They seem just inches away from hiring me. When I hear, you'll be the first to know. Why don't you go to the concert in the park and tell me how it was? I have some business to attend to anyway."

"Business?" She teased. "In the evening?"

He shrugged, checking his Rolex. "Time to get back. Oh, and I had a word with Sam. He won't be bothering you anymore."

Her heart sank slightly as she forced an appreciative smile. Had he doomed her to finish the job herself? *Plumbing Repair for Dummies?*

With a hand squeeze and a wink, he turned to go. She watched him disappear into the storefront, then headed back toward the theatre. Sauntering up the sidewalk, she enjoyed the evening breeze that always seemed to waft through town at about this time. With a sense of leisure, she commenced climbing the steep porch steps.

Reaching the top, she turned and leaned on the pillar, a dreamy smile forming on her lips as she thought of Devon. She hated lying to him, but surely when the time came to fill him in, he'd understand. He'd probably applaud her courage and ingenuity, not to mention the twist of fate that had brought them together.

She perched on the railing, leaning her back against the pillar, and took in a restorative breath. There was still a good half hour till intermission, and it was nicer out here than inside.

Relax. All she had to do was get through the next few weeks.

As her body loosened up, Ruby's comment slipped back to the forefront of her mind. She gritted her teeth. So what if Ruby had noticed she resembled Tracy? She hadn't seemed to think much of it. If she ever realized how right she'd been, Grace would be long gone anyway.

She shifted on her narrow perch. What if Ruby mentioned her observation to other people? It wouldn't take much for somebody to Google "Tracy Fontaine" and come up with all kinds of interesting information. Turning her head, she glanced at her image in the window and ran a hand through her hair. The short Warm Cinnamon was a far cry from the long blonde of just a few weeks ago. Would that be enough to deter the curious?

She scoffed. What was the worst that could happen? It wasn't like she was a fugitive with a reward on her head. Or was she? If Kirk had his feelers out.... She shivered. He'd bought the loyalty of people she'd trusted in the past. Who knew what might happen?

Her stomach churned. She couldn't waste any more time. She had to get the painting shipped to an art dealer so it could go to auction and she could get the money that would buy back her freedom.

Just then a movement across the street caught her attention. The door on the corner that looked like it led to an apartment over the hardware store swung open. Out stepped Sam into the lengthening shadows.

Grace narrowed her eyes. What was he doing up there, fixing the plumbing? Not likely without any tools. He looked one way down the sidewalk, then the other, like a spy on a secret mission. Head down, he thrust his hands into his pockets and strode toward his truck. He climbed in, revved it to a start, and drove off.

It was probably nothing, and why did she care anyway? Maybe he lived up there, but hadn't he said something about a yard? Could be they had an office upstairs, but the frilly curtains in the windows made that seem doubtful.

She shook her shoulders, in an attempt to free herself of all thoughts of him. Why would she even care? He was of no consequence to her now.

The churning abruptly graduated to a knot. Why hadn't she thought this through? If Devon had warned Sam to stay away from her, that meant she had nobody to build her crate.

She pressed her hand to her forehead. This was terrible. Now she was stuck finding someone for both jobs and time was of the essence.

She expelled a breath. Might as well go inside and get ready for the intermission crowd. It was a good house tonight and, as usual, most of them would want a coffee drink. She moved to the door, but something compelled her to look across the street one more time. A lacy curtain fluttered as if someone had been looking out.

Her forehead crinkled. Who was up there, and what did they have to do with Sam?

Chapter 24

"I heard a rumor about you." Lucy put her hands on her hips, a look of confidentiality dancing in her eyes.

A bead of sweat ran down Grace's forehead, not just from the ninety-degree heat, as she stepped into the potluck line. "I thought you said you didn't gossip."

"This isn't gossip," Lucy chirped. "It's publicity."

Grace twisted her fingers together. "Publicity?"

Lucy appeared ready to burst. "There's a petition circulating to convince Nancy to open your concession stand for more than just show times. Your iced mochas are developing a following."

Grace let out a long, slow breath. "You're kidding. That's fantastic news."

"I thought so." Lucy hooked her arm through Bob's and beamed at their vivacious little boy, Casey. "If people come into the lobby, they'll be tempted to buy theatre tickets. You could do some kind of special deal."

Grace wiped her forehead with her wrist. "That's what I've been saying."

Lucy leaned on her husband's arm. "Bob and I are seeing *Wait Until Dark* on Saturday. We can't wait to try a couple of iced caramel lattes."

Grace looked sideways at Bob. "I thought you only drank

instant."

His smile was taciturn. "I'm willing to branch out."

She flashed him an appreciative grin as the line shifted forward, forcing them to step out of the shade. Grace looked ahead at the row of people which wrapped around three huge trees and a swing set. She groaned. "I hope there's still food left when we get up there."

Lucy chuckled as her eyes turned to Casey, who bobbed impatiently next to her. She slipped her hand into the large straw purse she had flung over her shoulder. "Case, hold still a sec."

Grace smiled to herself as Bob shot the boy a listen-to-your-mother look. Grace had always thought marriage and children would be a second act to her own life, after she achieved a certain level of career success. Now as she watched Lucy slather sunscreen on Casey's neck, she wondered why she hadn't placed more value on being needed.

Lucy wiped her hands on her husband's arm. "Bob, why don't you take Casey over to the seesaws? Nobody expects an eight-year-old to have patience in a line like this."

Casey tugged at Bob's arm, giving him no option but to take Lucy's suggestion.

Grace watched the happy but gaunt child, whom she would have taken for six based on his size, lead his father to the playground. "What a nice family you have. Eight—such a fun age. Is he into sports?"

Lucy sank into her shoulders. "He would be if it was safe for him."

"Safe?"

Lucy's zest seemed to falter. "He has something called Barth Syndrome. He's had it since he was a baby."

Grace's stomach jolted. "I'm sorry, I—"

Lucy's manner was unruffled. "Oh, most people have never heard of it. It's a genetic disorder that weakens the heart. He gets tired just from walking, so sports are pretty much out of the question."

Grace struggled for words. "I'm so sorry."

Lucy's posture heaved like a marionette whose strings had been tugged. "Everyone has their cross to bear."

What an unusual phrase. Old fashioned. Grace rolled it over in her mind, trying to picture what it would be like to have a child with a serious ailment. "Will he get stronger?"

"It could go either way." Lucy seemed resigned, almost unaffected. "He'll never be free of it, and we have to be careful about infections. It affects the immune system, so it's just a day-by-day proposition."

"That must be hard on you. How do you stay so cheerful?"

"Believe me, it's not always easy. It just comes naturally to protect our loved ones, especially family."

Family. A guilt-tinged sadness covered Grace's heart whenever she thought about her mom. She felt so helpless to protect her from the pain of her dad's death, and from the problems Kirk had caused.

"You have to have faith in a greater power." Lucy's voice was soothing, as if she sensed Grace's own need for comfort. "That's what will see you through."

"I suppose." Grace tried to make sense of Lucy's words. Was that what Lucy told herself to make it easier?

Lucy seemed to brighten. "We don't know what He has in store for us, but one thing's for sure. He's always in control."

Control? Grace had always held a belief in some sort of higher being, but never to the extent that she'd wanted Him in control of her whole life. How could she put that kind of faith in something she couldn't see?

Lucy giggled at Bob teetering opposite Casey on the seesaw, a light of protectiveness in her eyes. "I hope you get to meet Taylor today. She's sixteen, and she doesn't want to be seen with us in public. Like she thinks people don't already know we're her parents."

Grace smiled. "I remember going through that phase. Now what I wouldn't give to—" She drew in her breath, reminding herself not to talk about her own family. What would she say if Lucy started asking questions? "I mean, she'll grow out of it."

Lucy's eyes did a half roll. "I hope so." Her gaze homed in on Grace. "You know, you haven't said anything about your own family. Are they still in Seattle?"

"Um, yes. My parents. And my…brother." She bit her lower lip. *I'm not lying. I'm creating a character.*

"You must miss them. Will they come out to visit now that you're settled?"

Grace gave a feeble nod. This improvised family tree she'd created seemed as fictitious as she knew it to be. Why hadn't she thought up a story that would make sense when the inevitable questions arose? What plausible explanation could she give now for leaving an exciting metropolis for a place whose idea of high art was preceded by a potluck?

Lucy looked at her earnestly. "You intrigue me, Grace. Most people leave small towns to head for the big city, not the other way around."

"I guess I'm just unusual." Her neck grew even hotter as she forced a half-smile.

In that instant, a cute blonde inserted herself between the two women, bubbling with excitement. "Mom, there you are."

Normally, Grace would be irritated by a teenager's disrespectful interruption of an adult conversation, but under the circumstances she wanted to hug her.

Lucy's eyes flashed as she gently turned the girl to face Grace. "Sweetheart, be polite. Grace, this is Taylor. Taylor, I want you to meet Grace Addison, our new neighbor."

The girl gave her a halfhearted greeting before turning back to her mother. "Can I get a kitten?"

"A kitten? Why on earth—"

"Stacy's dad found a litter out behind the hardware store and if they don't find homes for them, they're going to wind up as barn cats out at the Osborn place. Please!"

Her whiny elongation of the last word reminded Grace of a piccolo, and she found herself rooting for the girl. She had been tempted a time or two to get a cat herself, but hadn't wanted to deal with boarding it out whenever she left town.

"Oh dear," Lucy rolled her lips in and wrinkled her forehead, as if the fate of the free world rested on this decision.

"I'm going to go get Stacy and tell her to bring them over. They're sooo cute!" The girl darted off, her youthful exuberance trailing behind her.

Lucy let out an exasperated breath. "If those kids bring home one more pet..."

Grace plotted to avoid returning to the previous subject. "Speaking of pets, have you seen that stray dog that's been hanging around the neighborhood?"

Lucy's forehead creased. "I don't think so."

"He's mostly brown. Maybe a border collie or something. Do you know where he might have come from?"

"That's weird. I know all the dogs around, and that doesn't sound familiar. Either he wandered in from a farm or someone dropped him on their way through town."

"Hmm." Grace shook her head. Why did she feel a responsibility toward that mangy mutt? She had enough real problems on her plate.

Taylor returned with an equally cute brunette who balanced a box in her arms. Taylor reached in and pulled out a ball of blonde fur the size of a slipper.

"Aww..." Lucy put her hands to her cheeks.

"I know. Cute, right? But check out this tortoiseshell one." Taylor shoved the blonde kitten into Grace's hands, freeing her own to dip back into the pile of mewing fur.

"Oh..." Grace held the squirming animal at arm's length. As she tried to deposit her back into the container, a distant movement caught her attention.

It was Sam, pacing like a duck in a shooting gallery under a tree near the park's edge. On a blanket next to him sat the woman from the bar. She was fussing with something behind a big cooler, and Grace strained to get a better look.

The woman lifted a squirming bundle from behind the cooler and Grace's stomach plunged to her toes. A baby. So. Hardware Boy was a family man.

A little boy of about three ran over to the woman, who said something to him and handed him an apple. Grace tsked. Sam still lived at his dad's house with this brood?

Taylor's voice pierced her thoughts. "I'll take good care of her. Please...?"

Something troubled Grace as she observed the distant tableau. Sam's nervous eyes darted around as if he'd rather be someplace else. Couldn't he at least focus on his family?

Her stomach suddenly clenched as it dawned on her. Lucy had said that their friend who was being led into drug dealing and was desperate for money was a family man. And a churchgoer. *Sam.*

It had to be true. Hadn't she seen him with Carson twice in the short time she'd been in town? Her throat filled with disgust. That explained so much. The erratic behavior, the outbursts. It probably even explained why he was sneaking around the other night. No wonder Devon wanted her to stay away from him.

Her brow creased in contempt. To think she had felt guilty about buying the painting from him. Was it her fault he had sunk to the lowest possible means of generating cash when a fortune had sat right under his nose?

Sam's pacing subsided as if something had caught his interest. He took a couple of long strides toward a man who now approached him. They exchanged words. Grace held her breath. Was she witnessing a deal?

She opened her mouth to say something to Lucy, but the man made a move toward the woman and Grace's voice stopped short. Sam grabbed the man's arm, pulling him back. They assumed a showdown stance, as if waiting for someone to yell "Draw!" Instead, the man gave Sam an icy stare and lunged toward the blanket. The woman clung to the baby and grabbed the little boy's wrist, drawing him closer to her.

Grace braced herself to shriek if the woman needed help. Sam appeared ready to spring forward as the man reached—not for the woman, but for the cooler. He put his hand in and pulled out a brown bottle. Sam charged ahead and yanked him by the arm until they stood several feet from the blanket having words. Grace strained, but their voices failed to carry over the happy din of the picnic.

Sam wrenched the bottle from the other man's hand. Grace released her breath.

"Can I keep her, Mom, please?" Taylor's high-pitched plea underscored the drama which played out in the distance.

"How can I say no?" Lucy's voice dragged in resignation. "We'll have to pick up some supplies tomorrow. How about you, Grace?"

Grace's circle of attention snapped back in like a rubber band. "What?" She looked at Lucy, who was petting the small back of the tortoiseshell kitten clasped in Taylor's hands.

"Will you be joining us on our kitty supply shopping spree?"

A warm rumble vibrated against Grace's chest. She looked up to see that the man had gone and Sam was sitting on a camp chair with the bottle at his feet.

The kitten clawed her way up Grace's torso, resting her paws on her shoulder and purring in her ear. Talk about salesmanship.

"I really hadn't planned on getting a pet." Her protest sounded weak, even to herself.

"Well," Lucy reasoned. "Sometimes the best things in life are the things we didn't plan for."

The *best?* The best things about her own life had been systematically stripped away from her. How could something cute and furry fix that?

Tiny pinpricks kneaded her shoulder, and she nuzzled the velvety fur. Maybe Lucy was right. She was due for something good to come her way.

She looked again at Sam, who had moved to the blanket and was playing with the baby.

Turning to look the kitten in her contented little eyes, she shook her head with a sense of inevitability. Looking once again at Sam, she gave the kitten a kiss. It was decided. She *had* always wanted a cat.

Chapter 25

"Let's see...hair replacement, hair styling, *handyman*...ow!"

Grace's hands flew from the computer keyboard to her leg, which burned at the injection site of eight needlelike claws. She grabbed the warm handful of playfulness that had apparently mistaken her leg for a scratch post.

"Kitty!" She shifted the squirming ball of cuteness up to face level. "Until you get your acupuncture certification, I'll thank you to quit practicing on me." She deposited her pet on the dining room floor, a safe distance from her exposed skin, and returned her focus to the screen.

"Okay, I have plenty of handymen to choose from in Missoula. How am I supposed to know who's good?"

The kitten responded by hurdling from the floor to the mantel and sprinting across it like an Olympian. Grace leapt to her feet and bounded into the living room, making a lunge for the water globe as it teetered to its near demise. She flashed the kitten a futile frown as the young animal ricocheted from the mantel to the side table, then landed spread eagle on the polished floor.

Grace sighed, grateful that none of her recent decorative touches had succumbed to her new roommate's acrobatic display.

"Where did you get your training, Cirque de Soleil?" She looked at the globe, then around the room for a safe haven. "I still need to come up with a name for you, you know." She walked around testing out various horizontal surfaces while the kitten licked her paws. "How about Brunhilde? No, too much name for such a little girl. Ariadne? No, someone might ask where that came from, and well...wouldn't want to tip my hand, now would I?"

The kitten looked up at her with curious eyes.

Grace set the globe on the side table and knelt down, offering her hand as a plaything. "That's right, baby. You don't know my secrets yet. Well, I think you're trustworthy. If you promise not to tell anyone, I'll fill you in on the whole sordid yarn, okay?"

The kitten rolled onto her back, grasping Grace's hand with all four paws and her needle teeth.

"Ow! Speaking of 'yarn.'" She pulled her hand from the cat's prickly clutches and grabbed a catnip mouse to dangle over her.

"So, I had this really bad thing happen to me. Well, it didn't exactly happen *to* me, but I was there. Anyway, things were going really well in my life right up until—"

The doorbell made her jump like a scared rabbit. Cautiously, she pulled herself to her feet, crossed to the door, and peered through the window. She paused as Sam glanced up, making eye contact through the glass. *Great.* Why hadn't she looked through the front window, like she usually did? Now she was faced with having to open the door to the drug dealer's apprentice. She heaved a sigh and pulled it open just enough to see out.

"Morning." Sam held his tool box in one hand and a box of supplies under the other arm. His hair was shorter, and he smelled vaguely of fabric softener.

"What are you doing here?" She clipped her words, the scene from the park the day before still fresh in her mind.

He worked up a snide smile. "Are we playing this again? I wouldn't have to come here, except the kitchen is too big to take back to my shop."

She firmed her mouth. "Didn't Devon tell you not to come back?"

"He said something about staying away from you, but I didn't pay any attention."

"You got fired, and you didn't pay any attention?"

"Oh, he was firing me? See, I didn't get that, considering he wasn't the one who hired me." His expression switched from mocking to apprehensive. "So, what does Devon have to do with—?"

"Never mind."

"Okay." He gave a hesitant shrug. "You want me to go?"

Her eyes darted toward the computer on her dining room table. It *would* save her a lot of grief if she didn't have to find a replacement. "N...no, actually. You're almost done, right?"

"Closer to 'done' than when I started."

She heaved a resigned sigh. "Then come on in. Just don't tell Devon."

He angled a half-smile. "I'll resist the temptation when we meet later for tea."

She made a point of keeping her face a blank slate. If they had to spend time together she wasn't about to give him the satisfaction of thinking she was happy about it.

He stepped inside and gave a quick shiver. "You want me to check your thermostat? It's in the nineties all over town, but in here there's a chill in the air."

She folded her arms. Did he think he was funny?

"I'll just get to work." He tilted his head toward the back of the house. "Kitchen still this way?"

She pursed her lips and followed him. The door to the kitchen was already propped open, and he knelt down just next to it. He started to pull some gadgets from the box he'd brought.

Grace sat down at the dining table and gave her keyboard a few perfunctory plunks. At least now she could forget about the floor and focus on hiring an art dealer.

"Don't feel like you have to stay in here on my account." Sam leaned down low to examine the floor.

Irritation chewed at her. "You're not affecting my plans in the slightest. I happen to have work to do here."

"My mistake." He tossed her a slight smirk.

Grace slipped him a sneer. Guys like that had always galled

her. They thought they were so macho because they knew the right screwdriver to use. They'd crack their first beer before noon and think the ladies couldn't live without them. Then they'd demonstrate their complete lack of ability to treat a woman with any respect.

A sudden image of that poor woman's face as she held her baby on the picnic blanket flashed through Grace's mind. How could he resort to dealing drugs when he had kids? This was an awful situation and somebody had to do something.

"How's the family?" She spit out the question, her genuine concern swathed in sarcasm.

He gave her a sideways glance. "Not bad. You know family. You love 'em, but sometimes—"

"You think life would just be easier without them?"

"*Oh* yeah." He raised his eyebrows and nodded. "So, I'll do what I can today to stave off the damage, but we're going to have to keep the water shut off in here until the rest of the parts come in."

"Oh. When will that be?"

"Well, I ordered from a place called Speedy Plumbing, so I have high hopes for tomorrow." He pondered. "If not tomorrow, next week."

"Next *week?*" Annoyance seethed. She'd just have to hope Devon didn't ask about the project. "Fine."

"Your homeowner's insurance will cover the extra cost of eating out till this is fixed."

She shrugged and focused on her screensaver. "I eat out most of the time anyway."

"Most of the time?" He gave her a quizzical look. "Wow."

"Not everybody's a chef."

"True. Must add up though."

She fired him a glare. "I manage."

"Okay. Just trying to help." He returned his attention to the floor. "So have you discovered all the fine cuisine Madison Falls has to offer?"

"Some of it's decent."

"A lot of it's actually pretty good. There's a place called the Fountain—"

"Been there."

"Really?" He looked up.

"You sound surprised."

"No, it's just that people around here sort of think of that as a special date destination."

What was he implying? "You don't think I would have gone there on a date?"

"No, I'm not saying that. It's just—"

"Because, for your information, I did have a date."

"Oh. Well. Good." An array of emotions flashed across his face, landing on something that resembled indifference. "The guy who owns it is a chef from Chicago. Did you like the food?"

"Mm-hmm..." She glued her eyes to her screen, unable to focus but hoping he'd get the hint.

A sudden crash from the kitchen disturbed her planned silence. She jumped up, then darted to the doorway and looked past Sam. "No.... Don't tell me I've got rats."

One of the lower cupboards eased open. A bag of cat food fell out, its contents spilling perilously close to the damaged area of the floor. The kitten followed the bag, looked around with fiery eyes, and darted out onto the sun porch.

"Cutest rat I've ever seen." Sam smirked. "You ought to replace that cabinet latch."

Grace clenched her fists. "Argh. That cat's nothing but trouble." She snapped her fingers. "That's it, the perfect name."

"For the invisible rat?" Sam smiled as he continued to work.

She slid him a *very funny* glance, silently repeating the name. It held a secret comforting connotation from her real life, but nobody would decipher the reference. "I'm naming her Trouble."

"Nice." He grabbed a wrench and pried at a pipe. "That reminds me of something.... It's like that opera. What's it called?"

Her heart fell like a broken elevator. "*You* know *Madame Butterfly*?"

He chuckled. "You think we ain't got culture out here in the

Wild West?"

She harrumphed back to her chair. What did he know about culture? And who did he think he was, making fun of her for thinking he wouldn't have it?

Peevishly, she typed out "art dealers, New York City," and raised her fists to her chin as a list appeared. There were so many. How was she supposed to know who was reputable?

A pounding noise from the next room jostled her. All she could see now of Sam through the door was one work-boot-clad foot as he worked. She was tempted to ask Mr. Culture over there if he knew anything about art.

The thought forced an arrow of guilt to perforate her gut. Of course he didn't know anything about art. If he did, he wouldn't have to fix pipes to bring in extra income. He would have sold the painting for its true value and he wouldn't be mixed up with people like Carson.

She leaned back, placing her hands in her lap as the list of art dealers vanished behind her screensaver. It was awkward doing this research while he was there. It could wait.

"So, I haven't forgotten about that other thing." His voice sounded strained, as if he were muscling a pipe into place as he spoke.

She looked up, confused. "What 'other thing'?"

His face appeared in the doorway. "The crate. It's on my list. Are you in a hurry for it?"

"Oh." She'd honestly pushed that to the back of her mind. It suddenly seemed cruel to expect him to build it, given the circumstances. "You know, you don't have to do it. Really."

He gave her a sideways glance. "Are you firing me officially, or should I wait to get word from Devon?"

A genuine smile found its way to her lips. "I speak for myself," she said. "Don't worry about Devon."

"Don't worry about him?" He arched an eyebrow. "If only that were an option."

He returned to work, leaving Grace's question hanging between them. *Why on earth would he be worried about Devon?*

Chapter 26

"You're avoiding my question." Grace wrinkled her nose at Lucy as she tossed a stack of cat food tins into their shopping cart.

"What question?" Lucy was far too honest to convincingly feign ignorance. "Oh. Clay. Go with the clay litter."

"Not *that* question." Grace resisted a laugh as she hoisted two bags of cat litter into the cart.

"I know, I know." Lucy sighed. "But the theatre already *has* a piano player. Myra Henderson has played for every musical that theatre has done since—"

"Since Civil War times?" Grace jeered.

Lucy twisted her mouth. "I know she's not as good at counting as some people prefer—"

"'Some people'? Like the non-hearing-impaired?"

"And she can't see as well as she used to, but she loves it so much. I can't imagine who would be heartless enough to fire her."

"Oh, I can." Grace made a slashing gesture across her throat.

Lucy brushed her off with one hand, guiding the cart with the other. "I should pick up some paper towels. You go through a lot when you have an eight-year-old boy and an amateur mechanic in the house."

They rounded the corner of the paper goods aisle.

Grace refused to give up. There wasn't a lot she could do with the cast, but some actual talent in the orchestra pit would at least mask some of their flaws. "We have to step up the quality of our productions, Lucy."

"Step it up?" Lucy made a face at the paper towel selection. "I swear, Grace. Bob might as well just give his paycheck directly to this market. They get most of it eventually anyway."

"Lucy, this is really important. We need to show Mr. Roberts that the theatre can be a money maker for him. Otherwise he'll..." She stopped herself. This was no time to break her promise to Nancy. "The show needs a decent pianist."

Lucy shook her head. "I don't know..."

"You know you want to. It's supposed to be a fast-paced show. The way Mrs. Henderson plays, we'll have to tell the audience to pack in a meal and a pillow."

Lucy tittered nervously. "Well, you're enterprising. You could start selling sandwiches at your little stand."

"Please. It's all I can do to handle the espresso." Deflated, Grace folded her arms. She had expected Lucy to jump at the chance to help the theatre. She had talent, and it was a shame to waste it just playing at church once a week. Why wouldn't she want to put her skills to better use? "You know you're changing the subject."

Lucy lowered her voice. "To tell you the truth, I'm not comfortable performing without other musicians. I'm more of a team player."

"But..." Grace pictured Lucy onstage at church. She'd looked so at ease, but she'd had the band around her. Suddenly, it hit her. "That's a great idea! It would be even better if we had a full band."

Lucy's eyes opened in wide contemplation. "That *is* an idea." She stopped perusing the paper products and weighed the proposition. "Let me see what Sa...what *people* think."

Grace clapped her hands together. "Terrific."

"Okay." Lucy was silent for a moment, as if she had something more significant to say but was holding back. When she did speak, it was with a disproportionate fervor. "So, how's the floor coming?"

Puzzled by the gusto with which she spoke of home repair, Grace chuckled. “Just fine, thanks.”

Lucy’s head bobbed as she sorted through various brands of wax paper. “Good, good. It sounds like some project.”

“Yes, apparently I bought some pretty ancient pipes. Sam says the plumbing is practically older than the house.” Now it was Grace’s turn to weigh her words. “Lucy, I—”

“Sam mentioned—” Lucy spoke at the same time. “Sorry. Go ahead.”

Grace rolled in her lips and started over. “I just wanted to tell you that I figured out who your friend is—the one who’s mixed up with Carson.”

Lucy stopped pushing the cart for just a second as she blinked sadly. “Oh. I probably shouldn’t have said anything.”

“You obviously really care about him, and I just put two and two together. I had already seen the signs.”

Lucy gave her a curious glance. “I didn’t know that you.... Well, it *is* a small town.”

“That’s for sure. So you see why I was leery about Sam doing that work on my floor.”

Lucy’s brow creased. “I’m not sure I—”

Grace backpedaled, not wanting to wade in too deeply. “Well, it’s a big job.”

“Oh.” Lucy’s eyes softened in understanding. “I don’t know how Sam manages to get so much accomplished considering what he’s facing. Trust me, though, he always puts his all into his work. He’s a perfectionist.”

Grace gave her a puzzled look. Lucy had said herself that Sam’s behavior was inconsistent, and Grace had witnessed it more than once. How could you trust that someone involved in drugs on any level might not just snap?

“Anyway,” Grace continued, as casually as she could. “He was going to build something for me but I was wondering if maybe Bob might have time. It shouldn’t take long.”

“What is it?”

“A crate. Just a small one.”

"A crate?"

"Just a small one."

Lucy shrugged. "I can ask. But he wouldn't be able to get to it till next month at the earliest. He's pretty swamped with this ranch project."

"Next month?" *Darn ranch project.* "I guess I'll try to find somebody else."

Lucy looked tentative. "There was one other thing...about Sam."

Grace's stomach clenched slightly. "What?"

A look of culpability played on Lucy's face. "He knows we're friends, and he asked if I thought you were spending time around that director. What's his name?"

Grace's brow furrowed. "Devon?"

Her nod was hesitant. "I said you hadn't mentioned him."

Uncomfortable with this line of questioning, Grace wandered to the end of the aisle, pretending to hold an immense fascination with the pyramid of facial tissue they had on display. She shook her head. "Uh-uh."

Lucy let out a small sigh. "Good."

Grace's focus was pulled to the front of the store by a high-pitched titter that would have put any good soprano to shame. She looked up to see Sophia standing at the checkout several yards away, her back to Grace. She tossed her brunette mane to the side in a flirtatious laugh.

The warmth rushed from Grace's face so quickly she must have looked like the plug on her blood supply had been pulled. There next to Sophia, also laughing playfully, stood Devon.

Grace's heart pounded out a bewildered *recitative*. She nearly ripped the plastic off the package of Kleenex she'd grabbed to keep from lunging at the little viper's throat. She stepped closer to the pyramid, peering around and trying to get a view of the bag boy's hands as he filled a canvas tote with their apparent purchases.

A long baguette, two kinds of cheese, grapes, and a tall slender bottle of wine—cabernet sauvignon, if her eyes didn't deceive. She huffed, her throat clenching. What did this mean?

"So, I'm really relieved about that." Lucy had been talking, but Grace hadn't heard a word. She faked a smile and nodded in agreement.

Lucy seemed in better spirits. "Anyway, don't think we're nosy, but we just want to make sure you're okay."

Grace looked again toward the front of the store. Still engaged in lighthearted banter, Devon and Sophia walked out the front door, his hand on the small of her back.

Grace bit her quivering lower lip, forcing herself to speak. "Yes. Yes, I'm okay." She tipped her head, watching as the pair strolled up the sidewalk. "Just peachy."

Chapter 27

Grace paced in front of her fireplace, stopping to watch Trouble attack a ray of sunlight that danced across the living room rug. She hated being lied to. Devon could have at least been honest with her. She expelled a small growl of frustration. The thought of Sophia getting the guy she wanted was too much for her to take.

The clang of the doorbell sent her heart into a sprint. Was Devon finished with his picnic already? Squaring her shoulders, she marched toward the door, hastily rehearsing her charges against him. Crimes of the heart should not be easily dismissed.

Peeking through the cut glass, her heart fell. It wasn't Devon.

She groaned. The sight of Sam reminded her that she still hadn't found anyone to build that silly crate. Why hadn't she just let him go ahead and do it? Using more might than necessary, she turned the deadbolt and flung open the door. Surprise forced her to take a step back.

"Morning, Miss Addison." Mr. Roberts stood next to his son, a warm smile gracing his face. She instantly lamented her hostile stance.

"I told my dad about your cupboard door." Sam spoke in a tone that was gentle, almost apologetic. "He pretty much insisted on fixing it. I hope you don't mind."

Her fiery attitude from the moment before was partially

doused. "Of course not." She stepped back, allowing them to enter.

Mr. Roberts slipped Sam a sly wink. "I'll be in the kitchen." He disappeared around the corner, while Sam lingered next to her in the foyer.

Grace laced her fingers together, leaning back on her heels. Sam put up a decent front, but knowing what she knew about him made her want to keep her guard up. He couldn't fool *her*.

"So, good news." He fixed her with a look that could melt chocolate. "'Speedy Plumbing' lived up to their name. I have all the parts to finish the repair. It shouldn't take too long. I'll be able to get the tile down this morning too and your kitchen will be good as new."

"Oh." Her voice felt thick. She hadn't expected the project to be done so soon. Why did she feel a little let down?

He flashed a reticent smile. "Then as soon as the Roto Rooter guy does his thing, I'll come back and fill in that hole. I hope it hasn't been a hazard for you."

A hazard? She'd practically forgotten about it. "Only when I have the gang over for a rousing game of 'tag.'"

The corners of his mouth twitched in amusement. "I'd be happy to resod it for you, as a favor."

Indignation gave way to confusion. Why did he want to do her any favors?

She thought again about Devon and realized her head was starting to hurt. Maybe some caffeine would help. She lifted a hand toward the kitchen. "Will I be in the way if I make coffee?"

"Coffee?" He gave her a quizzical look as he rubbed his neck. "In this heat?"

"You've never heard of iced coffee?" She couldn't keep the tease from her tone. Something about Sam made it difficult to stay irritated with him. *How annoying.*

He chuckled. "I guess not."

"I've been making iced mochas for everybody in town." Folding her arms, she pinned him with a snappish taunt. "Maybe you should stop by the concession stand once in a while."

Hope flashed in his eyes. She bit her lip. What she'd intended as an admonition had come out sounding like an invitation.

She quickly recanted. "I mean, your dad does own the place."

The glint of hope dwindled slightly. "I know. I should be more supportive." He tilted an innocent glance. "Maybe I'll stop in this weekend."

A tingle of anticipation danced across her back. She shook it off. "Suit yourself." Why on earth had she even brought it up? The further away he stayed, the better. Resenting the urge to linger and chat, she started for the kitchen.

He followed, his toolbox clanking as he walked.

Pushing through the kitchen door, she smiled at Mr. Roberts, who was crouched in front of the errant cabinet. Gingerly, she made her way into the room, thankful that her kitchen would soon return to normal and she could stop feeling like she was moving across a river on stepping stones every time she entered it. She pulled open the fridge, and grabbed a jug of water. "It'll be a relief to be able to use the sink again."

Sam set down his tools and started to peruse the work he'd already completed. "I hope it hasn't been too much of a hardship."

She shrugged, speaking under her breath as she poured water into the pan on the stove. "I've lived through worse." She crossed to the counter and grabbed her jar of Nescafé.

Mr. Roberts chuckled. "You're making coffee in this heat?"

"Come on, Dad." Sam glanced up. "You've never heard of iced coffee?" His eyes met Grace's with a shrewd wink.

The older man held up his hands. "Matter of fact, no."

Grace's face relaxed into a smile. "Would you care for one?"

Pulling a screwdriver from his box, Mr. Roberts nodded. "I'm game."

Suddenly feeling awkward, she looked over at Sam, who was kneeling on the floor, putting the new piping into place. "Sam?"

He looked up. "Oh, no thanks. I have a lot of work to get done here."

"Son," his father shot him a pointed glance. "When a woman offers you a cold drink on a hot day, you should accept. Haven't I ever told you the story of how I won your mother's heart?" He turned to Grace, who blanched at the implication. "It involved an unseasonable heat wave and a thermos of pink lemonade."

Sam tossed his dad a glare, his face turning a color to rival the lemonade in the story. "Yes, Dad. You've told me."

"Too bad." Mr. Roberts cocked his head. "It's a good story."

Grace reached up into the cabinet next to the sink and grabbed the glasses she'd gotten six-for-five-dollars at the Peach Basket. "I'd like to hear it."

The older man looked at her with a pleased glint. "I love a willing audience." Holding the counter for balance, he stooped down and began to remove the screws from the latch. "It was the summer of seventy-six and I was building a fence out on the Sutton Ranch. A part of the fence line runs along Hanson Road, and I couldn't help but notice that a young lady rode her horse past at some point every day. Now, being the bright young buck that I was, I made sure that part of the fence got built to perfection. In fact, I put extra effort into that particular section. Took me a solid week to finish that chunk of the project, but I was there every day, waiting to flash that young lady a smile."

Listening intently, Grace took the ice from the freezer and leaned on the counter while she popped the cubes.

Removing the latch from the door, Mr. Roberts continued. "Since I never knew exactly when she'd ride by, I was constantly on the alert, but one particular day, it was hotter than blazes and I was about ready to give up and move on to a shadier section of the line. Right about then, a shadow appeared from out of nowhere, giving some much-needed relief. I turned around, and realized that the horse was standing right behind me. I'd been so caught up in what I was doing that I hadn't even noticed. I about fell over. This gal was even more beautiful than I'd realized."

Grace smiled at the image. Her eyes lit on Sam, who kept an uncomfortable focus on his work.

Mr. Roberts' voice grew animated. "Then, she reached into her saddle bag and pulled out a thermos. She handed it down to me with a single word. 'Lemonade?' It was like an angel's song, the way she said it. I was smitten. I reached up and took it, and to make a long story short, that was the beginning of a beautiful romance."

Grace swallowed hard, blinking her dewy eyes. She glanced again at Sam, who had stopped working and seemed lost in thought. She took in a ragged breath and crossed to the stove, where bubbling water made her pan dance.

Mr. Roberts looked up, a mischievous glint in his eye. "Here's the capper. About twenty years later, that fence blew over in a windstorm. The only part they didn't have to rebuild was the stretch that runs along the road." He chuckled. "I guess my diligence paid off in more ways than one."

Grace snickered, but Sam looked away solemnly. His voice crackled when he spoke. "I, uh, have to go get the tiles out of the truck." He stood, running a hand through his hair.

Mr. Roberts set down his screwdriver. "I'll go with you."

Sam held up a hand. "No. You'll never get that done if you stop to help me." Without waiting for a response, he bounded out of the kitchen.

Grace watched, puzzled, as she grabbed her jar of Nescafé and shook loose the residual crystals that stuck to the bottom. She looked at Mr. Roberts. "I'll be right back."

He nodded. "Take your time."

Moving through the house, she questioned her own motives. Something was clearly bothering Sam, but that wasn't the reason she was going after him...was it? She felt obligated to help carry in the tiles, that was it. Pulling open the front door, she expected to see him hoisting boxes from the back of his truck. To her surprise, he was standing on the porch with his head down and his hands on his hips. He looked up.

She smiled tentatively. "Hope I didn't startle you."

He faced forward, his gaze distant. "I just needed a second."

She nodded, not really understanding. "Are you okay?" As if she expected him to tell her what was bugging him.

He shook his head with a sad smile. "I'll be fine." He hooked his thumbs on his belt loops, apparently lost in his concerns.

Feeling awkward now, Grace drummed her fingers on her

thighs. "Was it something your dad said?"

He looked at her as if gauging whether to share his thoughts. "My dad talks a lot about my mom. I guess that's good in a way, but..."

Impatience gnawed at her. Did he realize how lucky he was to have great parents? He probably drove them crazy with worry, the way he behaved. "Why wouldn't that be good?"

He looked away again. "He talks about her, but he's not really dealing with it."

Confusion bubbled in her throat. "Dealing with *what?*"

His look registered surprise. "Oh, sorry. I forget you're new here." His eyes dropped along with his volume. "My mom died last year."

His words were like a blow to her gut. Now she recognized the emotion that welled in his eyes as the all-too-familiar pain that had been a constant in her own life for months. She swallowed hard to keep from shouting out *I know what you're going through. I know how it feels to lose a parent.* She wanted, for both their sakes, to tell him she knew exactly how he felt. The words were there. All she had to do was back them up with a breath of bravado.

Chapter 28

Grace toyed with the temptation to tell Sam she'd lost a parent too. It would have been a relief to just say it, but instead she held her tongue. Her good intentions weren't exactly in sync with Grace Addison's made-up life story.

She studied his face as his mind seemed to wander to a different time. She understood that too.

Silence settled for a moment. She knew how it felt when you just wanted to forget, at the same time wanting to confide in someone. Maybe Sam would welcome the opportunity to talk.

She cleared her throat, then took the plunge. "How did she die?"

His gaze dropped, and a tear glistened in the corner of one eye. He seemed to struggle for the right words. "She was helping out a family from church. They needed to sell their place, and their barn was a real mess. Mom offered to clean it out for them and she wound up breathing in a lot of dust. We didn't figure out till she got really sick a few days later that she'd inhaled some kind of deadly bacteria." He glanced up at her. "Something to do with rodents. Anyway, once it got her, that was pretty much it. We took her to the hospital but she was gone in a couple of hours."

Grace felt her breath leave her. "Oh..."

His face lifted subtly. "The good thing is, I know where she went."

Confusion colored her gaze. "Where she...?"

"*But the gift of God is eternal life.*" He finally looked at her. "See, she'd accepted the Lord the year before. It's good to know she's with Him."

Accepted the Lord? Unsure how she should respond, Grace fumbled for comforting words. "That *is* good."

He went on, his voice raspy. "Trouble is, I'm the only one in the family who sees it that way."

"What do you mean?"

"My dad and my sister, they..." His eyes welled up again. "They totally blame me for what happened."

"Blame you?" Her heart ached at the injustice. "She breathed in dust. How could that be your fault?"

He let out a controlled breath. "If it hadn't been for me, my mom wouldn't have started going to church. If it hadn't been for the Holy Spirit guiding her to help that family—"

"She wouldn't have died?" Grace's mind boggled. "But she was doing a good thing. How could anybody have predicted what would happen?"

"I know. And I know the Lord allowed it and that He uses everything for good. I'm just having a hard time figuring out how He's using this because the whole thing has really hardened my family against God and against me. I'm not sure they'll ever forgive me."

Grace pressed two fingers to her brow, then pointed her thumb toward the house. "But, your dad doesn't seem like he's mad at you."

A sardonic smile crept over his lips. "It comes out. Mostly in small ways. I can tell it's still eating at him." His face grew remorseful. "Look, I really didn't mean to burden you with my problems."

"It's not a burden." Her hand brushed his elbow. "It's good to talk about things."

He nodded. "You're a good listener. Thanks."

Their eyes locked for a moment. With a start, he looked away.

"I should grab those tiles."

Her stomach clenched. What was going on with her? "Right."

He moved from the porch and toward his truck, which he'd backed into the driveway.

Lingering at the crest of the steps, she watched him with fresh eyes. She hadn't wanted to admit it, but he had more than his share of positive attributes. He wasn't bad looking, if you pictured him in something designer with his hair gelled just a touch. In fact, under the right circumstances, she might even consider him a hunk.

He reached into the back of his pickup and unhooked the tailgate, his biceps clearly bulging under the fabric of his work shirt. She took in a resolute breath. *Okay, fine.* He *was* a hunk.

She scolded herself. Looks weren't everything. True, he was witty, in his own way. Now that she'd seen his vulnerable side, she had to admit she found it appealing. He even knew something about music. She hovered on the porch steps, warmed by this unexpected attraction to him.

A sudden jab to her heart brought her to her senses. What was she thinking? How could she possibly overlook the facts? He was, by the look of things, an abusive, neglectful husband who had turned to drug dealing. Even if he had his reasons, they couldn't possibly be good enough to justify any of that. A tsunami of irritation washed over her. Why was she feeling drawn to a guy who, for so many reasons, was clearly not a candidate for romance? Besides, she already had that area of her life covered.

At least, she'd *thought* she had it covered. Anger twisted in her stomach. A vision of Devon's hand on Sophia's back as they'd exited the Peach Basket that morning burned into her brain. She wanted to strangle that little wench.

"Oh, and I have something for you." Sam called out from across the yard, tugging her out of her homicidal thoughts.

She frowned. What could he possibly have for her? She heaved a sigh, hoping against hope that this wasn't going to be one of those awful moments where a guy tried to win her over with an inappropriate gift. Didn't she have enough problems?

She stomped down the steps and over to the driveway,

determined to tell him that whatever this *gift* was, he could just take it back. She didn't want or need anything from—

Staring into the bed of the truck, her mouth fell open.

"Lucy mentioned that you still needed it." He spoke with a swift, almost apologetic tone. "And since Bob doesn't have any time right now, I thought that..."

Much to her surprise, her eyes started to well up as she stared at an intricately constructed wooden crate. It was exactly what she'd described to him.

His voice was uncertain. "So, if you think this will work for you, I can take it inside."

Afraid to speak for fear of signaling her emotional state, she nodded with a close-lipped smile.

He let out a breath. "Okay. I'll just grab it then." He balanced the crate on a box of tiles, picked them both up, and began walking to the house.

She followed his departing back with her eyes before finding a steady voice. "What do I owe you?"

He turned around, his eyes warm. "I just used some scrap wood from the store. Consider it a gift."

Her knees felt weak. "But I asked you to do it."

The corners of his lips rose. "That's true, but you also fired me from doing it, remember? It's no big deal." He turned again and moved back inside.

She felt like a hot air balloon that had been deflated and left puddled on the ground. It was just so strange—him making this for her. She was touched by the apparently unselfish gesture, but the irony left her more confused than ever.

She hoisted a box into her arms. It was okay. Sam had helped her get over a hurdle. Soon, she'd have the painting shipped off, it would sell, and she'd have her life back.

Surprised by the weight of this small box of tiles, she stepped gingerly into her house. Sam had propped the kitchen door open with the crate, and she stopped to peer through the doorway. When he saw her, he stepped across the floor to relieve her of her load. His arms brushed against hers as he took the box, and their eyes met. Her heart beat like a steel-drum band.

From across the room, Mr. Roberts let out an audible breath. Grace and Sam both looked at him, and he flashed an innocent grin. “Getting a lot of work done, I see.”

Sam’s face flushed as he quipped. “Just worry about your own project.”

Mr. Roberts clicked the cupboard door shut. “I’m all done. Why are you so slow?”

Sam rolled his eyes, placing the box on the floor. “Excuse me. I have to get that other box of tile.” He edged past Grace. She followed him into the living room.

“Sam.”

He turned. “Yeah?”

“It’s just...I didn’t really say ‘thank you.’”

He smiled. “It was nothing.”

“It was huge.”

He tipped a casual shoulder. “And don’t think I’ve forgotten about your bathtub.”

A twinge stirred inside. “My bathtub?”

He tilted a sideways glance. “The leak...?”

“Oh. Right.” She shook off her unwarranted recollection. “And thanks for telling me about your mom.”

He nodded, his eyes glistening. “Thanks for listening. Not everyone understands.” He smiled his reassurance, then made his exit.

She stood for a moment, looking at the door through which he’d just walked and would shortly re-enter. Turning her head, she stared at the crate. Sadness filled her. Yes, she understood. If only there was something she could do about it.

“I can make that á la mode for fifty cents more.”

Grace slunk down lower into the comforting vinyl of the booth. “Why not?” She handed over her menu, content to celebrate her repaired pipes by visiting the Country Kitchen.

She leaned forward, placing her elbows on the table and her chin in her hands. She glanced out the window as Sam helped a customer load some wood into a flashy orange pickup truck. He'd apparently gone back to work after finishing her floor. Didn't that guy ever take a break?

She heaved a sigh. She appreciated that he'd confided in her, but that didn't change the kind of guy he was. Why was he constantly perched on the periphery of her mind like a sentinel?

"Here you go, honey. Peach pie, fresh baked this afternoon."

The pastry the waitress placed in front of Grace was as tall as a slice from Pie in the Sky stacked on top of one from Pie Heaven. New York should be ashamed of itself.

Her mouth watered as she picked up her fork, a little daunted by the task at hand. "Thanks, ah..." She glanced at the waitress's name tag, embarrassed that she hadn't thought to do so till now. "Thanks, Gloria."

The waitress smiled. "Call me Glo. Everyone does."

"Glo. I like that." Grace cracked the golden crust with her fork. She put a bite of ice cream-swathed pie into her mouth and closed her eyes. The taste of sweet peach burst on her tongue like a flavor firecracker.

"Good, isn't it?" Glo said.

"Mm-hmm." Grace nodded, unwilling to rush through that first bite.

"Well, you just take your time and enjoy. The dinner rush won't hit for a good half hour."

Grace nodded again, appreciative not just for the satisfying meal, but the companionship.

"How's that job working out for you?" Glo retreated behind the counter, a few feet from Grace's booth.

Grace swallowed. "Fine *now*. It's everything else that's confusing."

"Anything I can help clear up for you?" Glo picked up some stray coffee cups and swabbed the counter.

Smiling, Grace prepared another bite for launch. "I just have a little money problem."

Glo nodded as she turned to start a fresh pot of coffee. "Not enough?"

"A little too much, actually."

Glo shot a questioning glance over her shoulder. "Well, that's a new one."

It was far too complex a situation to do justice between bites. "I'm just trying to figure out if I should share it with someone. It's complicated."

"Oh. Well, you know what the Bible says. 'Store up your riches in heaven, for your heart will always be where your riches are'."

Her fork hovered midair. "That's really beautiful. I'm not sure it answers my question though."

"Well, think about it. Pray about it." Speaking over her shoulder, Glo filled a coffee filter with dark grounds. "What else is on your mind, honey?"

Grace looked around. A couple seated by the window paid her no attention, but she picked up her pie and moved to the counter just the same. She kept her voice low. "Glo, how well do you know Sam?"

"Sam?" The question appeared to catch her by surprise. "He's a dear. One of my best customers."

"I'm sure." Grace swirled her fork in the rich vanilla ice cream. "So, how long has he been married?"

Glo's well-mascara-ed eyes flew open wide and she nearly dropped her coffee pot. "Sam isn't *married*."

Grace swallowed a thick slice of peach without chewing. Coughing, she felt the blood rush to her face. "He's not?"

"Oh, gosh no, honey." Glo grabbed a glass and filled it with water, then handed it to Grace. "He's a catch, that's for sure, but he hasn't been lassoed yet." Glo picked up her coffee pot and went to welcome a couple of teenagers who had just walked through the door.

So Sam wasn't married? Why did that news make her even happier than the taste of fresh peach?

Her next thought twisted her stomach. She let her fork rest on the side of her plate.

Glo returned, tilting a concerned look. “Something wrong with the pie?”

Grace looked up. “Oh, no. I’m just confused. I’ve seen Sam with a couple of kids.”

“Kids? Oh, you must mean Jill’s kids.” Glo rested the coffee pot on the burner. “He’s like a dad to them in a way. Goodness knows those kids need one.”

Jill. So Sam was dating a woman with kids. And dealing drugs on the side. Who’d want to lasso that?

Watching as Glo clipped an order up for the chef, she weighed her words, not wanting to appear too ignorant. “Glo, what does it mean to ‘receive the Lord’?”

“Now there’s an easy one.” She gave Grace a warm smile and leaned on the counter. “It means to believe Jesus died on the cross to pay for your salvation.”

“And ‘salvation’ means going to heaven? It’s really that simple?”

“Simple as pie.”

Grace pushed a flake of crust across her plate, contemplating Glo’s words.

Glo spoke matter-of-factly. “All you have to do is pray for Jesus to come into your heart.”

She left to greet the start of the dinner rush and Grace pushed her fork across the plate to pick up the last of the crumbs.

All you had to do was *pray?* Finally, it was starting to make sense.

Chapter 29

Grace tossed a filter basket into the nearly full busing tub, where it landed with a *clunk.* Since realizing that keeping the stand open after the show nearly doubled their daily revenue, she'd fallen into a nice routine. Act two was just long enough for her to clean up from the intermission rush and prepare for the after-show and post-rehearsal crowd.

Muffled music from the rehearsal next door seeped into her stand. She gritted her teeth. The enthusiasm of the performers hadn't boosted them much above high school level, and the sound of their efforts only reminded her that Devon was in the next room. He hadn't even stopped in to see her. She imagined him flirting with Sophia as they rehearsed, while Grace sweated it out in her tiny stand. There was no justice.

She opened the half-door, raised the unwieldy tub, and carried it out into the lobby. It slipped between her damp fingers, and she imagined a cavalcade of clanging pitchers and filter baskets dropping to the floor. Wanting to avoid that added step to her clean-up process, she quickly set her load down on a table next to the front window.

Pausing, her eyes lifted to the scene outside. She loved this time of the evening when the sun had set and the sky turned to a deep purple. Casually, she craned her neck to glance up the street.

The lights were on in the hardware store. Frowning, she checked her watch. Sam must be working late. What was with that guy, anyway? He had so many problems, but sometimes he just seemed so...different. He worked hard for his dad, and he'd done so much to help her.

His story about his mom had weighed on Grace's mind all day, especially after Glo had helped her put that final piece into the puzzle. She wanted to believe in something, and what they said just made sense.

Another nagging thought had taken up residence in her mind. *The painting*. How could she sell it without admitting to Sam what she'd done? His dad needed money. Maybe if she offered him a portion of the proceeds he'd reconsider selling the theatre. It was worth a try.

She checked her watch again. There was still a little while before the show ended. This would be a good time to catch him. Cleaning up could wait.

As she readjusted her grip on the tub, something across the street caught her eye.

The light had flicked off in the windows of the hardware store. The door opened, and Sam stepped out into the shadows. Her heart quickened. If she wanted to talk to him, she'd have to move fast.

Leaving the tub on the table, she moved quickly for the front door and bounded out to the porch. From the top step, she looked up again, expecting to see him walking toward his truck, which was parked up the street as always. Instead, he was walking briskly in the other direction—toward the theatre. She smiled. Maybe he was on his way to see her.

She took a step down and a light popped on in a lace-curtained window above the hardware store. She stopped as Sam looked up, then stepped into the shadowed entryway of the second-floor apartment. He reached out to press the doorbell, then shoved his hands into the pockets of his jacket. Grace's stomach jumped as she moved back into the shadows of the porch.

A moment later, the corner door swung open, unveiling a bathrobed woman silhouetted by a dim light. Grace peered around the porch railing as the woman flung her arms, speaking animatedly. Both she and Sam cast watchful glances up and down the street, before she grabbed his arm, pulled him inside, and shut the door.

Grace's breath vacated her lungs. Even in that dim light she could see what was going on. Back to pick up his tools, perhaps? She didn't recognize the woman, but she was definitely not *his* woman.

Another woman. An *other* woman. *The worm.*

Feeling a little numb, she withdrew to the lobby. Just when she'd been ready to give the guy a second chance, his true character came shining through again. She retrieved the tub and slammed it down on the counter. Boy, if that didn't just prove that you could never trust what a person appeared to be on the outside. Everybody had secrets.

Music echoed from the rehearsal next door, jarring Grace into action. At least now she could shake her conscience free of her guilt about the painting. Sam had said it was his dad who needed the money, but had he just said that to mask his own greed? She sneered at the thought, pushing a stray hair from her face as she resumed cleaning. He'd probably go ahead and sell to Langley even if she did offer him half her money. What would be the point?

She closed the lower section of the door and turned to tidy a stack of cups. This building was old anyway—a firetrap, Nancy had said. Maybe it would do the town good to get a makeover. The casino wouldn't be so bad. It would provide jobs and lots of tourist trade. Besides, it wasn't her problem.

A noise from behind escorted her out of her thoughts. She turned to see a masculine figure appear at her counter.

"I wanted to beat the crowd." Devon gave her a warm smile, as if he expected warmth in return.

Grace firmed her mouth as tension rose from her like mist on the moors. She wanted to have it out over his deception, but this wasn't the place. The audience would be pouring out soon and she expected some business from the rehearsal crowd as well.

She tightened her lips. "Hello, Devon. What can I do for you?"

His eyebrow tweaked slightly. "Decaf Americano with a warning."

Grace's cheeks caught fire. A warning? Had Ruby said something to him? Adrenaline surged through her like electricity.

"What kind of warning?" She lowered her voice to conceal its nervous vibrato.

He leaned in, his face scant inches from hers. "The cast and crew from next door are going to bombard you with coffee orders the second they get out of rehearsal. I thought you should know."

Grace closed her eyes and gulped in air, then forced a weak smile. "Thanks." She turned and started to scoop coffee grounds into a filter basket.

"Tip jar's paying off." Though his words were casual, his tone sounded tense.

She cocked her mouth to one side, intentionally avoiding his gaze. "Seems to be." She poured his drink just as the theatre doors swung open, spewing out the happy post-show crowd.

Devon took the cup she offered, brushing his hand against hers. He set down the cup and pulled out his wallet, then handed her a five. "Allow me to add my own show of appreciation." He dropped something into the jar, and stepped back just as Lucy and Bob reached the counter.

In spite of the flash of harshness as she eyed Devon, Lucy was aglow with theatrical delight. "Grace! The show was so well-done. I was on the edge of my seat. That poor girl." She shook her head at the plight of the main character. "We can't wait to see how they do with *Pirates*. And you're not going to believe this, but Bob wants another latte."

Grace raised her eyebrows at Bob. "Oh, a convert."

Out of the corner of her eye, she saw Devon lingering by the window. Was he waiting for her? Nerves pinged through her like a pinball. She hated confrontation, but it had to be done. She would not be two-timed, and if he really wanted to cast her as Carmen, she'd have to make it clear now that their relationship was strictly professional.

The lobby was soon packed with patrons and pirates. Grace's

fingers flew as she tried to satisfy their beverage needs. A flutter of anxiety twitched in her chest. This was the biggest crowd she'd had so far, and Salvatore was getting feisty.

A moment later, she whirled around with a double mint mocha in her hand and nearly smacked into Lucy, who had edged her way into the booth with a pen and a pad of post-its.

"Lucy, you don't have to—"

"I'm here to serve. Besides, we're walking you home, and we'd be here all night at the rate you were going." She grinned and stuck a pink paper square to Grace's forehead.

Grace chuckled. Who was she to argue?

A whir of brewing and steaming followed. Lucy's line of post-it orders on the countertop soon dwindled, and Grace scrambled to pour the final drink.

"Double tall nonfat decaf latte," she announced. "The espresso stand I used to go to calls this a Double Tall Nothing." She turned to hand the hot cup to the one remaining patron, but stopped mid-spin.

On the other side of the counter stood Sophia, her lips pinched in a wicked glower and her eyes bright with ire. She reached out her claw-sharpened hand. A self-satisfied look spread across her harsh face like butter on a hot grill.

"Thanks for the coffee, dear." Her voice sounded pinched. "Next time, be a little quicker." A condescending perusal of Grace was her parting shot before she turned and walked toward the window.

The lobby was so packed, it would have resembled a gallery opening had there been any artwork left on the walls. Grace struggled to see through the mingling crowd. Devon still hovered by the window, but when Sophia approached, he stood at attention. Sophia said something to him and kept walking but his eyes fixed on Grace.

She weakened at the sight of his pleading gaze. Her heart told her to go to him, but her feet remained planted in place. In her moment of indecision, he turned and followed Sophia out the front door.

"Well," Lucy sounded uncharacteristically snide. "She always has been the jealous type."

Grace's eyes snapped toward Lucy. "Yes, I guess so."

Lucy gave Grace a wide smile. "Nice to see you giving her something to be jealous *of*."

Surprised at Lucy's apparent turn-around in her opinion of Devon, Grace regretted not going to him. Her heart ached. She and Devon seemed so perfectly suited for each other, and he was worth fighting for.

Lucy picked up a towel and started to wipe the counter. "By the way, I've considered your offer. I'll play under one condition. That Myra gets to stay. We have two keyboards. It'll be fine."

Grace tilted a smile. She had so much else on her mind, she'd nearly forgotten her concern for the show.

"And," Lucy continued, "I've talked to the band members, and they're all excited to do it too."

A wave of renewed hope rolled through Grace. "Lucy, that's wonderful. That'll make all the difference."

"You about ready, ladies?" Bob tipped his cup back to liberate the final drops of his latte.

"I still have some cleaning up to do." Grace wiped her hands on a white towel. "Do you want to wait?"

"Only if you let us count your tips." Lucy's eyes were like saucers as she picked up the full jar and shook it.

"Be my guest." Grace tossed some long twist spoons into her overflowing bus tub.

"Oh, look." Lucy removed a small envelope from the jar. "Someone left you a love note."

Grace's eyes rolled to the ceiling. *Great.* Most likely one of the stagehands had a crush on her and was too timid to admit it.

"Let me see." She took the unadorned envelope from Lucy's hand and pulled open the sticky flap. She slipped out a piece of unlined white paper that had been folded to fit into its undersized packet. On it was printed not a declaration of love, but a simple sentence that sent the room into a nauseating spin.

"Grace...are you all right?" Lucy's voice filtered in from

another dimension.

Grace's knees buckled, and the walls closed in. Someone grabbed her arm and a jolt of panic surged through her. She stepped toward the exit, pushing whoever had a hold on her into the counter.

"Ow! Grace..."

She wrenched her head around and saw Lucy frowning and rubbing her arm.

"I'm so sorry." Grace reached out to steady herself, horrified at her momentary loss of control. "I guess I just got lost in my thoughts."

"You looked like you were about to pass out. Are you sure you're okay?"

"Yes, fine." Grace refolded the note and stuffed it into her back pocket. She picked up her busing tub and opened the lower door. "I've got to wash these. I'll be right back."

"But..."

Lucy's concerned voice trailed off as Grace hurried through the lobby and down the hall, then slipped through the door marked "Backstage." Immediately, she set down the tub and pulled out the note.

There was no writing on the envelope—no clue as to whom it was from. She spread out the paper and looked at it, terror gnawing at her heart. One thing was certain. She wasn't safe.

She read the note again, this time mouthing the words.

I'm onto you.

Chapter 30

R*ed ink.*

He'd written the note in red. Like blood. Like last time.

Grace drummed her gnawed nails on the bare mantel and tried to map out a plan. She needed to pack whatever she could fit into her car and just go. Go somewhere safe.

Safe? Panic threatened to choke her. No place was safe.

She brushed her hair from her eyes with shaky fingers. This was such a familiar pattern with Kirk. He'd toss out some small threat with no immediate follow-through. Then just as she'd let her guard down he'd materialize in a manner as unpleasant as it was unexpected.

Trouble brushed past Grace's ankle. She knelt down and gave the kitten an absentminded pat. How could Kirk have found her? He couldn't have followed her, she'd been too careful. The new name. The new hair color.

She had to face facts. He had found her anyway.

Fear churned in her belly. How could she have been naive enough to believe she could outsmart him, after everything he'd done? He was clever and cruel, and that was a lethal combination.

Her hand visibly quivered as she stroked Trouble's plush fur. If Kirk hadn't cooled off after she'd disappeared, that meant he'd gotten angrier. She'd taken that chance, and now she was paying the price. She knew what he was capable of—

An abrupt knock at the door nearly catapulted her to the ceiling. Scooping up the kitten, she stood, wavering in indecision.

Another knock sounded, more insistent than the first. She padded to the front window, uncertain of her next move. It seemed unlikely that Kirk would just show up at her door. That would be too easy. She grabbed her phone out of her purse, preparing to call for help.

Peeking between the slats of the blinds, she let out a long, trembling breath.

It was Devon, shifting nervously from one foot to the other. Her heart lifted. Her anger over Sophia hadn't cooled, but at least she wouldn't have to go through this alone. She put her phone away and took her time opening the door.

"Grace," he exhaled her name. "I was worried about you."

His words pinched her nerves as she scanned the dark street behind him. "Worried? Why?"

He nodded toward the living room. "Can we talk?"

She stepped aside, allowing him entrance, then quickly bolted the door.

He crossed to the sofa. "I could tell you were upset." There was an agitation in his mannerisms that she hadn't seen before. "Then Sophia said something about you that made me think I needed to see you."

She sat on the edge of the cushion, not wanting to let down her guard. Trouble pulled away from her grasp and darted off to live up to her name.

"Sophia—"

"I know." He held up a hand. "Let *me*, please."

She nodded, her nerves still raw as steak tartare.

His face grew somber. "I just want you to understand that my life is complicated."

Grace arched an eyebrow. He thought *his* life was complicated?

"Please understand that whatever else happens, I feel like you and I have a special connection." He took her hand. "There are certain things that..."

Her temper flared. She pulled her hand away. Was he about to tell her he wanted to date them both?

He rested his hands on his lap. "Things that need to be kept quiet. Whatever Sophia said..."

Grace was too overwrought for this right now. She stood, chewing her thumbnail with absentminded disregard for her most recent manicure. She crossed to the window and peeked out into the blackness. A cringe crept through her. If someone lurked in the shadows, would she be able to see them?

"Grace." Devon was now standing a few feet behind her. "If Sophia told you something, please give me a chance to explain."

She whirled around. "She didn't have to tell me anything. I know."

The lines near his eyes deepened. "You know.... Look, if Roberts said something to you, I'll—"

"Sam? Why would he say anything? I have eyes. I saw you two together."

He looked at her sideways. "*Saw* us together? Wh...when?"

She blew out a jagged breath. She hated sounding like a green-eyed female, but she had to get this out. "This afternoon."

A look of genuine confusion swept across his face. "I don't..."

"At the market." She folded her arms. "You were buying what looked like a romantic lunch, complete with wine, and you were flirting like you were at a speed-dating marathon."

His face slowly lifted as his eyes softened. "You're kidding." His voice lilted. "That's what upset you? You think that *Sophia* and I..."

Her stance eased slightly. "Well, yes."

He laughed, taking a step closer. "Grace. Sophia is my student."

"Your student?"

"Right. We were just working on a scene. I'm her acting coach."

"Her acting coach?" She lowered her arms, weighing this information. "Boy, does she need one." She tried not to get flustered. "Okay. But why the *pranzo?*"

He rolled his eyes. "We're working on that scene from *Picnic*—do you know the play?"

Her temples throbbed with confusion. "I know the opera."

He nodded, his whole manner lightening. "Sophia has this obsession with a Stanislavski sort of realism. She thinks that if you're rehearsing *Picnic*, you have to *have* a picnic."

"Oh." Grace bit her upper lip. "Lucky you weren't doing *Murderers*."

"Yes." He chuckled lightly. "I thought you believed me when I told you earlier that Sophia and I weren't involved."

"I did. It's just that when I saw you like that..." Her voice trailed off as she tried to recall all her reasons for reaching that conclusion. "Wait a minute. If Sophia isn't jealous of me because of *you*, then why—"

A flicker of some unidentifiable emotion shot from his eyes as he held up a hand. "She might have gotten the impression that I was considering her for the role of Carmen."

"What?" Grace's jaw dropped like a broken elevator. "How would she get that impression?"

He rolled his eyes upward. "It's just that when I first met her, I was struck by her look. The way she moves, and that beautiful hair. I was a little overzealous and I might have mentioned that she looked like the Carmen type."

"Was that before or after you heard her sing?"

His eyes turned sheepish. "Before, I'm afraid. I offered to coach her, but I never really promised her anything. When I mentioned you were a singer too—"

"*Too?*" Her ego twisted in a painful knot at the inference that she and Sophia were even close to the same level.

He seemed to catch his faux pas. "Of course, the difference between you is night and day. Sophia has a long way to go before she's ready for something that big."

Grace folded her arms and curled her lip. This was all just too much for her.

Devon put a comforting hand on her arm. "There's something

else, isn't there? Something you're not telling me."

She nodded slowly, looking into his eyes. She had to tell him. However their relationship evolved, he had a right to know how dangerous her life was. She braced herself. This was the moment of truth. If Devon really cared for her, he'd understand.

She cupped his hand with hers. "I have to show you something." Pulling away, she went to the sofa and picked up the folded note from the end table. After a moment of careful contemplation, she turned and handed it to him.

Slowly, with a look of consternation, he took it.

Relief and fear intermingled in Grace as Devon's eyes swept the page. She needed to get it all out. "There's so much I haven't..."

She caught herself, disbelief clouding her thoughts. Why was he smiling?

Levity trickled into his voice. "I can't believe you took this seriously."

"Of course I did. I—"

"Grace." He held the note up and glinted an incredulous smile. "Do you know who wrote this?"

Her head swam. "I thought I did."

"The paper. The stupid red pen. She leaves notes for me every day. She's big on notes."

"*She?*"

"I don't know what you thought this was about." Devon tossed the note onto the table. "But it was written by my housemate."

Chapter 31

"Wish me luck, Troubs." Grace called out to the snoozing ball of fur curled up on her living room rug as she bounded toward the front entry. Now that her fears about Kirk were temporarily sidelined, she had other business to attend to.

In one swift motion, she undid the bolt, yanked open the door, and stopped with a gasp.

Sam jarred back, apparently as startled as she was. One hand hovered near the doorbell and the other held his toolbox. "Morning. This a good time?"

She downshifted from alarm to annoyance. "Don't people in this town ever call first?"

"Would you have said this was a good time?"

"No."

"Good thing I didn't call."

She twisted her mouth, disdain prickling her skin. She couldn't believe that just last night she'd been ready to hand over part of her wealth to him. Thank goodness she'd seen him go into that woman's apartment before she'd acted so rashly.

He cocked his head and raised one eyebrow. "I'm going to be busy for the next few weeks, with the show and all—"

She frowned. "What show?"

"*Pirates*." His brow creased. "Lucy said you asked us to play."

She let out a sigh. "I asked *her* to play." Was there no getting rid of this guy?

"Oh." His face fell subtly. "Anyway, I'm going to be pretty tied up and I'd feel better knowing that your bathroom pipe's not going to explode before I can get to it."

His vivid verb choice was hard to ignore. She'd prefer to steer clear of any sort of explosion if possible.

"I was just on my way out," she said in feeble protest.

"Then chances are I'll be gone by the time you get home."

She dropped her head back in surrender. "Fine. Just lock the door when you go."

Giving her a tentative smile, he eased past her. He opened his mouth to speak then looked away, his mind clearly changed. He stepped into the hallway and disappeared into the bathroom. There was a clattering *thunk* of toolbox meeting tile floor.

Staring after him, Grace folded her arms and contemplated his motives. He'd been so nice to make that crate for her, not to mention all that work he'd done on the floor for half what she'd expected to pay. Now this. Why on earth would he care more about her bathroom pipes than she did?

She caught herself smiling, troubled by the compassion she felt for a man with such obvious character flaws. Expelling a sigh, she headed out the door.

Casting her customary gaze up and down the block, she descended her front steps and started down the walkway. She looked both ways before stepping off the curb, a ridiculous habit, considering that traffic in her neighborhood was infrequent and snail-paced. She angled across the street, anxious to get this over with.

Consulting the slip of paper Devon had given her the night before, she set off. The walk would surely warm her up for battle.

She rolled her tense shoulders as she walked. Her anxiety from last night had waned, thanks to Devon's timely explanation, but she'd slept fitfully nonetheless. There was nothing like fearing for your life to knock your sleep pattern askew.

She'd been so overwhelmed with a brew of confusion and

relief, that she hadn't pursued her goal of telling Devon the details of her life. There would be plenty of time for that later. For now, she needed to proceed with her plan to sell the painting and go home. Her stomach tingled at the thought of what might lie ahead for her and Devon, both professionally and personally.

She crossed Main and went another couple of blocks before turning down a tree-lined street much like her own. All the houses around here were quaint and well-looked-after. Grace got the feeling that people here really cared about their town, and that comforted her. She'd miss this place when she returned to the bustle of the city, where you could go all week without running into anyone you knew by name.

She checked the slip of paper again, noting the house numbers as she walked. Her steps slowed as her gaze fixed on a little rectangle of a house that blushed a garish shade of pink. Seemingly embarrassed by its brash paint job, it attempted to duck behind black trim. Grace knew even before checking the address that this was the place. It was so like its owner—sickeningly sweet with dark around the edges.

She lifted the latch on the gate, swung it open, and walked up the curved path to the front stoop. With a bold and confident knock on the door, she braced herself for Sophia's pointed scowl.

Instead, the door opened to an unfamiliar masculine form. Grace pulled in her breath as she adjusted her gaze up a few inches. He was tall, with a football player physique and an air of cockiness that immediately set Grace's nerves on edge.

"Oh," she said. "Maybe I have the wrong house." She took a step back, confirming the number.

A pleasant expression masked the subtle once-over he no doubt assumed she hadn't noticed—or worse, had been flattered by. "You want to see Sophia or Devon?" He leaned a muscular arm against the door's edge. "You've got the right place." He moved back to allow her to enter.

"Oh...okay." With inexplicable discomfort, she stepped into the entryway. Who was this guy? "I'm here for Sophia. Devon told me he'd be at a meeting all morning."

"Right. A *meeting*." He pushed the door shut and gestured toward the next room. "Sophia's still in the shower, I think. She should be out any minute."

Grace nodded, taking a seat in the prim but cute living room. It was pretty much what she'd expected of Sophia.

Her makeshift host sat in a chair near the window. "I'm Ty, by the way."

"Nice to meet you, Ty. I'm Grace." She put on a polite face. "So you live here too?"

Surprised amusement flashed across his face. "Me? No. I'm actually on a road trip to Seattle. I just thought I'd swing by and see what Devon was up to. I haven't seen him since he disappeared off the face of the earth."

His words kicked her stomach. "Disappeared?"

"Yeah." He chuckled as if there was a highly entertaining story behind his comment. "That guy.... You know him very well?"

Her cheeks flushed. "Well, we've been seeing each other."

His eyebrows shot up like prices on an old-fashioned cash register. He huffed out a laugh and shook his head. "That dog."

Her heart *ka-thumped*. "I'm sorry?"

He looked at her as if he hadn't realized he'd vocalized his thought. "Forget it. I just meant I'm not surprised. You seem like his type. Some things never change."

Blood rushed to her face with such intensity that the rest of her went slightly numb. *His type?* What did *that* mean? She firmed her mouth. This guy was probably just one of those jerks who hadn't moved on past college days. The kind that never let his friends forget their foolish frat boy behavior. She couldn't let it get to her.

Glancing up, she pretended to admire a painting above Ty's chair. Where was that Sophia?

Apparently aware of her gaze, he looked at the wall behind him. "Beautiful piece."

"Hmm? Oh. Yes, isn't it?" Couldn't they just sit in silence?

"Sophia says it's by a local artist." He faced her again. "I'm an art collector, myself."

Grace tried to smile. "Really? How interesting."

He nodded pleasantly, apparently under the impression that anything he might have to say about himself would be riveting.

Just then Sophia strode into the room, her wet hair hanging straight over her shoulders. With no make-up to accent her hawk-like features, she actually looked pretty. A flash of unease gave way to a self-satisfied sneer before she spoke. "Well, what a surprise."

Grace stood. "Oh really? I thought you'd be expecting me. You did leave me a handwritten invitation, after all."

Sophia's lips pursed as her eyes landed on Ty, who sat with his ankle on one knee and his hands intertwined. Seemingly startled by the realization that he wouldn't be allowed to stay, he pushed himself to his feet. "I should...uh...get my things packed up." He stood and headed down the hall.

Grace looked at Sophia, who folded her wiry arms and glowered.

"Sophia, why—"

"You have no right to horn in." Sophia's voice sharpened.

"Horn in?" Grace nearly lost her cool. "And you have no right to threaten me. How dare you write that note? Who does that kind of thing past the age of ten?"

"I wanted to get the point across. I'm onto what you're doing. I've seen the way you flirt with him and I know exactly what you're up to."

Grace worked her jaw. So this *was* about who got the guy. "Sophia, let it go. He just isn't into you."

The fire in Sophia's eyes cooled, giving way to a look of actual pain. "How would you know?"

"He told me." A pang of sympathy cooled Grace's rage. "Don't you think it's up to him to decide who he wants?"

"Things were going really well for us." Sophia's voice came out barely above a whisper. "Until you showed up."

Grace felt for her. Devon *was* a great guy, and Sophia seemed genuinely heartbroken. "I'm sorry."

Sophia regained her composure. "It's just that men are easily swayed by...by..."

Grace raised a practiced eyebrow.

"By temptresses."

She spurted out a laugh. "Oh, is that what I am?"

"Yes, it is. There are loads of single guys around here. You should set your sights on one of them."

Grace fumed. "I'll set my sights where I choose, and there's not a thing you can do about it."

"Oh, really." Sophia's nostrils flared like a bull. She crossed to the window and reached into a basket on the floor. She picked up a magazine and held it up in front of her.

Grace's self-assurance shattered. The bold white letters before her screamed a warning like an air raid siren.

Opera Times.

"Look familiar?" Sophia's tone had lost all trace of hurt.

"What are you getting at?" Grace's voice quaked.

An evil smile spread across Sophia's gaunt face. She flipped the magazine open and turned it around, revealing a photo and article that Grace knew very well.

"I just thought you might like to find out a little more about that opera singer that Ruby thinks you look like." She turned it around again, studying the picture. Her face took on a sardonic scowl. "I do see some resemblance, although I don't know. Tracy Fontaine is so *pretty*."

Grace was livid. This little lightweight had no idea what she was dealing with. "Just tell me what you want."

"Oh, you know what I want. I want you to steer clear of my man. Leave him alone."

"Sophia—"

"If you don't, I'll tell him everything. And I mean everything." She reached for the basket, pulled out a stack of papers, and thrust them at Grace.

Slowly, Grace took the stack, then lowered herself onto the couch and started to flip through it. It was all there. Opera reviews—*Madame Butterfly* in San Francisco, *Aida* in Seattle, several from the Met. Newspaper articles about Julie's murder—the sensationalized accounts of why the police had suspected her.

She glanced up to meet Sophia's malicious glare. So she could do research. Big deal. Anybody with too much time on their hands could sit down and find this stuff.

As she flipped another page, Kirk's embittered mug shot nearly leapt out at her. Her eyes shot up again. "How did you get a copy of a police report?"

Sophia feigned nonchalance as she twirled a strand of damp hair. "I made friends with a detective. You can get anything if you're willing to pay for it."

Grace iced her with her eyes. "This isn't going to work. Go ahead and tell him. I was getting ready to do that anyway."

Sophia took a step closer to her, her look defiant. "I think you misunderstood. What I meant was..." She grabbed the police report from Grace's hands and held up the mug shot. "I'll tell *him* everything."

Grace froze. Could this woman really understand the gravity of the situation? Had she actually *read* this police report?

She met Sophia's unyielding stare for what seemed like a full minute. When she looked away, she did so with the full conviction that she had very little choice for now but to leave Devon alone.

Sophia meant what she said.

Distracted, Grace navigated the curb. What would happen to her if Kirk found her?

She crossed Main, barely conscious of the people who milled about. Her encounter a few minutes before had shaken all her anxiety back to the forefront, even worse than the previous night. Add to that her outrage that Sophia had intentionally researched her life, digging for something to hold over her. That woman was more than a nuisance—she was downright evil.

Grace shivered in spite of the morning sun. *The police report.* For all the good it had done. It had only made Kirk angrier with her. How could a man pull a woman into an alley, threaten her, stab her, and leave her for dead, then just be set free? She'd suspected Kirk had "friends" on the force, just like everywhere else. Friends tend to be awfully loyal when they're on the payroll.

Acid percolated in her throat. If given another opportunity, he would make sure she didn't walk away.

She couldn't let him find her, nor could she just let Sophia win. Devon had come to mean too much to her. Her mind raced. She'd write Devon a letter and give it to him privately. He knew how Sophia was. Once he knew the circumstances, he'd understand. When she had her money and could set up a safe situation for herself, they could get together in New York. Make a fresh start. By then, Sophia would have no power over her because Kirk would already know Tracy Fontaine was back in town.

The thought sent a shudder down her spine. What if her security plan didn't work? Her building back home had been secure. Her door had been locked. He'd gotten in anyway, and she still didn't know how. She hadn't stuck around long enough to find out. Did she really want to live with that constant fear? To never be able to walk into her home or a hotel room or even a dressing room without anxiously checking every closet and corner?

What was her alternative?

None. She had no choice.

She wrapped her arms around her middle as she approached her house. The thought of growing old all alone in Madison Falls while Devon and Sophia rode off into the sunset made her queasy. She needed an antacid.

Thankful to be home, she unlocked her door and stepped inside. As she turned the knob of the lock, she watched the bolt slide into the socket. Taking a cursory glance around the front rooms, she bounded toward the hallway. She gave the half-closed bathroom door a small shove and stopped cold.

No. She blinked quickly, a second glance confirming that this time it wasn't her imagination. A spattering of deep crimson dots lined the bathtub.

Terror drew her backward as she let out a guttural wail. Suddenly her arms were ensnared by the unyielding clasp of two powerful hands.

She screamed again.

Chapter 32

Grace fought to free herself from her assailant's grasp and spun around to face him. As her muddled mind registered recognition, she crumpled into a heap on the hardwood floor.

"Grace! Are you okay?" Sam's hands steadied her shoulders.

Recoiling from his touch, her palms found the cool floor. She quickly regained her balance and pushed herself up to her knees.

Sam released his hold on her and rose to his knees as well. His warm brown eyes fixed on her.

She lifted a shaky hand toward the bathroom. "What...happened in there?"

"It's not a big deal." His voice remained steady. "I was trying to pry the spout loose so I could replace it with a decent one. I was being a real lunkhead, using my Swiss army knife. It slipped, and I got the artery in my thumb." He held up his neatly bandaged left hand.

"Oh..." Getting her feet under her, she forced her weight onto her trembling legs.

"I called Lucy and she ran me over to the hospital." He scrambled to his feet, his gaze still set on her. "I just came back to clean up and finish the job."

Relief and rage battled in her heart for top billing. "You scared me out of my wits."

"I'm really sorry. I was in the kitchen looking for paper towels." His face broke into an uncertain smile. "By the way you screamed, you'd think you found a dead body or something."

Her breath caught in her throat. She lifted her arm toward the front door and forced her words out in measured doses. "Get...out...of my house."

Confusion mixed with concern on his face. "But—"

"Go!" She jabbed a finger in the direction of the exit.

His eyes sharpened as he raised his hands to shoulder height, palms toward her, taking a step back. "Okay, I'm going. But I'm getting Lucy to check on you, all right?" He sidestepped toward the entryway.

Emotion boiled in her veins, exploding in a lava flow of torment the second he was out the door.

Stumbling to the kitchen, she splashed cold water over her face as her sobs reverberated like a siren. Incapable of silencing them, she submitted to the long overdue emotional release.

Memories assaulted her, flashing through her mind in rapid-fire succession. San Francisco. The shock. The body nestled in the blood-splattered white of the old-fashioned tub. The parade of policemen.

She pulled herself upright as it all came pouring over her. Julie had been an opera office employee who'd offered her place while she was away on leave. *Some leave.*

Grace closed her lids to the recollection of detectives asking thinly disguised variations of the same questions until she'd gotten so worn down she couldn't make sense of her own words. No one had empathized with her vivid realization that different timing could have resulted in her own untimely demise.

Why was she reliving this nightmare?

Propping her elbows on the edge of the sink, she lifted her eyes to the backyard on the other side of the glass. If only she could go back to the time in her life before it had all gone so terribly wrong. She would make different choices, be a better judge of character. Not let things happen the way they had.

She'd made that wish more times than she could count and

things had only gotten worse. So much worse.

Straightening, she turned and took in a deep breath. She had to take things one step at a time. The first step, unfortunately, was to clean up Sam's mess. Then, she could get online and make her decision about an art dealer. There was no time to waste, especially now.

With bold resolve, she marched into the bathroom, trying not to look at the tub. Her image in the mirror caught her eye and she stopped, running a still-shaking hand through her hair. It was a safe bet that when it grew back to its natural shade it would come in pure white.

Letting out a jagged breath, she faced the bathtub. Her brow furrowed. Why had what she now saw to be just a few red drops seemed so horrifying? She shook her head as she stepped into the hallway and picked up the paper towels that Sam had apparently dropped before he'd grabbed her. She moved back into the bathroom, pulled a towel off the roll and perched on the edge of the tub. What was wrong with her? Couldn't she at least have insisted he finish this before she tossed him out?

Catching a flash of something black from the corner of her eye, she turned. Much to her annoyance, her crowbar was hooked over the inside doorknob. A breath of pure affront huffed from her throat. *The audacity*. Not only had he clearly made himself at home, going to the sun porch to get the tool, but he hadn't even bothered to put it away. The thought of him acting on a perceived familiarity with her personal space made her blood boil.

As she reached for the tool, the stabbing toll of the doorbell injected a fresh dose of adrenaline into her system. Sam must have run straight to Lucy, like he'd said he would. The last thing Grace needed right now was Lucy asking questions, however well-intentioned.

Leaving the crowbar, she hurried to the front window and heard herself gasp. It wasn't Lucy.

Her pulse quickened as she stood back from the window and deliberated. *Devon*. How could she talk to him without the risk of Sophia making good on her threat?

She wavered. Now was as good a time as any to fill him in, but she'd have to act quickly. Flinging the door open, she grabbed his arm and yanked him inside. She slammed the door and whirled on her heel. "Does Sophia know you're here?"

"No..." Surprise transformed instantly to confusion. "When I got back from my meeting, she'd gone over to her mom's." His tone grew tentative. "Ty said you and she had a cat fight. What did she say to you?"

A *cat fight?* She cringed. Leave it to a sophisticated guy like Ty to dredge up such a flattering phrase. She braced herself, fear overcoming her need to defy Sophia's brazen tactics. "Devon, we can't see each other right now."

His face blanched. "Look, whatever she told you about me—"

"It's just that..." She put her fingertips to her temples. "There's so much I have to say to you, but I'm not sure it's even safe for us to talk."

"Not safe?" He pierced her with a pleading gaze. "I know things are crazy, but I wouldn't let you be in any kind of danger. You can trust me."

His reassurance struck a chord in her. "I do. I do trust you. I was going to write you a letter, but if you're sure Sophia won't know you're here..."

"How could she?"

"Ty might say something."

"Ty took off for Seattle. Grace..." He brushed her hair from her forehead, his gentle touch causing her trepidation to melt like ice cream on a hot day. "Let's sit down and talk this out."

"Okay." As she allowed him to lead her to the sofa, her head swam. Where to begin? "Sophia has figured some things out. Things that are none of her business, but..." She glanced at him, noting that the spark of interest in his ocean-deep blue eyes was focused beyond her. Was he even listening? She turned, following his gaze to the sheet of paper she'd left on the end table.

The appraisal. How could she have been so careless?

"What is that?" He squinted toward the page.

She weighed how much she should tell him. "It's an appraisal for a piece of art I bought."

He picked up the paper, his eyes widening like exit lanes on the Jersey Turnpike. "You own a painting that's worth one point two million dollars? What is it, a Van Gogh?"

She shook her head, holding up a *wait-here* hand. Crossing to the bedroom, her stomach danced with anticipation. She wanted Devon to know.

As she reached under the bed, a sickening thought wormed its way in to defile the last. What if Sam had seen the appraisal as well? He'd helped himself to the crowbar. How did she know he hadn't poked around in her belongings while he was at it?

Pulling out the crate, she took in a decisive breath. What difference did it make? He most likely wouldn't confront her about it, not after the way she'd yelled at him. If all went as planned, there was no reason for them to even speak again. Ever.

The moment she entered the living room, Devon leapt to his feet and bounded toward her, still clutching the appraisal. He took the crate from her and set it down on the floor, then anxiously lifted the lid and brushed aside the tissue paper Grace had nested around the artwork.

"Ahh..." He smiled in amused recognition, followed by a burst of laughter. "You're kidding me. Does Roberts know?"

Her chest pinged. "I haven't told anybody." That much was true, whether he *knew* or not.

His eyes remained fixed on the painting. "I mean, I paid him what...ten bucks? How did you know it had actual value?"

Her stomach tightened. "I used to know a collector. I recognized the artist." She wrung her hands, nervously gauging how much she should reveal. "Kirk has two Blackthorns that are worth a fortune. He made a big show of telling us how much he wanted to find a third by that artist because they're so rare. He had the spot all ready on his wall. He's infatuated with opera, and Blackthorn only painted opera themes."

"So—" He chuckled. "—it's good to have friends who know these things."

"He wasn't exactly a friend." Her stomach lurched at the

thought. “He was obsessive about three things—art, opera, and me. He’s the reason I came here.”

Devon looked up from the appraisal, his eyes soft with compassion. “We all have a past.”

“True, but I came here for safety.” She braced herself. “He was stalking me.”

A visible tremor ran through him. He took her hand, his touch soothing. “Grace, that’s awful.”

She relaxed into her recollection, relieved to have his sympathetic ear. “There’s more. I haven’t been completely honest.”

He offered a comforting chuckle as he squeezed her hand. “Honesty is highly overrated.”

She smiled lightly, appreciating his attempt to diffuse the seriousness of her situation. “Maybe, but there’s a time to come clean. I’m not who you think I am.”

A hint of apprehension flashed across his face. “Oh?”

She shook her head. “No. See, I’ve been a professional opera singer for about five years now.”

He lifted a shoulder. “That’s not so surprising.”

“And I’m from New York, not Seattle.”

A look passed across his face that she couldn’t identify. “Okay. But why didn’t you tell me?”

“Because I didn’t want anybody to know who I am. I couldn’t take the chance that Kirk would find me here.”

“Kirk? That’s the stalker?”

She nodded. “He’s dangerous. And he has so much money he’ll stop at nothing.” Her eyes fell to the painting. “It’s funny really. I mean, if Kirk had found this painting, he would have offered a bazillion dollars without even blinking.”

A spark glinted in Devon’s eye. “So...he’s wealthy?”

Grace blew a laugh out of her nose. “He’s so rich, money has ceased to have a realistic value to him. It’s more important to him that he own the thing he wants—like a painting.” Her thoughts chilled. “It’s the same way he feels about me.”

Devon paused as if weighing his words. “That’s flattering—in an odd way."

"In a sick, repulsive way."

"Yes, but how many women are viewed like a work of art?"

She shuddered. "I'd really rather not be bought and sold."

A silence fell for a moment while they both gazed awkwardly at the painting.

When he spoke again, his tone was almost businesslike. "What's his last name?"

She raised a cautious brow. "Silverman. Why?"

"He's a wealthy art collector...a patron of the arts. I thought I might have heard of him." The silence stretched between them for another long moment. "So, was he your boyfriend?"

The thought sent a shiver through her. "No, not at all." The police had tried to force a confession of a personal relationship, as if they thought they could use that to justify his abuse of her. "He was just a fan. He seems to think there's something more between us, but believe me, there's not. There never was."

"But the guy was obsessed with you?"

She nodded. "It went on for close to two years." She paused, considering the importance of her next words. "He tried to kill me."

His head snapped up, a look of alarm washing over his features. "How?"

"He pulled me into an alley and stabbed me."

With a visible swallow, he reached for her other hand. "You survived."

"Yes. So far."

"And that was why you left?"

"No." Her voice quavered. "About a month or so ago, I decided I'd had enough. I had just gotten home from doing a show in South Carolina—my first since the stabbing—and when I opened the door to my apartment..." Her voice cracked under the weight of emotion. "I live in a studio, and when you open the door, you can pretty much see the entire apartment. My table was set for two, complete with candles. The bed had been stripped back to the white sheet, which was sprinkled with something that looked like red rose petals." She swallowed hard.

Devon gently drew his thumbs against the backs of her hands, his eyes intently focused on her.

"The pillow in its white case was propped up at the head of the bed. He'd written across it in what must have been red lipstick."

Concern tinged his brow. "What did he write?"

She shuddered. It felt so strange to say this out loud. "He wrote 'I never lose.'"

He let out a low whistle.

"The worst part was that he'd stuck one of my headshots to the wall over the bed using a switchblade right between my eyes."

His hands communicated support. "What did you do?"

"I turned around and ran. All I took with me was the suitcase I still had in my hand and my computer. I don't know if he was inside the apartment or if he just wanted me to discover it that way, but I didn't stick around to find out. I ran to a payphone and called this police officer who had promised to help me go into hiding. That's how I wound up here."

He took a moment to compose his words. "This might seem like a strange thing to say, but I'm glad you ran." His eyes danced. "If you hadn't, we wouldn't have met."

She smiled, consoled by his line of thinking.

"So…" He searched her face. "What are you going to do?"

She pulled her eyes from his, focusing on the painting. "My plan is to sell this and go home."

"This is just perfect, Grace." He stood, pulling her to join him. "I happen to have a friend who's an art collector—"

"Ty? I know. He mentioned that."

His eyes glowed with enthusiasm. "He has a dealer he works through. He could handle the sale for us."

Her heart fluttered. It had sounded so natural, his use of the word *us*. "But, I thought you said Ty left for Seattle."

"He did, but he'll be back home by the time I get there. If all goes according to plan, I'll be returning to New York to start *Carmen* rehearsals just as soon as *Pirates* opens. The timing will be perfect."

"Well..." A creeping uncertainty nagged. "You're sure we can trust him?"

"He's been my buddy since college. We've done some business deals together. Believe me, we can trust him." He wrapped his hands around her upper arms, instantly shifting her doubts to a lower gear.

She toyed with the front of his collar. "So, a minute ago, you said 'us.' Does that mean you see a future for you and me?"

A smile played across his lips. "I know it's a little soon, but who can argue with fate?"

"Good, because I'm starting to really..." She stopped herself just short of saying too much. "*Care* about you."

He tilted a smile that indicated he understood her meaning. "And I *care* about you too."

"I love fate." She gazed into his hypnotic baby blues. "Oh! I almost forgot." She snapped back to the ruthless reality of their situation, pushing away from him. "Sophia threatened me."

He almost laughed. "She *threatened* you? With what?"

"She found out about Kirk. She's threatened to tell him where I am, unless I stay away from 'her' man."

A smirk skipped across his handsome face. "*Her man*, huh? She has a good imagination."

"Yes, but with so much at stake, we can't afford any risk."

He smoothed her hair, bathing her with an admiring glance. "I agree. Fortunately, avoiding contact with *her man* shouldn't be too difficult."

"Yes." Relief washed over her. "You know, I really like the idea of the two of us playing it cool. I don't want the whole town talking."

"I agree." His tone soothed her. She was so lucky. "What goes on between us is nobody else's business. And I do mean *nobody*."

"I'm so glad we see eye to eye. Besides, pretty soon we'll both be back home and it won't matter. We can be free."

"Free. I can't wait." He smiled, then turned serious. "I should go." He looked down at the painting. "Why don't you let me take that and prepare it for the trip? It should be properly wrapped. I've helped Ty with that before. We wouldn't want it to get damaged."

Her stomach clenched with apprehension. Did she dare let it out of her sight?

He seemed to read her hesitation. "Of course, I understand if you don't trust me—"

"No, it's not that." She touched his arm to reassure him. "Actually, I'd love to just get this thing off my hands. I really don't know what I'm doing, and I'd be grateful for the help."

His smile conveyed his genuineness. Kneeling down, he replaced the lid, and picked up the crate as if it were a newborn. His eyes sparkled. "Don't worry a bit. It's in good hands."

She glowed as she walked him to the door. They had so much to look forward to.

Finally fate was doing her a favor.

Chapter 33

Her plan couldn't have been working out better.

Grace had bided her time for the past several weeks, playing it cool with Devon for Sophia's benefit. She'd honed her focus on the concession stand which, thanks to Salvatore, had collected a group of regulars—the *Cheers* of the Bitterroot Valley.

Today she felt breezy as she took what had become her daily afternoon stroll in to work. The July sun felt rejuvenating on her face, and she tipped her head back slightly to gain fuller exposure. She allowed a long blink, an unthought-of action when she'd been a hurried city dweller in constant fear of being followed. She must be loosening up.

Sauntering a little ways further, she caught a glimpse of herself in a shop window. Her hair had grown out a little, and looked ruffled and casual. Her make-up was minimal, much less fussy than had been her norm, and she liked it. She looked like an ordinary small-town girl.

Taking a few more steps, she caught herself. She'd neglected to make her customary cross to the other side of Main at the corner of Pine View, and was now about to pass the hardware store. What should she do? She'd intentionally avoided Sam since her unpleasant and, in retrospect, rather embarrassing freak-out over the blood that had turned out to be more smatter than splatter. At first she'd expected him to mention that he'd seen the appraisal she'd so carelessly left out. Now that nearly three weeks had passed and he'd politely stayed out of her way, it felt just plain childish to continue to ignore the elephant on the coffee table. She really should apologize.

She stepped forward, allowing a casual glance into the window, as if the arrangement of garden hoses held a particular interest. She slowed up. Where was he?

Taking a deep breath, she opened the door and stepped inside.

"Well, well." Mr. Roberts stopped whatever he was doing at a nearby shelf and walked toward her. His deeply creased eyes filled with tenderness. "Is there something I can help you with, or did you just stop in to brighten my day?"

"That's sweet of you, Mr. Roberts."

"I hear from Nancy that your snack stand has turned into the place to be seen in our little burg."

Grace smiled. "It's doing quite well. Word's gotten out that I'm opening in the afternoons, and I convinced Nancy to open the box office too. We've been talking up *Pirates*." She tipped an insinuating look. "I'm sure you've heard, opening weekend is sold-out."

A slow smile extended across his face. "I've heard, and I couldn't be more pleased. That old theatre deserves a hit."

Grace smiled too. She knew Mr. Roberts cared about the theatre. A successful show would surely sway his thinking, whatever Sam thought. She just couldn't believe Mr. Roberts would be so greedy as to let the theatre be torn down when there was a chance to save it. She opened her mouth, but he held up a hand like a New York traffic cop.

"He's in the back."

Grace's brow creased. "The back?"

His focus shifted to something behind her, and she turned to see Sam approaching from the rear of the store, a large box in his arms. His eyes held a tentativeness that increased her unease.

"Afternoon." His voice quavered as he set the box down on the floor near the front display window. "Is my dad helping you?"

"I'm busy at the moment." Mr. Roberts appeared to have assumed a sudden fascination with the Juicy Fruit display next to the cash register.

Sam tossed him a look. "I'll watch the front now, Dad, if you want to check in that shipment."

Mr. Roberts slanted a knowing nod. "I can take a hint." He waved a hand in the air. "I'll be in the back room if you need anything."

Grace turned to Sam, shifting nervously.

Clearly feeling as awkward as she did, he began removing sprinkler heads from the box and placing them on a shelf. "Heading in to work?"

Did she want to let on that she'd come in just to see him? She took a few steps, lessening the gap between them. "In a minute. I just stopped in to pick up..." Her eyes darted around. She grabbed the first item her hand touched. "One of these."

"No kidding." His face broke into a snide grin. "It's a darn good thing we keep a stock of blacksmithing guillotines on hand."

She grimaced, feeling even more juvenile than before.

His grin turned to concern as he continued to empty the box. "Are you okay?"

She twisted her mouth. "I'm fine."

"I'm glad to hear it." Removing the last sprinkler from the box, he started to rearrange them on the shelf. "Because I've been worried."

Taken aback by the sincerity in his voice, she stammered. "W...why would you be worried?"

He made no attempt to conceal his too-keen perception. "It's just that the last time we talked, you threw me out of your house, remember?"

"Oh, right." Now that he'd brought it up, it hit her that she couldn't give him the real reason for her strong reaction. Why had she opened this can of worms? "You caught me on a bad day. I try to limit my raging outbursts to one a week."

He leaned a hand on the shelf and looked at her. "Oh. Well, if you actually schedule them, remind me to check your appointment book."

"No, spontaneity is so much more effective." They shared a restrained smile. "I'm sorry, Sam."

"It's all right. It was a weird situation, I'll admit." He paused, facing her. "Can I ask you another question though?"

Her stomach buckled. Was he about to ask about the appraisal? What could she possibly say? She nodded, fearful that her voice might betray her anguish.

As he opened his mouth to speak, the bell over the door jingled, and his face dropped. Grace pivoted around just as Devon entered the store. A startled look crossed his face before turning to amusement. He took a few slow steps toward them.

"Good afternoon, Grace." He arched an eyebrow, his icy gaze shifting toward Sam. "Roberts."

Sam's demeanor remained unshaken. "What can I help you with?"

Devon assumed a professional air as he cast an uneasy glance at Grace. "Actually, I'm here to drop something off for your father." He patted his briefcase. "Is he in?"

Sam's face remained neutral while his eyes filled with disdain. "He's in the back." He reached out a hand. "But I can take it."

Devon's lips parted in protest, then he shot Grace a quick glance and appeared to reconsider. Slowly, he opened the case and stepped toward Sam, blocking her view of what he passed to him. "If he has any questions, he has my number."

Sam moved back, roughly clutching a stack of papers. "Oh yeah," he sneered. "We've got your number."

Confusion burrowed in Grace's temples. What business did Devon have with Mr. Roberts?

Devon watched as Sam retreated toward the back of the store. He turned to Grace. "Well. Fancy meeting you here."

She shifted uncomfortably, her eyes scanning the street outside. What if Sophia happened to walk by and see them together? She kept her voice low, pretending to examine the tiny bins of nails in front of her. "We haven't gotten to talk. Is the painting ready?"

Devon relaxed his stance. He pegged her with a Bob Dylan squint, the corners of his mouth lifting in mirth. "There's nothing to worry about."

Nothing to worry about? That would be unusual. She kept her concern concealed. "But what does that mean?"

"It means it's all taken care of." His nonchalance could have rivaled Gandhi. "Just relax and think about what you can do with all that money."

Her eyebrows shrugged. It wasn't like the money was going toward anything fun. Still, knowing it was coming was a relief, and Devon's efficiency reassured her.

"Everything is going according to plan." He looked around casually as he spoke. "*Pirates* opens tomorrow, then I'll be free."

"That's great." A nervous flutter reminded her that they really hadn't formed a plan for her departure. "So when—"

"In the meantime, I have things to do." He raised his voice slightly, as if to remind her that this was too public a place for them to hold this conversation.

"Yes." She twisted her fingers. "What were those papers about? Theatre business?"

His gaze shifted away, then immediately returned to her. "Yes. Theatre business." He flashed a perfect smile. "Well. See you at rehearsal."

A vague unease filled her as he walked out the door. She heaved a sigh. That annoying Sophia had really managed to postpone her developing relationship with Devon. *Oh well.* Things would be different in New York.

Alone now, she glanced at her watch. It was past time for her to start prepping for business. She'd have a line waiting for coffee if she didn't get a move on.

She turned to go, then stopped. For some reason, she felt awkward leaving without saying something to Sam. She started toward the back of the store, secure that at least now she had an excuse not to pursue their previous conversation. She'd just let him know she was going.

Treading around a case of paint stir sticks, she approached a door, aiming a knock beneath the hand-lettered word *Office*. As her fist was about to make contact, a female voice stopped her cold.

"I'm sick of it, Sam!"

Grace's breath caught in her throat. Who was in there with him?

"I'm not exactly crazy about it either." Sam's voice was hushed, forcing Grace to lean in. "What do you want me to do?"

The woman's volume pitched. "You know what needs to happen. We can't go on the way we've been."

"I just don't—"

An involuntary gasp escaped Grace's throat. The conversation came to an abrupt halt, and Grace panicked. She whirled around, intent on diving for the front door.

The office door clicked behind her. "Grace!"

Sam's voice stopped her. Could he tell she'd been listening? She turned slowly, tilting her head just enough to catch a glimpse of a woman standing in the office. It was the woman from upstairs.

He took a few steps toward Grace. "Is something wrong?"

"Wr...wrong?" She knew her voice concealed nothing, as she backed awkwardly up the aisle. "Not at all. I just have to get going."

Sam seemed unconvinced. He followed as she hurried toward the door. "Okay. Well, maybe sometime we could—"

"I just have so much work to do." She looked at him as she spoke, reaching behind her for the door handle. The bell over the door jingled, and Grace flicked her head around, facing the stony gaze of Sophia. Her heart fell. Something in the woman's accusatory stare told her she'd been right to worry about her catching her with Devon. Thank goodness she hadn't arrived five minutes sooner.

Sophia's eyes remained fixed on Grace as she spoke. "Hello Sam."

Grace looked away, flinching at the attempted superiority in Sophia's tone.

"I'll be right with you, Sophia." Sam sounded tired.

She shouldered around Grace, stepping between her and Sam.

"I'm afraid I need your help. Now."

Who exactly did she think she was, the Queen?

Grace caught the door before it shut, edging her way out. "I have to just..."

Sam reached around Sophia to grab the door, holding it open. "Aren't you forgetting something?"

She cautioned a glance. What was he talking about? "I don't..."

He raised an arm toward the wall. "Your guillotine. Would you like it gift wrapped?"

She shot him an incredulous glare. What kind of guy would joke around after she'd all but walked in on him fighting with his courtesan? She turned on her heel and stormed out.

She didn't get him, and she never would.

Chapter 34

Craning her neck, Grace searched the throng of people exiting the rehearsal. Seeing no sign of Devon, she leaned back, disappointment heaving in her chest.

She forced an attitude check. *Pirates* would finally open tomorrow, and that meant one thing—soon, she and Devon would be going home. Sophia was not going to win.

The auditorium doors swung open one more time and an excited buzz escorted a group of cast members across the lobby. Grace smiled in encouragement. Despite her previous surrender to the inevitability of the casino, a fresh hope had blossomed over the past few weeks. Since *Wait Until Dark* had closed and *Pirates* rehearsals had moved into the auditorium, the show had actually gotten really good. Sam might not know quality theatre from a hole in the ground, but his dad would have to see things differently.

Glancing at her watch, she startled at the lateness of the hour. She'd been so caught up in preparing for opening, she'd ignored the onset of fatigue. Just as she turned to survey her cookie inventory, a noise from the lobby forced her back around. Sophia stepped up to the stand and glowered at her.

Grace's nerves suddenly jolted to attention. Why was she allowing herself to be intimidated by that little minx when she'd been so careful about not letting her see her with Devon? Was there no pleasing her?

"Sophia." She injected the word with a forced pleasantness. "How are you this evening?"

Sophia's upper lip curled in a way that failed to flatter her. "Oh, *I'm* just fine."

She reached into the sky-blue Capezio bag she had flung over her shoulder and Grace leaned back, entertaining a Godfather-like image of Sophia riddling her stand with machine gun fire.

"I thought you might enjoy this." Sophia brought out not a gun but a newspaper, which Grace quickly recognized as the arts and entertainment section from the *New York Daily News*. Sophia jabbed it at her. "Hot off the presses."

"What's this?" Wanting to appear cooperative, Grace took the paper.

"Just a little reminder." Sophia readjusted the strap of her bag on her bony shoulder, aiming her body toward the door before bringing her spiteful glare around to join it. She marched out.

Perplexed, Grace slowly opened the paper, half expecting a dead fish or a horse's head to fall out. Relieved at Sophia's apparent lack of carcass creativity, she scanned each page for clues. Suddenly, there it was in front of her. A half-page spread on Kirk and his art collection complete with color photos.

She turned away, acid gurgling in her throat. So he'd been featured in the paper. That was nothing new, really. He craved the limelight, and he had friends in the press. Sophia just wanted Grace to think she was clever for spotting it. Let her have her ego boost.

Steadying herself, she snagged her sweatshirt off the counter and folded the paper inside it. No point in leaving it lying around here for everybody to see when she could so easily dispose of it at home. She tossed her purse strap over her shoulder and exited the stand, eager to get some rest. All she needed to do was make it through tomorrow and she'd be home free.

Halfway across the lobby, her ear strained toward a faint hint of music. Was a band member staying late to rehearse?

Curious, she veered toward the house. She pulled open the

door and peeked into the mostly darkened auditorium.

Shrinking back into the shadows, she held in her breath. It was Sam, sitting on the edge of the stage strumming his guitar. Good sense told her to sneak back out before he saw her, but his soft playing seemed to cement her feet in place. She paused as the gentle wave of music coated her emotions.

Her stomach clenched. In spite of her desire to flee, her eyes stayed glued to him. She eased back a step, as he played a complicated combination then tried again, making an adjustment. He scribbled on a piece of paper and returned to playing. She watched in awe, grateful for the darkness that concealed her.

As he began to sing, a whisper of excitement stirred in her. Even though she'd seen him play at church, this was a side of him she hadn't expected. He was actually a *singer*.

She leaned on the door's edge and pictured him charming an audience with his talent and good looks. As she watched and listened, her predominant impressions of him tried to crowd their way in. Outside the bar and that time at Carson's place. The woman he kept above his store. Her stomach churned at the thought. It was as if he was a different person here, creating music under the soft glow of the work lights.

Without realizing it, she started to sway with the rhythm of the music, causing the aged floorboard under her feet to let out a discordant squeal. Sam's head jolted up and a prickle charged down her neck.

"Hey." He squinted, his slight smile testing the waters. "You trying to get me back for sneaking up on you?"

She wavered. It was too late to back away, and she did want to hear more of his music. Almost against her will, her feet moved her fully into the room and the door eased shut behind her. What now? She took another small step. "That song. You're *writing* it?"

His smile grew a bit more certain as he stood. "The spirit moved me to get this one down." He braced a foot on the edge of the stage and began strumming again. "It's a little thing I do when I'm not busy selling plungers."

"It's nice." Taking a few more steps down the aisle, she

twisted her fingers together nervously. Something—gravity, maybe?—necessitated her continued movement toward him. Since the auditorium was no bigger than the ladies' lounge at Saks, she soon found herself standing just a few feet away from him. He looked down, strumming lightly and shifting in a way that indicated he felt as ill-at-ease as she did.

She glanced at the lyrics he'd written on the paper. It didn't take a genius to see that this was a love song. Her pulse spiked. Did he write it for both of his women? She sterned her look. "So, whoever you're writing it for must be very *flattered*."

He slid her a sideways glance. "I hope He is."

Her head snapped involuntarily. "You hope *he* is?" He had a complicated love life, but this unforeseen twist totally sideswiped her.

His face slid into a mischievous grin as his hand stilled the strings. "It's a song of praise. I'm writing it for Him." He pointed upward.

She pulled her eyes away with a measured blink. "Oh. Of course." Her face warmed. "You're really into this God thing, aren't you? I mean, the lyrics are so passionate." Setting her sweatshirt down on the stage, she reached for the paper with a *may-I?* look.

He tipped his head in consent. "It's worship music. That's my thing." Lowering his foot, he lifted his guitar case from behind the piano and set it on the stage.

She studied the page, noting how easily this could be misconstrued as an ode to a woman. She'd never really paid attention to the lyrics of the hymns she'd sung in choir beyond the basics of proper phrasing. "It's very soulful."

"That's a nice thing to say." He placed the instrument in the case.

She flipped over the paper and saw that he'd utilized the back of a flier for his notes.

"*Heritage Songwriting Competition*." Her eyes lifted. "So you're a songwriter?"

He took the flier, a sad smile crossing his face. "Yeah, in my dreams." He put the paper on top of his guitar and closed the case.

Confused, she tipped her head, coaxing him to meet her gaze. "But you're really good. Are you entering the competition?"

He clicked the case shut. "I thought about it." His face grew suddenly somber. "It takes a lot more than talent to make it as a singer." He held a beat, finally looking at her. "But I'm assuming you already know that."

Alarm jolted through her. "Why would you assume that?"

He cocked an eyebrow. "I heard you in church, remember? Obviously you're no stranger to performing. You don't develop a voice like yours just singing in the shower."

She wrapped her arms around her middle, pressing back her nerves. "So I sing a little. That doesn't make me a singer."

"Maybe not. But with a gift like that, it's a shame to just bring it out once a week at church."

His eyes bored into her like he was seeing her for who she really was. For a split second, she wanted to tell him, but caught herself.

"But, why not at least enter the competition? You never know."

"Look, I'm just a small-town guy who writes music for fun." He waved his hand past his cheek. "I don't want to talk about me." Suddenly, he had her gaze. "Can I ask you a question?"

She braced herself. Was he about to confront her about the appraisal? "Go ahead."

"The other day at your house..." His words were slow, considered. "Why did you get so upset?"

Her jaw clenched. She didn't want to talk about this again. "You startled me."

"I get that, but you freaked before you knew I was there. You weren't reacting to me. You were reacting to a few drops of blood."

How could she answer that? She contemplated. "It's just that...I had something really bad happen to me a few years back." She reined in her words. "And I'm still paying for it."

"Oh." Concern welled in his eyes. "I'm sorry."

"My life has been such a struggle." A slow breath steadied her nerves. "I just want it to be easy like it used to be." She perched on the rim of the stage, surprised at her ease with him.

"Life is supposed to be hard." He sat, keeping his guitar case between them. "God made it that way to build our character for eternity."

She looked up, puzzled. "If that's true, I must have enough character for six eternities."

He chuckled. "I know what you mean." He searched the dark expanse of the empty house as if a new subject might appear in the rafters. "I'm sure going to miss this old place."

She jolted. "What?"

He looked at her with questioning eyes. "You know. When they tear it down."

"But..." Her tongue felt like it had been tied in a knot. "This show is going to be really good."

"I know that—"

"And this theatre means so much to the town. Don't you think you could convince your dad to reconsider?"

"Grace, nothing has changed." He stiffened his shoulders. "It's not about how good the show is. It's not about the theatre or the community."

"Then what *is* it about?"

"It's about the *money*." His face turned hard. "I'm sorry, Grace, but that's the bottom line." He stood, picking up his guitar case with an end-of-conversation finality.

Stunned, she rose to her feet. "So I guess that makes you a hypocrite."

He lobbed her a look that said he was ready to accept her challenge. "Meaning?"

She fired back a glare. "It's just that you talk big about this God thing, but doesn't the Bible call money 'the root of all evil'?"

Anger rose in his face. "It says 'the *love* of money.' That's what God has a problem with. When people put money before Him."

"But aren't you doing exactly that, putting the money first? I mean, you could sell to someone who understands how to run a theatre, even if it meant less money for you. At least you could feel good about the deal."

Emotion pooled in his eyes as he leaned his case against the stage. "I admit that the moral part of this whole thing has me on edge."

She spurted out a terse laugh. "The 'moral' part? You don't seem to be letting that get in the way of your *other* business."

His forehead creased. "You've got a moral issue with hardware?"

Indignation swelled in her throat. "Yeah, *that's* what I'm talking about." Though her gut warned her to stop, the dam had already burst. "I *saw* you, Sam. I know what you've been doing."

His mouth formed a question that remained unvoiced as she pinned him with an accusatory stare. She knew about it all—the abuse, the woman on the side—but now was the time to hit him where it would really hurt. "Everybody needs money, but there are limits to what a person should do. What could you be thinking?"

His look of confusion grew. "Well, right now I'm thinking 'Huh?'"

She folded her arms. How could he play dumb? "I saw you at Carson's house...or *shack*...or whatever you want to call it."

He looked around as if trying to make sense of her words. "How could you have seen me? It's clear out on the old highway."

"On the way to the falls. I have eyes." She pointed to them for effect.

He shrugged his brow. "Okay, so you saw me."

"And since Lucy had told me about Carson—"

"She did?"

"And about her *friend* who's going into 'business' with that creep."

"*Her* friend..." His look registered realization. "You thought she meant *me?*"

She ignored his feigned innocence. "I know you need money. Everybody does. But there are limits to what a person should be willing to do."

"Grace..." He chuckled, fueling her anger.

"This isn't funny, Sam."

"You're right, it isn't." He curbed his amusement. "What Carson does is evil. He has to be stopped."

Chapter 35

It took all of Grace's resolve not to slap Sam. He knew Carson was evil, yet he'd been doing business with him.

She frowned. "Then why—"

"When you saw me at his place, I was talking to him about my buddy Caleb."

"Oh." She paused to process. "Who's he?"

"My best friend since we were kids." His voice softened. "He's been going down the wrong road lately. I've been doing my best to bring him back."

"You mean, you're not—"

"Dealing drugs?" He said the words as if the suggestion was ridiculous. "Absolutely not. Lucy was talking about Caleb."

"Oh..."

"Forgive me for laughing, but...drugs...me? I don't even drink."

She plunked a fist on her hip. "Oh, come on. I saw you stumbling out of the town bar with my own eyes."

He laughed. "I don't think so."

"You think I'm lying?"

"I'm not saying you're lying. I just think you're mistaken."

She had him now. "It was as plain as day. I saw a woman run out onto the sidewalk, then you stumbled after her and grabbed her. You were yelling at her too. Explain that, Mother Teresa."

Comprehension covered his face. "I know exactly what you're talking about, because I remember seeing you watching us. That was the night Caleb didn't come home and we went out looking for him. Jill was certain that he was off somewhere with Carson, and she wanted to find him. I had to convince her to go back home and let me deal with it."

"That's why you grabbed her like that, to stop her?" Righteous anger eased out of her argument like air from a pricked balloon. "So, did you find Caleb?"

"Did I ever." His face pinched, as if the memory was painful. "Remember that shiner I had a while back?"

"Carson hit you?"

"Not Carson. Caleb. He punched me right in the face. I got him to go home, though."

"Your best friend hit you? What did you do?"

He raised a shoulder. "Anger doesn't solve anything."

"No..." Determined to justify her diminishing outrage, she flipped through her mental file labeled *Sam's indiscretions*. Her eyebrows shot up. "What about that day you were on your cell phone in my backyard?"

"You mean that day I yelled at Caleb to get his act together? You're right—I kind of lost my temper that day. Sometimes he just doesn't hear me unless I yell at him. Sorry about that."

"It's...it's okay. I didn't realize the situation."

He closed his eyes, a slow smile glazing his mouth. "You know, it all makes sense now."

"What does?"

"Why you've been so cold to me."

Chagrin rattled her to her core. He was right. "I thought you were being selfish and greedy."

Anticipation twinkled in his eyes. "So, has your opinion of me changed, now that you know the truth?"

She studied him. "No. I still think you're selfish."

His eyes turned narrow. "How so?"

Did the guy really want an inventory of his shortcomings? She clasped her lower arms in front of her. "For starters, I still think it's greedy to sell out to Langley."

"Grace—"

"I mean you said yourself that there's a moral issue—"

"Yes, and—"

"You're just thinking about yourself."

"This isn't about me."

"Then who *is* it about?"

"It's about my dad." The shift in his tone was abrupt. "He has cancer."

Silence settled as her face froze in a stare. *Cancer*. Emotion welled in her throat.

Sam's voice lowered and he dodged her gaze. "He, um...he doesn't want people to know. He's sure that chemo would kill him and he doesn't want anybody to try to talk him into it."

A subtle shock consumed her. She lowered herself onto the stage edge, remembering how awful chemo had been for her own dad. Her mother had relayed every painful detail. He had suffered so much and hadn't survived long after. "What's he going to do?" Her voice felt frail.

He eased down next to her. "There's this clinic in Germany. It's unconventional, but their track record with his type of bone cancer is phenomenal."

"That's encouraging."

"Well yeah, but the cost isn't. Then there's the follow-up."

Her brain felt rattled. "He doesn't have insurance?"

"For what it's worth. Insurance won't touch alternative treatments like this."

Her heart ached. The pieces of the puzzle were all falling into place, and the picture they formed wasn't pretty. "So, those smaller offers for the theatre wouldn't be enough?"

"Not by a long shot. Lucy and Bob and Nancy and I prayed for months, and then Langley's offer came from out of nowhere. I've been asking God for confirmation that this is the right thing to do."

He looked up and caught her studying him. Her stomach knotted, but when his eyes didn't waver, her own gaze stayed strong. Her defenses abandoned her. She wanted to open up to him, to tell him she knew exactly what he was going through. She knew because she'd been through it too.

She gravitated toward him, giving in to the magnetism of his rich, mocha eyes. He leaned in as well, his countenance seeming hopeful. For a moment, everything else faded to black. All that existed in the world was Grace, Sam, and the gradually diminishing space between them.

Just as their lips were about to meet, a noise jerked them apart. They both looked toward the audience, but there was nothing there—just darkness covering empty seats, and the dim outline of the exit. They looked at each other in confirmation that the sound had been the dull thud of the door shutting.

"Must be Nancy." Sam's tone held more curiosity than concern.

Grace bit her lower lip. He was probably right. Who else would still have reason to be there?

They sat for a moment, not looking at each other, but letting the reality of what had passed between them simmer. What was she doing? Sam was involved with someone else, and that just wasn't right.

When he finally spoke, his voice was soft. "I know you think it's a mistake."

A mistake? She drew in a sobering breath. Did *he* think it was a mistake? "Sam—"

"Please just listen." His look beseeched understanding. "My dad deserves a chance."

His dad? Grace could practically hear her mental gears shifting. Of course. *That* mistake.

An edge of desperation crept into his voice. "I just don't see any other way."

Her mind raced. There *was* another way. She was the one who'd been selfish. An image of her own dad the last time she saw him took center stage in her head. What she wouldn't have given for the chance to help him. She looked into Sam's eyes and firmed her resolve.

"Sam." She touched his bicep. "I have to tell you something."

A glimmer of expectation twinkled as he looked at her. "What is it?"

She let out a long breath. "I think I know of a way that—"

The door at the back of the house whooshed open and Devon's prominent form appeared backlit by the muted light. Tension thickened the air like smoke as Grace let her hand slip from Sam's arm.

"Grace." Devon's voice was firm but strained. "I don't suppose you've seen *Sophia*."

Puzzled by the question, she shook her head.

Devon stepped fully into the auditorium, allowing the door to ease shut behind him. "No, I didn't think so."

Grace stood and Sam followed her lead. Devon strode slowly down the aisle, his eyes fixed pointedly on Sam.

Grace looked from one to the other, feeling like she'd stumbled onto the set of *High Noon*. She stepped between them, forcing a casual tone. "We were just talking about the theatre."

Keeping his eyes on Sam, Devon stopped by Grace's side. "Don't let me interrupt." He placed his arm firmly around her shoulders, turning her so that they both faced the stage.

She wanted to pull away, her attraction to Devon suddenly diluted. Whatever the problem was between these two, she couldn't let Devon blow their cover. What if Sophia walked in? "Devon, I—"

"You're kidding me." Sam stared at them, his voice rumbling like distant thunder.

Devon remained cool, resisting Grace's subtle attempt to remove herself from his grasp. "Too bad for you, Roberts. Some guys have all the luck."

Sam's eyes widened with controlled rage. "Grace, do you even know what this guy is like? He's the one who—"

"Watch it, Roberts." Devon took a step toward him, his arm trailing off Grace's shoulder.

"No, I'm sick of keeping this quiet. She needs to know." Sam looked at her, his eyes earnest. "He's behind this whole casino thing. He's the one who's orchestrating it."

Grace's breath left her. She looked to Devon for some sort of denial.

His eyes shot fire at Sam, but his voice remained steady and controlled. "Don't blow this, Roberts. Your dad needs this deal."

Sam stared, a tightness forming around his eyes and mouth.

Devon smiled slightly. "I think you'd better leave before anything unfortunate happens."

Grace interceded. "Devon—"

"I'm thinking about you, Grace." His gaze on Sam stayed firm, as if looking away would signal defeat.

Sam shook his head, then looked at Grace with something that resembled pity. After reaching back to grab his guitar case, he retreated up the aisle and out the door.

The second Sam was gone, Devon turned to her. "I'm so sorry you had to witness that."

Her words exploded in a fireball of rage. "Is it true? You're in charge of this casino fiasco? *That's* your 'deal'?"

He nodded almost imperceptibly. "Grace, hear me out, please. Mr. Roberts is sick. He needs money for his treatment and this is his only chance. You think this land is worth anything near what Langley's offering? He's being very generous."

"But what does this have to do with you? You're a director."

"I'm a businessman. You know how it is with the arts. You need to develop other skills to keep yourself afloat at times."

Her head swam. "So you do what? Work out deals for real estate developers?"

"Exactly. They tell me what they need and I scout out locations. When the deal closes, I get a finder's fee."

She pushed him away. "And you don't care what the casino's going to do to the integrity of this town?"

"I think you're overreacting. People might be upset at first, but it's going to do wonders for the economy here. Pretty soon they'll be happy about it."

Her gut ached at the memory of her own version of that ugly thought. "Maybe, but why didn't you tell me?"

"I wanted to wait till the time was right. Mr. Roberts and I agreed to keep it under wraps for the sake of all concerned. It's not like I lied to you. I just didn't give you all the details."

"And now I'm supposed to trust you?"

"Grace. I hate to point this out, but aren't you the one who lied in the beginning?"

Her voice caught. "That was for a justifiable reason."

"Yes. And I still trust *you*. Please tell me you can give me the same benefit of the doubt."

She wanted with all her heart to accept what he was saying. He was right. She had lied to him and he hadn't even blinked when she'd come clean. Why couldn't she be as understanding with him?

She clutched her lower arms to her belly. "I'm just not sure..."

He moved closer, his eyes softening into that expression that siphoned away all her will power. "Things are happening just the way we've planned." He reached out, catching her wrists and pulling her toward him. "I got the job."

Her eyes met him in a moment of confirmation. He'd gotten the job. Was he telling her she'd gotten the job as well?

A coy smile pried at his lips. "You'll make a lovely Carmen."

She could hardly believe it. Not only would she be returning to New York, but she'd be launching a new phase of her career. It was almost too much to believe. Letting loose a laugh, she threw her arms around him. "I don't know how to thank you!"

"You already have." Easing back from their embrace, he clasped her upper arms. "From now on, just roll with the flow."

Her doubts melted. What had she gotten so upset about? The casino was going to be a reality, she had to accept that. To Devon it was purely a business deal, and it wasn't fair for her to expect him to see it any other way. He was enterprising, an admirable quality in any man.

Looking into his eyes, she knew she'd behaved rashly with Sam. It was better for everyone if she kept her focus where it belonged—on her singing and on romantic prospects who were available and appropriate. Anything else was just an invitation for trouble, and she didn't need any more of that.

"So…" His tone was efficient and upbeat. "If all goes well, I'll be ready to leave for New York the day after tomorrow, right after Roberts and his lawyer sign the papers."

Her heart pinged against her chest. "That soon? I have so much to do." There was packing, and getting the house ready to rent. Pushing their plans forward would necessitate hiring and training her replacement at the theatre.

Devon held up a palm. "Don't worry. You should have at least a couple of weeks."

Her brow furrowed. "But, you said we'd be leaving the day after tomorrow."

"You misunderstood." The back of his hand grazed her cheek as his eyes betrayed a slight discomfort. "I meant me. I want you to stay here until we have the money to set things up right. I want you to feel safe."

Her heart fell to her shoes. This wasn't how she had planned it. She had envisioned taking the painting herself, not sending it with Devon.

"It's really for the best this way." Devon's voice soothed.

"But, won't I be needed for rehearsals?"

His voice remained steady, confident. "I'll have them overnight the music to you. You've got weeks before you'll be needed for blocking."

Something felt unsettling to her, but she couldn't say what. "Okay. But—"

"Don't worry." He rubbed her arms. "Life is going to be amazing. I can't wait to get away from this Podunk place."

Curiously, his condemnation of the town stung. Hadn't he once expressed a fondness for Madison Falls?

She pulled back from him, sorting through everything that had transpired in the last few minutes. Her fists clamped together. If she had gained anything from her experience with Kirk, it was the ability to recognize her own intuition. Something here wasn't right.

His face was difficult to read, but his voice quivered with impatience. "Grace, what's wrong?"

"I'm not sure." She frowned. Thinking straight was impossible in such close proximity to him. She pivoted, paced a few steps up the aisle, then turned and gave him a long look. "I trust you, Devon, but I need you to trust me with just one thing."

"What's that?" His eyes entreated.

She pulled in a deep, strengthening breath. "When you go, it will be without my painting." She firmed her stance. "I want you to give it back to me."

Chapter 36

Grace bit down hard on her upper lip. Her hand flew to her face and she quickly checked her fingertips. Relieved that she hadn't drawn blood, she scoffed at her own negligence. Thinking about Kirk always did that to her.

She scanned the roomful of opening night revelers. From her position behind the concession counter she could see most of the lobby, but no Devon. He still hadn't given her the painting, but she couldn't exactly go hunting for him, not with Sophia lurking.

Perusing the room again, she couldn't help but wonder if Sam would make an appearance. That moment they had shared the night before had been a mistake—that was painfully clear. He had a girlfriend after all, and Grace was...well...leaving soon.

She rearranged the cookies on the platter in front of her, thinking again how timely Devon's entrance had been. What if she had promised Sam the money before realizing the full implications? She had been moments away from causing the downfall of Devon's deal. She hated to think it, but would that have cost her the role of a lifetime?

Laughter and music permeated the cheerful space, and she tried to ignore the image of a wrecking ball swinging through the window. She forced back the ache in her throat that had been fighting for her attention all day, reminding her that the money from the painting could still save the theatre. Her gaze drifted to the ceiling. How could she possibly make this decision on her own?

Smiling mechanically, she handed a cookie and a soda to a patron and scooped up the change he'd plopped on the counter. She pondered. If Mr. Roberts needed the full million that the sale of the buildings would provide, would half the proceeds from the painting even make a difference for him?

She opened the till. Not only that, but she still had herself to think about. Would a mere half a million provide for her own protection? Having no idea how long the Kirk threat might continue, she had to assume that her need would be ongoing. What if his obsession never let up? She might need a bodyguard for the rest of her life.

Massaging the back of her neck, she turned to survey the concession stand mess. On top of everything else, Salvatore had started spurting out coffee grounds near the end of intermission and she had no idea why.

Now, standing amid the post-show clutter, she folded her arms and surveyed the large silver cylinder that stood next to her beloved machine. Hank had come to her rescue, toting the urn from the green room to act as coffee understudy. Crinkling her nose, she inhaled the pungent odor that had worried her at first, until Hank had assured her that was normal for such an old appliance.

She glanced at the heavy rope-like cord that stuck out its backside like a frayed tail and wound its way down the counter and to the outlet in the lobby. This machine looked old enough to have served at JFK's memorial, or at least its local equivalent.

"Grace."

Snapping around, she looked into the eyes that brought out a reluctant yearning for a grande mocha. "Sam." She gulped, frantically swabbing the counter between them.

He looked down at her hands as if resisting the urge to reach out and still them. His words were slow and guarded. "Can we talk?"

"Uh...sure." A wave of apprehension passed through her as she navigated a small mound of crumbs into her hand. He was the last person she wanted to talk to right now.

"It's probably none of my business." His delivery seemed carefully rehearsed. "But last night, you..." He wrinkled his nose like a rabbit. "What's that smell?"

Grace sniffed the air. "I don't know. What's it smell like?"

His features contorted. "Burnt coffee and chemistry class."

Grace patted the top of the coffee urn. "Sal's on the fritz."

"Oh." He sounded concerned, like they were discussing an old friend. "What's wrong with him?"

"I don't know." Grace said. "He just started spitting out coffee grounds."

"You want me to take a look?" He gazed past her, as if already developing a diagnosis. "I can probably fix him."

"Oh..." Of course he could. He could fix anything. "That would really help. Thanks." She pressed against the side of the stand to make way for him.

Taking his Swiss army knife from his pocket, he started to remove Sal's side. "Anyway, I've been thinking about it, and—"

"There you are." Lucy popped into view, with Bob close behind. "We're heading home." Her eyes darted to Sam, then back to Grace. "I don't suppose you'd like to walk with us."

"Oh, no thanks." Grace watched as Lucy and Bob shared a look. A blush crept down her neck for no logical reason. "I mean, I have my car right out front."

Lucy gave her a smile that implied a shared secret. She hooked her arm into Bob's and they strolled away like a pair of college kids on a date. Envious of the air of romance that seemed to hover over them wherever they went, Grace trailed them with her gaze.

She let out a sigh as she contemplated Sam, whose frowning focus was on the now partially degutted Salvatore. *What was it about him?*

He glanced over to where Lucy and Bob had been, then sent a look her way. "So, I was trying to say that..." He stopped himself, catching her studying him.

As their eyes met, her heart rolled over in her chest. His face held such intensity that she felt her breath being pulled from her lungs. She retracted her gaze. If she allowed herself to get trapped in the vortex of his eyes, she might say something she'd later regret.

"It's about Devon." His voice was low and somber.

She shot him a look. *Devon.* Of course.

Suddenly, a pair of giggly women stepped up to the stand. Grace turned, gawking in recognition. What was Sam's hardware store hussy doing with his girlfriend?

Looking more glamorous than she had in her bathrobe, the tall attractive blonde lit up like a Christmas tree when she saw Sam. "Hey, there's our boy."

Grace turned a dumbfounded glare on him, expecting a reaction that conveyed the appropriate horror of the situation. Instead, he gave up a tight-lipped smile and turned his attention back to his repair job. *Talk about a poker face.*

Grace scoffed. A mighty casual response for a guy facing the allegiance of his apparent paramour with his partner.

"Sam!" Jill, a petite brown-haired girl-next-door, leaned in to claim his attention. "Aren't you going to introduce us?" She tipped her head toward Grace.

Sam looked up as if he'd been caught unawares. "Oh, sorry." He turned his body just enough to gesture to each woman in accord with her name. "Grace, this is Jill and Colleen."

Grace stammered out a greeting that utilized no recognizable words. Didn't these women know about each other?

The blonde—*Colleen*—smiled warmly. "Nice to finally meet you, Grace." She shifted her focus back to Sam. "We're taking the party across the street." Her nod indicated either her apartment or the bar. "I'd invite you, but we're having girl talk."

"Yeah, it's really not his style." Jill gave Colleen a friendly nudge.

Grace frowned. Colleen deserved a punch, not a prod. Jill had every reason to hate her, and they were sharing girl talk?

Guilt pierced the pit of her stomach. She had seriously

considered kissing Sam. Jill should hate *her* too. Grace's eyes washed over the poor girl, as she fought the urge to grovel for forgiveness.

Suddenly self-conscious, she considered beating a hasty retreat. Just as she was about to excuse herself, Sophia entered her line of sight. She looked vixen-like in a slim cream skirt and ruffled pink blouse. Like a cupcake with all the sugar left out. She scanned the room as if she were looking for someone in the thinning crowd. Devon, no doubt.

Grace's face must have registered her disdain, as first Colleen then Jill turned to follow her gaze. Sophia's eyes shot Grace a quiver of poison arrows before she stormed out the front door, decidedly Devon-less.

"She has *got* to learn to lighten up." Jill said good-naturedly.

Colleen furrowed her brow. "Give her a break. Unrequited love does things to a girl."

Grace startled. Colleen knew about Sophia and Devon?

"Cole, be nice." Sam gave her a warning glance.

"Oh, Sammy." Reaching over the counter, Colleen lightly backhanded his arm. "It's all in good fun. Just because you're all work and no play—"

"And a very dull boy." Jill lightheartedly pursed her lips.

Sam jerked a glance over his shoulder toward Grace. "You see what I have to put up with."

Put up with? Her fists clenched.

"You love it." Colleen's tone remained playful. "Where would you be without the two of us?"

Sam squirmed. "Look, you two, if you don't mind, we were just..." He motioned toward Grace.

"Oh!" Colleen's face lit with instant comprehension. "We're totally interrupting."

After a swift but friendly valediction, the two departed, leaving Grace feeling as if she'd stepped into either *The Twilight Zone* or a Pinter play.

"Sorry about that." Sam tipped his head toward the departing women, his back still to Grace.

She gave him a long, hard stare. What kind of man played two friends against each other? To make matters worse, he was clearly willing to involve her in this too. Did he think she was an idiot? She hauled off and cuffed his bicep, trying not to notice how firm it felt against her palm.

"Ow!" He grabbed his arm and pivoted around. "Why'd you hit me?"

Feeling like her mental filing cabinet had been ransacked, she lifted her hands to her temples. Where to begin? "So, Colleen lives above your store?"

His look begged her to get to the point. "Uh...yeah."

"And Jill. She knows about that?"

"Knows?" His brow furrowed. "It's not exactly a secret."

Not a secret? The need for comprehension seized her mind. "Colleen seemed so upset."

"Upset?" *Mr. Innocent*. "When?"

"Yesterday. It sounded like you were fighting."

His brow creased, then understanding dawned. "Oh, yeah. We were." His eyes rolled to the side. "I appreciate your concern."

Her *concern?* Sure she was concerned that he was a rotten two-timer. Strange that Jill didn't seem to share her concern.

He returned his attention to Salvatore. "We fight all the time. Mostly about Dad."

His last sentence caught her by surprise. "So, she's concerned about your dad."

"To put it mildly. She thinks he should do the chemo. The last thing he needs is for her to be yelling at him that he's crazy for wanting to do this other treatment."

Grace bristled, mystified and disturbed by the casual inclusion of this woman in his personal life. "Why is she so involved?"

His brow furrowed. "She really misses Mom. When you've lost one parent, you kind of cling to the other one."

Grace swallowed a gasp as his meaning became clear. Colleen was his *sister?* He wasn't a rotten two-timer. He wasn't a hypocrite. Her jaw dropped like a backdrop during a scene change. He'd stripped away her last reason not to trust him.

"Of course"—he went on, apparently oblivious to her recent revelation—"it doesn't help that she blames me."

"Blames you?" Her voice was barely a squeak. Suddenly everything started to make sense. "For your mom?"

"That, and she thinks it's my fault Dad won't do chemo. Plus she's totally against selling the theatre to Langley. That's why she was acting so crazy tonight. 'Moving the party across the street.' She thinks the casino's going to ruin the town."

The tingle of guilt returned. What had Glo said about storing up your riches in heaven? "I hope she's wrong."

"Yeah, well." Turning his back once again, he began suturing up Sal's side. "Sorry for the mess. I thought I could fix the problem myself, but no such luck."

Funny. She could say the same. "Sam, I—"

"I'd like to take him over to my shop." His voice was strained. "If that's all right."

"Oh, sure." She waved a hand. Sal was the least of her concerns at the moment. "Sam, I...I'm so sorry."

He tipped her a bemused grin. "You are?"

"Yes. You were right."

"Okay. About what?"

"You said God uses everything for good. Even your mom's death."

"I'm not quite following."

What was she trying to say? The harsh memory of her near-death in the alley assaulted her mind. What would have become of her if she'd died? "You told me that story to help me understand about salvation, and..." She straightened, looking him in the eye.

The most important question of her life waited in the wings. She had to be sure.

Chapter 37

"Will you pray with me?" Grace's question came out on a near-whisper.

A tentative smile found Sam's mouth. "You're serious?"

"I'm serious." She nodded. "Show me the way."

He took her hands. "Just repeat the words I say and ask Jesus into your heart."

She closed her eyes and listened to the gentle cadence of his voice as he led her in prayer asking Jesus to be her Savior. Something moved through her—something even more powerful than the rush of filling an opera house with her voice. Whatever it was filled her soul, and she knew she'd never be the same.

When she opened her eyes, she realized that tears were streaming down her cheeks. She looked up at Sam, whose broad grin had taken over his entire face. He enclosed her in a warm hug, and she willingly wrapped her arms around his waist.

"Congratulations on your new life."

She felt light, like a burden had been lifted. "*New life*." To think she'd been fighting all this time to return to her old one.

He pulled back, maintaining his grip on her upper arms, and looked into her eyes. His face turned serious and for a moment, she was unsure what he was going to do. Suddenly, he let out a holler that could have carried to the upper balcony of the Met, lifting her off the floor and spinning her out of the stand.

She let loose with an operatic laugh. He set her down and she caught onto his upper arms to regain her balance.

"I have to admit, I've been praying for you since..." His eyes grew large as something behind her caught his attention.

Turning, she followed his gaze to the lobby, which was now completely vacant except for an indignant-looking Devon. He held the crate in front of him.

"Well." His sarcastic tone cut through the quiet room. "This is a cozy scene."

Grace jumped out of Sam's arms. Why did her timing have to be so off?

"Terrific." Sam's countenance of joy had been replaced by a look of pure primal challenge.

"Calm down, Roberts." Devon's air of affront evaporated into impatience. "I'm here to see the lady."

Jaw firming, Sam nodded. His eyes grazed over the crate. "I didn't exactly think you were here to see me."

Devon shook his head. "No. That appointment can wait until morning."

Grace's heart filled. Mr. Roberts was signing away the theatre in the morning. If the money from the painting was going to make a difference, she'd have to tell Sam about it tonight. Whatever it was that had filled her soul now filled her with the courage of her conviction.

"Thanks for bringing the painting." She looked at the crate. "Because I have to tell Sam about it."

Devon's face blanched white as a diva's petticoat. "What do you mean 'tell him'?"

Her heart threatened to pound a dent in her ribcage. "I decided to give him half the money. I know I should have told you first, but—"

"What…?" Devon's eyes flared. "The million they're getting for this place isn't enough?"

"Whoa." Sam waved his arm like a referee. "What's going on here?"

Devon's eyes flashed an icy warning at Grace. In one awful second she realized she had to risk everything—the safety afforded by the money, the career-changing role, even the possibility of love—all because it was the right thing to do. She looked into Sam's questioning eyes and took a deep breath.

"Sam." She firmed her resolve. "Remember that painting I bought from you?"

His look grew more confused. "What about it?"

"Well, it's worth more than you realized."

"Yeah?" A hopeful glint flashed across his face. "How much more?"

She pulled in a wince. "About one point two million more." Swallowing hard, she allowed that to sink in.

His eyebrows lifted as he looked at the crate, then back at Grace. "Wait a minute. You're telling me that the painting—the one that hung on that wall over there since who knows when—is worth over a million bucks?"

Grace nodded, a smile tugging at her lips. "I have the paperwork to prove it."

He cautioned a chuckle. "So what exactly are you telling me?"

She turned slightly in an attempt to block out Devon's disapproving glower. "I'm telling you that your dad can afford to take one of those lower offers for the theatre because I'm going to give you half the proceeds from the painting."

His jaw dropped as a tentative laugh escaped his lips. "You're not kidding?"

She shook her head. He grabbed her again, this time pulling her into a serious bear hug. When he drew back, Devon held out a hand to him.

"Congratulations, Roberts."

Sam looked at his hand a moment before accepting his shake. "You seem awfully calm for a guy who just wasted two months on a deal that's not going to pan out."

Devon shrugged. "Deals sometimes fall through. Besides—" He scanned Grace from head to toe, skillfully lingering at certain points. "—it's not like my time here has been wasted. I've had a lot of fun."

Sam's jaw firmed and his center of gravity seemed to shift as if he was fighting the urge to lunge. He regained his composure, and huffed out a laugh. "So, Sinclair. You're leaving tomorrow. Can't say I'll be sad to see you go."

A potpourri of emotions fought for Grace's attention. What was with these guys? Devon was willing to take the high road. Couldn't Sam just get over it?

Sam turned to Grace, his stern expression melting slightly. "I'm going to grab Sal and head home to tell my dad." He turned his eyes on Devon while still speaking to Grace. "Will you be okay?"

She startled at his question. Why wouldn't she be? Her head bobbed in reassurance.

"Good." His eyes lit on the crate, which Devon still held tightly. "Did you want me to carry that to your car for you?"

Devon blazed him with a glare, and Grace reached for the crate.

"No," she said, taking it from Devon and turning toward the stand. "I'll just put it in here till I'm ready to leave."

Sam stepped in front of her and grabbed the crate, his hands lingering on her arms as he met and held her gaze.

Devon reached for Grace's upper arm. "That's all wrapped for shipping."

The sharpness of his tone took her by surprise. "Great, but I'm not shipping it. It's going with me." She released her hold on the crate, allowing Sam to take it.

"Even so..." His grasp on her arm still tight, Devon shot fire at Sam. "I followed Ty's exact specs for protecting it—sealing up the crate. He really knows what he's doing when it comes to art. It would be a shame if you damaged it before it gets to the dealer."

She nodded, perplexed by his insistence. "Got it."

Sam's eyes fixed on Devon's claw-like grip on Grace's arm. Devon released his hold, and Sam took the crate into the stand.

Grace sighed, her eyes lingering on Devon. He seemed to avoid her gaze.

In a moment, Sam emerged from the stand, having exchanged the crate for Salvatore. He gave Grace a concerned look. "You're sure you'll be okay?"

She nodded. Why did he keep asking her that?

After a disapproving nod toward Devon, Sam headed out the front of the theatre.

Wanting to avoid an argument, she floundered for an explanation that Devon would accept. "It only seemed right to share the profit, considering—"

"Yes, of course." He let out a caustic chortle. "I can't think of a more fitting gesture."

Her mouth froze around her rambling justification, leaving her speechless. She didn't have to convince him. He actually seemed to like the idea.

Devon sounded almost giddy. "I love the poetic justice."

"You're not upset about the casino?"

He tipped a casual shrug. "So my deal falls through." He chuckled as he reached for her hands. "What's fifty thousand dollars compared to..." He cut short his thought. "I mean, it's only money."

She raised her brow. "Langley was going to pay you fifty thousand dollars?"

He shrugged. "As finder's fees go, that's pretty modest." He smiled slyly. "I've seen better, believe me." He glanced out the window. "I really should go."

She jolted. Did he think Sophia might see them together? "You're still leaving in the morning?"

"I need to get back."

"Okay. But—"

The sound of Nancy's office door opening jarred them apart. Devon's face became instantly businesslike. "Grace, it's been a pleasure." He turned toward the hallway, holding out a hand to the now-approaching Nancy. "Good luck with the run."

Nancy accepted his shake. "Mr. Sinclair. Thank you for everything."

"The pleasure"—he slid Grace a meaningful glance—"has

been entirely mine."

He nodded farewell to them both and slipped out the front door.

Grace felt as if the wind had been knocked out of her. How could he leave so abruptly?

"You about done?" Nancy sounded spent.

"What?" Grace tried to bridle her focus. "Oh, almost."

"I'm too tired to wait. Mind locking up?"

Grace nodded, her smile vague. Devon's hasty departure must have been a show for Nancy's sake. Surely he wouldn't leave town without a real goodbye. Maybe he'd be waiting for her at her house when she got there.

"So…" Nancy had worked her way toward the door. "I'll get the main switch. Just leave the lamp in the window on so you can see to get out. And would you unplug that old coffee contraption? I don't trust it."

Grace agreed as she headed for her stand. She'd finish quickly and hurry home.

She tried to shrug off her doubt. Fifty thousand dollars was a lot to lose, but Devon hadn't been mad at all about the deal falling through. It would be just fine.

She grabbed a wet towel and finished wiping down the counter. Renting out her house should be easy. She'd call Spritz in the morning. Now that it looked like the theatre would be staying open, she'd happily donate Salvatore and train her replacement.

The important thing was that she had the painting back. She smiled to herself. If she planned carefully, she could find a safe place to live in New York before Kirk got wind of her re-emergence.

Tossing the towel onto the counter, she looked around the clean-enough stand and flicked off the light with a satisfied smile. Soon she'd be going home, even if it was to some high-security version of her real life.

She threw her purse over her shoulder and sighed. She'd managed to help Sam, but she still had concerns about him. She shrugged. That was none of her business. There was only so much that money could fix.

Suddenly, a screeching noise pulled her right out of her skin. She reeled around, her eyes darting to the ceiling in recognition of that frightening sound.

There was no doubt about it. It was the smoke alarm.

Chapter 38

***S**moke.*

The lobby air grew murky in the split second it took Grace to propel herself toward the front door. Her mind raced as she clutched her purse and reached for the doorknob. Then a terrible thought forced her abrupt halt. *The painting*.

Whirling around, she saw bright orange flames lapping at the wall between her stand and the box office. *The cord.* Why hadn't she unplugged it?

Fear surged through her veins. Precious moments were wasting in indecision. She had no choice. She had to go back.

Taking a deep breath, she bolted in the direction of the stand, unable to see clearly through the thickening air. Eyes burning, her fingers frantically felt the doorframe and the counter beyond. Her mind raced. Where had Sam put it? Panic propelled her to feel her way along the wall.

Something bumped against her abdomen as a rough surface scraped her palms. *The crate!* She grabbed at its rough corners, rotating around and thanking God for her luck. Struggling to see through the dark haze, she loped forward. In spite of the diffused lamplight penetrating the smoke, she could barely see through her slit-open eyes. She reached out a hand and felt for the doorframe.

The moment her fingers touched its edge, an orange flame

blazed up from out of nowhere, igniting the edge of the crate. She shrieked, tossing the enkindled object away from her and stumbling backward.

What had she done? She surged forward, intent on rescuing the painting, but flames illuminated its distinct shape as the wood flared up like a bonfire. Her hope for the future was going up in smoke.

Distraught and disoriented, she allowed the blazing heat to drive her back into the stand. The flames overtook the lobby, blocking her way to the exit. There was no way out.

Hot smoke seeped into her lungs. Thinking fast, she grabbed for both halves of her door, slamming herself into the stand and shutting out all light but the pinstripe of orange that outlined the doorway.

Drowsiness encasing her, she hit the floor, nearly overcome with the pungent air. Through slit eyes, she caught sight of something hanging off the edge of the counter and thrashed for it. She fingered soft wet fabric and silently thanked herself for ignoring her own instructions about hanging up the wet bar towels. As quickly as she could, she shoved the towel into the space under the door, slowing the rush of smoke. That bought her some time, but now what?

Heaving herself to her knees, she felt something weighing against her leg. Her purse. Her *phone!* Why hadn't she thought of that sooner?

She touched the familiar softness of leather and plunged to the breathing space near the floor. Sputtering for breath, she pawed at the pocket she had opened a million times but now struggled with. At last the snap gave way, and she fumbled with the phone. Something was wrong. There was no comforting blue glow. It was dead.

No! She always kept her phone charged. Why now? Terror surged in her throat as she sat up, trying to revive the plastic promise of hope to no avail. Gasping, she fell back, her head hitting the rough wood of the floor. Soot filled her mouth like a bellows, but a gut-wrenching cough did little to clear her passages.

Desperation and lack of oxygen swamped her judgment. What if no one noticed the building was on fire? She let out a voiceless moan, feeling herself slip out of consciousness. Her eyes burned and she lidded them to a fast-forward version of her life.

A picture flashed in her woozy mind. A similar moment in her recent past when she had lain in an alley, blood oozing from her abdomen where Kirk had plunged a switchblade. She had all but blocked out that horrible moment when she'd felt life leaving her, but now a critical detail came to mind. She had drawn on some hidden source of strength and had managed to pull herself to the street where people had finally helped her. Where had that strength come from?

In a wisp of memory, it came to her. She had, for the first time in years, cried out to God. It had helped her then.

Her voice failing her, she silently pleaded. *Help me, God. Help me now.*

She sputtered, struggling for air that seemed to come a little easier. She forced the thickness into her lungs.

As if beyond her will, her lids peeled open. The heaviness in the room burned her nose and eyes, but an unfamiliar calmness gave her clarity. As she studied the floor in front of her face, a narrow strip of dim light caught her attention. She reached out a weak hand to touch it, and the wall above the light seemed to give just a little.

The door.

She'd paid such minimal attention to the passage from her stand into the rehearsal space that, like Nancy, she had forgotten it existed. Now, its discovery breathed fresh life into her.

With tremendous effort, she raised her leaden body.

Keeping her head close to the floor, she flung her hand upward, fumbling for the doorknob. Her hand enclosed the orb, which had already absorbed heat like a branding iron. She forced her hand to twist before pulling it away. *Locked.*

A wail of frustration sat tacit in her lungs. *God, please.*

Then she remembered. The drawer. That old key ring.

With the determination of a swimmer about to take the gold,

she filled her lungs with air and pushed herself to her knees. She felt for the handle and gave it a too-forceful yank, sending the drawer and its contents plummeting. *No*. She groped across the expanse of floor, causing twist spoons to go clanging across the room.

Falling forward, she struggled for breath, giving in to the need to melt like butter on the floor. As she did so, her hand touched something metal. A spoon. Moving her fingers ever so slightly, she felt the shape of something familiar. Not a spoon. A key.

She flailed, finding the ring with flaccid fingers. So many keys. Would any of them fit this door? She forced herself up to her knees, fumbling. A jingling noise. She pulled the edge of her sleeve over her hand and felt for the doorknob, struggling to separate one key from the others on the ring. There were too many of them. She didn't have time or strength to guess wrong.

The tip of the first key found the keyhole, but refused to go further. She felt for the next one along the ring and prayed for a miracle. Touching the hole in the door, she held up the tip of metal, and pushed. It went in.

Sputtering a laugh, she turned the key and pushed open the door. She fell onto the landing and went no further. Where was her strength?

Smoke filled her nose, and darkness overtook her.

In the next instant, she was vaguely aware of strong hands grabbing her shoulders and pulling her upward.

"Come on, stand up!"

A familiar voice. Her groggy mind failed to identify it. She got to her knees, then, with help, to her feet. Someone had their arms draped around her, forcing her to hobble. Her knees gave a little. Steps...that's right...from the landing. Clumsily, she navigated her way down. A vague light. The windows...the outside door.

A rush of fresh air filled her lungs, and her legs dragged her as far as they could. A scuttle of noise...shouting. She collapsed onto hard pavement.

"Breathe, breathe!" A voice from somewhere above her commanded.

Flat on her back, she coughed uncontrollably. A siren wailed amid frantic shouts. She looked up into a face, its features still unclear. She forced herself to focus.

Directly above her was a pair of piercing eyes. She knew them well.

Those eyes belonged to Kirk.

Chapter 39

"I love you, Tracy!" Kirk screeched at the top of his voice. "I love you! Don't you get that? Why are you doing this to us?"

He pounded a palm on the steering wheel of her Beetle before gripping it again with a maniacal fierceness. His other hand clenched the handle of a switchblade, which he pointed in her direction. She stared at it—a grim reminder of their last encounter.

She lifted her eyes, momentarily transfixed by the huge diamond stud in his right earlobe. A new ornament since she'd last seen him. By the light of the dashboard she noticed another, more disturbing, addition to his usually impeccable appearance. He was wearing gloves. *Gloves*. The implication sent her fuzzy mind into a tailspin.

Squirming in the passenger seat, she averted her eyes from the dizzying darkness as her car careened along the curvy country road. She cleared her soot-caked throat and summoned her courage. "Kirk, I—"

"Why did you leave me?" Angry and hurt, his voice was as terrifying as his presence.

She leaned her shoulder against the door, distancing herself from him as much as she could. "I just—"

"Why didn't you tell me about your little problem? I could have helped you."

Her *little problem?* Was he serious?

"I could have bought that theatre for you if it would have made you happy. I could have bought that whole town. All you had to do was ask."

A pressure started to build inside. How did he know about the theatre? Her only hope was to calm him down. She feigned composure. "How did you find me?"

His sideways look implied the idiocy of that question. "I always find you."

Her heart chilled.

He chuckled, the topic clearly improving his mood. "It was so easy. All I had to do was wait. I knew someone would come to me sooner or later. You've got friends here. Did you know that?"

Coldness encased her body. *Sophia.*

He let out a cackle that seemed alarmingly detached. "Hey, at least you did me a favor."

"A favor?" Her voice sounded small.

"Sure. I never thought you'd buy a car, but I'm really glad you did. It handles nice for an old piece of junk."

She withered a glare. What was he getting at?

"I thought I'd have to use my rental car, which would have presented a serious problem. Not that it would have made much difference to me, but this just makes so much more sense." He tipped her a raised eyebrow. "Good thing I don't mind walking."

"I don't understand."

He faced her with a disgusting leer. "You will."

Trying futilely to still her pounding heart, she looked out at the dark masses passing by the window. *Mountains.* She recognized this route. It was what Sam had called the old highway.

Suddenly, her blood ran cold. They were headed toward the falls.

Her voice quavered. "Where are we going?"

A sly smile played on his thin lips. "I got a tip on a great romantic spot. I think you'll find it inspiring."

The menacing insinuation chilled her to the bone. What was she going to do? If she let him take her to the falls, she wouldn't stand a chance. She closed her eyes, bringing back the vivid images of that day with Devon. The roar of the water, the feel of the slippery rocks under her feet, her dizzying loss of balance.

"Hey." Kirk's sharp voice cut into her thoughts. "Have you got any paper in here?"

"What?" Her groggy mind failed to comprehend.

"Paper. Do you have paper?" He stabbed at the air in her direction.

Her head spinning, she reached into the glove box, then pulled out an old receipt and a pencil.

He nodded eagerly. "That'll work."

Fear made a slow climb up her spine. "What do you want me to do with this?"

"I want you to write what I tell you."

Reluctantly, she poised the pencil, waiting for him to speak.

"Let's see, where should we start?" He drew the blade across his chin. "Might as well start at the beginning." Using the blade, he pointed toward the paper. "Start with 'I'm sorry about what happened in San Francisco.'"

She jerked her head toward him. "What?"

He chuckled. "Trust me. Now, how should we say this? I know. 'I need you to understand that I did it for love.'"

Her heart crashed against her chest. How did he know about San Francisco? "I can't write that."

He slammed on the brakes, hurtling her forward. The seat belt kept her lower body in place, but couldn't prevent the cymbal crash of her head to the dash. Stars danced all around as he grabbed her by the shoulder and shoved her back into her seat. The cold tip of the blade touched the hollow of her throat as he leaned into her. She let out a terrified yowl.

"Don't you get it?" His voice dripped with an almost inhuman force that drenched her with sheer terror. "You made a huge mistake when you left me. You narrowed down your options."

His eyes flared. She slid as far as she could to her right as the blade pressed deeper into her flesh, threatening to pierce it. She flailed, wanting to push away his hand but not daring to.

A nauseating smile tightened his lips. “Are you going to make this harder than it needs to be?”

Ultra-aware of the pointed metal that threatened to puncture her skin, she shook her head almost imperceptibly from side to side.

Looking pleased, he sat back, keeping the switchblade aimed carefully at her neck.

She let out her breath and reeled back, her elbow banging against the door. An electric jolt shot up her arm. Suddenly, her thinking turned crystal clear. This was her chance.

She watched as Kirk struggled to keep the blade honed on her while reaching awkwardly across his body for the gearshift. She had to act fast. Finding the seat belt latch, she clicked it open and reached with her other hand for the cold metal of the door handle. Bracing herself, she gave it a yank and pushed her shoulder against the door.

It didn’t budge.

Joanie’s words rang in her head. *The passenger side door tends to stick.*

Kirk’s laughter peeled through the small car as it jolted into motion. “Nice try.”

Tears of exhaustion pooled behind her eyes. Thrust back into her seat by the forward momentum of the vehicle, she redid her belt. What now?

“Pick that up!” He pointed the blade toward her feet, where the paper had come to rest when she’d slammed forward. She bent to retrieve it, along with the pencil.

“Where were we?” Kirk’s voice was cold, mechanical. “Read me what we’ve got.”

Her voice quavered. “‘I’m sorry about what happened in San Francisco. I need you to understand that I did it for love.’” Her heart pounded and she nearly choked on the words. Why was he making her do this?

“Good. Now.” The knife jabbed toward the paper. “‘I know what I did was wrong, but Kirk needed to be free of Julie.’”

Horror seized her. “You *knew* Julie?”

"Knew her?" He sneered. "I lived with her."

An icy shudder passed through her. *Impossible.*

Her mind started to spin, the details of her first encounter with him blipping through her memory. A chance meeting at an opening night party, months after Julie's death. They'd literally run into each other as she stepped away from the bar. Her drink splashed onto his lapel and they laughed about it. He seemed to know who she was, but had acted casual, just like any other opera donor.

She couldn't stop shaking. "You knew? All along, you knew that I was the one who found her?"

"Of course I knew. Why do you think I wanted to meet you?"

Her breathing grew shallow. *Meet me?*

He'd been equally friendly to everyone at the Met in those early months. Inviting them all to his cottage in Chappaquiddick. Hosting cocktail parties at lavish restaurants for the cast and crew. He hadn't paid her any special attention, but he'd *known*. He'd known all along.

"Why didn't you ever mention that you knew?"

A smile broke through the grimness of his features. "I didn't want to make you jealous."

Jealous? Why would she have been jealous?

"Come on, Tracy." A stomach-turning tenderness overtook him as he lifted the blade toward her face. Still clutching the weapon, he ran his index finger along her jawline. "You knew what you were doing. It was more than fate that brought us together."

Us? There was no *us*, as far as she was concerned. He was just a fan, nothing more. A crazy, maniacal fan.

Memories came at her in earnest now. How he'd started sending her notes that had grown progressively more intimate. Casual references to personal details of her life that she'd only revealed in emails and phone conversations with other people. Even changing her number and address hadn't helped.

She'd done nothing to encourage his advances. When she'd told him tactfully that she wasn't interested, he'd backed off for a time. Then the real nightmare began.

Threatening notes. Expensive champagne delivered to her dressing room with a box of chocolates that she'd given to her dresser. News the next day that the woman was in the hospital after having spent the night in the ER.

Grace's clammy hands shook beyond control as she recalled Tristan, the tenor she'd dated for a short time, being mugged and beaten in a subway station.

Then it had been her turn.

She'd tried so hard to be careful, never to be alone in a vulnerable situation, but it hadn't mattered. He'd grabbed her one night as she stepped out of her building, pressing a knife to her side and telling her not to scream. That was when he'd stabbed her in the alley next to her building, and left her for dead.

That troubling thought raised a question. With as much force as she could muster, she blurted it out. "Why are you doing this? Why not just let me die in that fire?"

A lunatic smile crossed Kirk's face. "You know me better than that, Tracy. I wouldn't deprive myself of the satisfaction of knowing that the last sight you saw before taking your dying breath was my face."

Disgust filled her being. What chance did she have against that kind of evil?

He stared at the road ahead as he continued his dictation. "'Kirk needed to be free of Julie. She loved him so much, and there was just no option. Now, Kirk is ready to be free of me, and I need to let him move on. I'm sorry if this hurts anyone, but you'll have to understand. There's no other way.'" He glanced down at her scribbling hands. "Good. Now sign it."

She let out a whimper, shutting her eyes tight. She couldn't.

"Sign it!"

Letting the tears flow, she scrawled out her name, panicked thoughts reeling through her mind. All her time here in Madison Falls flashed before her like a social studies filmstrip. There had been no way for her to know that those would be her final days, but still.... Why hadn't she appreciated them more?

Her mind touched on random memories, lingering on that

morning she'd gone to church with Lucy and Bob. She'd felt good there. She wished she could be there now.

That young singer had said something that morning—what was it? *God is always with us*. If that was true, where was He right now?

"Besides..." Kirk pointed at the paper she held loosely between her fingers. "I wanted this. Just in case there's ever any question about who killed Julie."

She looked up, alertness suddenly kicking in. "*Who* killed Julie?"

A satisfied smile curled up his lips. "You really don't know?" He chuckled in a low and menacing rumble. "I guess I'm better than I thought."

Her eyes opened wide. *Kirk had killed Julie?* All this time she had known he was dangerous, but the realization that he had committed murder—committed *the* murder—filled her with renewed horror.

Something prodded at her to focus—to remember the words of that young man. She honed in her thoughts with laser-sharp clarity.

All we have to do is ask, Lord, and You'll lead us.

That was it. *Ask*. She'd asked for help that awful night in the alley and she'd survived. Was that God?

With no time to debate or overanalyze, she lowered her head and centered her thinking.

Help me, God. Help me now. Please.

Her head snapped up. Without thinking, she reached over and grabbed the steering wheel, cranking it to the left as far as it would turn.

"Hey, what the...?" Clearly caught off guard, Kirk released the wheel, as the car reeled out of control.

Grace held fast, and the vehicle spun like a top, veering off the road and careening down the embankment. An amazing calmness caressed her spirit as they hurtled downward. Down—she remembered without emotion—toward the river.

With a deafening *crack*, the car came to an abrupt halt, giving her a sickening re-enactment of her earlier encounter with the dashboard. This time though, there were no stars. Just an awareness of the stillness surrounding her.

Pulling herself upright, her attention turned instantly to Kirk. He was hunched forward in an unnaturally motionless pose, his head draped across the top of the steering wheel and his arms flung over the dash. She stared, adrenaline filling her like helium in a birthday balloon. Soon she noticed a glistening in the moonlight—a flow of thick, dark liquid streaming down the side of his face. *Blood.*

The sound of rushing water caught her attention and she looked toward the windshield. The car sat at a severe angle, its front end considerably lower than its rear. A tall object directly in front of her blocked her view. *A tree.* She could barely make out what remained of the front end of her car, smashed against the evergreen like a soda can. She squinted. To her horror, the rushing river ran several yards below their stopping place, at the bottom of the abrupt drop-off on which they were perched.

The realization that the tree had saved her from making a rapid and decidedly *un*inspiring visit to the falls just a few miles downriver all but paralyzed her.

Hysteria seized her mind. She had to get out of the car. Turning hastily to free herself, she felt the car shift. She froze.

Slowly, warily, she reached for her seat belt and pulled up the latch. She turned a careful head toward Kirk, certain that at any second he'd spring to life like the killer in a bad horror movie. Reaching behind her, she felt for the passenger door handle, hoping against hope that it would choose this moment to tend *not* to stick. No such luck. She let out an unintentional sob. The only way out of the car was the driver's side.

Taking in a lungful of air that would have sustained her best money note, she pulled her feet up under her, then reached behind Kirk's hunched form. Using extra care not to touch him, she carefully stretched one arm toward the door handle, bracing the other hand on the back of the seat. With all her strength, she pulled the latch as she gave the door a shove. It swung open, creating a terrifying momentum that pulled the car forward. Flailing and letting out a small cry, she inadvertently grabbed a hold of Kirk's shoulder.

He moved, not of his own volition, but with the thrust of the car. Grace released her grasp of his shoulder, firming her grip on the edge of his seat until the car was once again still. She let out a long breath, folding further into her hunched position behind his unmoving form.

She prayed again. *Please just get me safely out of this car.* This was no time to lose control. She had to focus. She pulled her body fully behind Kirk, trying to make herself as small as possible, but rubbing against him nonetheless. No response. She tried not to notice that he didn't appear to be breathing. Those thoughts could wait for later.

With all the care she could muster, she swung first one cautious foot, then the other onto the steep spongy ground. The sound of rushing water reaffirmed her desire to get out of the car before it shifted further.

Pulling herself to a tenuous standing position, she held onto the side of the car until she was certain of her footing. Her breath wavered. She was out.

A glance back reassured her that Kirk hadn't budged. There was no time to waste. She looked upward, unable to see the summit of the gully she was in. She had no concept of how far they'd fallen. Using her hands for added support, she pulled herself up the crisscross of tree limbs that swathed the earthen wall. She winced as the cold mossy ground both scraped and soothed her burned palm. She had to keep climbing.

Hoisting herself upward, she gasped for breath. Her arms ached, but adrenaline propelled her on, until at last she reached up and felt a ridge. She put her forehead to the earth for a moment, giving silent thanks.

Just as she pulled whatever energy she had in her together to hoist her body onto blessed level ground, someone grabbed her wrist from above. She gasped hard, tipping back her head. Her feet slipped out from under her and she started to fall, but the strong hands that now gripped both her arms held tightly enough to prevent it. A scream formed in her throat with no breath to support it.

"Grace!"

A deep voice pierced the night. Grace fought to get a toehold as she whimpered in recognition.

"I've got you. Hold on!" Sam firmed his grip, pulling her upward until one arm slid around her back. She felt her body go limp as he pulled her over the crest of the rock face.

Everything went black as he scooped her up and she wilted into his arms.

Chapter 40

"That's some story." Sam cast Grace a sympathetic look as he leaned his elbows on his knees. The metal chair creaked under his shifting weight, sending a reverberation through the otherwise quiet office. "Sorry it had to end the way it did."

She tipped up a melancholy smile. "Tragic operas generally end with a death. Only it's usually the diva who succumbs."

He gave her a consoling wink. "Good thing we're not in an opera."

She smiled, weary from spending the last two hours answering the sheriff's questions. He'd been so kind, nothing at all like the big-city detectives she'd dealt with in the past.

Her clothes still reeked of smoke, and her skin felt greasy. Without thinking, she reached her gauze-covered hand to her face, wincing as pain shot up her arm.

Sam looked concerned. "You sure you don't want to go to the hospital?"

"It's not a serious burn." She raised her hand. "You must have been a Boy Scout."

He nodded sagely. "I've built a campfire or two in my day."

The door eased open and Sheriff Drew walked in, rubbing his temple. "There's news, Miss Addison." He stopped, catching himself. "I mean, Miss Fontaine. My boys pulled your car out of the river. It's a good thing you got out when you did, because it was completely submerged. Would have been darn near impossible to fight your way to shore against that current, especially at night."

Grace's stomach jolted. She gave Sam a pained glance.

As if reading her thoughts, he spoke up. "What about Kirk? Did they find him?"

Sheriff Drew stroked his chin, his eyes sorrowful. "Oh, they found the body, all right. Didn't look too pretty after a few hours in the water."

A surge of nausea pressed at her gut. What an awful way to go. Then a horrible thought made the queasiness worse. "You won't need me to...*identify* him?"

He shook his head, his eyes rimmed with sympathy. "He matches your description right down to the diamond stud. I don't see any reason to put you through that."

Sam reached over to give her arm a reassuring squeeze, and she returned a weary smile.

The sheriff took his jacket from a hook on the wall. "Now why don't you go home and see if you can get some rest. There'll be plenty of time for questions in the light of day." He peered out his office window as he slipped his arm into the jacket sleeve. "Which will be in about three hours if I don't miss my guess."

Sam's chair scraped against the cracked linoleum. "Come on." He took her elbow. "I'll drive you home."

"You know," she said, pulling herself onto still-unsteady legs. "I could really use the walk."

He tipped her a sideways glance. "You sure?"

She nodded. It had been one thing allowing him to drive her back to town earlier. Now that she had her wits about her she was a little afraid of the vulnerability she'd feel alone in his truck with him.

A few minutes later, Grace wrapped her arms around her middle to stave off the night chill. Sam removed his Levi's Trucker jacket and placed it over her shoulders. Too exhausted to refuse, she slid her arms into the warm sleeves.

"That Kirk was some character," he said as they started up the sidewalk.

"You could say that." She fell into pace next to him.

"I still can't believe he threatened you with a switchblade. Where did he think he was going, to a rumble?"

Grace shrugged. "When you're a Jet, you're a Jet all the way."

He tipped an ear to his shoulder. "I'm guessing you weren't a part of his *gang?*"

She angled a sideways smile. "Very funny."

"I try." His tone turned somber. "At least now I understand why you said you wouldn't be hanging around Madison Falls."

Her face fell slightly. She *had* said that.

When she didn't respond, he continued. "You must be anxious to get home to see your friends."

"Yes. Well. I don't have that many friends." She considered. "Or *any*, actually."

He shoved his thumbs into the pockets of his jeans. "Except Sinclair, of course."

"Right. Of course. Except Devon."

His words seemed calculated. "So, you *want* to go back."

"Of course I do. It's all I've wanted since I got here."

"And I guess you'd have no reason to stay."

She tilted him a glance. What was he getting at? "No reason at all."

He nodded, his eyes set on the dark sidewalk ahead. "So, you think you'll go back with Sinclair in the morning?"

Her tired nerves pinched. Would she? She looked at her watch. "He'll be leaving in a few hours." Anxiety fluttered in her stomach. "I can't even think after what just happened to me."

"Right. Sorry." They kept walking. "I'm so sorry you had to go through that. You must have been terrified."

How could she describe it? "It was like being in a *Die Hard* movie, only John McClane stood me up."

His stance turned rigid. "I should have gotten there sooner."

"Gotten there *sooner?*" A niggling question worked its way to the surface. "How did you even know where to look for me?"

They stopped on the corner of Pine View and Main. "After I

talked to my dad, I realized I'd left my guitar at the theatre. On the way back, I noticed your car wasn't in your driveway."

She turned to him in mock dismay. "Don't tell me you were spying on me."

"Not *spying*." He held up a hand in defense. "Just concerned that you'd gotten home safely. Anyway," they started across Main. "It was right about then that I heard the sirens."

She shuddered, the terror returning in spite of her attempts to suppress it.

"Don't tell the sheriff, but I made it from that corner to this one in record time."

"Oh?" Her eyes sharpened on his moonlit face.

"Andretti would have been jealous." He tossed her a soft look as they reached the curb. "From this vantage point..." He turned, nodding toward the theatre. "I could see the flames through the windows."

He didn't look at her, but she could see his eyes glistening under the streetlamp.

"It had only been, what, fifteen minutes since I'd left you there." A tremor crept into his voice. "I thought my heart was going to beat a hole in my chest."

She felt a little breathless. "My, that's a vivid image."

"Yeah." He turned, and they started to walk again. "Anyway, I saw your car was gone from where you'd been parked. I was so relieved."

"Relieved?" Warmth wafted through her. "Really?"

"Of course." He eyed her tenderly. "Now, if I had known what was really going on..."

"How could you possibly have known?"

"I don't know." He held a beat. "John McClane would have known."

"True." She tipped a smile. "So, what happened then?"

"I got out of my truck and ran over there." He pointed back with his thumb." Nancy ran up to me in a panic and asked who the man was that you'd left with."

She jolted. "She saw?"

He blinked a nod. "Good thing too. I figured it must have been Sinclair but that just didn't make sense."

"So, you followed us." A warmth radiated from her chest in spite of the night chill. "But how did you know where my car went down?"

"I didn't at first. I must have driven past right after it happened. When you weren't parked at the falls, I started back. I was praying all the way that you were safe, and I don't know. Something just told me to stop when I did. I heard a noise and when I walked over to the edge I looked down and saw your hands." He paused, softening. "Sorry if I scared you."

She fought back a lump in her throat. "You have a way of doing that, you know."

"I could wear a collar with a bell on it."

She chuckled, relieved that he'd broken the seriousness of the moment. She looked at the street ahead, then stopped in her tracks and held up her unbandaged hand. "Wait a minute. Are you walking me home?"

"You noticed."

"But isn't your truck back there—in front of the sheriff's office?"

He gave a slow nod.

"You mean you're going to walk me home, walk back downtown, then drive home right past my house? What's the point of that?"

He looked at her sideways. "I guess I just feel sorry for you because you don't have any friends."

A sardonic smirk found her face as they started walking again. "Thanks a lot." Her voice turned quiet. "I'm really sorry, Sam, but the painting burned. I saw it."

He shook his head. "I figured. It's not your fault."

"It was my fault for not insuring it." A thought struck her. "Maybe your business insurance..."

He shook his head. "My dad has no use for insurance." He held up a hand toward her. "I told him we needed full coverage, but our policy is pretty bare bones. We'll be lucky if it pays ten percent of the value of what was lost."

"Oh." Her heart sank. "So, what are you going to do?"

"It looks like we're at Langley's mercy again. That is, if I haven't totally alienated his yes-man."

"You mean Devon? I could talk to him for you."

His face turned somber. "If I had my way, you'd never talk to that guy again."

"I'm sorry you feel that way."

"Since you brought it up." He stopped, facing her full-on. "Grace, I just wish you'd reconsider your involvement with him before you get hurt."

"I don't want to talk about Devon." She looked away. "Whatever he did to you—"

"Not to me," he said. "To Colleen."

The fatigue jolted from her body. "Colleen?"

He paused, a cavalcade of emotions plying for top billing across his forehead.

Her heart warned her not to ask. "What did he do?"

"What didn't he do?" Emotion welled up in his voice. "Swept her off her feet, lavished her with gifts. Promised to take her 'away from all this.'" He waved his arms, mocking the sentiment.

Grace's throat clenched in incredulity. "But, he wasn't even in town all that long."

His whole face had turned stony. "A testament to his speed. The guy'd be a shoo-in at NASCAR."

"So..." Acid bubbled in her throat like a third-grade science experiment. "What exactly happened?"

"He wined and dined her to get to Dad. Along with all the fine cuisine, he fed her a convincing argument which she passed on to us. We never would have taken Langley's offer seriously if she hadn't been so persuasive on that Casanova's behalf."

"But, you said she was dead set against it."

"She is—now. Funny how much clearer things are by the light of day."

"Meaning?"

"As soon as Devon had Dad on the hook, Colleen apparently

didn't look so enticing. See"—he turned to her—"my sister's an old-fashioned girl and Devon is, like I said, *speedy*. Why waste time hanging with the pit crew when there are so many pretty little cars willing to go for a spin?"

Her mouth contorted. *What a cute analogy*. "But your dad could have just dropped the deal. He wasn't committed."

"No, but by that time he'd pinned all his hopes on it. Colleen was so humiliated. We couldn't burden Dad with the sordid details."

"Oh." *Poor Colleen.*

"So, you see why it's hard to stand back and watch someone I..." His voice was soft and disarmingly intimate. "To watch *you* get mixed up with him."

Her heart suddenly cooled. What concern was it of his, when he had a girlfriend who was probably lying awake at this very moment wondering where he was? She clenched her jaw. "Thanks for your concern but it's really none of your business."

"It *is* my business because I care about you."

She tried to ignore her pounding heart. "Yeah, well maybe you should start caring a little more about your own life and leave me alone." She increased her pace.

He stepped up his own to keep up. "Why would you think I don't care about my own life?"

"Well for starters..." She wanted to scold him for betraying his girlfriend, but the words wouldn't come. "There's your music. You're keeping your gift hidden. 'Under a bushel'—isn't that the term?"

"It's not exactly hidden." His voice betrayed his pain.

"Bringing it out once a week at church. Is that really what you want?"

"What if it is?" He was holding back his anger, she could tell.

"If that's true, great," she snapped. "I just think you're kidding yourself."

Anger was clear on his face. "Look, I'm just a small-town guy—"

"So you don't like cities, is that it?" Her pitch went up a half-step.

"Not a big fan. Besides, my dad needs me here—"

"You just don't want to leave Madison Falls."

"Is that so terrible?"

She felt flustered. Why did this suddenly matter to her so much? "I think you're wasting your talent."

"Okay, I get that." He steadied his voice. "But what did you mean, I should leave you alone?"

She pulled in a breath. Stilling her pace, she faced him. "You say you care so much about me not getting hurt, but what about *Jill?*"

His brow creased. "Jill? You think I'm not doing everything in my power to protect her too?"

"Oh." Her diva fire was back. "Like she won't get hurt as long as she can't see you walking around in the dark with other women?"

"I don't walk around in the dark with other...*other* women?" A wave of realization rolled across his face. "Wait a minute. You don't think that I'm..."

She folded her arms, bracing herself for his rationalization.

He almost smiled. "You think I'm involved with Jill."

Her gaze dropped to the sidewalk, then back to his face. "You mean, you're not?"

"No." His eyes entreated. "Where did you get that idea?"

"Well, I..." She dove deep into her memory. Where *did* she get that idea?

He held up a hand like a professor at the lectern. "Let's get this straight. Jill is married to Caleb, my best friend."

"*Oh.*" Her head suddenly felt much as it had a few hours ago, when it slammed into the dashboard of her car. "So there's nothing between you?"

"Nothing. She's Caleb's girl." His voice now dripped with emotion. "That's why she was so bent on going after him that night you saw us outside the bar."

Another puzzle piece snapped into place. She'd assumed the guy in the park was there to score a deal, but now she understood.

"And why she acted the way she did at the potluck when he showed up."

"You saw us at the potluck?" He smiled. "What have you been doing, surveillance work?"

"Sorry. It's a small town."

"And we wonder why small-town gossip is such a cliché."

"Right. Sam, I was really wrong about you. I'm so sorry."

"It's okay." He chuckled. "So, you thought I was involved with Jill. No wonder you..." His voice trailed off.

"No wonder I what?" Her jaw constricted.

"I don't know." His eyes grabbed onto hers. "Acted like you weren't interested."

She opened her mouth to speak but all that came out was air. Suddenly and unexpectedly, her heart ached for him. She looked into the chocolate-brown eyes of a man who was attractive, accomplished, and available. Heaven help her if she moved on to the *B* words.

Though the distance between them was just a few feet, it felt like an unbridgeable gap. He was solidly grounded here in Madison Falls. She was a city girl. *Green Acres*, we are there.

"Sam..." How could she explain how she felt? "I came to Madison Falls to hide."

He nodded. "I know. I get that."

What was she trying to say? "I really just wanted to keep to myself, and then you.... So many things changed for me." She huffed out a laugh. "It's been such a short time, but I feel so different."

He nodded. "That's what they mean by being 'reborn'."

Her voice caught in her throat. He had told her about salvation. Was that where these warm feelings were coming from? Was she mistaking them for something else?

"It's just that..." She wanted to say more, but where was her courage? "I'm going back to New York."

He lowered his eyes. "I understand."

She took another step before realizing they were standing in front of her house. She turned up the walkway, then a new thought brought her back around. "By the way..."

His head snapped toward her.

"I haven't 'gone for a spin' either. In case you were wondering."

His eyes flitted down, then met hers with a slow smile. "Don't leave without saying goodbye."

She nodded her assurance.

As he lifted a wave, his smile turned sad. Blinking, he turned, then headed back in the direction from which they'd come.

She drew in a long breath as she dug in her purse for her key and climbed the porch steps. Why was she feeling this way? She had a plan—a good plan. It was finally safe for her to go back to New York. Sure, she had accepted Christ here, and it seemed clear now that God had used her situation with Kirk toward that end. Maybe He had even used Sam. But now it was time for her to return to her life, and there was no room there for him. Was there?

Maybe it had been fate that she'd misunderstood him all that time. It would have been wrong for her to act on her feelings toward him. She lived in a different world. Turning the key, she pushed open the door.

It was all for the best. She felt sad, but that was only natural. She'd lived in Madison Falls for nearly two months and had gotten to know people. She pressed the door shut, leaning her forehead on the cool wood.

A pang of realization twisted her insides. She had told Sam she didn't have any friends, but that wasn't true. She did have friends. She'd made friends here. Turning, she leaned the back of her head against the door.

She looked around. Something wasn't right. Trouble always met her at the door, but the tiny rabble-rouser was nowhere in sight. Grace shook off the thought. The kitten had probably sensed that they'd be moving soon and cats weren't exactly big on relocation.

Expelling a sigh, she hung her purse on the closet doorknob, then wrapped her arms around herself. She followed her practice of scanning the living room, noting that the lamp near the window glowed just as she'd left it. She appreciated its elucidation of every corner as she turned to take a step into the room.

Her head popped up. Something was wrong.

Eyes snapping into sharp focus, she took in the outline of the dining room arch and the darkness beyond it. Hadn't she left the light on in there?

Cemented in place, her mind raced. She was certain she had followed her careful routine before leaving the house. Her memory of flipping the switch to illuminate the Craftsman fixture over the table was clear. The death of one light bulb was an unavoidable gamble, but eight all at once?

Her stomach jumped to her throat as she gazed into the unlit room. To her tired eyes, it looked like the table had been set.

Impossible. Kirk was gone.

Recoiling, her eyes fixed on the darkened room. Suddenly, a shadow stirred. As she fumbled backward, the shadow resolved into the shape of a man and lunged at her.

Her nightmare wasn't over.

Chapter 41

Grace froze in a stare.

There under the archway, looking slightly frazzled, stood the man she had hoped would play a significant role in her future.

She felt her legs slowly thaw. "How did you get in here?"

Devon advanced toward her. "That's not exactly the greeting I had hoped for."

As he moved into brighter light, she drew back. He had always been so well-groomed, but now his face was scruffy, and the tail of his Armani shirt flapped over the waist of his wrinkled silk slacks, something he would never allow ordinarily. His normally coiffed hair stuck up in spikes on one side, as if he'd just woken up.

She fought to find her voice. "I'm sorry. It's just that you really scared me." Her heart pounded like a bass drum as she took a halfhearted step toward him. "It's the middle of the night. What are you doing here?"

"The theatre burned." His face seemed hard. "I was worried about you."

Of course. She let out a breath. "I'm fine. Can't we talk in the morning?"

He angled a sly smile. "We won't be here in the morning. It's time to go home."

"Right." She rubbed her brow. "You're leaving."

"Not just me." He moved toward her and caught her wrists. "You're going with me."

This was more than her tired mind could process. "What do you mean?"

"I heard what happened." He tried to draw her closer, but she resisted. "You don't have to worry about Kirk anymore."

"No." Pulling away from him, she twisted her fingers together and stepped into the living room. "So much has happened."

He followed. "You got what you wanted. There's nothing to keep you here." The look in his eye seemed to mix desperation with affection—or maybe it was just the lighting. Had he sensed her uncertainty about Sam?

She wavered before speaking. "Yes, but after what happened, I need some time to catch my breath."

He tossed his hand in disregard. "You can do that on the way home."

His persistence set her teeth on edge. "Devon, I really don't want to drive across the country tomorrow."

"I totally agree." He assumed the manner of a salesman refusing to hear 'no.' "We can take a cab to Missoula and fly home together. There's nothing to keep you here."

That was what she'd been telling herself for weeks. Why was she hesitating? "You're right." She eased closer. "I'm glad you're here, and I can't wait to get home."

"Good, because I booked our return flight. We'll leave as soon as you can get your things together."

Her heart thumped. "You mean leave *now?* But I'm not ready."

"That's not a problem." His tone dismissed her concern. "I'm here to help."

"That's nice of you." Her head swam. At the very least, she needed a long shower and a good night's sleep. Then there was her job. And her friends. She'd promised Sam she wouldn't leave without saying goodbye. No, this wasn't going to work for her. "Why don't you go on ahead. I'll meet you there in a day or two."

He jutted his chin. "Grace...Tracy. You don't understand. We need to get to rehearsals."

"Rehearsals? Devon—"

"I'm going out on a limb giving you this role. If you don't come with me now, I'm afraid—"

"I didn't realize it was so urgent." She tried to focus her tired mind. "You mean I'll lose the role if I don't leave with you now?"

He lifted his hands, agitated. "This role is going to be a tremendous break for you."

That was true but still...something didn't seem right. Only yesterday he'd been intent on leaving without her. Why was he pressuring her to go with him all of a sudden? She put her hands to her temples, trying to ignore the throbbing of her burned palm, and crossed to the sofa. "I just need to sit down for a minute." How could he possibly expect her to leave on a moment's notice, especially after what she'd just been through?

"Of course. You must be exhausted." He followed her, but remained standing. "Do you have any wine? I could pour you a glass."

The suggestion held no appeal, except that it might buy her some time to think. "Sure, sounds nice."

"Good. Why don't you relax and I'll see what you have." Something caught his attention on the coffee table. "What's this?"

Her gaze shifted. She'd forgotten she'd left the newspaper Sophia had given her on top of the stack she'd intended to discard. The glimpse she caught of Kirk's smarmy grin made her stomach curdle. "It's an article about Kirk. Sophia thought I needed a reminder."

Devon's demeanor grew visibly darker as he picked it up and studied the photo. "So, this is him."

Grace tipped her head. "That's the gallery wall I told you about. I know it's really blurry, but you can see his two Blackthorns right there."

"Amazing." His voice was steady, devoid of feeling. He folded the paper, article to the inside. "Look, I don't want you to have any reminders of him. Let's get rid of everything like this and put the past in its place. In fact—" He wadded the paper into a ball and pitched it into the kindling basket. "—let's turn it into a nice fire to enjoy our wine by. Then we'll get going." He produced a book of matches from his jacket.

"Oh." Her nerves jolted as he thrust the matches into her hand. Did he realize how insensitive the gesture was, considering that she'd nearly been kindling herself a few hours ago? All she wanted was to unwind and get some sleep, but she'd light the fire if it would make him happy.

As their hands touched, a knock at the door caused a mutual flinch. Her pulse kicked into high gear as she recalled Sam saying he'd be driving back this way. Had he decided to stop? This was going to be very awkward.

Exchanging a look of alarm with Devon, she sprang to the window and gasped. Turning to him, her mouth formed a single word. 'Sophia.' Now *this* was going to be awkward.

Steeling herself, she moved to the door and pulled it open.

Looking considerably less self-assured than usual, Sophia's eyes flitted from Grace to Devon and back. "I'm sorry." Her voice was barely above a whisper. "But I need to talk to him."

Grace turned, expecting Devon to register consternation. Instead, he folded his arms and firmed his stance. "What is, Sophia?"

"Could we speak in private?" Sophia's normally steady voice shook like a pom pom at a pep rally.

His jaw hardened in a moment of quiet thoughtfulness. With exhaled exasperation, he took her by the elbow and piloted her to the kitchen.

Grace made a move toward the fireplace with a vague intention of completing her assigned task, then paused. The muted voices drifting from the kitchen tweaked her nerves, and she wondered for a second if Sophia was one of the "pretty little cars" Sam had referenced. She tried to cast off the thought. What had that woman come here to discuss at this hour?

Glancing casually at the dining table, she traveled on tiptoe toward it. She feigned a preoccupation with the placemats Lucy had made for her, as she strained an ear.

"But it's just not *right.*" Sophia's tone was biting.

"Get over it, Sophia. I've made my decision."

A satisfied smile crept across Grace's face. They must be talking about the role. *Get over it, Sophia.*

The sound of footsteps urged her back into the living room. As the kitchen door opened, Grace folded her hands. There was no point in gloating. Poor Sophia was upset enough as it was.

Head down, Sophia moved slowly through the dining room. She paused, her gaze catching Grace's for a split second. Some unidentifiable emotion flickered in Sophia's eyes, and Grace's polite smile fell.

The brief exchange left Grace with an odd sense of foreboding completely unlike her normal post-Sophia disquiet. This time, the antagonism in Sophia's demeanor hadn't been directed toward her.

"We wish you well, Sophia." Sounding like a casting director after an unimpressive audition, Devon escorted her to the door.

She stepped slowly through the foyer, her hands knotting in front of her abdomen. She paused just short of her exit.

"Grace and I are leaving soon." Devon's tone was stern with finality.

Sophia tilted a parting glance at Grace—a slight shake of her head barely discernible—she and was gone.

Grace creased her brow. That was odd, even for Sophia.

"Well, that's that." Devon turned, as if nothing about this encounter had been out of the ordinary.

"I feel bad for her." Grace said, an unanticipated burst of compassion forming in her chest.

"Sophia will be fine." Devon shrugged. "I admire her ingenuity. I mean, the lengths she went to, keeping you away from Roberts." He turned, speaking over his shoulder as he headed back to the kitchen. "Threatening you to stay away from him. As if he had any interest in her."

What? Was he saying that Sophia didn't love him, but *Sam?* If that was true, Grace had spent the last three weeks steering clear of the wrong guy. How could she have been so foolish?

Groggy and confused, she ambled into the living room. It all started to make sense now. Why Sophia had given her the *little reminder* after seeing her in the hardware store with Sam. How Kirk had suddenly shown up when he did. Sophia had made good on her threat because Grace hadn't understood the ground rules.

Kneeling in front of the fireplace, she grabbed a piece of newspaper from the basket and crumpled it into a tight ball. Sophia had been nothing but a sharp bone in Grace's corset since the moment they'd met. Yet she had seen the truth that Grace herself had been blinded to. Sam was drawn to *her*.

What was she going to do? She placed the paper on the grate, then laid the kindling sticks and a crisscross of wood on top of it. She grabbed a match, struck it, and touched it to the paper.

Fighting back reflections of the theatre fire that by now seemed like a lifetime ago, she focused on the soothing glow. An ache at the base of her skull had started to crawl upward, and she rolled her head back to ease it. The role of Carmen was at her fingertips. Why was she suddenly so tempted to stay put?

She grabbed another piece of wadded paper and drew her hand back, stopping just short of launching it into the flames. Something compelled her to uncrinkle it, and she held the image of Kirk's sickening smirk up in front of her.

She jerked her eyes away. Devon was right—it was best for her to get rid of this. Mementos of him would do nothing to ease her pain.

She tried again to feed it to the fire, but stopped. The temptation to take one last look pulled at her. She smoothed out the paper. Forcing her eyes into sharp focus, she realized something wasn't right. What was it?

Images from that weekend in Chappaquiddick rolled to the forefront of her mind. She squinted, making out the details of the two Blackthorns Kirk had been so swollen with pride over. Since the finer points of the other artwork he owned had made no real impression, they remained fuzzy to her eye.

She studied the photo, unable to shake the feeling that something was different—wrong—about it. It was obviously recent, judging from the diamond stud on prominent display in his right earlobe. She concentrated her focus.

Then it hit her like a maestro's downbeat. Something was hanging in the spot that had been vacant when she'd visited—the spot Kirk had reserved for a third Blackthorn. Her stomach clenched. Pulling the paper closer to her eyes, it became clear. *The painting in the photo was her Blackthorn.*

Her mind raced. What was going on? The painting had burned. She'd seen it. *No.* She'd seen the *crate* burn. Realization stabbed her heart. It wasn't really her painting that had burned because Devon had already sold it—sold it to *Kirk.*

"I hope you're in the mood for Merlot. I..."

Her head snapped up as Devon entered the room carrying two glasses of red wine. He flicked a glance at the paper in her hands and his expression subtly shifted.

"Tracy—"

"You sold my painting." She stood, the paper quivering in her grasp. "How could you do that?"

He set the glasses down on the end table and held up his hands in defense. "Just listen to me. I knew we could get more money from Kirk than from another collector in an auction and I was right. The guy practically jumped through the phone the first time I called him."

"You contacted him." She weakened like a rag doll at the thought. Add Devon to the list of people who had betrayed her by sidling up to Kirk. A rage burned in her stomach. "But how could you sell it without asking me? It was mine."

"Tracy, I knew you'd never agree. You would have let your fear stand in the way of making a wise financial decision. I knew I could sell it without ever letting your name enter into the transaction."

A bitter taste filled her mouth. To think she had entertained romantic notions about this man. That she'd trusted him.

"Besides, don't you see the beauty of it?" He gave up a carefree grin. "You would have been building your safe fortress against Kirk using his money. Don't you love the irony of that?"

Her stomach roiled. She'd refused Kirk's money and gifts for so long, desperate not to be beholden to him. Now he was dead because of her. How could she feel right about taking his money?

Her mind clouded in confusion "So you just gave me an empty crate?"

"Not empty exactly. It had Sophia's swap-meet find in it. I needed to buy some time."

"Buy some time? I don't understand. If the painting was already gone, why didn't you just tell me?"

He sputtered a laugh, looking sideways as if to imply that the answer should be obvious. "Because I wanted to surprise you."

"*Surprise* me?" As if she hadn't had enough surprises. "You undermined me."

"Don't you think you're overreacting?" He let out a nervous chortle. "It's not like I wasn't going to give you the money."

The money. Her wrath softened. The painting wasn't gone after all. She'd been so focused on her outrage that she'd overlooked her restored hope for the money. Maybe this situation wasn't as bad as it seemed. "How much did you get?"

He hesitated. "You know what it's worth."

"Yes, but you said you got more. How much did Kirk pay you?"

His eyes darted around nervously. She held up her palms. Enough with the surprises—why couldn't he just tell her?

Nerves tingling, she lowered her head in an attempt to catch his eye. "You must have a receipt—a bill of sale. Something like that."

Letting out an audible breath, he reached for his briefcase, then produced a sheet of paper which he held out to her. She stepped toward him, hand extended, and took it.

A tremble of excitement enveloped her. *Two point five million!* She could give Sam all he needed and more. She could stop the casino deal. She could start a foundation for victims of stalkers. Maybe Devon's actions hadn't been so ill-advised after all.

Just then her enthusiasm blurred. Something wasn't adding up. She looked into his silver-blue eyes. "So, what changed?"

His already-tentative smile grew fainter. "What do you mean, 'what changed'? Kirk is dead."

"I know that." Her pulse made an alarming *ka-thump* as she forced her tired mind to focus. "I'm talking about *Carmen*. Why do I all of a sudden have to leave this minute or lose the role?"

Almost imperceptibly, a storm crossed his face, filling her with a sickening sense of dread. She'd seen that look on Kirk's face the night he stabbed her, and again a few hours ago in her car.

Her chest tightened as the situation gained a frightening clarity—she was in danger and Sophia knew it. Sophia had been warning her.

Her dull mind instantly whipped into a whirlwind. What was she going to do? Her eyes darted toward the front door as she did a quick calculation of how long it would take her to reach it if she bolted. It was no good. He was too close. He'd cut her off.

"Look." His voice took on a demanding tone. "I'm offering you a major role. I don't think you're in any position to be asking questions."

She straightened her spine, faking a confidence she didn't feel. "I can leave tomorrow, but I'd like to handle my own travel arrangements." Forcing the tightness from her shoulders, she stepped toward the door, as if intending to see him out. "Just give me my money and let me get some sleep."

He stood fast, the storm in his eyes brewing. "You don't want me to look like a fool, do you?"

"Of course not, but—"

Suddenly, he charged at her, grabbing both of her arms as she let out a terrified shriek.

Chapter 42

"Stop it!" Devon's voice was filled with an unearthly rage. "You're stalling. It's too late. You're trying to ruin everything, but it's not going to work!"

Grace gasped, fighting futilely against his powerful grip. "Just...just give me my money and get out of my house!"

"So you think I'm stupid?" His voice dripped with disdain. "You're the stupid one—handing over a valuable piece of artwork to someone you barely know. What kind of idiot does that?"

She cringed. He was right.

"So you sold my painting." Her voice was barely a whimper as she writhed. "Why didn't you just leave me alone?"

"Because I'm not that dumb." His eyes crinkled in condescension as he wrenched her in closer. "I knew that pretty soon you'd figure out what happened. When you realized it was Sophia's swap-meet junk in the crate instead of your Blackthorn, I knew you'd try to find me. See, I have enough people gunning for me after my last investment deal went down the drain. You're not the only one who's been lying low."

She drew in a sharp breath. Was that what Ty had meant by "disappearing off the face of the earth"?

"Besides," one corner of his lip curled up. "Turns out you're worth almost as much as that painting."

A cold weight settled in her heart. She felt the pull of evil in his voice that brought with it a portent of doom. "What do you mean?"

Coldness filled his eyes. "Isn't it obvious?"

Grace's head spun in a dizzying whirlwind of comprehension. Sophia hadn't told Kirk where she was. It had been Devon.

His face registered her realization. "Business is business, Tracy. It was a simple business transaction. A 'finder's fee', if you will."

Nauseated, she forced her over-adrenalized body to stand strong. "How much?"

"You want to know how much you're worth? I might as well tell you." His chuckle was disturbing in its glee. "A million up front and a million upon delivery."

Delivery? Her knees gave way and it was all she could do to remain upright. She choked back a gasp. *How could he deliver her to a dead man?*

Given the choice, she'd rather not find out.

She'd have to focus. Pulling in a breath, she forced her arms to relax, which mercifully loosened his grip on them.

Without warning, she sliced her hands up through the space between his arms, then twisted them down, forcing him to release his grip. Spinning around, she bolted toward the dining room, then pushed through the door into the dark kitchen. Sensing Devon on her heels, she increased her speed, heading for the sun porch.

Just as she was about to run through the doorway, a figure appeared, blocking her way. Unable to stop her momentum, she collided with the solid form. Reflexively, she stumbled back, squaring a horrified look at the tip of a switchblade. The shape stepped from the darkened sun porch into the dimly lit kitchen and Grace froze. It was Kirk.

"Surprised to see me?"

Shock filled her chest. She raised her hands to her mouth, feeling the heat of Devon's presence at her back. She was trapped.

Looking like he'd returned from the dead, Kirk towered over her. His jeans and T-shirt were torn and filthy, and the gruesome gash on his forehead was impossible to ignore. Even in this light, she could see that blood had dried on his face and shirt.

"Sinclair." Kirk spoke past her while his eyes remained set on her. "Get the rental. It's parked around the corner." He pulled something from his pocket and tossed it over Grace's shoulder.

A sickening *jangle-thud* was followed by the sound of Devon moving through her house and out the front door.

Kirk released a low, maniacal chuckle. "Imagine my disappointment when I opened my eyes to find you gone." He raised the tip of the blade, pointing it at her throat. "If you were smart, you would have taken my cell phone with you. It was just plain luck that your friend Devon answered when I called."

She took a backward step toward the kitchen door, her foggy mind fighting to form a plan.

Kirk let out a laugh. "I suppose you heard they found my expired body in that beater car of yours?"

She managed a weak nod, confusion narrowing her eyes.

"Obviously, they didn't really find me. They found some guy who was unlucky enough to look like me."

Grace's blood ran cold. *Carson?*

"It was Sinclair's idea. He saw that guy at his cabin."

Grace's stomach curdled as the story unfolded. *Poor Carson.*

"Devon...*killed* him?"

"You catch on fast. We knew a Podunk operation like the local sheriff's office wouldn't check dental records or anything that sophisticated, but we did think they might make you identify the body. We had to be thorough."

She shuddered. Faking an interest in his story might buy her some time. "So you traded clothes and put his body in the car and—"

"Gave it a little push. Simple."

"Aren't you afraid they'll check for footprints, or tire tracks?

"Nice of you to worry, Jessica Fletcher. Let's just say we covered our tracks. We both know what we're doing when it comes to making things go our way." He assumed a look of mock regret. "Oh, sorry about your car. Good thing you won't be needing it anymore."

She calculated. If she made a dash for the front door, he'd have her before she hit the foyer. She'd have to distract him, and she'd have to be quick.

Hours of acting class congealed in her mind. Her flair for the dramatic was about to come in handy.

In one swift movement, she pinned her gaze on the kitchen window behind Kirk and, as if she suddenly saw something horrendous beyond the glass, let out a blood-curdling scream.

Her action served its intended purpose, catching Kirk so off guard that he momentarily lost focus and turned to look. She was off like Secretariat, racing through the dining room as if her life depended on it and trying to forget that it did.

She'd made it to the foyer when he caught her by the arm, whirling her off her intended course and into the hallway. He somehow whipped her around, forcing her to face him. One hand gripped her arm like a vice while the other leveled the point of the blade directly at her throat.

"Bravo." He spoke through gritted teeth, his eyes flaring. "Quite a performance. Too bad the diva has to die in the third act."

Fear coiled up her spine as she tried to pull away, but his grip only tightened. She let out a sob. The futility of her struggle fueled her panic.

His eyes flickered in a quick double take toward the bathroom. "Hey, I have an idea for the climax scene."

Grace felt her body grow weak.

He pulled her into the bathroom, slammed her back against the open door, and released his grip. He held the blade in front of her nose. "This could be the greatest performance of your career." He sneered. "Too bad there won't be any critics to commemorate it."

Her chest heaved with pure panic.

He sent a cold glance toward the bathtub "Remember Julie—how you found her? I like the poetry of you going out the same way."

Grace heard a mournful wail of a voice she barely recognized as her own. The sharpness of the blade pushed at her throat and she felt her air being cut off. An acute pain shot through her, along with the awareness that she was going to die.

But the gift of God is eternal life. Sam's words flew into her mind. Thank God he'd spoken to her—led her in prayer. They'd almost been too late. One more day and—

The thought brought with it more thoughts of Sam, and something he'd done that had irked her at the time, but now jolted her with revived hope. There *was* something she could do.

With movement so slight she prayed Kirk wouldn't sense it, her hand edged across the smooth varnish of the door behind her. She forced a swallow against the pressure of the blade and moved her hand a little more.

Reassured by the placid late-night sounds of the house—the refrigerator motor, the gentle drone of a car going by—she bent her elbow and reached around the door's edge.

"Goodbye, Tracy." Kirk leaned in, his breath hot on her cheek. "It's been a pleasure."

All at once, the stillness was broken by a drawn-out screech from outside followed by a heart-stopping crash. Kirk jarred back as the sound reverberated through the entire house.

The distraction bought her the second she needed to grip the crowbar, unhook it from the doorknob, and raise it up high. He looked up just as she swung it down hard on the top of his skull.

Grabbing his head and shouting in anguish, he staggered backward into the hallway, blocking her path to the front door.

Wasting no time, she took off at a sprint toward the kitchen, thanking God for that Central Park training program.

As she ran through the house, time moved in both slow motion and at double speed. Miraculously, she made it to the back door. Fingers flying, she managed to unlatch it and leapt down the steps into the darkness. Cool air surrounded her. She was outside. All she had to do was get to the front of the house.

Her lungs filled with predawn dampness as she propelled her body through the narrow side yard. As she neared the corner of her garage, she realized that something was wrong. There had been an accident. A truck was smashed into the tree in front of Lucy's house. Her heart threatened to break free of her ribcage. It was Sam's truck.

All thought of her own peril lifted as she tried to get to him. Lucy and Bob bolted out of their front door, but there was no movement near the truck. Fear seized her. Why wouldn't her legs move faster?

Her heart pounded like a kettledrum in her head. She braced herself to jet down the driveway and across the street. Just then an awful awareness hit her like a fist to her solar plexus. There was a car in her driveway. *The rental.*

In a split second, Devon appeared around the corner of the garage, enslaving her arms and squeezing so hard she struggled to breathe.

"What do you think you're doing?" His voice grated in her ear as he dragged her back into the darkness from which she'd come. "I have another 'mil' coming, and I mean to collect."

Fighting to fill her lungs with supportive air, she summoned a scream. Devon must have felt her abdomen inflate, because just as she was about to release an operatic bellow, he thrust a hand across her mouth. A pitiful hum sounded in her ears as he maneuvered her around to the backyard, out of sight of anyone who could help her.

Horror filled her as a dark form hobbled down the steps from her back door and approached her. She struggled futilely to pull away from Devon as Kirk's grunting breath grew louder.

Devon's voice reverberated in her aching head. "Kirk! Look what I found. I didn't let her get away."

Kirk ambled up to her, his vengeful eyes aglow in the pale light. As he neared, he raised a hand above his shoulder.

Adrenaline fired her fight but it was no use. She twisted her head as Devon let his hand slip from her mouth and settle on her throat. Her heart sank. Even if she broke free, what chance did she have? A wisp of air remained in her lungs. She powered it out with a barely audible sob.

"Please don't..."

Kirk let out an angry roar as he brought his palm down across her face with a forceful smack.

"You should have done what I told you." His voice was like gravel. "It would have been so much easier."

He raised his arm again, this time high over his head—an ordinary motion made terrifying by the moon-glinted blade in his hand. She opened her mouth, a scream trapped somewhere between her lungs and her larynx. Before she could produce a sound, Kirk's eyes grew wide and a roar swooshed through her ears. To her amazement, Devon released his grip and she stumbled forward. She swiveled around in a clumsy attempt to get her footing.

There on the ground in front of her, two forms grappled in the darkness. Confusion enclosed her head like a vice as Devon's panicked cries bit through the night. An unearthly growling sound, the likes of which Grace had never heard, resonated through the darkness and rendered her powerless to move.

"Grace!"

The muted cry of her own name seemed otherworldly, like an offstage chorus providing unseen support. Kirk barked out an expletive and backed off, lowering the blade. She lifted her eyes in confusion as the voices grew louder and three figures darted from around the side of the garage. She recognized Bob as he pulled Devon into what looked like a wrestling hold. In a flurry, she saw that someone had gotten a hold on the other form.

Her heart leapt. *Sam*. He was all right. *Thank God.*

"Steady boy, steady." Sam's voice sounded soft and jittery.

Grace blinked as he soothed the stray dog she had worked so hard to expel from her life several weeks back. Thank God for canine disobedience.

"You've got this all wrong!" Devon pleaded. "That animal attacked me."

Sam made a show of petting the dog's scruffy back. "Good boy."

Hearing a thump behind her, she whirled around just as Kirk bolted across her yard. Sam let go of the dog and took off after him, but Kirk had a good lead.

Just as he was about to round the corner of the house, Grace lost her breath. *The trench!* Unless you knew it was there, it was invisible in the dark, and Kirk was headed straight for it.

Instantly, his arms flew up in the air and he splayed forward, moonlight reflecting off the blade as it flew from his hand. He landed face down on the hardened sod with a dull thud. In a second, Sam was on him.

The two men struggled and Grace prayed that the strike to the skull she'd given Kirk a few minutes before would hobble him enough to give Sam the advantage. Letting out an unearthly wail, Kirk reeled back and gave Sam a punch to the jaw that sent him toppling, giving Kirk the momentum he needed to get to his feet and search for his weapon. Sam managed to pull himself up, quickly shaking off the damage and pummeling Kirk in the stomach. Just as Kirk folded forward, Sam's fist met his jaw with a cracking blow. Kirk's knees folded and Sam grabbed his arms from behind, gripping him in a hold similar to the one Bob maintained on Devon.

Grace's nerve dripped away like melting frost. As her body wilted, Lucy's firm but gentle grasp enclosed her. "Are you okay?"

Grace nodded mechanically, still coming to grips with the actual answer to that question. Her voice found its way out, bathed in surprising control. "No, I'm not. They wanted to kill me."

"What?" Lucy said with appropriate disbelief.

"Luce!" Sam maintained an unwavering grip on his opponent while tipping his chin toward the pocket of his shirt.

Making a wide arc around the thrashing Kirk, Lucy reached a cautious hand between the two men and managed to retrieve Sam's cell phone. Punching it with her finger, she stepped to the patio and spoke urgently.

Devon struggled, but Bob had a firm grip on his arms from behind. The moonlight illuminated a trickle of blood down one side of Devon's face.

"The sheriff's already on his way." Lucy returned to Grace's side, clicking the phone shut and encircling her with a supportive arm. "Apparently, Sophia called him."

Grace lifted her brows. *Sophia?*

"I love you, Tracy!" All eyes shot toward Kirk as his pleading screech pierced the early morning. "I love you! Say you love me!"

A wave of pure relief buoyed her as she squared him a hard look. "I remember falling in love, Kirk." Still speaking to Kirk, her eyes locked with Sam's. "Just not with you."

Even in the faint light of predawn, she saw one side of Sam's mouth quirk. She melted into a smile as the sound of a distant siren grew more distinct.

Chapter 43

Grace wrung her hands. She'd been through more opening nights than she could possibly count, but none as important as this. She flicked a look at her watch and steadied her overzealous heart. It was nearly time for the show to end. Time to get moving.

A quick check of the mirror confirmed that the hairdresser Spritz had recommended really did know her stuff. Grace smiled at her image. It felt good to return to her blonde roots.

Stepping from the bathroom to the office with a disgruntled *tsk*, she vowed to organize that space later in the week, once she made it through tonight. She smoothed the front of her lavender-gray silk sleeveless sheath and took one last strengthening breath before descending the stairs.

"That sauce could use just a pinch of nutmeg."

Grace couldn't help but smile at the familiar voice drifting up from the kitchen along with the aroma of huckleberry cobbler. She reached the bottom step and put a hand on her hip. "Mom. What do you think you're doing?"

A perky woman with hair the color of mahogany turned from the stove, her eyes lighting up as they landed on Grace. "Honey, you look beautiful. That dress was worth every penny."

Grace arched an eyebrow, walking toward her mother with the careful stride necessitated by her two inch heeled strappy sandals.

"Thank you, but you're avoiding my question." With a wink to the chef, Grace placed her hands gently on her mother's shoulders and guided her from the stove.

"Tracy, you said you wanted my input."

"I know, Mom. But tonight you're a guest."

As they neared the saloon doors that separated them from the evening's main event, Grace's nerves reminded her who was boss.

Clearly, it showed on her face.

Her mother enclosed both Grace's hands in her own. "I'm so proud of you. You have nothing to be nervous about."

Grace resisted. "But—"

Her mother squared her in the eye. "Anyone who can sing opera at the Met, survive what you've survived, and make it down that staircase in those heels should think nothing of running a restaurant. Now let's go."

In unison, they reached out to touch the swinging doors. Grace shot up a quick prayer and they made their entrance.

Emotion welled in her throat. They'd actually done it—gotten the place ready in time for the opening of the first show of the new season. Thank goodness for Nancy. Starting two new businesses at the same time would have been impossible for Grace without a reliable artistic director to take care of the theatre side.

She forced her muscles to relax, and scanned the room which, in spite of the fire, hadn't changed all that much from its days as a rehearsal hall. The high-beamed ceiling still sported the rows of hanging antique lights, now on a dimmer switch, thanks to Bob. The soaring front windows gleamed, seemingly pleased to be rid of the years of caked-on grime that Hank and Carl had needed an entire afternoon and two very tall ladders to eradicate.

It had been Lucy's concept to use the theatre memorabilia from the rummage sale to decorate the walls. The effect was charming, and Grace loved the touch of local history it added.

She tipped her head, pleased that the light jazz music she'd so carefully chosen set the mood perfectly.

Her mother put an arm around her and gave her a reassuring squeeze. "Everything looks just right."

Grace agreed. She stole a glance at her favorite feature of the room. The landing that had been her oasis the night of the fire. Softly gelled Fresnels cast their glow on a tall stool and a mic in a stand. Miss Kitty would have to make her entrance elsewhere.

Reminding herself that she was now an employer, she cast a critical glance at the refinished general store counter which had found new life as a dining bar and espresso stand. She firmed her tone. "Taylor, how's it going back there?"

"Terrific." She bobbed with youthful anticipation. "Salvatore's ready for action. Thank goodness Sam saved him."

Grace couldn't help but smile at Taylor's choice of words. Salvatore's salvation had been only slightly less opportune than her own.

Her stomach fell into her shoes at the sound of voices. She quickly raised her eyes to the new arched doorway that opened to the lobby.

"Mom, why don't you grab a seat." She gave her mother's shoulders a squeeze. "I need to meet and mingle."

Grace moved quickly across the room. A surge of relief filled her when Lucy and Bob appeared in the doorway.

"Welcome to the Backstage Bistro." She opened her arms with a flourish reminiscent of a Vegas showgirl.

Lucy looked around admiringly as they descended the ornate steps. "Grace, you'd never guess this place auditioned for a remake of *The Towering Inferno*. And the candles are perfect."

"My decorator calls that the 'finishing touch.'" She gave Lucy a wink. "She's good. If you're nice to me, I'll give you her number."

Lucy lilted a laugh. "My favorite part is still those squeaky old theatre seats." She nodded toward the front corner, where she'd set up a conversation area utilizing seating and tables that hadn't been smoke damaged. "I can't believe we actually used to sit in those things for two hours at a shot. The new ones are so much more comfy."

"They ought to be, for the price I paid." Grace chuckled.

Lucy and Bob stepped away just as the gang from the Banque

entered, alit with enthusiasm.

"Grace, I love your hair!" Joanne put her hands to her cheeks. "So long, Anne Hathaway, hello, Katherine Heigl."

Grace ran a hand through her locks, grateful that her do-it-yourself cut from early summer had grown into a stylish shag. "How did you like the show?"

They all chimed into a chorus of approval.

"It was my first Shakespeare!" Joanne spoke as if her viewing the show was a component in its success. "I never knew *The Taming of the Shrew* was a comedy."

"I'm so glad you liked it."

"And Sophia has never been better. Talk about perfect casting."

Grace had to agree. Sophia had worked hard and made a formidable Kate.

In no time, the room filled up. Like a bride at a wedding reception, Grace acknowledged a blur of congratulations.

A firm hand touched her shoulder and she spun around to the plump but pretty face of the first person she had met in this town. "Spritz!" She gave her a long hug.

"I can't keep my handsome hubby waiting." Spritz turned a wave in the direction of the dashing red-haired man. "I just had to tell you how happy I am for you. Buying real estate in Madison Falls is always a sound investment."

Grace laughed. "Thanks for writing up the offer."

"I wouldn't have missed the look on Mr. Roberts' face. One point five million. Priceless!"

Grace's heart warmed. "He deserves every penny." She recalled the day her attorney had given her the check—her profit after selling the painting to a legitimate buyer. The thrill of seeing all those zeros and realizing what she could finally do punctuated her whole ordeal with a lovely twist of fate.

She'd never be able to change the past, but thanks to Kirk's art expertise, Mr. Roberts was successfully receiving his treatment in Germany, and Madison Falls was not playing host to a posse of roulette-wheel habitués.

In fact, Main Street looked prettier than ever with a renovated playhouse and a bistro smart enough to put any sidewalk café in Paris to shame.

"How's it working out having your mother as a housemate?" Spritz's query drew Grace from her reverie.

"Couldn't be better. I missed her so much."

"Well, you just let me know the second you're in the market for a bigger house."

Grace smiled warmly. "Will do." Suddenly, something in the center of the room begged her attention. "Excuse me, I see somebody I need to talk to."

Bracing herself, she wound her way through the crowd, then sidled up to the table where Sophia sat solo, sipping a soda. Her eyes brushed over Grace, then quickly flicked away.

Grace pondered, choosing to stay in spite of Sophia's obvious reluctance. Although she'd sensed a change in her over the past few months, the two had barely spoken.

"You know…" Grace's attempt at breeziness felt forced, but she pulled back a chair and sat anyway. "I haven't said a proper thank you."

"You're thanking *me?*" Sophia's jaw flexed, although the tenseness in her slender shoulders seemed to ease.

"You tried to warn me about Devon." The warmth in Grace's solar plexus felt genuine. "I never told you how much that meant to me."

Sophia lowered her eyes, giving her an uncharacteristically humble appearance. "That was the least I could do." Her voice sounded strangled. "I wish I had figured out sooner what a fraud Devon was."

"A fraud?" Grace's throat pinched. While her emotions had moved on, the embarrassment over her miscalculation of his character still stung. "I know he let greed lead him to make some despicable choices, but why do you call him a fraud?"

Sophia's eyes widened as she leaned her forearms on the table. "When he came to town last spring in his fancy clothes and all, I totally bought the act. I was so in awe, I didn't even question it when he offered to rent out my second bedroom in exchange for acting lessons. I didn't realize he was completely broke."

"He was? I knew he had complicated finances, but..." Grace shook her head. "Boy, was he smooth."

"As ice." Sophia's shoulders tensed again. "And, lacking the proper mental traction, I conveniently slipped and fell for it. He convinced me to put his car in my name and to make the payments for him until his big 'deal' came through. I was so naive."

"Wow." Grace leaned in. "So you didn't know what the deal was either?"

"No." Sophia rolled in her lips as if to quell a quiver. "I was sick when I thought the theatre was going to be torn down..." Her voice trailed off to a near-whisper. "I grew up doing shows here."

Grace nodded her understanding.

Composing herself, Sophia drew in a deep breath. "Then you came along. I'm sorry I was so mean. I saw the way Sam looked at you, and I got a little carried away. I really had no right to pry into your private life."

"I've forgiven you, Sophia." Grace reveled in the truth of her words. Then a niggling thought rose to the surface. "How much did you know about what Devon was up to?"

"Not much." The corners of Sophia's mouth lifted as she lowered her chin. "When Devon told me about selling the painting, I thought that sounded pretty good if it meant he could pay me back. Believe me, I didn't realize he was *stealing* it from you."

"Go on."

"I knew he had sold it to Kirk and that he told him where to find you, but I didn't know Kirk was really dangerous."

Grace pulled in her brow. "But, you'd seen the police report."

Sophia let out a jagged breath. "See, Devon made it sound like you and Kirk were a couple and that you were making him prove his devotion. He said the police incident was just some lovers' quarrel. From the way Devon talked, it was like he was playing cupid. Being all magnanimous and helping Kirk."

Grace shuddered. "That wasn't true at all. Kirk and I were never a couple."

"I know that now." Sophia let her eyes take a slow journey around the room before going on. "When Kirk showed up at my house the day *Pirates* opened, I got a bad feeling about him. Not from anything he said, just from the way he was. He and Devon made a plan for Kirk to hide in the rehearsal hall." She looked around. "In this room. It was supposed to be a surprise."

Grace heaved in a breath. *These men and their surprises*.

"Then the fire happened and I wasn't sure where you had gone. Devon and I were frantic until Nancy told us she'd seen you leave with some guy. I didn't get why Devon was still so keyed up till he said something about Kirk taking off without paying him. I said, you mean for the painting, and he said no, for *you*." She pointed a slim finger at Grace.

A hard weight churned inside Grace's gut. "So how did you wind up at my house later on?"

"Well, I was pretty upset about the fire, so I couldn't sleep, and Devon was pacing the floor like a crazy man. I kept saying he should get some rest for his drive the next day, but he said he had more important things to deal with. Then his cell phone rang at one in the morning, and I knew it was Kirk."

"Did you hear what they said?"

"I overheard enough to know that Kirk was in some kind of trouble and that Devon was going to help him." She shook her head. "It was weird. At that point, I was just glad Devon was planning on leaving my house the next day."

"So, what did you do?"

"I fell asleep. I woke up about two hours later because Devon and Kirk were making so much noise."

"Noise?"

"Rifling through Devon's things. I stayed in my room and eavesdropped and I heard them talking about finding Devon's key to your house. Did you know he had one?"

Grace shook her head as an eerie tremble scuttled up her back. So that was how he'd gotten in.

"Kirk told Devon to do whatever he needed to do to get you into the car so that he could dispose of you out in the woods. That was the word he used. *Dispose*."

Queasiness surged in Grace's belly. What exactly had he intended to do?

"I was just sick about it, and I knew I was partly to blame."

Grace cocked her head. Sophia had been nosy, but how could she be to blame?

Sophia's cheeks darkened. "See, I was the one who found Kirk's phone number so Devon could call him. Remember, I told you I'd endeared myself to that detective? He was happy to help when I mentioned your name."

Grace's heart surged. Sophia *had* sold her out. Why did she just feel sorry for her?

Sophia continued. "I realized I had to try to warn you. That's why I went to your house. To try to stop you from going with him."

"I appreciate that."

"I'm so sorry I couldn't just say it." Tears buoyed her voice. "But I was scared. I didn't know what he'd do."

"It's good that you didn't. He and Kirk could have killed us both."

Fear flashed across Sophia's face. "At least now Devon's only facing *one* murder charge"

"Right." Grace shuddered. "Poor Carson."

They shared a mournful look. Carson had been trouble, but he hadn't deserved to come to that end. Nobody did.

A silence stretched as Sophia looked away. "There is one other thing." Her rueful eyes returned reluctantly to Grace. "Not as bad as the rest, but...I knew it all along and I really should have told you."

A cold weight rolled down Grace's throat before settling in her belly. "What?"

Sophia drew in a long breath. "He was a real womanizer. Thank goodness I saw it from the start, or I might have..." She cut herself off as she met Grace's eyes. "I'm sorry."

Grace nodded, hurt by the confirmation of what she'd suspected after Sam had told her about Colleen. Devon had no real regard for women.

"Not only that," Sophia's tone consoled. "He's *married*."

Grace's head snapped up, the word piercing like a spear. "M...married?"

Sophia gave a slow nod.

Disgust rolled through Grace's belly. Thank goodness she hadn't gotten any more involved than she had. "His poor wife."

"Fttt..." Sophia scoffed.

Grace jarred at the reappearance of the old Sophia, in her apparent lack of sympathy for a woman scorned.

Sophia regarded Grace, seeming to read her thought. "She's well rid of him." She arched a narrow diva-like brow. "Don't you think?"

The women shared a smile before Grace startled to attention, glancing at her watch. "Oh, I'd better go check on my 'talent.'"

"Careful." Sophia's tone was wry. "I hear 'talent' can be pretty temperamental."

With a parting grin, Grace rose and worked her way to the corner landing, where she gave the door to the former concession stand a light tap.

When she pulled it open, Sam was leaning back in a chair with his feet on the make-up counter, casually strumming his guitar. The brown dog, who lounged on the floor next to his chair, lifted his head lazily to look at Grace before going back to sleep.

Grace folded her arms and leaned on the doorjamb. "Well, aren't you just a bundle of nerves."

He stilled his hands, lowered his feet and stood. "Trust me, Gracie. I'm a wreck on the inside."

Smiling at his pet name that combined her two identities, she stepped in and shut the door. "Yeah, right. I think *I'm* more nervous than you are, Mr. Competition Finalist."

He set his guitar on the counter and took her hands. "You've got nothing to worry about." He nodded toward the door. "It's just friends out there. They want us to succeed."

"Good, then they should buy lots of sandwiches."

"If the food's as good as it smells, you've got nothing to worry about." He flashed her a dimpled grin.

She forced a businesslike focus. "Okay, I'm going to get back out there. Are you all ready?"

"Anything you say, boss."

"I love it when you call me that." She wrapped her arms around his shoulders. As they drew closer, they were abruptly muscled apart by a force separating them at knee level.

"Angel!" Grace looked down at the no-longer-stray dog, who smiled up from between them, his lovingly groomed tail wagging. "How do you like that? He's my guardian angel *and* my chaperone."

Sam let out a laugh. "And a public speaker. I didn't tell you he's got a gig."

"What?"

"Mrs. Finch stopped by the hardware store the other day and asked me to speak to her sixth-grade class. They're doing a unit on heroes."

"Wow. That's quite an honor."

"Sure, but I told her Angel here is the real hero. If he hadn't darted in front of my truck the way he did, and forced me to run it into Bob's tree, I never would have known you needed help."

"John McClane would have known." She quirked an eyebrow.

"I guess Mrs. Finch doesn't have his number." His mocha eyes were rich with humor. "So anyway, can I borrow Angel a week from Tuesday?"

"Take him to the park afterward and he's all yours."

"Deal."

She pulled herself away. "Enough stalling. It's showtime." She turned, beckoning Angel to follow.

Sam grabbed her wrist, pulling her back into an unhurried kiss.

Angel barked a protest, and Sam looked down in defense. "Give me a break. It's for providence."

A few minutes later, Grace leaned on the espresso counter and watched Sam onstage, his cappuccino-smooth voice lulling her. She had to admit she'd fallen in love more than once in the last few months—with Sam of course, but also with Madison Falls and the people there. They in turn had accepted her for who she really was.

She'd always thought of her ability to plan as her saving grace, but it wasn't until she stopped planning that her life finally made sense. She could do an opera or two a year for God's glory, not her own, and have a real life to come back to. She smiled. It was a real plan—God's plan.

Relaxing at last, her heart filled with joy. It felt good to be home.

The End

Thank you for taking the time to read *Saving Grace.* If you enjoyed it, please consider telling your friends or posting a short review. Word of mouth is an author's best friend and much appreciated. Thank you.

Please enjoy this sample chapter from

Jill Came Tumbling After
Book 2
in the **Madison Falls** Series

Sample
Chapter 1

Jill Martin flung open her front door with a burst of uncharacteristic boldness, then whirled around to face her husband. "Get out."

Caleb's bloodshot eyes widened with either surprise or amusement. "Ge'out?" The two words slurred together into one. "Where am I supposta go?"

"You seem to be an expert at finding places to be other than home." She dug her nails into her palms, determined to hold her ground. It was about time she did this. In fact, she should have done it ages ago.

"Bu' honey." Taking a step toward her, he reached for her cheek but staggered, giving her nose a decidedly unromantic flick.

She slapped his hand away. "Don't call me that. I'm not your 'honey' anymore. I'm not your *anything* anymore."

"Hey." He held both palms out from his sides like a statue of the Virgin Mary. "Wha'd I do?"

Disbelief puffed out between gritted teeth. How could he be so incredibly manipulative? And why had she put up with it for so long?

"What did you *do?*" Planting her hands on her hips, she braced herself against the cold October night air now gusting into their entryway. "For starters, we don't have any food in the house, and you just blew my grocery money on beer."

"Jilly…" His attempt at the boyish grin that had won her heart all those years ago in high school faltered under the influence of the two six-packs he'd just polished off in front of the TV. "I tol' you I'd pay it back."

"Oh really? Well, that's going to be a neat trick, considering you don't have a job."

He dropped the grin along with what looked like his hope of sweet-talking her. "You can't kick me outta my own house."

"Maybe not." She reached for the cordless phone, perched in its stand on the hall table next to the stairs. "But I'm sure Sheriff Drew would be happy to do it for me."

Fear flashed across his face like a brushfire. He'd had enough encounters with the sheriff of Madison Falls to know that if he found him in this condition, he'd haul him away to cool his heels overnight in a jail cell. Jill grimaced. It wouldn't be the first time.

Giving her a glare that was no doubt intended to intimidate, Caleb stumbled past her and on out the door, then nearly tripped down the porch steps.

Firming her jaw, she glanced up and down the street. A couple of curtains parted and faces peered out. If this had been his first public display of drunkenness, she would have been mortified. As it was, the neighbors were probably wondering why she hadn't kicked him to the curb years ago. She shivered. At least she wouldn't have to announce the news of her situation. Between the gossips and the prayer warriors, news traveled fast in this small Montana town.

Caleb hit the bottom step and whipped around to look up at her, waving an arm and probably thinking he looked threatening.

"I'll be back, Jill," he growled. "You can't keep me from seein' my kids."

A pain shot through her heart at the reminder of the two innocent little ones sleeping upstairs. At least she *hoped* they were still sleeping, with all the yelling that had gone on for the past fifteen minutes.

As he turned and stumbled toward their car in the driveway, her stomach buckled. She quickly glanced at the hooks that edged the bottom of the vintage white mirror hanging next to the door. Her keys were there as usual, but where were Caleb's? He was always losing them.

She looked back out to see him pat the pockets of his jeans then roll his gaze toward the house. Their eyes met in a mutual acknowledgment of the situation. He was keyless, and he shouldn't drive in his condition anyway. Not that that ever stopped him.

He sneered, then started down the sidewalk on foot.

Releasing a prayer of thanks, along with the breath she'd been holding, Jill rested the phone on the table next to the door. She would need the car more than he would, what with the kids and all.

The kids. Keeping an eye on Caleb as he swaggered into the night—probably to hit the Spur before last call—she strained her ears for any sign of wakefulness upstairs. She let out a long breath. Nothing but blessed silence.

Shaking from the dissipation of adrenaline, she shut the door and twisted the deadbolt, hopeful that Caleb wouldn't find his keys somewhere and be able to get back in. She made a mental note to track down Sam tomorrow and tell him not to give Caleb the spare set of keys for their house, no matter how much he begged him. Sam would do that for her, she was certain of it.

She sighed. Even though Sam had been Caleb's best friend since they were kids, he saw through him. He wanted to help Caleb, but he was more concerned with keeping Jill and the kids safe. It was good to know she could trust him.

She sighed again, leaning her back against the door. Too bad she couldn't trust her husband the same way.

Running her hands through her unkempt hair, she let the silence soothe her ears. She'd done it. After years of thinking about it and making halfhearted threats, she'd finally made her husband leave. Closing her eyes, she sent up a quick prayer, thanking God for the surge of strength that had apparently lasted just long enough this time to get him out the door. Even as she said a silent *amen*, her knees turned to mush and she sank to the cold hardwood floor.

Relief gave way to a wave of anger. She picked up a mountain ash leaf that had blown in while the door had been open and crunched it in her fist. She'd been such an idiot for marrying him. And then for having children with him.

No. She wiped her palms across her thighs, flicking away the bits of dried leaf. She couldn't go there. Couldn't regret having her precious children.

Her hands dropped to her lap and she expelled a breath, then twisted the band around her left ring finger. He had promised—no, *vowed*—to take care of the family. *Right.*

Did he really think that "taking care" of them meant spending half his time drunk, losing his job…then getting into trouble with the law for associating with a drug dealer?

Her jaw clenched at the memory. It made her sick to her stomach to know that her husband had put food on the table for weeks using the money he'd earned making deliveries for Carson. Claimed he didn't know what he was delivering and had gotten out of doing jail time because there was no concrete proof that he'd been directly involved with either using or dealing. Not even Jill had anything to go on but her suspicions. She would have pressed the sheriff to put Caleb behind bars if she'd known he wasn't going to make good on his promise to look for honest work. What a waste.

And now that he was out of the house, how low would he sink to ensure his own survival?

Oh, come on, Jill. She shot a glance into the darkened living room, at the family portrait hanging above the fireplace. A reminder of happier times.

She rubbed at a dull pain in her chest. *He's got a drinking problem, but he's not a monster.* It was just that it had been so long since she'd been able to trust him. Perpetual suspicion had come to feel like a normal condition.

With her head throbbing like it might explode, she pushed to her feet. She took a step, realizing too late that Riley's mini soccer ball had rolled underfoot. She stumbled, catching herself as exhausted frustration surged afresh.

Unable to control the new groundswell of rage, she hauled off and kicked the ball, aiming for the hall table as if it were a pintsize goal. The ball ricocheted off the table leg, amputating it from its top and sending an accumulation of mail—along with the phone stand—plummeting. Jill lunged, catching as much of the load as she could before it thundered to the floor.

With her arms full, she held completely still. No sound came from upstairs, and she eased out a breath.

An uncharacteristic curse word rolled around in her head and landed on her tongue, which she bit down on to silence. She'd been asking Caleb for weeks to fix this table leg, but of course he hadn't gotten to it. Another empty promise. Life with him had been full of them.

Leaning forward, she propped the table on its three good legs and held it there with her hip while easing her load down onto it. Then she braced it with one hand and retrieved the wayward leg with the other, and slid it under the fourth corner. It seemed okay, but the slightest provocation would jar it out of place again. Just like her life. It looked fine, but it had no security.

Who was she kidding? Her life didn't even *look* fine anymore.

As she started to tidy up the papers, something colorful snagged her attention. She pulled a bright yellow sheet from the pile and just about choked.

A shut-off notice? She gaped at the red print screaming from the page. Their power was going to be shut off? *When?*

Her eyes darted around the paper. *Ten days from this notice.* She tried to read the details, but her mind boggled and her vision blurred. Where was the date? Why couldn't they at least make it clear?

There it was…ten days from…*October thirteenth.* And what was today?

Clutching the rest of the papers, she hurried to the kitchen and the calendar on the wall next to the back door. *October twentieth.*

Her lungs pushed out air like a spent bellows. By the look of things, she had two days to come up with…how much? She surveyed the paper in her hands.

"Three hundred and eighty-seven dollars?" She could barely breathe out the words. It might as well be a million.

Her teeth gritted. Caleb had to have known about this. Of course he had—he'd opened the notice. When had he intended to tell her about it? Was he going to let the man from the power company break the news when he came to shut off their service?

She fumed. No wonder Caleb had gotten smashed tonight to escape reality. Their reality stank.

Focusing now on the rows of numbers on the page, she tried to decipher how long it had been since a payment had been made. Caleb had been out of work for so many months, she could barely even remember what it felt like to know that money would be coming into their account on a regular basis.

Giving up, she tossed the papers onto the kitchen table like they were on fire, afraid to check if anything else was going to be shut off or taken away. Her stomach clenched. Exactly how bad had he let things get while she'd kept her head buried safely in the sand?

A wave of panic rolled over her. What had she done? Here she was with a three-year-old and a baby to feed, a stack of unpaid bills, no money, no job, and no husband to help her. Where was the hope she had expected to feel when she finally took control of her life?

Swallowing a sob, she sank into a kitchen chair. Telling Caleb to leave had taken all her reserves. What was she supposed to do now?

End of Sample

I hope you enjoyed this sample chapter from *Jill Came Tumbling After,* book 2 in the Madison Falls series. This book can be found at my website:

www.lesleyannmcdaniel.com

Or on my Amazon author page:

www.amazon.com/author/lesleyannmcdaniel

My Thank You Gift to You…

High and Dry

CRESCENT COVE Series Prequel
Available only to my newsletter subscribers. Get your copy for FREE!

Do you love Inspirational Fiction? Join my Newsletter family and receive all the latest news about my books, plus contests, giveaways, and insider info.

www.lesleyannmcdaniel.com

LESLEY ANN MCDANIEL

While earning a degree in acting at Willamette University in Salem, Oregon, Lesley fell in love with theatrical costuming, and pursued that as a career while nurturing her passion for writing on the side.

Between working as a homeschooling mom and professional theatre costumer, she has completed several novels and screenplays. She would have done more by now if she didn't also occasionally stop to clean the house and fold laundry. Fortunately, she loves to cook, so no one in her family has starved yet.

In her spare time (ha!) she chips away at her goal of reading every book ever written.

Lesley loves to hear from readers. Please visit her website at: **www.lesleyannmcdaniel.com**
…or on Facebook at
www.facebook.com/LesleyAnnMcDaniel

www.ingramcontent.com/pod-product-compliance
Lightning Source LLC
Chambersburg PA
CBHW021443240626
47153CB00001B/273

* 9 7 9 8 9 9 8 8 4 8 8 5 8 *